Praise for *On the Bright Side*

'Warm and wise'
JULIE COHEN

'Big. Beautiful. Incredible. A moving story of personal
strength and learning to love yourself'
ANTON DU BEKE

'A hygge hug: a story of how to love the who-you-are,
not the who-you-have-been. An elegantly crafted story
that we all need right now'
ANSTEY HARRIS

'Great story and characters . . . the kind of read you can
settle right into and just love'
SUSAN LEWIS

'Tender and tangled, exploring the grey areas and
nuances of life . . . it's such a pleasure.
Warm, sage, heartfelt and real'
BETH MORREY

'The book of the year for me'
ANNA McPARTLIN

'This tender tale of love and finding your inner strength
is a balm for the soul. Beautifully crafted, this book and
these characters will stay with me for a long time'
CLAIRE ALLAN

NELL CARTER

On the Bright Side

WELBECK

Published in 2021 by Welbeck Fiction Limited, part of Welbeck Publishing Group
20 Mortimer Street London W1T 3JW

A CIP catalogue record for this book is available from the British Library

Paperback ISBN: 978-1-78739-520-6

Printed and bound by CPI Group (UK) Ltd., Croydon, CR0 4YY

10 9 8 7 6 5 4 3 2 1

For Esme, who's shown us all a thing or
two about love.

PART ONE

Chapter One

The first email arrives on Thursday.

Sent to my work address in chambers, I'm still staring at it the next day, Friday 10th August. The invite is under-stated in style; just the simple naming of a time and place to celebrate Alice's birthday. As the letters spelling her name blur on the screen, a fleeting memory of our last dance catapults forward thirty years – I'd held her, kissed her hair, fragrant, soft beneath my lips.

Mabel, after a typically timid knock, enters the wood-panelled office, and I'm grounded back in the present, Alice's form already banished. The woman who's worked alongside me for more than a decade offers a smile and a cappuccino on a small silver tray and I nod a thank you. After she's left, I stand up, pace the space. The three monkeys on the shelf just to the left of my mahogany desk aren't quite right and I move the middle one just a fraction to the left. Hear No Evil now sits exactly ten centimetres from both of his blind and silent brothers, right in the centre of a long line of leather-bound legal tomes.

Today is the day Alice would have been fifty . . .

Back at my desk, my hands curl around the coffee mug and I sip through the frothy milk, glance again at the computer, as if to check the date one more time. Within seconds, it reverts to the default screensaver, an image at a charity event a few years ago; me in black tie, my parents flanking me. I force myself to concentrate on that evening, a fundraising event at a local rehabilitation charity where I'm patron. As if on cue, my eyes pinch tight, and pain detonates from the nerve endings where my lower left leg used to be.

From inside my desk drawer, I remove two tablets from a blister pack and swallow them with coffee. Then, before the sounds and images of my last night with Alice overwhelm, I print off the invite, pick up the phone and remind Mabel I'll be out until much later this afternoon.

*

I take my time. Sensing I'm going to be late, I still drive within the speed limit, unwilling to tempt Fate. She and I have been strange bedfellows throughout my life. I've never been able to embrace Her; preferring to control every tiny element to keep Her at bay. I'm a man who likes certainty, checks facts before I take them as truth. If numbers prevail, I like to count things two or three times to be sure. If words matter, like they do when I'm in court, I read them quietly, read them aloud, and study them until I know them by rote. If something feels off, I search until I find what it might be and fix it. I check and recheck and, as such, leave little room for error, or Chance, to upset things.

The old primary school is a turn-of-the-century red-brick building with a tarmac play area to the side and a parking area just beside a small green space. From the nearness of a new housing development, it looks like some of the land was sold off and the rest is about to be. Faded red 'sold' signs loom on large advertising boards. I fill my head with useless housing trivia, roll my shirtsleeves down, fold my jacket across my arm and hurry towards the main door.

At the entrance, I stop, can't help imagining a little Alice coming here in her school uniform, her long hair hanging in loose plaits by her side, her shoes scuffed at the toes. To my right, there are two pots of unloved geraniums. I deadhead them while I'm standing there, pocket the debris, straighten them up. Symmetry is important.

Then I head indoors towards the music, perfecting my gait as I go. There are days I have to work to ensure there's absolutely no hint of my prosthetic and this is one of them.

When I push open the swing doors to the main hall, there are people scattered around a large projector image. Alice's face fills the screen and I'm rooted to the scarred parquet floor. Her face . . . My instinct is to look away towards an area where trestle tables are lined up, laden with food. The invite had said something about Friday lunchtime being Alice's favourite time of the week and I remember it was. Food and the arrival of a weekend, two of her biggest loves. Music from our era is playing in the background as I'm drawn to her image again. She's just as I remember; her ruler-straight, walnut-coloured hair falling down her back covering the tiny scattering of freckles I loved. Her head is thrust back in laughter. Vibrant. Alive.

A woman I know immediately to be her younger sister, April, approaches me, offers a hand. 'Jack,' she says. 'I recognise you from your picture on the chambers' website, though, to be fair, you're just an older version of the man back then. You've not changed.'

'You neither,' I reply, quickly scanning the room for her parents.

'Thank you for coming, I wasn't sure you would.'

My smile is half-formed. 'If I'm honest, I'm really not sure I should have, I—'

'Alice and I went to school here, and both of my children too. It's being sold now, but I was on the PTA for years, so they let me rent the hall for the day before they exchange contracts. Look at me, I'm babbling.' She grins at me, her smile a lot like her sister's.

I haven't moved, my eyes still darting anxiously around the hall.

'Mum and Dad both died last year, Jack.'

'I'm sorry.' The words are instant, sincere, but a shameful, relieved blush reaches my face. I've not seen Alice's parents since her funeral, after which I went home to Surrey, leaving York University where we'd met, transferring my course to Royal Holloway, where my own parents could keep an eye on me. I've been terrified of ever meeting them again.

Though they never said so, I always thought they held me responsible for her death. And I hadn't ever wanted to see that in their eyes because, even now, decades later, I see it in my own.

'Don't be. They were as happy as they could have been, in the circumstances. He had cancer and Mum had a heart attack only six months after Dad passed. They'd both reached eighty . . .' Eyes sad, she shrugs and raises a hand. 'This was my idea. I'm still in touch with a lot of Alice's friends and we thought: To hell with it, let's have a party. Can I get you a drink?'

I mimic the turning of a steering wheel. 'I've got to get back to the office.'

'It's only soft drinks, tea or coffee – what's your poison?'

After asking for a black coffee, I watch April move away towards a makeshift café area before my eyes are pulled back to Alice. I focus on the projected picture of the only woman I have ever loved, powerless against that crushing memory: *Oblivion. Now. Please*

Before long April's back, handing me a small white cup and saucer, and I refocus.

'So, what are you up to nowadays, Jack, apart from working with baddies?'

'I'm a defence barrister – not all of them are baddies.' I smile.

'There it is, the grin she used to talk about.'

My free hand rubs my neck.

'You married, Jack? Any children?' She frowns at my head shake. 'I confess I tried to find you on social media – no sign of you. Did you *ever* marry?'

More head shakes. I wipe my clammy hands on the napkin that came with the cup.

'That's a shame.'

Before I know what's happened, she's looped an arm through mine.

'Come, sit. We can talk over there.'

'April.' I dig my good heel into the floor. 'I'm sorry, I think this was a mistake.'

'Nonsense,' she says. 'I don't bite. And I've wanted to talk to you for over thirty years and never plucked up the courage. I'm not letting you out of my sight now. Come. I won't put you through meeting the wider family. Just you and me, having a catch up.'

*

'She loved you.' April has told me this several times. I'm not sure why, because if there's one thing I'm certain of it's that Alice and I loved one another. I *know* we both felt the same.

I drain the dregs of the bitter coffee.

'I suppose what I'm trying to say is that she was happy when she died. If someone had to die at twenty, isn't it wonderful that she'd known love?'

I agree, make suitable noises, one eye fixed firmly on the exit. Thirty paces and I'm out of here.

'Can I ask you something?'

She's going to anyway, so I mutter an, 'Of course.'

'Why did you never settle down?'

'I never loved anyone else enough.' My reply is typically factual and blunt, but Lynn springs to mind. She'd been the one to come closest. We'd lived together; she and I with her teenage son, Antony, and I'd screwed up that relationship as if I'd followed a bullet-point plan on how to do so.

And suddenly all the moments since Alice, millions of them at once, create a noisy stampede in my brain.

'I should go. Thank you for thinking of me.' I glance at my wristwatch. 'I'm needed in chambers this afternoon, so I'd better head back.'

'Can we keep in touch?' April asks.

'I'm sorry.' I pick up my jacket. 'I'm glad you invited me, but I'm not sure that's a good idea.'

After a polite but awkward hug goodbye, I walk away from the school hall, where once Alice had stood in attendance during assembly; where she and her girlfriends would have played hopscotch on the tarmac, or kiss chase with the boys. In the car, I close my eyes, clasp the steering wheel tight and try to refocus on work. It's easier than allowing myself to dwell on what might have been.

*

Back at the office I scroll through messages on my desktop before I have to read the new client file that Mabel has left on my desk. Immediately, April's name appears on the second email from her in as many days. Despite the urge to pretend today never happened, I click on it:

-----Original Message-----
From: AprilFahy272@gmail.com
Sent: 10th August 2018 15:55
To: JackTate@WhittardChambers.com
Subject: Today

Jack,

I'm so terribly sorry. Upsetting you in the way I did was the last thing on my mind today, when I really wanted to celebrate Alice. She lived a short life, but a full one, and I, for one, still miss the enthusiasm she had for absolutely everything. I could tell from the time we spent together today that you do too.

Forgive me. I'm writing this on my phone and, before I began, agreed with myself that I'd just spill what I was feeling.

Over the years you were mentioned, and not in anger as I suspect you think. My parents never blamed you. I never blamed you, yet seeing you today, I think even after all this time, you blame yourself.

Oh, Jack. Life is never easy, is it?

What is it I still want to say to you? Something simple.

I think you're stuck, stuck in that moment when she died. And I'm asking you, on her birthday, please do whatever you can do to live this next half of your life. I mean LIVE from this moment on – as if life for you begins in the middle.

For God's sake, Jack, change it up. See how the wider world works. Do something big! Let love into your life. Make her proud.

And forgive me if my saying any of this makes you want to scream abuse at me. Who the hell do I think I am, etc.

I'm Alice's only sibling. Had life been kinder, I think you and I would have been friends. Because she loved you so much, Jack.

Dare I say, you owe it to her?

Take care of yourself,

April.

Pulling open the drawer nearest me, I grab one of the miniature bottles of whisky I'd kept from some plane journey, swallow it in two gulps. I never drink during the day but today feels like an exception to the rule. Today feels as if someone took my rule book and put a match to it.

I try ignoring April's unsolicited advice by opening the manila file Mabel left and skim-reading the contents. The new client is a guy in his twenties accused of aggravated assault, his third offence, so the CPS are going to want to throw the book at him. The resulting message I type to Mabel is probably a little blunt but mirrors my mood: 'Get him in for a meeting asap. J.'

My head lowers to my hands, my elbows rest on my desk and, with them, I nudge the keyboard away. It feels as if just one reading of April's words is enough to hear them

reverberate around the office. The loudest echo is, 'Do
something big. Let love into your life. Make her proud.'

As my thumbs massage my tired temples, I wonder how
exactly I might do that.

How the hell does one actually do *that?*

I'm half tempted to write back and tell her to keep her
feelings to herself, but she's just saying it as it is; an almost
stranger who sees me trapped in a time warp, someone
who thinks that three quarters of a body is enough to love.

'Do something BIG.'

Like what?

'Let love into your life.'

*It's laughable. I've tried. I'm damaged, not whole. Neurotic
and a little OCD. Unable to love. Ask Lynn. Hell, ask Antony
too . . .*

To distract myself, I reopen the work file and this time
I read it properly. And I learn nothing new, apart from
one important fact. For the first time ever, I don't really
care what happens to this guy, which really isn't right at
all. Thoughts collide. I pick up the phone and feel instant
relief when the call is answered.

'I'm just sending you a copy of an email,' I say.

'Yes, hello to you too, Jack.'

'Sorry. Hi, Ollie. You got it yet?'

'Maybe I'm too busy to read your email right now.'

'Are you?'

Ollie sighs down the line, feigning impatience with me.
It's part of his thing; pretending to be irritated if I need

him in any way, when he has always been, and always is, there for me, on the end of a phone or in person. The bond that ties us started back in primary school, but since the accident, it's an unbreakable thing.

'Right, got it,' he says. 'Just reading now.' He makes little 'aha' and 'hmm' noises, finishes with a stretched-out 'Ok-a-a-y.'

'What do you think?' I nibble on a stray hangnail.

'I think she's right. I like this lady.'

I say nothing.

'So, she sent you this after you went to the party that you said you weren't going to go to, yes?'

'I changed my mind.'

'I see that. What do *you* think she means?'

'Haven't a clue. It's why I'm calling you.'

'Something big ... I'd tell you to stop buying plastic, help eliminate global warming or donate to food banks and charities, but you do all that already. And size matters, I mean, she's talking BIG. Hang on, just rereading it,' he pauses. 'Yeah, look, she's right about the love bit. It's time, mate.'

'Please,' I'm visibly wincing. 'Please don't go lining up friends of friends for dinner parties where you sit me next to some singleton. I'm not interested.'

'Right.'

I can almost hear him nodding down the line.

'Jack?'

'Yes?' I hold my breath, brace myself for whatever's coming, knowing I probably need to hear it.

'There's nothing really new here, apart from the prospect of doing some BIG THING, which is probably a good idea . . . but most of it is what I've been saying for a long time and what you already know. How was it the Rolling Stones put it? "Time Waits for No One" and maybe now *is* the time to really move on. You want my advice? Don't ignore this. It's happened now for a reason. Let what she says marinate with you for a few days.'

'Marinate . . .' I imagine the email swirling about in my brain.

'Look, sorry,' he adds, 'but I've a meeting in five minutes. Let's talk later in the week, OK?'

With that, he's gone and, immediately, I'm plunged back in time, to the moments that are filed deep in my psyche; to the memory that's relived second by second any time I allow it out.

We're slow dancing, her head resting on my chest, both her arms circled around me. I'm that geeky guy, just out of his teens, who stoops to hide his six-foot-four frame and plays trumpet in a blues band; someone who went through school being called weirdo, believing the tag.

Alice, a petite brunette, completely confident in her soft velvet skin, is wearing red pedal pushers with a unicorn T-shirt because she 'totally believes in magic'.

Alice loves me.

I love Alice.

I'm wondering how her hair smells of Christmas in July when she whispers, 'Let's go.' Leading me through the crowd at the night-time, open-air concert, we run to the car park, towards the Mini I'd borrowed from Ollie. We both giggle as I bend my long limbs into the narrow driver's seat.

She's humming some song we heard earlier and I'm just about to say something, something I'll never remember later, when my left hand shoots up to shield my eyes. Ahead, too close, lights glare from a car on the wrong side of the road. Swerving, the only thing I do say is her name.

Tyres squeal. Metal grinds metal. Alice's right arm, in some maternal manner that will never flourish, flails across me barrier-like, as if to protect me from what's to come.

The embankment is steep; jagged branches whip through the open window as we nosedive. Headlamps explode when the car shudders to a vertical stop – the front folding in pleats. My left leg twists into the crushed metal and mid-scream, I taste blood.

Alice's head is slung forward at a peculiar angle. I reach for her beautiful face and panic flushes through me because instantly – I know.

And all I want is oblivion.

Chapter Two

WhatsApp Grace & Tim

Dad, please, no trouble, OK?

How & why would I make trouble?

U said u'd stay away.

If that's what u want but am allowed to feel sad ☹

I know . . .

Nah, Gracie, u don't. U won't know til ur older & love someone & they just decide they don't love u any more, just like that. No warning, just announce it & ur supposed to just take it. I hope u never know what that feels like.

I'd say Mum remembers it differently.

U know nothing. Gotta go, might see u tomorrow.

No, Dad! U said U wouldn't. Dad?

Chapter Three

Clare felt like her gut had twisted around itself during the night. When she woke, trying to rub her tummy better, trying to embrace the first minutes of the day, she couldn't help but wonder what drama it might bring. Though it was school holidays, Grace needed a lift to a hockey tournament, so she busied herself, first making an instant coffee, then some lunch for Grace. Two slices of white bread, no butter, ketchup and some salami. She would swear that her only child had been born without taste buds.

Washing the six pack of soft drink cans under the tap, Radio 1 in the background, she was aware of being watched. 'Rat's piss,' she told her daughter without looking up. 'I read an article about it. These cans sit around in warehouses and you never know what's been crawling on them and then you drink from them and—'

'Right,' Grace took one from her, wiped it dry and packed it in her bag. 'You ready?'

'I'm always ready,' Clare said, smiling.

'Yes, but are you ready to leave the house now, Mum?'

'Your carriage awaits, my dear.' Clare ushered her through their front door and pulled it shut behind her.

The carriage was a twelve-year-old Nissan that had seen many better days. Most times, she chose to walk places rather than risk the engine coughing like a tired old man with respiratory disease.

'So, rat's piss,' Grace said as soon as they were driving down their narrow car-lined street.

Clare laughed. 'Tease away, but there could be something lurking!'

'Not now that you've taken care of it, Mum.'

'Don't I always? Take care of things?'

'You do.'

A weighted silence sat between them until Grace spoke. 'You'll be all right today?' she asked, and Clare knew it was less of a question and more of a statement.

'Of course.'

'You'll call me if there are any problems?'

'There won't be any problems. I'll pick you up this afternoon at 5.30.'

'And if anything—'

'Grace, go play, have fun! Be fifteen, my love! Everything is fine, I promise.' Clare pulled up outside the school playing field just beyond the zebra crossing. 'See you later,' she called after her only child, who blew her an over-the-shoulder kiss.

Clare had no idea where she'd got her from. Grace was an old soul; someone Clare was convinced had lived another thousand lives. From the time she was little, she'd always talked before other children, walked before other children, read books and wrote her name before other children. Apart from her dark eyes, the girl was nothing like her father and even less like her, yet between them they had managed to produce a kind and caring teenager. And for all of Tim's bad points, and there were many, he tried to be a good father.

Just thinking of Tim made her insides gripe again. She glanced at the clock on the dash – just enough time to get home, check the mail, finish outstanding work admin and then get to the hall to set up for her midday dance class. It was one of her favourites – waltz lessons specifically for the over-seventies; somewhere for them to practise their rise and fall, somewhere for them to improve their footwork, somewhere for them to have a weekly laugh with friends.

As soon as she opened her front door, her senses pitched. The radio she knew she'd left on was silent. The mail that had been delivered while she was out sat in a small pile on the radiator cover next to her.

'Hello?' she called out, leaving the front door open behind her.

Tim's large frame appeared at the entrance to the living room. 'Hello,' he replied.

She sighed. 'Tim, you can't keep doing this.' She kept her voice calm, her speech deliberately slow. 'You said you'd drop the key back.'

Her very-soon-to-be ex-husband held out a hand with a key in it. 'Come and get it,' he said.

'I'm not playing your games. What do you want?'

'I wanted to be here when you open it.'

Clare glanced at the post. Six weeks after her decree nisi had been granted, somewhere in there lay the decree absolute ending their marriage. She shook her head. 'That's just weird. Can't you see that that's weird?'

'I want to watch your face.' He picked up various envelopes, leafing through them before handing her one – white and starchy, her name and address typed on the front, the franking mark of the solicitors in the top right-hand corner.

'Go home, Tim.'

'*This* is my home.'

'Not any more.' She had tried hard during their long separation to keep the house. With free legal aid, she'd taken him to court for child support and his part in mortgage arrears, but he never paid. In the end, unable to meet the debts alone, the house had been repossessed by the lender. The date on the final notice was less than two weeks away.

She didn't flinch as he neared her, determined not to show fear, not today.

'Open the letter,' he said.

'I'm not opening it with you here.' She counted the tips on the fronds of the palm leaves on the hall wallpaper. It was one she'd chosen with him years ago, when they'd both had a bit of a fancy for Miami-style art deco.

'Please. I'd like you to. Read it. Nice and loud.'

Clare ripped open the envelope and began to speak. 'Referring to the decree made in this cause on the 18th of June 2018 whereby it was decreed that the marriage solemnised on March 18th 2000 at St Margaret's Church

Twickenham between the Petitioner Clare Bryanson and the Respondent Mr Timothy Bryanson has dissolved—'

'Dissolved,' Tim took hold of her chin and turned it towards him. 'Makes us sound like an Alka-Seltzer.'

Clare jerked her head, moved away towards the front door. 'I think you should go now.'

'Aren't you even a little bit sad?'

Despite herself, her eyes met his, an image of them both on their wedding day prompting a lump in her throat. 'Of course, I'm sad. If you hadn't been here now, I'd probably have had a small cry into my coffee.'

'So have a coffee and a cry with me.'

'No.'

'Why not?'

'Please, Tim? I really can't do this any more, especially not today.' She held the paper in front of his face. 'It's over. It's been over a long time, but today even the law agrees it's *absolutely* over.'

Before she knew what was happening, his hands, swift as ever, had grabbed it and ripped it into small pieces. Staring at her, he held them high before dropping them slowly. Clare watched them fall, filtering through his hands like some ironic confetti. Then he turned and walked into the kitchen.

'I can get a copy, Tim,' she called after him, wondering if she'd have to phone the police. It wouldn't be the first time. When he appeared back in the hallway, he had a rucksack slung over his shoulder and a can of lemonade in his hands.

'I'm leaving now,' he told her. 'Please tell Grace to be ready at six on Friday.'

Clare nodded, reluctantly. Friday-night curry with her father was something Grace seemed to endure rather than enjoy, but keeping regular contact with him seemed to be important to her.

Just as he passed her, Tim lowered his face to hers. She flinched at the feel of his kiss on her cheek. 'Take care, Clare. You got what you want – you're a single woman now. We both get fuck all out of our house. I'm living with my parents and you can't afford to rent the worst local shithole there is. Congratulations.'

She held her breath, bit back the reply she would love to have made, instead softly saying, 'Can I have that key, please?' just as he crossed the threshold. 'The bank will want all copies.'

'I think I'll hold onto it,' he smiled, pushing it low into his front jeans pocket. 'Safekeeping.'

Clare closed the door behind him, slipped the lock into place and rested her forehead on the faded paint. She'd known. Grace had known. They'd both known he'd make an appearance today.

'If I'd got what I want, you'd never have hit me,' she whispered. 'I wouldn't have spent my life second guessing what was going on in your head. If you'd helped me, I'd never have lost the house . . .' She blinked slowly. 'And I would never now be wishing a serious dose of rat pee poisoning on you.'

Clare straightened up, looked at her watch. Thanks to Tim, there was no time for admin, but she had a few minutes for a solo coffee and a call to the solicitors for another copy of the absolute. Then a much-needed uplift from the waltzing septuagenarians in her life . . .

*

By 10 p.m., fatigue was making her yawn continuously. She switched the news off and unfolded her legs from under her. Hearing the thumping tread of Grace coming downstairs, no doubt for late-night toast, Clare lifted her phone from the cushion beside her, deleting a recent text without reading it. Tim had said enough for one day.

'Mum,' Grace was stood in the doorway. 'Do you remember the time you bought that ticket from Gladys in the church hall?'

Clare yawned, ran a hand through her hair. Gladys. Her dancing pupil – partnered with Phillip. Lovely old lady she'd seen earlier today. 'Ticket?' she repeated.

'You bought one from her. The lady whose son was injured in Afghanistan. Remember?'

It was coming to her. Gladys had been selling tickets for a charity her son used in Wiltshire, an organisation that helped with amputee rehabilitation. 'What about it?' Clare was bone tired, unable to think straight.

'I must have followed them on Twitter because it's on there that a ticket has won but not been presented yet.

Where would it be?' Grace had walked into the galley kitchen and was riffling through cupboards.

'What was it for? I probably tossed it, love.'

'Mum! The prize was ten thousand pounds. The tickets were a fiver each.'

'A fiver!' Clare shook her head. 'Gladys saw me coming!'

'Ten thousand quid, Mum.'

She joined her daughter in the kitchen, the memory returning, Gladys telling her all about her son's injuries. Clare parting with a fiver she couldn't afford to part with. 'Grace, it could be anywhere.'

'Think, Mum.'

'I am. You're my only luck in life, love. Now, have your tea and toast and get to bed. We both have an early start in the morning.'

'God, you're maddening,' Grace said as she shook the kettle.

'I love you too,' Clare kissed her cheek. 'Turn everything off before you come upstairs.'

*

Clare was woken by the sound of drawers opening and closing in her bedroom. Bleary-eyed, she threw off the duvet, the feather one Tim had tried to claim was 'his', even though it had been a birthday present to her from him.

'It was a Saturday and I was with you. I'd helped out with the teeny-tots before you had the oldies.' Grace, her blonde hair tousled from sleep, her too-small pyjama top flashing her midriff, stood with both hands poised on her hips.

Clare sat up slowly, lowered her legs to the floor and opened a window, breathing in the dewy air. She walked from her bedroom to the bathroom down the narrow landing, pacing a path in the centre, where the green carpet pile had flattened over the years.

'You had your blue handbag, the one with red stars, I remember!' her daughter called after her.

Clare placed her head in her hands, her elbows on her knees as she sat on the loo. After washing her hands, she switched the shower on and ambled back in. 'You or me in the shower first?'

'Jesus, Mum. Ten thousand quid would be really helpful right now! Don't you ever dream of getting out of here?'

Clare stood very still. She'd fought Tim hard to help keep a roof over their heads and lost. She'd fought the local council to be housed, but rightfully, had to take her place at the back of the long queue. She was trying her level best to make ends meet and to ensure Grace's life was disrupted as little as possible – that she could stay in the same school, have her bedroom with her pink mosquito net shrouding her bed and stay near the selection of odd teenagers she sometimes called friends, but there was no way she could afford a local market rent. Her eyes blinked slowly. Yes, she had dreams. But struggling to keep her marriage afloat over the last few years, and dealing with Tim when they separated, meant she could no longer remember what they were. 'I'll go first then,' she said quietly.

'That bag,' Grace yelled. 'Where would it be?'

Clare ignored her, turned the water up to just beneath scalding and stepped under. Some people used their morning shower to wake – Clare preferred to think of it as a cleansing ceremony. She would wash away anything that had happened in the last twenty-four hours. This morning that meant she scrubbed hard because it sent Tim and all his shit, and all Grace's disappointment, down the plughole. And the thought that her only option might be to contact her estranged mother and ask for help – that required such a scouring of her thighs that it almost hurt.

Ten minutes later, she walked back into her bedroom, a large towel around her body and another wrapped around her blonde curls. 'Bathroom's free,' she said without looking at Grace.

'I'm just checking this,' her daughter replied. She was hunched over her phone but there was nothing new in that.

'I have to get ready for work.'

'Mum.'

Clare walked around the pile of handbags Grace had left at the foot of the bed. 'I have a class this morning at nine.'

'I found the ticket. The numbers don't match.'

'I could have told you that. In fact, I did tell you last night – you're my good luck.'

'Mum.'

She turned to face her. 'What?'

'What are we going to do?'

Clare sat on the bed beside her and put an arm around her shoulders. Wiping away the tears that formed in Grace's eyes, she held her face with her free hand. 'I'm going to do what mums do and I'm going to sort it.'

'We have two weeks before we have to move out.'

Clare nodded slowly. 'Yes.'

She would call her mother today. She'd file away all of the hurt and pulse those numbers that she still had written on an old piece of paper. 'Mum,' she'd say, swallowing every ounce of pride she'd ever had. 'I need your help.' That's what she'd say. Much as it galled her, that's what she'd do. Today.

'Grace, you have to trust me. OK?'

She felt her daughter's head move ever so gently on her chest. It was a yes. And it was all she needed. She couldn't let her down.

Today, she'd call the woman whom *she'd* spent her earlier life letting down. She'd call the woman who'd instructed her when she was ten never to love someone or never to have children because 'people you love will always disappoint you.' She'd have it confirmed that she, Clare, was the failure her mother had predicted she would be.

And then she'd ask for a loan.

Chapter Four

'There's a delay on the glass.' My builder, Tony, sucks on the end of a cigarette after saying the words and I can't help glaring at his casual demeanour delivering bad news.

'How long a delay?' I ask. I'm standing in the two-metre aperture that should have a single floor-to-ceiling window, meaning the entire barn conversion would be watertight. Its refurbishment has been a hobby for many months but now I want it finished.

'It's coming from Sweden, Jack,' Tony replies, before tossing his cigarette on the ground.

I stare a little longer. It's a strategy I've learned during years of handling people in court. When the opposition know that they haven't actually answered your question, just wait. Wait.

'I don't know,' he finally relents, wiping his sweating brow with the back of his hand. 'But if I was a guessing man, at least another fortnight.'

'I'm not paying you to guess and I don't have another fortnight,' I say, bending to pick up his stray cigarette butt. I hand him what is a fire hazard in a parched garden that hasn't seen rain for weeks, before walking away. 'Fix it, Tony,' I say, adding a last-second 'Please' before I leave.

His eyes bore into my back and I can imagine the unspoken expletives on the tip of his tongue. Making my way around the newly erected fence and line of planted shrubs separating the properties, I move the hose that has been watering their roots and head up the garden towards the main house, where Ollie is due soon.

*

I've cooked dinner, although Ollie's steak barely touched the pan.

'I don't know how you do it. That thing is practically mooing.' I point at the offending item with my fork after we've sat down at the table in the kitchen.

Ollie grins. 'It's great!' He continues talking as he slices into the meat. 'So, have you decided what you're going to do?'

He's been my sounding board for the last few days while so many things, prompted by April writing to me, have marinated in my head. 'Yup . . . I'm going to take a sabbatical, somewhere between six months and a year, travel, destinations yet to be decided.'

'Still sounds a bit vague, Jack.'

I shrug. 'I can't fill in the blanks until I talk to Marsha and work out the details with the office. Then it'll be *exciting*.' As I say it, I'm not quite sure that Marsha, Head of Chambers, will agree that it's as thrilling as I think.

Ollie is staring at me as he chews. 'So, is the travel a "thing" or *the* "Big Thing"?'

My brow puckers as I consider the question. 'I'm not sure. All I know is I really feel the need to do it.'

'You're not running away?'

'No.' I sigh. 'I knew you'd think that. I wasn't sure *what* I wanted to do until I had an interview with a new client this week . . .' I want to explain this properly and put my cutlery down by my plate. 'From the moment I met the guy, hell, even from the first moment I read his file, I just found myself not caring what happens to him. And the tenet of him deserving the best defence possible, whether guilty or not, *depends* on my caring. So, it's not running away, it's more . . .' I find myself focusing on a scarred spot on the oak table next to my glass. 'I'm tired, Ollie,' I admit. 'I suppose the idea of a break, of getting away from everything, once it began to form, just grew more and more until it became a very loud voice in my head.'

He's nodding slowly opposite me. 'I get it. But what's different about April's email was the mention of some grand gesture to yourself, or to the world, or both – the Big Thing.'

'I was thinking I might do a fundraiser for the local rehabilitation centre.' I check his expression across the table.

He looks unimpressed. 'Or you could write them a cheque.'

'Frankly, I think travelling would widen my world, which might mean being able to move on from the past,

which would be huge, enormous. Titan.' I hold my arms
out as wide as possible and offer a weak smile.

'Granted, but is taking yourself off on a big holiday
enough?'

'I prefer a "learning, life-broadening travel experience"
rather than "big holiday". Who knows?' I shrug and begin
to nibble my cooling food, my appetite already waning.
'But it's a start.'

Ollie smiles, clinks his water glass against my Merlot-
filled goblet. He's driving and neither of us ever drink
alcohol if we're driving; a nod to the past, an acknowledgement to Alice, to me – both victims of a stranger who
made a different choice so long ago.

'How's the Barn coming along?' he asks, staring out at
its silhouette.

From the tabletop, my phone vibrates and, after a quick
glance, I jab the disconnect button.

'Tony, the builder, is trying my patience,' I reply. 'He
doesn't seem to understand the word "finish".'

'What will you do with it when it *is* finished?'

'The plan was always to sell, but the market's awful, and
now, I'll probably rent it for a year.'

'And this place? What about when you go away?'

I take a moment to look around the home I love – at my
country-style kitchen with the Aga that I still struggle with,
the old oak dining table that we're sat at, next to the ticking
grandfather clock I picked up at a local auction. The room
next to us, visible through an open archway, is the snug – a

small sitting room with a sofa and an armchair, a record deck and a music stand. The walls there are painted white and the rear one has a single-glazed door to the garden.

Ollie clicks his fingers in front of my face. 'Earth to Jack.'

I look at his plate and see he's finished, yet I'm really no longer hungry. We clear the plates together.

Minutes later, we're both sitting in the snug. I'm on the sofa, sunk into a dent the exact shape of my ass. Just behind the armchair Ollie's in sits a big old blanket box where I store all my records and sheet music. The door is open and, outside, the August day is fading to dusk.

'I was asking what you might do with this place?'

'I'll leave it empty, have someone check it often, but I couldn't bear the thought of other people living here.'

Ollie nods, sips his coffee, and I pour myself a brandy. He's suddenly quiet, and before I can ask him what's wrong, he blurts the words: 'I've been thinking.' There's a pause and his eyes tell me that he's remembering the night of the accident.

Over the years, we've had many brandy-fuelled evenings and it's rare that we don't end up talking about the role Chance played in events. What if I'd never borrowed his car? What if I'd driven home ten minutes later? What if Ollie had never got the flu and he'd come with me to the concert, which was what was supposed to happen. His being ill meant Alice and I went together. Which one of us would have driven if he and I had gone, and which one of us might be dead?

I watch his face computing the facts before he continues, 'About everything that's led you here and . . . I have an idea.'

'Oh God . . .'

'Look,' he says to me. 'Hear me out, OK? I've just been appointed to the board of a charity set up by someone I knew in uni. It's a small endeavour, helps relocate families who've lost their homes post-divorce and houses them for a while to help get them back on their feet. Years ago, she found herself in that situation and later set up the organisation to help others.' Ollie looks straight at me. 'She really believes it's a chance for new beginnings, convinced me to join the board.'

Immediately I sense what's coming. 'I don't think so, Oliver.'

'April did say BIG.'

The brandy burns my throat. 'Is this what prompted the unusually last-minute visit from you?'

His right leg sits on top of his left and his foot moves gently, rhythmically. The odd click in his ankle is the only sound until he speaks. 'Busted. Jack, I get the travelling, but you're also chasing the "BIG". This is it, my friend. Give fate the two fingers it deserves and help change someone's life for the better.'

I roll the idea around my head. As he knew it would, it stays put and I don't dismiss it because it *is* BIG, and it *could* work. 'Tell me more,' I say. 'More about this charity. Just talk. I'll listen.'

Two coffees later and I know almost all I need to know, and he's done talking as silence crackles between us.

'How would I vet who goes in?' I voice what worries me most.

'You don't.' He shrugs. 'Like I said – people apply, they have to meet the recently divorced criteria, loss of home, et cetera, and then it's timing, luck. Obviously, the charity meet them . . .'

'Could you be involved – talk to whoever is put forward?'

'I could do that . . .' Ollie grins, sensing a win, whereas I'm still unsure.

'I mean, the Barn space isn't huge – you could really only have an adult and child, or two small children at a push? And children, shit, all that glass . . .'

'Stop worrying. You'd be gallivanting all over the world.'

He's right. I would. And without realising what I'm doing, I find myself telling him that I'll think about it, which, in typical Ollie fashion, he assumes to mean that I will actually do it. To the tune of him slapping his hand on his thigh, I repeat, 'I said I'll *think* about it, Ollie. And it could only be for max a year and you'd have to personally oversee it.'

'Of course!' He stands and pulls me up from the sofa into an embrace.

'Jesus, what part of "think about it" did you not get?' My face crumples.

'It's a really Big Thing and you'd *really* be helping someone.'

I pull away, reach for my glass and drain it. 'I help people every day.'

'Jack, you charge people for your work.' He shakes his head and some of his unruly hair falls from his ponytail and I realise that though he's the most unlikely-looking chartered accountant ever seen, he is the person I trust most in the world. 'You charge people a shedload of money,' he continues. '*This* would be altruistic, philanthropic.'

Sitting down again, I remove my prosthetic, and rub my stump. There's always a time in the evening where I take it off for a bit, just to feel the freedom. Oliver watches me before taking his seat again.

'You think I have the making of a philanthropist?'

He laughs. 'You certainly have the money.'

It's not something I dwell on. I'm already generous, I think, donating a large monthly sum to a local rehabilitation charity, and once a year raising other funds for them. I support a few other charities in a more minor way, yet it's a point my mother is always making to me. Having come from a much humbler background than I live in now, her favourite retort to me is, 'How much can one man spend?' She chooses to forget one of the main reasons I have it. I've earned well, sure, I've earned lots of money and have no dependants to spend it on, but a large amount came from an initial compensation that I've invested wisely. From an insurance payout after a drunk driver halved my left leg.

'Stop.' Ollie wags a finger at me.

'Stop what?'

'Overthinking things. You have that look.'

I scrunch my nose and try to rearrange whatever the look is.

'Thank you,' he says. 'For *thinking* about it.' He raises a placatory hand. 'So, potential Big Thing discussed, let's talk about the love part. The "let love into your life" bit of the message.'

'I can do that,' I nod reassuringly.

'Jack, there's been no one since Lynn.'

'And?'

He shrugs. Ollie likes his facts simple, even more so than me, a worn-out barrister.

'I do still know how things work, Oliver.'

'But you have to dip your toe and then you have to want to—'

'I'm ready – at least readier than I've ever been before.'

'That's good.' He leans forward and stares at me, deep in thought. 'You have to be open.'

'I'm an open book.'

'Open to anything the world throws at you. I mean it, Jack, and . . .'

'And what?'

'And you've been closed for so long. Terrified fate will fuck with you again. You're going to have to risk your battered heart.'

'Jesus! Who made you the love guru?' I start to laugh, try to drown out the echo of that last 'Fate' sentence.

'I think I envy you,' he says. 'You have all the adventure and excitement of finding and getting to know someone, the falling in love, the early sex, the—'

'You are so full of shit.' Jennifer, his gorgeous wife, and his two beautiful healthy children register in my raised eyebrows.

'I know,' he admits.

'You wouldn't swap a moment of what you have.'

'Not a second.'

'You don't have to lie to *me*, Ollie. It's not what we do.' I eyeball him. 'Whatever happens, whatever comes my way, I'm ready.'

He nods and it's like a full stop, a point that marks the end of the conversation. A lengthy silence later, he stands. 'I should get back. Jen will be waiting up.'

'What, now that you've potentially got my Barn for a year and given me my instructions, you're off?'

'Ouch . . .' He mock winces. 'It is getting late, I should get on the road.' Ollie squeezes my shoulder as he passes. 'Don't get up.' By this he means that there is no need to reattach my prosthetic and walk him out.

'Go on, go before you start declaring love for me and embarrassing yourself.'

'I do love you, man,' he calls back.

'Good night, Ollie. Give my love to the family you wouldn't swap a moment with.'

The room is totally silent when he leaves.

Rolling my trousers up, I replace my prosthetic and walk over to the record deck. I open the blanket box and, from the pile of jazz albums, I pick the first one, play the first track – Herb Alpert and his band. From the green, velvet-lined box next to my record collection, I remove my trumpet. With my left thumb over the saddle, finger through the ring, and my right fingers on the first, second and third valves, my lips buzz into the mouthpiece and soon joyous jazz fills the room. At the open rear door, I arch my back, working my instrument. As always when I play, my cares vanish. Escape from my broken body is possible with the sounds my lungs and working hands can make. There have never been any neighbours to be bothered, and as my injured heart rises, soars above the boundary that now separates the Barn from the house, I sense that might change very soon.

But by then, I could be anywhere.

*

The next day I see no point in prolonging the decision I've already made.

'Marsha?'

'Yup?' The Head of Chambers is a little curt on the phone. I imagine her in her office, looking at her wrist, knowing it's nearing the end of the working day and wondering why I'm bothering her at this time.

'Quick drink?' I ask.

'Hell yes,' she almost gasps before adding a wary, 'Why?'

'Something I want to run by you.'

'Oh, God. The last time you said that it meant two new hires.'

'Nothing like that. Don't worry.'

After hanging up, my shoulders feel as if some weight has been shed. I walk to the three monkeys and place Speak No Evil face down, angled in the opposite direction to his mates. It takes a few seconds to be certain that I *can* leave him like that before I head down to meet Marsha in the foyer.

Waiting for her, I practise my most winning smile, the one I reserve for court appearances, and when I see her come down the stairs, she immediately frowns.

'Shit, I'm going to regret this, aren't I?'

I laugh, air-kiss her cheeks. 'Of course not. You're going to be helping me. I'm doing something big.'

Marsha keeps pace with me as we walk through Lincoln's Inn Fields towards the Wig and Pencil. Birds are singing in the trees. People, young and old, are sitting on the benches in the café as we walk by. The sound of laughter is all around. I take her arm, the one she's not carrying her briefcase with, and link it through mine.

'You're going to love it,' I tell her, fearing she's really not. '*Because* you're going to be helping me.'

She's silent, though she leaves her arm where it is, and soon we're on the only spare stools, perched at a tall narrow table in the pub, two iced G&Ts ready to go.

'Come on, sock it to me,' she says before taking a long gulp from hers.

Suddenly, I'm not sure what to say, where to start, unsure when the last time I ever asked for help was. And the realisation that, outside of medical assistance, I never really have mutes me momentarily. Yet when the words flow, Marsha listens and is surprisingly agreeable to the plan, even admits to being a little jealous, laughingly begs me to take her with me. She assures me that the other partners will come on board before finally sharing her opinion that this is my midlife crisis and is probably all centred around my own looming fiftieth birthday. Before we leave, she bets me fifty quid, one for each of my living years, that I'll be back within three months.

I smile, and silently look forward to taking it from her.

Chapter Five

Instagram

GraceD15, Croydon

. . .

We are moving! No details yet but leaving the area and am ☹

#housemove #willmissyouall #hockeygang

. . .

View four comments:

    SonyaFarr Nooooooo!

    CarolBonham Good luck, Gracie ☹ #stayintouch
      #willmissyoutoo

    PinkieBrown When u off?

    GraceD15 Will WhatsApp u.

Chapter Six

The recent heatwave has scorched the grass to burnt hay and the shower now falling offers only a brief respite. The weathermen say this August will break a previous record set in 1976. I was seven back then, can remember peeling the tar that grouted road patches outside my parents' house – the stink of bitumen on my hands that would linger way past bedtime. The memory makes me scrub my fingernails at the kitchen sink. I stare out the window at the parched lawn finally being nurtured by much-needed rain, thinking about how far we've all come, my parents and I. Nowadays it's verdant golf courses in sunny Florida that my father frequents, while my mother alternates between playing tennis and teaching her 'American ladies' to play bridge.

The Barn looks back at me – seems to stand proudly behind the new hedge, as if to announce that I'm doing something good with my new life. There's a family moving in today; a woman named Clare Bryanson and her teenage daughter, Grace. According to Ollie, who has met them a few times, I could not hope to have a more perfect 'tenant'.

I resisted telling him that perfection would include a rent payment. I'd have thought it was funny but Ollie, who worries he's pushed me into this, wouldn't have laughed, so I stayed schtum.

What *is* funny, or weird, is how this thing has taken on a life of its own since I agreed to do it. Within ten days, the woman had been informed by the charity and I raised the legal papers and they were signed and suddenly, she – they – will be here tomorrow. I can't deny I feel both a frisson of excitement and full-on terror, alternately.

Turning towards the rear of the kitchen, I'm faced with some of the reasons I haven't packed yet. The wall – some of it still with fashionably exposed brick, but most of it a plastered finish which has been painted with blackboard paint – reveals my very own chalky mind map. Though to look at it, it looks like the meanderings of a middle-aged fool. Even I can no longer follow the threads or see the reasons behind any suggested decision. One day, I'm going to the States first, then onto Australia, then back to Europe, and the next day, the other way around, and then another day, I hop all over the world in a completely nonsensical random manner – just because I can. It's so unlike me that I can't bear to even look at it, so, in the end, I've done nothing, because I want to meet the neighbours before I leave. I just need to look into their eyes.

Grabbing my nearest rain jacket, I head out to the pig pen, the bucket of scraps from the kitchen in my hand. The two pygmies, Walnut and Pecan, are waiting by the

gate. I'm convinced they have their own personalities –
Pecan being the bully and Walnut the pacifist. As if on
cue, Pecan pushes his way towards the bucket in my hand
before I get to the trough. 'Don't be greedy,' I rub his nose.
'Your brother has to eat too.'

They're making such a racket that I'm wondering if
they're attempting a high-pitched harmony to the baritone scales I'm singing, or maybe they're laughing – their
tiny squeals like the pealing giggles young children make.
I'm sloshing about in the pen with them, when different
noises sound from the Barn's direction – a car arriving, a
removal truck maybe. I hurry back up the garden as quick
as I can, and though I rarely bother with the top level of
the house, I take the stairs slowly. From a landing window,
I glimpse a white van. It's parked next to the small grey
Nissan that arrived last night, the owner leaving immediately in a taxi from the firm located at the railway station.
As I watch, my hands are trembling. Having handed this
whole thing over to Chance, what if it's a disaster and Fate
just decided at birth that I was somehow unworthy?

The rear door at the back of the Barn opens, which
means they've found the keys I left out for them, and I
see a young girl come into the garden. She's tall, wearing jeans and a T-shirt, and has a knotted headscarf over
blonde hair. Definitely no horns. Or cloven hooves. Or a
forked tail. She wanders around, smelling flowers, taking
in the view, and though she seems harmless enough, I find
myself wishing I'd put taller hedging or actual trees by the
new fence.

I move downstairs, collect my keys. It's time to meet the neighbours, as I'd promised Ollie I would.

Picking up the folder I'd prepared, I pull the door behind me, perfect my gait and head over. At the Barn, I push the bell.

'Hello!' the girl beams a greeting when it opens.

'Hi.'

'You must be Mr Tate, the landlord.' She offers her hand.

I have no reason to lie as I shake it briefly. I have no worldly understanding of why I *do* lie, other than some innate fear of this actually happening. It's no longer an event on a spreadsheet. It's a for-real thing, the 'Big Thing' made flesh and occurring right now.

'I'm, er, I'm Martin,' I say. 'I live next door.'

'Oh.' She looks a little disappointed. 'Mum!' she yells over her shoulder. 'Martin from next door is here.'

I'm just wondering if I'll be asked into my own house when she says, 'Oops, forgot my manners. Do come in. Do you mind wiping your feet on the mat though? This place is spotless!'

Up close she seems younger than I'd first thought, though she holds herself and speaks in such a non-teenage manner that I'm momentarily confused. Then again, my only teenage barometer is Antony, who barked at his mother, Lynn, constantly and who, on a good day, merely grunted at me.

'I seriously think Mum will make me carry a cleaning cloth everywhere I go!' she adds, looking around.

This is good, I think. I quite like the image of them both being clean freaks.

A woman appears in the hallway and, inexplicably, my tongue decides to completely knot itself at that exact moment.

'Hello, Martin,' Clare Bryanson greets me with another handshake.

I smile, afraid of the sound I'll make.

'Goodness, have you *seen* this place? Grace and I have been wandering around gaping. Everything, just everything, is so beautiful.'

Immediately, something just fills my soul. Her smile, the pleasure and gratitude they both exude, seeps into me.

'Do you know the landlord?' she asks me, looking at the folder in my hands.

'Yes, I know Jack . . .'

'Well, would you mind giving him this when you see him next?' She reaches across to the chrome table that stands up against the only nearby wall, the living space and kitchen beyond being totally open plan, and hands me a bottle bag with a card peeking out the top.

'Sure.' I clear my throat, beg my tongue to unravel as I stumble over my words. 'He, er, Jack that is, he, er, wanted me to give you this folder with everything you need to know about the house.'

Clare takes it from me, and I note they're both nodding simultaneously, which under any other circumstance might make me laugh, but here and now confirms that they think I'm strange. They think they're living next to an oddball, who, after today, they'll be glad to never see again.

'I'd offer you a cup of tea, but everything is still in the van!' She points to the self-hire van she must have driven here.

'No problem, another time.' I back up towards the door.

Clare fans her face with her hand. 'Is it hot in here or is it me?'

Grace laughs. 'Mum is always hot, Martin. She'll have all the windows open within minutes of you leaving.'

I don't normally take to teenagers, but she seems sweet. 'If you need anything . . .' I address the mother.

'Thank you, Martin. Oh, you don't happen to have Mr Tate's mobile number, do you?'

'You don't have it?'

'No, Mr Rantzen explained that—' Her face flushes and she tucks some loose hair behind her ears, stops herself saying 'the charity', not wanting Martin from next door to know her circumstances, and I'm appalled at myself for putting her in that position. I pretend to look up 'Jack's' number on my phone and call mine out to her. She keys it into an iPhone that looks older than the Barn. 'Thank you.' Her smile is wide and genuine.

'You're welcome,' I tell her, filled with a simple certainty that this – this has been the right thing to do. 'I'm sure Jack won't mind if you call him. And I'll make sure he gets the bottle.' It's only as I'm leaving that my tongue has managed to untie itself.

'Cheerio, Martin,' Clare says.

'See ya,' Grace smiles.

I leave them to it, wondering what in hell they're saying about me, deciding I really don't want to know.

Back at the house, I open the bag – a bottle of supermarket own-brand champagne that she can probably ill afford. I tear open the envelope, really wanting to know what this woman and her daughter have written to their benefactor, Jack Tate:

'Dear Mr Tate,' I read it aloud. 'I'm really not sure that there are words in the world to express our gratitude to you. What I can say is that, thanks to your kindness, the transition after divorce will be easier. We have (I'm led to believe by Mr Oliver Rantzen) the most beautiful home to move into and we have the chance to rebuild our lives after what has been a very difficult time. Both Grace and I are humbled and grateful. Thank you from the bottom of both our hearts.'

The card is signed by Clare and Grace Bryanson. I read it again in my head, study the flowery handwriting, and then place it on top of the kitchen table.

When my mobile rings, I flinch at the sound, take it from my front pocket. Afraid it might be her calling, I think about not answering, but then tell myself I'm being ridiculous and press answer. 'Hello?'

Nothing.

'Hello?' I repeat.

A faint rhythmic sound, someone breathing as if they're trying not to be heard.

'Who is this?' I glance one more time at the number before placing the phone back to my ear. I have no idea why, but these calls have been coming lately, and because I've nothing to say to anyone who won't announce themselves, I end the call.

To keep busy, I try to play, practising scales. I shut all the windows in case I disturb my new neighbours. The fingers are bad today, feel like they're sluggish and slow. I attempt to accompany an instrumental practice track. It's dreadful, really awful, and I end up chucking the trumpet back in its case and switching on the television. In the middle of *Blue Planet*, I eat a tasteless sandwich, wondering how Clare and Grace are making their way around the small, but state-of-the-art, kitchen in the Barn.

I glance at the mind map, relieved that, now the neighbours are here, I can fix it. I can sort out the best itinerary and pack my bags. It's time for the 'see how the wider world works' part to begin.

Chapter Seven

It was overwhelming. Everything about it.

Ever since the morning when she'd been battling with the idea of having to call her mother, listening to the echo of rock bottom in what used to be her home in Croydon, when fate had intervened and thrown her a lifeline, Clare's days had taken on a dreamlike quality. She may not have had the winning ticket with Gladys's raffle, but completing a form she'd seen at the Citizens Advice office had led to a call from a stranger named Oliver Rantzen, and *everything* had changed. Events then moved quickly and here she was – with Grace, in a stunning house in rural Wiltshire. One moment the horror of being homeless, the likelihood of temporary living in bed-and-breakfast accommodation loomed, and the next – this house, the views, the garden, the kitchen.

Pinching herself wasn't enough. It was so surreal she'd had to move through the rooms slowly; the enormous high-ceilinged living room with a kitchen at one end, the ground-floor bedroom and bathroom, Grace's bedroom upstairs. She'd stood in each one, just touching the walls and windows. In the kitchen she'd turned each ring of the gas hob on and off and flicked the light switch that controlled the twenty-six spotlights several times. Twenty-six spotlights . . .

Standing still by the huge opening to the rear garden, she stared at the view through the glass, remembering a childhood television programme where the presenters urged young viewers to 'look through the round or square window today'. There would be scenes of something interesting, narrated by the presenter. Clare inhaled the rural scene; a landscape of colours and shapes of trees, tall and small, and fields, ploughed and planted, like she had only ever seen in pictures. She listened for new noises. No more pneumatic thumping from the building site that had been next door to their home in Croydon for months. No more passing traffic. The only outdoor sounds she'd heard since moving in yesterday had been birdsong, the hum of a distant tractor and some tiny squeals. Piglets, Grace told her, having gone down the garden and peered over the line of fenced greenery that separated the two properties. Their house, a high-tech converted barn, was almost twice the size of the semi they'd left. Next door's turn-of-the-century thatched cottage, where Martin lived, looked like it might in fact be huge inside. She wondered if he lived there alone or with family.

Clare fanned herself with a skinny novel from the top of one of Grace's boxes as a sudden but powerful heat flushed through her. She leaned out the window, breathing in the still summer air as the moment passed quickly. Upstairs, her daughter could be heard singing in her bedroom.

Grace was already soaking up everything new, yet the new both thrilled and frightened Clare. She didn't know what to do with herself because things like this didn't happen, not really, at least not to her. And her meagre furniture in the big space seemed to scream the question whether she belonged there at all – whether she was worthy of this break. Why her, why not one of the thousands of other people who needed help? For just a second she wondered how she'd be able to run the house – it was rent-free, but utilities were down to her.

Stop, she told herself. Stop. She was worthy. She *was* lucky. Thanks to Oliver Rantzen and Jack Tate, she and Grace had the best of new starts and, somehow, she'd work the rest out.

The sound of trumpet playing made her look up towards the cottage. She recognised the tune and hummed along, raising herself up on her toes and pirouetting, before calling loudly up the stairs.

'Grace? I'm going out to get food. You want to come?'

'Nah, today is all about my room.'

Clare smiled. With one tap of a hammer and a single nail, Grace had installed her pink mosquito net above her bed and was busy nesting.

In the front driveway, Clare climbed into her Nissan and headed slowly to the edge of town – one-point-three miles on the dash. At the nearest end of the high street, she bought a half-kilo of mince in the butchers and some carrots and onions from a small grocer. Further up the street, she could see the signs for a supermarket and some recognisable stores, yet there were also smaller, charming shops – a tea rooms, a library, a church. Clare felt the sense of a close community moving around her, something she wasn't accustomed to but nor was she afraid of. Crossing over the road to one of two pubs, she glanced in the window, wondering if she would ever get to the point of sharing a glass of wine in there with some local friends.

'We don't open until 12.30.' She heard someone speak behind her and turned.

'Oh, I was just looking.'

The voice belonged to an extremely tall man with a mop of dirty-blonde hair, a darker, long beard and an accent she couldn't place.

'I'm Clare.' She thrust a hand forward.

'Nice to meet you, Clare.' He shook it. 'You passing through?'

'Er, no, I—' She glanced up the road she'd just driven on. Here on the edge of town, she realised she could see her house from the spot she stood in. 'We've just moved into a new house,' her head jerked towards it. 'The Barn.'

'Ahhh,' he said. 'I'm Jan, spelt J-A-N but pronounced "Yan", licensee here.'

'Nice to meet you, Jan.'

'So, you're the new tenant. Place looks lovely.'

Clare nodded, her eyes suddenly landing on a square of paper sitting in the window next to him. ***Help wanted, enquire within***. Never someone to wait around, she bit the bullet. 'You're looking for staff, Jan?'

'Bar staff, mostly evenings, some days. You know some-one?'

'Me,' she announced. 'It's been years since I worked in a bar, but I do have experience.'

Hire me. I need a job. I could roll down the hill from the house to here. Hire me.

Jan tried to cover a slight frown, but she caught it. 'I'm reliable, hard-working.'

'What are you doing tonight?' he asked.

'Unpacking boxes that can wait.'

He jangled keys in his hand. 'Come down for seven and we'll give it a try. See how you go. Wear black,' he said as he used his shoulder to push the door he'd unlocked.

'I'll be here,' she said.

On the drive home, she thought of the fact that she didn't possess a single black item of clothing, Tim always wanting her to wear bright colours. Grace would have something, she told herself.

She rubbed her hand over her stomach, touched her sore breasts with her fingertips. Her periods were all over the place and Google had informed her she was perimenopausal, a fact she was trying to ignore since it meant middle age was upon her.

'He plays the trumpet,' Grace was standing on the stairs looking at her as she came in. 'Next-door-man-Martin. I mean, it's nice and all, but he plays the trumpet for a lo-o-ng time!'

'You're not complaining, Grace, are you?'

'Me? Never.' Her daughter skipped down the last few stairs. 'What's for supper? I'm starved.'

Clare carried the bag through to the kitchen. 'Spaghetti Bolognese. I'll make it, but you'll have to eat alone – I'll be out.'

Grace's head whipped around. 'Out? Where? We've just arrived!'

'A sort of job interview. Guy who owns the local pub is letting me try out for bar staff tonight. You'll be OK here, won't you? Have you anything black? I need to wear black.'

'Breathe, Mum.'

Clare leaned on the countertop. 'It's all a bit surreal.'

'I know.'

'I'm afraid I'll wake up.' She gathered her daughter's tall frame in her arms. 'I'm scared someone will tap me on the shoulder and say "Wakey, wakey!" and that I'll be left with only the idea that this is maybe what we could have had if I'd done something specific, but I'm not even sure what it is I was supposed to do?'

'It's definitely real. You know how I know?'

Clare let her daughter pull away from her, felt her pinch her arm twice as she moved.

'Ouch!'

'Because if you were dreaming you'd have woken just now.'

'If I'm scared, you must be terrified.' Clare rubbed her arm.

'Nope.'

'Really?' Her eyebrows raised. 'You're not even a little bit scared?'

Grace shook her head. 'I probably will be on Monday starting school, but I'm glad we're here, Mum.'

'It's the worst time to move you, GCSEs next year, I—'

'Subjects are the same, curriculum is the same, just different teachers. It'll be fine, Mum.'

'You're right. Of course, you're right.' She unpacked the food and stared at the fridge. 'I just bought for tonight. I'll do a supermarket shop tomorrow.'

'You start dinner. I'll find something black.'

When Grace disappeared upstairs, Clare opened the fridge. There were eight shelves inside. She scratched her head, thinking she'd never, ever fill it. Instead, she filled a glass with cold water from its front, drank half of it down and began to chop an onion.

*

Jan, it turned out, was Norwegian and his wife, an English woman called Emma, told Clare all about how they met when she was in college nearby, and how her parents still weren't speaking to her for wasting her extremely expensive private education on a 'Viking'. It reminded Clare of her own estranged mother, something she could never have explained in a few simple sentences as Emma had.

Clare nodded understandingly, listened carefully as she was reminded how to pull pints. As the evening progressed it felt as if she'd been there forever. And she'd met so many of the locals, all pleasant to her, all welcoming.

Climbing into her car at the end of the night, Clare opened her palm and stared at the cash Jan had pressed into it: forty-eight pounds for four hours' work. He'd told her, with a squeeze of her hand, that the job was hers if she wanted it. She wanted it. The next day, she promised herself, she'd contact the local dance schools and see if there might be any teaching opportunities around.

Outside the Barn, she switched off the ignition, kissed her fingertips and tapped them on the steering wheel. It was a thank you gesture she'd developed a habit of, as if a quick appreciation towards the old car would be remembered by it the next time she turned the key. She still did it to her pillow every morning as an acknowledgement that she was grateful to be alive.

Tim slipped into her thoughts as she recalled the early days of their marriage, how she'd used to reach across their bed and tap him gently three times before he woke. She caught her breath. In so many ways, she missed him. She'd never had to think about practicalities, because he'd taken care of them; he'd taken care of her. The irony was laughable – how taking care of her had also meant raising his hands to her. That was some kind of twisted logic, missing anything at all to do with their union – but she understood that at the core of it she was terrified of the sole responsibility for creating a new life for her and Grace. Especially having already failed spectacularly to hold onto their home.

As she got out of the car, a security light beamed in front of the building and Clare blew the contents of her lungs through pursed lips. It *was* real. All of it. The Barn. Grace and her here. A job that had fallen into her lap within twenty-four hours. Luck had wrapped its arms around them, and she allowed herself to fall into its hug. Life was good and Tim was nowhere to be seen.

She had this.

Her phone pinged in her hand and, looking at it, she swore under her breath. It was as if he knew, as if somehow, even at this distance, he'd known that she'd allowed herself to think about him. She couldn't, wouldn't; she refused to let him seep back into her life, and as she locked the car, she shoved the phone deeper into her pocket.

'How was it?' Grace called from a sofa. Clare had placed both her sofas opposite one another, next to the wood burner. In front of the one Grace lay on sat a low coffee table with their small flat-screen television on top of it. The shiny pine dining table that Clare loved, because it was the first piece of furniture she'd ever bought, stood in front of the wide floor-to-ceiling window overlooking the garden. Grace muted the sound. 'You look like you could do with a cuppa.'

Clare looked at her watch. 'It's late. I shouldn't.'

Grace stood. 'Have a caffeine-free one. I want to hear all about your night.'

From the kitchen end of the room, Clare heard the kettle switch being flicked.

'Did Dad get you?' her daughter yelled.

Clare sat down, closed her eyes and sighed.

'Mum?'

Reluctantly, she pulled her phone free from her pocket and read his message, fighting the tears that threatened to fall as the words sank in.

Tomoro is Fri. No reason Grace n me can't still have curry. Will need a bed overnite – sure u have room. T

Grace placed a small tray next to the television. Two mugs of steaming-hot tea and a plate of digestive biscuits made Clare realise she hadn't eaten since lunchtime. She took two, sandwiched them together and bit into them.

'I found some chamomile.' Grace sat down. 'And I can tell by your face that Dad got you.'

Clare could only nod.

'I'll put him off,' Grace offered, 'tell him we're out.'

'Would you? Just until next week, I'm not saying that—'

'I get it, Mum. I'll tell him we have something on and rearrange for next week.'

'He's just curious, I know.' Clare felt her head shaking. 'But I need the time to get my own head around all of this without him being here, without—'

'His shit,' Grace filled in the end of her sentence.

Clare blushed. 'He's your father. Of course, he can stay over if he comes to take you out. It'll have to be the sofa though. He seems to think we have a spare room . . .'

'Mum, there's no reason that I can't go and see him in Croydon and . . .' Grace paused. 'This is a big school year for me. I've been thinking that when I see him next, I'll try to suggest every fortnight instead of every week.'

Clare sipped the scented tea, imagining how Tim not seeing Grace when he wanted to would somehow be all her fault. 'Maybe I'll just—'

'Mum. I'll see Dad next week. I'll tell him I have something on tomorrow.'

Clare faced her daughter. Guilt for the fact that Grace and Tim's visits with one another would inevitably be affected by their move prodded her, before being quickly replaced by a certainty that the move was the right thing. 'What though? We've only just got here. What could we have on?'

'The neighbours are having a "welcome to us" drink at theirs.'

She laughed. 'It's probably best to be honest, Grace.'

'Maybe by tomorrow, Mr Trumpet will have asked us over.'

'Just tell your dad the truth. We still have boxes to unpack and it's too bloody soon.'

'Then he'll only offer to help. He'll suggest a takeaway for all *three* of us.'

Clare scratched her head.

'Will you leave it to me?' Grace asked. 'I know how to handle Dad.'

She nodded, stood, took her tea with her. 'I'm heading to bed.'

'You never told me how the pub trial was? Did you get the job?'

'If I want it, yes.'

'You do, don't you?'

Clare leaned over and kissed Grace's worried forehead. 'What I don't want is to be out every night with you home alone. I'll see if I can work something out with them where I do two or three nights with some day shifts. And tomorrow, tomorrow I need to find the dance schools in the area.'

Grace smiled. 'Night, Mum. Sleep well.'

As Clare walked along the hallway, she heard the sound of the television again. Grace was still on school holidays for another week, Clare reasoned, no need to push her fifteen-year-old daughter towards bed at this hour until then. She walked into the small en-suite bathroom, where, looking at her reflection for a full two minutes in what was someone else's mirror, she brushed her teeth. Peeling off her clothes, she slid under the duvet, almost asleep before her head hit the pillow.

She dreamed Trumpet Man was having a party and everyone was invited. Except her and Grace. And she and Grace stayed home in the most luscious barn pretending they didn't care, eating lukewarm curry with Tim.

Chapter Eight

Instagram

GraceD15, Melborough, Wiltshire

. . .

Unbelievably excited about my new room and view.
See pic below!

#housemove #thatgarden #thatchedcottageview

. . .

View four comments:

> **SonyaFarr** Looks amaaaaazing! Parteeeee at
> yours?!
>
> **ReyaPurdite** Have messaged you on WhatsApp.
> See you still have the pink mosquito net?!
> #nomossiesheremate
>
> **MollyDunne** Too good for Croydon now?
> #forgotyourrootsalready #biggarden #sowhat
>
> **MattTheBat** Good riddance Beeeeattch.

WhatsApp Reya & Grace

Why u posting pics, G? Still think U left without proper goodbye & now Ur showing off. R

Reya, not showing off. Why U think that? Sorry, no time for long goodbye. U know that. Grace Xxxxxx

Ur right. Sorrreeeee. Just miss u. R x

Instagram

GraceD15, Melborough, Wiltshire

. . .

Missing all my friends ☹

#housemove #croydonrocks #oldfriendsarebest

. . .

View four comments:

> **MeenaKendall** Thought you were living it up somewhere else. Why the sad face?

> **AliTyler** R U alright? Hockey Tues nite not same without U.

CraigWatts That's a big fridge in the background. U been in? #eatingallthepies #porkerface not #pokerface

ReyaPurdite Ignore that #pindick G.

Chapter Nine

The girl ambushes me in the garden when I'm watering the hedge along the boundary.

'Hello.'

I hear the voice from just beyond the foliage, and one more time wish I'd planted a tall row of cypress trees.

'You're a neat trumpet player,' it says.

Her face appears through the top of the leaves and moves a little to her right to where there's a bigger gap in the greenery and, unlike yesterday, I take the time to get a proper look at her. She's about sixteen, I reckon, has long blonde hair tied back in a high ponytail and is wearing what seems to be her standard uniform of jeans and a black T-shirt.

'Snap,' she says, laughing at my matching casual attire.

I smile.

'You have pigs.' Her head nods towards the pen, where their snouts are now both in the trough. 'They're meant to be really bright.'

'Intelligent, emotional, cognitively complex,' I reply.

'But I do love a bacon sandwich,' she whispers.

'To be fair, it used to be my favourite way of starting the day before I had these guys. Now, I can't bear the thought.'

'Do they really eat anything?'

'They're not crazy about citrus fruit but, otherwise, not fussy.'

'What are their names?'

'Walnut and Pecan,' I tell her. 'They're both nuts.'

She grins, then catches sight of something in their garden and turns to face me. 'Do you happen to know what they're for?' She points to a row of ground-mounted solar panels. 'Are they solar thingies?'

'They *are* solar thingies – the Barn is completely self-sufficient.'

She folds her arms and looks back at the building.

'Everything runs off solar power,' I explain. 'This summer has been great, so I reckon you'll be selling back to the grid if you're lucky.' I'm wondering why they haven't gathered all of this from the pack I left for them. 'It's all in the information pack.' I can't help myself.

'Mum has it, but I'm not sure she's read it all yet. This week's been totally mad.'

'So, where have you guys come from, Grace?' I know all of their details from Ollie but want to hear it from her.

'Croydon.'

'I spent the first ten years of my life very near there.'

'Really?'

'Yes, I was born in Purley.'

'I've left all my friends,' she blurts, staring at Walnut and Pecan so much that I look down at them myself. 'Though one of them called me "Porker" last night. On Instagram.'

I'm not exactly sure how Instagram works, but her words make me wince. 'Some friend,' I say.

She chews her lower lip. 'You're right. Think I'll just block him.'

'Not a clue what you're talking about, I'm afraid. Other than the name-calling. That's just rude.'

She laughs, as if the idea of her neighbour not knowing about social media is cute somehow. I resist explaining. I mean, I *know* about social media – I just choose not to take part in it in any manner.

She makes to walk back to the house. 'Nice talking to you, Martin,' she says.

For a couple of moments, as I tug the hose behind me, we're both walking together, but on different sides of the fence and shrubs, before she heads up the slight incline towards the back of the Barn. Her tall frame is long and athletic, and I can't imagine why anyone would be cruel enough to try to fat-shame her. I remind myself it's not a new thing. I too had been teased mercilessly in school. And later, even in university, when people should have known better, the word 'cripple' had been tossed at me often.

'You'll make new friends.' My words are an attempt to reassure her, but with no reply, I'm unsure if she even heard them. She disappears through the rear doors in the Barn and I find myself wondering if there's something else I can do for these people. The girl has nudged something in me; something that makes me want to help even more, and I spend the afternoon oscillating between trying to figure out what that might be and telling myself not to be stupid – that I've already done more than enough.

*

It's only a few hours later and it's raining again when I see Clare Bryanson for the second time. She's responsible for the banging on my door that wakes me after I'd fallen asleep in front of the television.

Seeing her damp shape through the peephole, I open up. 'Clare,' is all I say. It's eleven at night and I can only assume there's a problem. 'Everything OK?'

She ignores my question and, without being asked, enters and drips all over my hallway.

'Come in,' I mutter.

'So, Martin, or is it Jack?'

My hand goes to my neck.

'I'm working some evening shifts down in the pub.'

'Oh.'

'Yep, getting to know the locals.'

'Right.' Heat rises under my palm.

'They talk, these punters – all happy to meet the new tenant in the Barn, all wondering how I get on with the landlord next door.' She shivers.

'Can I get you a towel, to dry off?'

'Is it you?' she asks softly. 'Are you, Jack, the person who's made this happen for Grace and me?'

I nod, silently pointing her into the kitchen, towards the Aga, where she'll at least be warm.

'Why didn't you just tell us?' she asks.

'I've no idea.' My laugh is nervous and part of me just wants to launch into the truth, that my tongue suddenly twisted around itself in front of her and I found myself unable to talk. That when I meet new people, especially women, I imagine them seeing me as lacking. It never happens with clients, only ever outside of work. I've realised over the years that it's the fact I know I'm not 'whole' that warps my thinking, but it doesn't seem to get any easier. 'I suppose I've never done anything like this before and . . . I don't know. Hold on a minute.' I walk back to the cloakroom and grab a hand towel. 'You'll catch a cold. At least dry your hair.'

She tosses her head over when I hand her the towel and does as I ask. The result is no longer soft damp curls but something more like a bird's nest. I say nothing.

'I want to say thank you . . .' She stops talking, her head shaking in tiny side-to-side movements, then eyes, blue as the darkest sapphire, fix on mine. 'Then that sounds so inadequate. Thank you for giving Grace and I this amazing chance is probably more what I mean.'

Clare is twisting the hand towel in her hands and I gently prise it from her, realising that Chance and I have somehow collaborated to help this family out.

'You're welcome. I mean that – you're both welcome. I hope it works out for you.'

'It will.' She smiles, and it changes her face, and I wonder who the man who let her go was. According to Ollie, she had a dreadful time with her ex. 'Would you mind giving me an hour of your time some day?' she asks. 'Maybe go through the utilities with me so I know what to expect? Grace mentioned solar panels, but I was late for work and didn't really hear details.' She rubs her mouth with the back of her hand before breathing slowly through spread fingers.

'Of course.' I'm not sure what else to say, so I opt for nothing. In my straightforward attempt at altruism, it never crossed my mind that someone might struggle to run the place. And yet, that's what I realise is hiding behind this woman's smile.

I'm about to tell her not to worry, that the place practically runs itself, when something catches her attention behind me, and she veers her head to her right to see past me. 'What . . .?' she squints her eyes. 'What have you got on your wall?'

I turn and look at the 'blackboard' with what I hope is a dispassionate eye, but I can see how it seems. Unfolding my arms, I remove my glasses, automatically clean them with the end of my T-shirt. 'It's a mind map, like a picture plot.' There are lots of spidery arrows and scribbles that to anyone else look like an explosion of chalk. 'They're my travel plans. Would you like a drink?' I point towards a few bottles sitting on top of a worktop nearby.

'No thanks. I should get back to Grace. I'll leave you to your . . . mapping.'

'Of course,' I repeat.

She turns, walks back to the hallway, and I follow.

'What did you do, Clare, before, in Croydon?'

'I was a dance teacher. Ran classes, all ages. I used to be . . .' She stops herself, palms suddenly airborne. 'I've taken up enough of your time, Jack.'

'People want to learn to dance in Wiltshire, you know.' I do a very bad upper-body shimmy to make her laugh because, for some reason, I want that before she leaves. I'm granted a wide grin.

'Let's hope so. I mean, let's hope people who might want to learn to dance in Wiltshire want me to teach them.'

'For sure.' If I were a younger, less inhibited man, with two fully functioning legs, I'd have this woman teach me to dance. Something from the way she holds herself, upright, poised, tells me she could probably out-move the best. 'Would you have liked to have your own school?'

'I tried it once. It didn't work out.'

'Why not?' It's possibly a nosy question but I ask it anyway.

She hesitates, lost in reflection for a moment, as if she's deciding how to answer. 'My ex,' she replies. 'If I'm honest, he never liked the idea. I was busy and he said I wasn't around for the family.' She says it slowly, as if she's trying the words out for size, as if it's the first time she has acknowledged it out loud or to herself.

Spurred on by the image of her daughter this afternoon, words that I've never given a moment's thought to spill from my mouth. 'You could try again,' I tell her. 'Set up your own school here in the garage next to the Barn. It's not included in the tenancy but there's no reason you couldn't have it. It's heated.' I pause, embarrassed that I had, until selling it recently, housed a very expensive car in said heated garage. 'It has glass doors at the back, so there's natural light and . . .' I stop talking, half worrying about what the hell has come over me, while also quite liking what I'm saying. For a moment I can tell she's thinking about the possibility. 'Do you believe in Chance, Clare?'

'I'm here so, yes, sure. I mean, what are the chances . . .' she says.

'I think you could maybe,' I begin, 'take a chance on dance.'

She scratches her head, looks at me as if she doesn't believe we're here or having this conversation. 'I've got to go,' she says. 'I'm sorry for calling so late and thank you once again – for everything.'

Before she leaves, I nudge her arm gently with my own. 'Think about it,' I say.

'Good night, Jack,' she says and runs through the rain to her car.

I close the door, realising that I'm glad they're here. I really want them to be happy and perhaps I've always wanted neighbours. And perhaps *they* were always meant to be my neighbours.

Maybe, just maybe, this is Fate befriending me.

Chapter Ten

There was, she thought, something fascinating about him, with his weird wall and his bookshelves full of classics. A few nights ago, Clare had cast her eyes over the shelves in his hallway, laden with names she would never read: Dickens, Mark Twain, Emily Brontë, just a few she'd seen. He was, she conceded, looking at him now, an attractive man, not her type, but someone who looked after himself; difficult to age, mid-forties maybe, and well-dressed in a quirky, bespectacled way. Sort of like an ageing Clark Kent, she thought, wondering if his posh-boy accent was something he was born into, or something he'd acquired along the way. Clare wanted to know more about him; the person who had gifted them a new home, a potential new way of life, the person who was sitting at her pine table drinking coffee, looking up the garden towards his home, frowning.

'You can really still see my place from here, can't you? Needs more shrubs, taller ones, and the shape of the hedging is all uneven. I can see that better from here.' Jack's frown altered in a split second to reveal a closed-mouth, apologetic smile. 'Uneven bothers me.'

Clare wasn't interested in looking at uneven shrubbery and didn't answer his rhetorical question. 'So, apart from my saviour, who *are* you, Jack Tate?' she asked.

'I'm not sure what you mean.'

'Tell me about you, the guy who lives alone up here on the hill. The man who plays trumpet and sings scales to his pigs.'

'When you put it like that . . .'

She grinned. 'What do you do for a living?'

'I'm a barrister, but I'm taking a sabbatical for a while.'

'A barrister, wow . . . And the career break explains the wall – when are you planning to travel?'

'I'll be leaving soon for a few months, but not sure exactly when yet.'

'How exciting!' Clare hoped she sounded excited for him. She couldn't imagine anything worse. One of the things she and Tim had had in common was the fact they were both home birds. They hated to fly, and on the one occasion they'd managed to get to Florida, her beloved father had died while she was away. 'Can I ask a personal question?'

Frown lines appeared like horizontal stripes on his forehead, yet he nodded.

'Why did you do this? Don't get me wrong – Grace and I pray we're not dreaming every day, but why invite strangers to be your neighbours?'

'If you'd bought the Barn, you'd still be strangers . . .' He gave a little shrug. 'It's not complicated. Someone I know suggested I make some changes in my life, recommended something big. Then another friend suggested this, and here we are.'

He made it sound so simple that Clare wondered if he even knew what he *had* done. She knew so little about him but doubted he had ever felt the dread she had felt only weeks ago; the sheer desperation of losing her home and panic over her and Grace's future. Where they found themselves now, helped by the kindness of this one man, still seemed fantastical.

He straightened the stack of papers in front of him. 'We should do this,' he said. 'I don't want to eat into your day too much.'

As well as coffee beans for the walled coffee machine he'd shown her how to use, he'd come armed with examples of bills for the Barn. Clare listened and made notes. The council-tax bill had almost made her eyes bleed, but the fact that there was no gas connection and that electricity was taken care of for most of the year with the solar panels was better news. The phone line, he explained, was really only there to provide internet and maybe Sky television.

'We don't need satellite television,' she interrupted, 'but we'll keep the landline for Wi-Fi.'

'Great,' he said. 'Look, I'll leave these here with you. It's a really easy house to run and, relative to its size, economical too. I still have the ride-on lawnmower and Grace can do the garden with it any time. So, that's the outside taken care of.' He grinned, as if to say his work there was done.

Clare glanced at her watch. 'She'll be on lunch break now.' She'd spoken the words aloud without realising it. 'Today's the first day in her new school.'

'You mustn't worry about Grace.' Jack, who seemed to have read her mind, was looking straight at her. 'We only children, we're an unusually capable bunch.'

'You're an only child as well?' she asked.

'I am.'

'Gosh, me too. Are both your parents—'

'Alive and kicking,' he answered, draining his coffee cup as he stood. 'Living the dream in Florida. Right, I'll leave you to the rest of your day. If you need anything else let me know.'

She stood too, waving her hands at the surrounds. 'Thank you once again for everything and for this morning. You've put my mind at rest.'

'I meant what I said about the garage too.'

She felt his gaze on her and blurted, 'I was a national dance champion once.' No sooner had she said the words than she wished she could pull them back on a string. All through the previous night she'd played around with the idea of setting up her own school again. While awake, she could almost see it as a possibility. In her sleep, all she heard was Tim yelling at her that she was never home, and her mother's scorn when it would inevitably fail.

'That's brilliant!' Jack removed his glasses and bright eyes, the colour of the damp grass outside the door, trained on her as she blushed.

'It was a long time ago,' she added.

'Ballroom or Latin?'

'Ballroom. Though I also competed at top level in Latin.'

'I'm impressed,' he said, putting his glasses on again and peering through them. 'Look, I'm not good at speeches,' he said. 'Not unless I'm in court, so I'll make this quick. Anything I can do to make this transition work for you, I want to, while I'm still here.'

'Thank you.' Clare wondered if she could ever come up with other words to say the same thing. 'But I'm incredibly grateful for everything you've already done, truly.'

Closing the door behind him, she refused to dwell on what he'd said about leaving soon. She refused to give airtime to her concern over being alone in rural solitude because she was Clare Bryanson and Clare Bryanson of Melborough was a strong, independent woman, determined to make shit happen and never again depend on any man.

It was 12.45 and she had a life to grab by its balls.

*

A few hours later, using Tim's old iPad that he had passed onto Grace, Clare looked up the two local dance schools. One, held in the town hall, seemed centred around pre- and early-school tap and ballet. The other offered classes of all styles to all abilities and all ages, and was based in a small theatre in the next town.

She read their websites from top to bottom, several times. On a notepad, she wrote down what she alone might offer, that was different, better. Though it was a short list, she couldn't ignore a new and strange fire in her belly. Jack had ignited it with the words, 'You could set up your own school here.' She underlined the top sentence. It was what Tim used to call a USP, a catchword he'd heard the salespeople using in the life-insurance company he worked an administrative role at.

National Ballroom Champion 1995 – 1998, four years from aged nineteen to twenty-two.

Before she could stop herself, she'd walked outside, turned left and up the path, and was knocking on the cottage door just as she had a few nights ago.

'Sorry,' she said when Jack appeared. 'I'm really, really, sorry to bother you again. The garage, were you serious?'

She noted every crease in his face and breathed out as they deepened when he smiled.

'Perfectly serious. Would you like to have a look?'

She could only nod as he turned to root in a big bowl of keys.

'It'll take a bit of work and you'd need to have PL insurance if you're working from there, get change-of-usage permission from the council too.' He turned back to her, waved a remote in his hand. 'Found it.'

She walked beside him. A look inside wouldn't kill her. Silent, she watched as he pressed the remote and one of the three garage doors rose.

'There's a proper door around the side too, you'd use that for people going in and out.'

Clare moved slowly, her eyes darting left to right. There was indeed a side entrance and there were two glass sliding doors on the far wall overlooking the garden and fields beyond, allowing natural light in. On two of the walls there were large radiators and next to one of them stood a black metallic drawer unit on castor wheels, with a neatly stacked pile of classic-car magazines on top.

'Who has a sweeping view of rapeseed and heating for their cars?' she asked him quietly. The words escaped before she filtered them.

'To be fair, there was only one car. An old classic that needed an ambient temperature, not so much the view.' He scratched his head, embarrassed. 'Anyway, I sold it.'

She watched a red flush creep up his neck as he walked the length of the garage and opened the sliding door before closing it and locking it again.

'I didn't say anything earlier, but I googled you last night.' He had turned back to face her, and it was Clare's turn to redden. 'You should do this, Clare. If you're even ten per cent as good as you once were, you should do it.'

Her head reeled with the cost of the changes she'd need to make to create a studio in the space. And her head reeled with the possibilities. Could it work in the eleven months and two weeks that she had left here? Even if she worked like fury and saved a rental deposit, could they afford to live near here afterwards? She rubbed her temples with her fingers, noticing as she did that Jack was unlocking and relocking the side door now, and seemed to be limping.

'Are you OK?' she asked. 'Have you hurt yourself?' She pointed to his left leg.

'No, no, just a slight strain. And don't change the subject. You should do this.'

Clare hugged herself. 'I can't.'

Jack was staring at her, waiting for her to say more, and when she didn't, he was the one to speak. 'In chambers, I can mostly tell when people are guilty or not. Good or not. Years of practice.' He paused. 'You're one of the good ones. You should do it.'

'And you're very kind, but hopefully I'll get a job teaching in one of the existing schools, maybe that—'

'I won't insult you by offering to pay for any alterations in here. And I hope I'm not offending you by saying that I think that's the reason you're saying no.'

Part of her wanted to yell at him. He didn't know her. He knew nothing about her. Yet he was right. The only thing that was stopping her grabbing the chance of her own dance school was the set-up costs. She had so little funds left and knew that she and Grace would need them. Even Grace's new school uniform had eaten into them more than Clare had anticipated.

'But would you be insulted if I paid for the works and you paid me back? A loan,' he asked.

The sudden sound of footsteps on the gravel made them both look up.

'Hi,' Grace said. 'What you both doing out here?'

Clare kissed her cheek.

'I'm trying to persuade your mother to open her own dance school in here.'

'That,' Grace peered into the space, 'would be really cool.'

'How was it?' Clare asked, aware she'd started to wring her hands.

'Same shit, different county. I'm heading in, I'm starving.'

Clare felt her daughter's loose hug. 'Do it, Mum, you know you want to,' she whispered before leaving them. 'See you later, Martin,' she called back.

'About that,' he said in a loud enough voice to make her turn. 'My name's actually Jack.'

Grace laughed. 'Oh, I know that. Mum told me. I just prefer Martin.'

When she'd left Clare shrugged. 'What can I tell you? She's wonderful *and* a little weird.'

She noticed he stood just far enough away from her, always aware of personal space.

'So, will you let—'

'Thank you. No,' she said emphatically. 'You've done enough, Jack. I'm grateful for the offer, but no.'

They parted at the top of the driveway to the Barn and Clare walked away, feeling his eyes on her back. It just wasn't feasible. The charity placing them in the Barn had been her stroke of good luck and, yes, Jack had been a pleasant surprise. She liked him, but Clare Bryanson trusted no one completely, and with the universe having bestowed one large heap of blessings already, she didn't want to push things. Nice as her ageing neighbourly Superman seemed, it wasn't good to start needing anyone. She'd look to take on some classes in one or both of the local dance schools and with her job in the pub, it would be enough.

And Jack, she decided, she would have to give him a wider berth.

*

'I could build a website for you,' her daughter told her. 'Then leaflet drops in the schools, the library, and I'm sure there's one of those local Facebook groups, you know, "Melborough People" sort of thing.'

'I'm not doing it, Grace.'

'Yeah, you've said.' Tim's eyes stared at her from Grace's face over a bowl of crunchy salad. 'But why not?'

'Lots of reasons.'

'A loan is a very generous offer.'

'I don't even know the man, Grace!' Clare rested her hand on her stomach, aware her voice was louder than she'd hoped.

'It's because of Martin we're here.'

'I'm more than aware of that, but he's done so much already, and I don't *know* him.'

Clare lowered her face, tilted her head and tried to catch Grace's eye. 'You know I'm right.'

She walked to the sink, busied herself washing the pot and dishes, and clanked them onto the draining board, not yet used to the dishwasher to her right. 'He's going off travelling soon. He said "sometime", don't know when.'

'Who? Martin?'

'His name's Jack, Grace. Yes, Martin. I mean, Jack. He'll be away for months.' She turned around to look at her daughter, who said nothing, just picked up her bowl and approached her at the sink.

Clare removed it from her hand.

'All the more reason to take his offer before he leaves,' Grace announced before heading upstairs. 'Mum, we're here to move on. He's not Dad,' she added from the third step, before taking the rest two at a time, leaving Clare staring in her wake.

Similar words, 'He's not exactly your dad, is he?' popped into her head. The sentence had been the first one out of her mother's mouth when she'd introduced Tim to her decades ago. She hated when her mother, Jean Hutton, dance school owner extraordinaire, was right, and that time, probably *only* that time, she'd been on the button. Tim wasn't even a poor version of her own father. He'd not come close.

Not for the first time Clare fantasised what it might be like to just call her mother and ask for help. What it might be like to ask for a loan to set up a dance school, to do it properly this time. She'd get the money, sure, but by inviting Jean Hutton back into her life, by allowing a situation where she would owe her mother – that cost would be too high.

She folded the tea towel into a tiny rectangle as random Jean-like sentences attacked from all sides:

'Must you have TWO pieces of toast?'
'I could have told you it wouldn't work.'
'Be a wife or be a dancer.'
'I hate to say I told you so . . .'

Clare shook her head firmly, tossing the memories aside. She wondered if there was anything on television. She wondered if the floor in her hypothetical dance school really needed to be fully sprung or if she could get away with a wooden one.

And with past details of their relationship foremost in her mind, she reminded herself that no situation, not even the chance of her own dance school, could possibly merit 'Mummy Dearest' being back in her life.

Chapter Eleven

WhatsApp Tim & Grace

U going to mug me off again on Fri?

No & sorry again bout last week.

I'll come there.

Fine but no room 4 u to stay over. B&B?

Sofa. Slept on it enuf when married to ur mother.

Dad u need to check that's ok with Mum.

U want to c me or not, Grace?

Course.

Send me full address.

K. After I check with Mum.

FFS child! Want to C U!

Late 4 class, gotta go now.

Love U baby mine.

U 2 x

Chapter Twelve

The walls of the rehabilitation centre in town are as familiar to me as those at home. If I close my eyes, like I'm doing now while I wait in reception for my physio appointment, I could tell you the colour of each of the treatment rooms. I could tell you the person most likely to be working behind the door of each one. I could tell you the names of their family members, the area they live in, what they enjoy doing outside of work. I could tell you the brand of scented candles they use, the preferred aromas of each therapist. This place has been my home from home since I arrived in Melborough twenty years ago – my place for physical training and my haven if I need to talk.

Dawn, on reception, takes an internal call, lifts her head and smiles at me. 'You can go through, Jack. Room four.'

I head down the corridor towards Jim's room. He has magic thumbs. His room will smell of bergamot and neroli and if anyone can relieve the muscle spasm in the upper part of my stump, it's him. I pass Simon's room – vanilla. A simple vanilla essence is what might help urge people to talk to the resident counsellor.

Knocking first, I enter Jim's room and he stares at my gait. 'You've not been doing your exercises, have you?'

Strangely, when I was in work, I'd set an alarm for ten minutes every morning and afternoon. Even when I was busy, I'd make the time for a small PT set. Not so much now – I've turned the alarm off and inevitably forget until I'm going to bed, where I hurry a slapdash version.

'Can't lie,' I reply. 'You're right.'

Jim lets out a dramatic sigh, shakes his head. 'Leg off. Up on the bed.'

I laugh. 'In no other life of mine could that comment make sense.'

'Yeah, but you love this life really, you wouldn't swap it.'

On my back, I'm taut with tension. Jim works on leg muscles, avoiding the tender scar tissue, as I recall a similar conversation with Ollie and ponder that comment. Would I swap it? If I had the chance to do it all over again, would I swap my life? Going back to my childhood with Mum and Dad in Purley, would I change anything? No. School, nothing – apart from a few cruel name-callers whom I learned to avoid, even young schooldays were pretty good. My scholarship to a private secondary school? No – it helped give me a confidence I'd never know otherwise. Meeting Alice? Never . . .

My heart still beats faster when I think of her all these years later. The night of the accident – it's the only thing I'd change if I could. Alice and me in some alternative version of my life would have been married with a family.

I'd still have had the legal career I've had, and she'd have been a Pulitzer Prize-winning journalist and the only arguments we'd ever have would happen when I wouldn't want her to travel to some war-torn world for work. We'd have had three children, two girls and a boy . . .

'You with me, Jack?' Jim's voice interrupts.

'Here,' I reply, as if answering roll call. 'Sorry.'

'It's looking tender. You need to use the salve and take the prosthetic off more often. Use your crutches. You know all this.' There's a mild chiding tone in his voice.

'I do.' I bite down on the word 'sorry' again.

'Are you in pain?' his voice is immediately softer.

I've had pretty intense pins-and-needles pain for the last week, nothing that's not helped by some meds, but I hate taking them.

'Nothing my cupboard full of pain relief and I can't handle,' I tell him before zoning out for the rest of the appointment.

*

April's emails are now a regular thing and often make me smile. Though I said after Alice's party that it might be better not to keep in touch, I felt I had to tell her about the Barn, about Clare and Grace – and her responses have a knack of making me feel good about myself in the same way her sister did so long ago. I'm staring at her last email, wondering if that skill is a DNA thing or something to do with the way their parents raised them both, or just a random batch of good people, when there's a tapping on my hall window. The kitchen door to the hallway is open and I'm visible from where Grace is looking through. My leg is resting against the chair next to me.

'Come around the back?' I say, and she nods, giving me the time to strap it on.

I beckon her inside the double doors to the rear. Immediately, her eyes narrow and she asks me if I'm all right.

'Just a bit of a migraine.'

'Ugh, Mum gets them too. Can I get you anything?'

'No, no, of course not.' I stand. 'What can I do for you?'

She has something in her hand covered by a napkin, which she theatrically removes.

'I baked a cake,' she grins. 'It's still warm and has lashings of jam. Want some?'

Not knowing what else to do, I tell her to sit at the table while I fetch a knife and plates. 'Tea, coffee?' I ask.

'You have the same coffee machine as us?'

'Of course.'

'Coffee, milky,' she says and slices two large chunks from the cake. 'Mum's working in the pub. I've done my homework. So . . . cake time.'

Something twitches inside me. This move can't be easy for a fifteen-year-old girl. She's missing her friends, her father. I know nothing about children, teenagers – I proved that when Lynn and her son Antony were living with me – but I do recognise loneliness when I see it.

I'm just working out what I should say, whether I should say anything at all, when, with the same look on her face as her mother, and virtually the same words, she stares at my mind-map wall and asks what it is.

'That's a plan,' I tell her. 'Still needs work.'

'Mum mentioned you were going away. That's your plan?' She says it in a way that suggests I'll be lucky to find Gatwick.

'I've had a very successful, very "organised" legal career, but I can't seem to come up with an ideal itinerary,' I hand her a frothy coffee, 'which, trust me, isn't like me.'

'Maybe you don't really want to go?' she says, before biting into the cake and licking jam from just beneath her nose.

'Oh, I want to go,' I assure her.

'Who's going to look after the pigs?'

I think of Steven, the man who farms the land next door and has already agreed to have the animals. 'I was going to ask you,' I reply. 'You could earn some pocket money if you're interested?' More little alien words in my mouth. I have no idea how they arrived there and don't recognise them from any previous thought process. What is it about these people that makes me take leave of my senses?

'Don't be silly. I'd love to mind them, and I do *not* want payment.'

'I'd much rather.'

'No! Crikey, you've given us a home, it's the least I could do. What would I have to do?'

She seems adamant, so I don't argue. 'Well, they'll need feeding twice a day. Vegetable scraps and dry feed. I'll just arrange with the grocer to deliver their leftovers once a week. That's what they usually love.'

'Sounds good . . .'

'You need to check with your mum that she's happy for you to do it.'

'Mum will be thrilled we can do something for you. Eat!' she says, nodding towards the slab of cake in front of me.

I do as I'm told. 'Still, I'd prefer if she gave you permission,' I add. The sponge is warm and sweet and melt-in-the-mouth.

'She will. Can I help you with that wall as well? I'm a really good organiser.'

'I'll sort it,' I tell her, before changing the subject. 'How are you finding the new school?'

She shrugs. 'It's OK. Year eleven, people have their friendships already. I'm the novelty new kid, but . . .'

'You'll be fine. It takes time.'

'There are a couple of girls I think will be pals and at least no one's called me fat, well, not to my face anyway.' She pushes the plate with the remaining cake on it away from her.

'You are not fat.' I shake my head. 'God, people can be cruel.'

'Yup.'

A memory of me hobbling through the university grounds flashes. People staring. People talking. The prosthetics available then were nothing like they are now. Today, I have a bevy of legs in my wardrobe. I can choose my foot: a lightweight blade with spring, a foot that will don any shoe, my water-activity leg, or one with more ankle movement, for tackling uneven ground – all state of the art. Yet, in the early days, I did limp. 'You have to learn to rise above people's ignorance,' I tell Grace. 'And don't change. It's all right being a bit different.' Immediately, I blush. What the hell do I know? Maybe she's the norm. 'I mean—'

'I know what you meant, Martin,' she says.

'I'm not sure *I* do.' My smile is apologetic.

'I'm not like the others, never have been. Even "others" I've known since I was little, friends in Croydon, I wasn't like them either. Most school friends have already forgotten me. I just keep in touch with a few from hockey.'

'I've been "different" most of my life.'

'I can tell.' She wriggles her nose. 'I have a snout for oddballs.'

'Speak for yourself.'

'You ever been married, Martin?'

I shake my head.

'Any kids?'

'No.'

'Girlfriend?'

'No.'

'Boyfriend?'

'No. What is this?'

'It's the inaugural meeting of the "Different in Melborough Society", from now on known as DIMS.'

I laugh out loud.

'So, girlfriend or boyfriend, which would you like?'

'Are you, my fifteen-year-old neighbour, really asking me about my sexuality?'

'I am. And I'm nearly sixteen. So, male or female?' She pulls her cake plate back towards her, takes another bite and looks up at me.

'Women, always.'

'And do you date?'

I think of Lynn. 'Not in a long time,' I reply, suddenly uncomfortable. 'Eat your cake, Miss Nosy-Neighbour.'

'I'm trying to help.'

'Why?'

'Because you need help. You should date. I can set up an app on your phone. You seem lonely.'

You should date. I can't. Apart from my working environment, if you put me in front of a strange woman, I become a blithering idiot. Case in point – the first time I met Grace's mother.

I can set up an app on your phone. One of those swipe-left-or-right things? No thank you. Just another way of people being cruel to one another.

You seem lonely. No comment.

'Martin?'

'Jack.'

'Martin suits you better.'

I lower my head to my hands. 'I don't want to date before I travel. What's the point?'

'Practice,' she says. 'You need to practise for when you meet the woman of your dreams, when you're skiing in Aspen, or climbing the Rockies. You should do both by the way. They look a-ma-zing online.'

I don't share with her why neither of those is an option to this amputee and I dare not ask what it is I need to practise – in case she tells me.

'And social media? I'm assuming you're not on any platforms?'

Groaning, I reply, 'The seventies was the decade for platforms. I was too young to wear them.'

She looks puzzled at first. 'Ahh, I get it. A joke! See? You're funny! Come on, hand me your phone. I'll ease you in gently with Instagram.'

Two hours later the place seems empty without the sound of her giddy laughter. My Instagram account has been set up with two photos taken by Grace, one of Pecan and one of Walnut. I have one follower, Grace. She has assured me that this is something I'll use daily on my travels, and though she might be right, I can't quite fathom the need for the hashtag shit.

I take a snap of the cake plate she left behind and type: Cake. All gone. #delicious. Moments later, my phone pings with a reply: #inauguralDIMS

I check out some of her recent posts, photos of the Barn, her room, the pigs from a distance, the view from the top-floor landing. Unlike her friends, who seem to be pouting posers, most of her posts seem thoughtful, considered.

And I hear myself exhale a long sigh, just for her, because she really is Different in Melborough.

It makes me head to the wall and do what I've been avoiding doing. With the duster I wipe every previous looping thread from the board, then from three carefully lined-up pieces of chalk, I choose the end one and begin again.

*

The trill of my mobile wakes me in the middle of the night. Heart thumping behind my ribcage, I switch on the bedside light, grab my glasses, instant concern for my parents flooding through me. The number, however, is unknown, and one that I've been ignoring for days. 'Whoever this is, please just piss off,' I speak into the phone. Ending the call, I sit up, wide awake, very pissed off myself.

With my hand on my chest, I steady my breathing, check the time: 03.10. The cool radiators under the windows tick. Outside, there's a rhythmic sound that makes me think one of the side gates is off the latch and is tapping against the outer wall. I look at my prosthetic resting up against my bedside table and decide I can't be bothered. Ignore it, I tell myself, but just before I lay back down, my mouth dries in an instant. There are other sounds, more like muffled movements coming from *inside* the house. I grab it, strap it on, stand and move towards the door. Naked, I take a dressing gown from a hook on the wall and opt for noise, knowing my leg won't allow for stealth.

'Who's there?' I call out, switching the lights on.

The only sound is the thrumming of my heart against my ribs.

I could almost convince myself I imagined it but for the strip of light underneath the door of my study down the hallway. I make my way, angry, scared, and push it open. And suddenly it all makes sense. I try to still my trembling hands by shoving them deep into the pockets of my dressing gown.

The boy, a man now, is sitting on my desk, his phone in one hand, a small ornament in the other. Next to him, on the leather surface, sits a house key.

'YOU piss off,' he glares at me.

'You should have left that here.' My eyes are on the key.

'No one ever asked me for it,' is his typically sullen reply.

'Antony, you obviously want my attention. You've got it.'

'You,' he stands, and I see immediately he's taller; a lot taller than he was two years ago. He must be nineteen now – his dark hair is cut in a military-style crew cut and his eyes are level with mine. 'You are a fuckin' bastard.' He's tossing the ornament from one hand to the next and I feel a deep spasm in my stomach.

'OK.' I turn, head towards the landline in the hallway.

'You calling the police again, really? You fuckin' owe me.'

I stop moving, close my eyes briefly, then turn around and focus on what he has in his hand. 'You were dealing drugs, hard drugs.'

'You dobbed me in. I was in that place for months.'

'You were dealing drugs,' I repeat. 'From my house! Can't you see that was wrong?'

'What I see is the fuckin' bastard cripple who dobbed me in.'

I flinch at the word, and feel my hackles rise. 'I'm a fucking bastard crippled *barrister*. You left me no choice. Now you've come into my house in the middle of the night, have been calling me and hanging up – what is it you want?'

He says nothing at first, before side-eying me. 'An apology.' He places his phone in his pocket.

Suddenly, I feel as if I'm whacked in the face by my reality. I'm a middle-aged lonely man about to go running all over the world to find something I could probably have had right here with his mother, yet I still insist, 'You're the one who should be sorry.'

He snorts. 'You never even loved her.'

'You should leave. You should call your mother. And give me that key.'

He picks it up and flings it into the far corner of the room. 'Fuck you. Get down on your good knee and find it.'

'Antony, stop!' My hands are raised, palms out. 'What's this about? Talk to me.'

'I don't want to talk to you.'

'Why come here, why keep calling, if you don't want to talk?'

'Just to piss you off, man. Just to let you know I can.'

He still has the ornament in his hand. 'OK. You've pissed me off. Now, can you put that down? Please.'

'What, this?' He holds the delicate ornament by its tiny ridged horn and swings it, before dropping it. 'I remember you always liked it.'

My hands reach my nose and mouth, prayer-like, as I watch it in slow motion.

'Oops,' he says as it shatters on the slate floor.

He barges past me and I'm left staring at the pieces as the front door slams behind me. I cannot move. Neither my good nor my bad leg will edge towards it. She'd given it to me for my twentieth birthday and it was the only thing that I was certain about with my upcoming travels. Wherever I went, that tiny unicorn was going to come with me. And if I ever needed to believe in magic, like she had, I'd look at it to remind me it might exist.

'I'm sorry,' I whisper to Alice in the dead of night.

Sleep, I realise, will not be an option, so I spend hours rearranging the books on the shelves in my study. They look off, uneven, and oddly enough for this *crippled boy*, I don't do uneven. I start with the old study books dating back to my first year in university, remove them from the shelf and rearrange them in height order rather than the chronological order they'd been in. My hands gather my old student planners – five of them from my years both in York and Royal Holloway. A memory prompts me to open number two, the planner from the year that Alice died. Inside there are pages and pages of nothing in the middle – where allegedly not much happened. I find a folded sheet with a typed poem she'd written and read the first lines:

There's a thing called love that scares and blinds

And best of type is one that binds – you to another being . . .

Unable to finish it, I flick to the back of the book where . . . there it is, what I knew I'd find, her handwriting, and I remember the exact moment as if she's sitting opposite me now:

'We could do it,' she's saying, 'no reason we have to go straight to work after graduation. Travelling is another form of education!' She has scribbled down the places she'd like to go to, the things she wants to see before she 'settles down'.

As always, when I think of Alice, I marvel at her certainty about us. It was a given that we'd spend the rest of our lives together without either of us ever having to say so. Except it wasn't. We didn't know then that she'd die within the year . . .

Her wishes are simple: The English and creative writing student wants to write a short story in the New York Public Library on Fifth Avenue. She wants to eat a sandwich on Harvard's lawn in Boston and pretend to be a student there. She wants us both to shout our names into the Grand Canyon just to hear the echo. I've added that I want to swim with pigs in the Bahamas and play jazz trumpet in New Orleans. It seems that day we only got to cover the United States – there are no further wishes for the travelling we never did.

The planner sits on my desk as I continue tidying. Hours later, slumping into the chair, I bend down and lift the tiny blue horn, still in one piece. I roll it between my thumbs, pocket it and head to the kitchen with the planner. There, as the house awakens, as the boiler clicks to heat the hot water for a shower, I stare at Alice's handwriting, occasionally glancing across at the wiped-clean chalkboard. The coffee I've made is strong and bitter, and as the burnt-orange sun stirs, with the backdrop of the warbling dawn chorus, I watch it slowly soar from just behind the inky shadow of the Barn. And amidst the first light, the beginning of my journey takes form in my head.

Chapter Thirteen

Clare's dreams had been poked awake.

It was as if there was no going back to the woman she'd left in Croydon. If she thought about it, there wasn't a single part of her that wanted to return to that person, but leaving her behind so abruptly also made her panic. That had been the Clare she knew well; the one who'd grown up with Tim, but also the one whose dreams had shrunk alongside him. Here in Melborough, she thought, as she walked into the pub to do a lunchtime shift, here, she felt freedom course through her veins. She felt chances and opportunity wave at her each day, tickling her provocatively as they passed. And though they frightened her, she was no longer able to ignore the fact that they excited her more. The dreams that she used to have as a young woman, the dreams that Grace had asked her about in the weeks before leaving Croydon, they had been well and truly roused.

Clare found herself wanting to make *plans*. And plans were all about proving that she could thrive in this new skin and have a wonderful life without having to rely on anyone as she had done, for so long, with Tim. The irony that she was living her new life at all because of fate and another man's generosity was not lost on her and made her all the more determined not to waste the opportunity. She wanted it all to work; not just for her and Grace, but to show Jack that what he'd done could truly make a difference.

She practised her new self on the punters in the pub. If someone asked her where she'd come from, she'd say Croydon, and smile and tell them that she was thrilled to be in Melborough now. If someone asked her about herself, she'd hold her neck straight and head erect and tell them she was divorced and mother to Grace. When one couple urged her to go on, implying there must be more to her, she confessed to being a dance teacher, an ex-national dance champion actually. After only one afternoon trying her new self on for size, she decided she quite liked this brave and independent Clare.

'You're an ex-national dance champion?' Jan asked only minutes after it was first mooted.

'I am,' she replied with more than a hint of pride.

'You *are* a dark horse . . .' Emma smiled.

'Not really. It's just something I never talk about.'

'But you must! If I were a national anything, I'd be shouting about it,' Emma said. 'Though thinking about it, according to my parents, I'm the best in the world at making shit decisions, so . . .'

'I have a mother like that,' Clare replied. 'She used to teach dance and lived her life vicariously through me. She was most put out when I chose love for a man above love for dance.'

'Your husband?' Emma asked.

'My ex-husband.'

'Don't you just hate it when mothers are right?'

They both laughed.

'Let's take a break.' Emma looked at Jan, who nodded without looking up from his order sheets. 'Come on out back.'

Clare followed her through the narrow corridor that led to the downstairs of their private living accommodation on the ground floor of the pub. She passed a door with a yellow picture of a skull and bones with the words KEEP OUT! shouting a clear message.

'The man child lives in there. We rarely see him. Always "studying".'

Clare noticed a tiny shake of Emma's head as she'd raised both her hands, making quote marks around her last word.

'Sit,' Emma pointed to a seat at the white circular table with four chairs and Clare sat down in the small kitchen. The room next door that she'd sneaked a glance at as she passed by had looked homely, more old-fashioned than where she lived – with floral sofas and lots of small occasional tables topped with framed photographs. The kitchen units were Shaker-style, painted in a soft green shade with oiled wooden worktops. Beneath her sandalled feet, the floor was tiled and spotless.

Clare's hands twisted in her lap as she suddenly realised what she was doing. It was a long time since she'd had a 'friend', since she had even thought of nurturing a female bond, and she automatically looked over her shoulder for some shadow of Tim in the background. In her mind, she heard the echo of past remarks about Gill, another dance teacher she'd been close to for a while.

'That bitch is talking about you behind your back.'

'I don't want that woman anywhere near Grace. Have you seen the way she treats her own children?'

Clare had seen, and Gill was a wonderful mother, but she had succumbed, and Gill became a thing of the past. She wondered where she was now.

'You all right?' Emma placed a mug of lemon tea, Clare's drink of choice when she was working, in front of her.

'Sure.' She lifted the mug and looked around. 'Don't I need to put something under this?'

Emma spluttered her own tea. 'Do we look like coaster people?'

'I think I just assume everyone is,' she replied.

Emma frowned.

'I'm sorry, I didn't mean that the way it sounded. With Tim, everything had to be just so and the thought of putting a mug down without a coaster underneath was unacceptable in our world, his world,' she corrected herself. Clare felt Emma's gaze, could almost hear her brain tick over, and wondered what she might say next.

'Let's not talk about your ex,' Emma suggested. 'Tell me about you, you *dancer*, you! I mean, you told us you taught dancing when we met you first, but *champion*. You left that bit out.'

'It was all a long time ago.'

'Champions are champions because they're the best at what they do.' Emma wagged a finger at her. 'Don't forget that. It takes grit, determination, to be the best at something. And it took grit and determination, to leave the person we won't be talking about.'

'He's had enough of my time,' she blurted.

'Hear, hear,' Emma chanted as she raised her mug to clink against Clare's.

Clare listened as Emma did what she often did, shift subject matters at just the right moment. Difficult customers were her domain rather than Jan's because of her ability to distil things. And now, she had switched to talking about a new drama on Netflix that she thought Clare might like, something that was apparently perfect for tuning out of real life.

As Emma spoke, Clare found herself staring at a picture on the wall next to her. It was an image of her and Jan's wedding day, somewhere on a powdery beach, just the two of them. She wondered if they had eloped. She thought of a wedding image that Tim had gifted her for her birthday once, remembered how she'd thought at the time that it would have been a wonderful anniversary present, but maybe not a birthday one. She'd convinced herself that she was indeed ungrateful, like he often told her she was, and she'd loyally placed it in the bedroom next to their bed. It was now in one of the boxes in the Barn, no longer on display.

The impulse to reach over and take Jan and Emma's photo down to study it, to try to decipher why and how it looked so different to her own, was one she fought to resist.

Emma's eyes had followed her own. 'Barbados,' she said. 'We ran away. No one else wanted to know, so we did it alone.'

'I have one like it,' Clare said, still staring, 'though it's nothing like it really.' It had hit her why, just in that moment, like a sharp stab to the chest. Emma and Jan were half turned towards one another, laughing, and the look that passed between them was one of love. There was, Clare realised, nothing else to call it except that. 'In mine,' she told Emma, 'we're facing the camera. Tim looks like the cat that got the cream, with an arm around my shoulder, gripping me really. I have a smile on my face, but I remember folding into him, even then, just folding into that clutch. Jesus, love is blind sometimes, eh?'

Emma stood, crossed around to her side and gave Clare a loose hug. 'You know what?' she replied. 'You're here now. Clare can begin again.'

*

After her shift, Clare turned out of the pub's car park and the gears shuddered up the hill as she made her way home.

The last time she had had a new home was the day she and Tim had moved into the house in Croydon. They'd both scrimped and saved for two full years to afford the deposit. They'd each lived at home with their parents,

Tim working in his uncle's insurance company and Clare turning away from her meagre dance-sponsored existence to teaching. For Tim, whose parents swelled with pride at the mention of his name, it had been easy. He worked an administrative pen-pushing job, and he saved hard. Jean viewed Tim's proposal as the death knell to Clare's championship potential, and for Clare, it had been the beginning of the end of her and her mother's relationship.

She turned the steering wheel around the looping corner just before her driveway, allowing herself to fantasise one more time about the potential in her imaginary dance school, which she'd simply called 'To Dance'. It said immediately why people might come, what she might be there to teach, while also being a sort of call to arms for the art of dance. She was musing how happy she was with the vision when, at the entrance to the Barn, she slammed on the brakes, her ageing wheels skidding on the gravel. Opposite her, casual as an extra lolling about on a movie set, Tim sat up against the bonnet of a car.

For two seconds she thought about reversing back out the gate. For one second, she thought about ramming him, sandwiching his lower body between her Nissan and his recently acquired company car. According to Tim's last text, he'd just needed to lose Clare from his life for his uncle to recognise that his true calling was in sales and not stuck behind a desk. She edged closer and parked just outside the garage that housed her dreams.

Yet, walking towards him, it started. Her reversal back to Croydon Clare was almost instantaneous. He was wearing her favourite shirt, the one she'd always said suited him. The western boots he loved to wear peeked out from under ironed jeans and were polished to a shine. He looked good, she thought as she approached, ignoring the nagging pulse at the back of her head, the one which asked, 'How did he know the address?'

It was the first time in twenty years that they had not seen one another for weeks. Clare tried as she walked towards him – she tried to hold onto the woman she'd only just been in the pub, the woman she knew she was capable of becoming. Yet, when her ex, the man she'd left for all the right reasons, the man who had helped her strangle her own potential, leaned in to kiss her cheek, all she could remember was the comforting scent of him. Not the physical and emotional abuse, not the bruises or the barbs, just the woody smell of him.

'Clare,' he whispered into her ear, 'you look lovely.' Standing tall again, he placed both palms upwards and looked around. 'And this place is amazing.'

Speechless, she scratched her head, because that was what Tim did to her. Apart from intoxicating her with his familiarity, he made her immediately question everything. What was she doing here? What was *he* doing here?

'Tim,' she spoke slowly, feeling Melborough Clare wither to a wisp. 'Why are you here?'

'Why not?' He looked hurt. 'I've come to see where you and our baby live now. Shit, you lucked out, didn't you?'

She said nothing, dug both her hands into her pockets, now begging new Clare to stay, to help. 'You should have called first.'

'You going to invite me in for coffee?' He ignored her, instead tilting his head, his comment laden with suggestion.

She scratched her head again, imagining his sarcasm if he saw the actual coffee machine that Jack had installed. He'd laugh. He'd sneer.

'No,' she said as loudly as she could.

'What?' Tim's head reared back in surprise.

Clare lowered her hand to her neck, ran her fingers slowly along the left-hand side of it. The picture of the last time he'd held her down, her gasping for breath on the sofa, his knee on her throat, arrived unbidden. Or perhaps Melborough Clare had called it forward for her, suddenly spelling out her real needs as if a small plane had looped it in silvery plumes above her. Melborough Clare needed to survive. No, she needed to thrive. And whenever Tim was around, Clare knew; she knew Croydon Clare was a mere moment away, waiting, just waiting to be rescued by Tim the knight.

She forced herself to focus on that feeling of not being able to breathe.

'No coffee. No invites inside. Grace is at school. The agreement we have is you have access to Grace, at times agreed with both of us. You're due to see her Friday night, that's *tomorrow*, and you shouldn't be here now.'

'You're kidding, right? You don't mean any of that.'

'How did you get this address, Tim?' She questioned in her mind whether Grace had sent it to him, but they'd both agreed that she'd send it on Friday, the day he'd been due to pick her up and take her out for a curry.

'Clare,' he began.

She walked past him, and his hand shot out, grabbing her hard on the upper arm.

'Everything OK?'

Clare looked towards the gate, to where Jack stood.

'Everything's fine, Tim was just leaving, weren't you?' She shook her arm free, chewed her right cheek to stop herself crying.

'Tell Grace, I'll pick her up at seven on Friday. I'm assuming it's all right to stay over.' Tim's voice spoke softly, quietly.

'You can have the sofa, but you need to leave early on Saturday. Grace and I have a busy day.'

She watched her ex-husband's eyes narrow before they glanced towards the man still stood at the gate.

'Clare, lovely Clare, you didn't waste any time, did you?' he whispered.

She shivered with the memory that Tim's lowered voice was always so much worse than his raised one. 'Jack is my *landlord*,' she replied.

'I'll see you tomorrow,' he said, getting into his car. 'You can show me around then.'

Clare watched him drive away, doff an imaginary cap to Jack and rev his engine down the hill. As Jack approached, she just wanted to run away, didn't want to have to explain.

'Nice chap,' Jack said, eyes on her arm where Tim's fingers had left a four-fingered mark.

She rubbed it self-consciously. 'My ex. It's fine.'

'Are you all right?'

'Of course, I'm all right.' Clare could hear the petulant tone, regretted it instantly, but she was still learning how to behave around her neighbour. She held a hand up to her eyes to shield her from the sun, looked out towards the fields of rapeseed blossom opposite the two houses, and took a leaf from Emma's book. 'I heard you play "Summertime" earlier. It seemed so right to wake to on this gorgeous morning.'

'September is my favourite month of the year and it *is* a beautiful day,' he nodded, and Clare was grateful that he understood her need to change the subject. 'I keep forgetting I have neighbours and am just playing like I always have.'

'Don't stop playing,' she said. 'Not because of us. I was singing along.'

'What, you can sing as well as dance?'

Clare smiled, despite herself, took her house keys from her bag. 'Not really. I only know the words of the chorus.'

'You should listen to the verses,' Jack said. 'There's a great bit in it, about spreading your wings and taking to the sky.'

She stood there, listening to Jack talking, keys in her hand, staring at the space where Tim's car had been, and patted her chest gently three times. She had felt it – that instant instinct to forgive and embrace. As soon as she'd seen Tim, caught a whiff of him, Croydon Clare was present; small, unsure and trembling. She would steel herself, she thought, rooting both feet to the ground. She would create a force field around her whenever he was there for Grace. She would never weaken again. Melborough Clare was here to stay, and she needed neither man nor mother.

'Clare?'

'Sorry, Jack.'

'You were miles away.'

'Not really.' She shook her head, suddenly prepared to be honest opposite this relative stranger. 'I just don't understand how, if I see him now, I slip back into thinking that things weren't really that bad when we were married.' She watched her benefactor's face compute what she'd just said.

'You were together a long time,' he offered.

'Most of it was bad . . .'

'People glorify the past. It's a coping strategy.'

Clare pondered how many times this man had loved a woman, because the difference was she had only ever loved *one* man and she'd been strong enough to divorce him, despite moments of doubting whether she could be alone.

Jack, probably sensing the need for another move away from discussing Tim, began talking about the plants at their feet with an encyclopaedic knowledge. Clare nodded politely, fanned her face with her hand, as one of her daily flushes of heat assaulted her from the inside out. Silently, she told herself she could reach high shelves by using a stool. She didn't need Tim or any man. She could earn her own money and quite easily carry the bins out on a Tuesday – no man was needed. She could even pleasure herself – no need for a man.

You, Melborough Clare, are more than enough on your own.

Chapter Fourteen

Today feels weird.

To start with, the cottage has been echoing with the sounds of Antony hollering at me, like the walls have suddenly developed memory banks of the time he and Lynn lived here too. I was strolling around outside to escape it, and to keep a look out for my visitor, when I bumped into Clare and her ex at the Barn – a nasty piece of work who left a handprint on her arm. Needless to say, I took a rare and instant dislike to the man.

So, when April arrives, she's a breath of fresh air. A woven bag swings from her arm and I soon discover it's full of shop-bought nibbles for a late lunch. She hands it to me, asks me to unpack it as she heads to the back doors and looks towards the Barn.

'That's it,' she says softly.

If I hadn't been looking at her and instead had my eyes closed, I'd have put money on the voice being her sister's, yet it's April staring across at Clare and Grace's new home.

'I can't believe it was Alice's birthday that set all of this in motion.'

And I can't believe that my reply to her 'let's catch up in person' email has resulted in her arriving with lunch in a bag, even though food was never mentioned. She sort of asked herself over to see the Barn and I sort of agreed that it would be lovely to see her here. Now she *is* here and I'm pouring a glass of sparkling water for her and making a large coffee for me.

'How are you feeling?' she asks as she approaches and starts to place the finger food on plates I'd taken out of the dishwasher. 'You want to eat inside or out?'

'The garden's good,' I answer as I follow her to the bistro table just outside and sit opposite her, 'and I think discombobulated is how I'm feeling.' I risk a smile in her direction.

She gets it immediately, claps her hands and laughs. 'Christ, she loved that word, didn't she?' Then I listen and laugh along as she lists so many daft examples of Alice's 'discombobulations'.

'You remember,' I ask April, 'the way she'd describe things like the "lemony lemon" or the "rusty rust"?'

'I still have that "lemony lemon" sweater she wore all the time.'

'I was allergic to that.' With the taste of warm coffee and nostalgia on my lips, I smile, recalling Alice wearing it. 'Mohair . . . I couldn't go near her in it. Your dad had bought it for her, and we used to call it her "chastity jumper"!'

She laughs again, before levelling a serious look in my direction. 'You seem a lot better than the last time we met.'

'I am.' I feel grateful for the first time for the birthday invitation that day. Yes, I've been plunged into a world of Alice again, but I feel alive in a way that's been absent for far too long. Still, my reply is deliberately simple because I don't want to tempt Fate, who's always listening.

She takes the hint from the short silence that follows, then asks, 'What are they like, your new neighbours?'

'Lovely. The mum is a dance teacher and the daughter's a hoot. Seems the husband's a bit of a prick . . .'

'How so?'

'They're divorced now, but I sense he's not the nicest of men.' I don't offer more because it feels a little like talking behind Clare's back. 'I feel good about helping them. Your email, and a few other things – they all lined up and here we are.'

'Here we are,' she agrees.

I watch her mouth move as she continues chatting and am appalled that I suddenly want to kiss it. I have a vivid, but thankfully brief, vision of us clinched together in a deep kiss, the sort of kiss I miss, and my groin reacts instantly. My knees cross themselves of their own embarrassed accord and I banish the thought as quickly as it arrived, helping myself to something that looks like a cold ball of risotto.

April doesn't stay for long, citing the journey back and having to pick up her eldest son from football training. At the door we hug. My groin behaves, and I hold her out opposite me. 'You look and sound very like her,' I say, 'hence the discombobulation.'

Her smile is sad.

'But you're *like* her too. I mean, you seem able to bring out the magic in people too.'

Her bottom lip trembles ever so slightly, so I pull her to me for another brief but tight hug.

'Take care of yourself when you're off doing whatever it is you'll be doing abroad,' she whispers.

Before I know it, I've typed my Instagram details and my phone number into her phone. We've only ever been in touch by email, so this feels big – like I've just agreed to be friends with my dead lover's sister, which is exactly what it is. It's another Big Thing. It's a strange thing in a weird day, yet it feels right as she drives away.

*

Later on, I'm perched on a stool opposite Jan, who's talking about his hometown, which he swears is situated just under the Northern Lights. I don't tell him that the Northern Lights, being a moving scientific phenomenon, can't possibly be situated in one spot. I just build two small identical towers of bright red beer mats side by side. Jan's in the right job; he likes to talk and this evening I'm more than happy to listen as I muse on the fact that I don't ever remember another time, outside of my work diary, where I've arranged to meet two women in one day.

I feel her hand rest on my shoulder before I see her. Lynn is dressed in her normal smart tailored suit. The pixie-cut hairstyle is new and suits her natural shock of red hair. It's just her eyes that let the image down, or maybe that's me. Maybe it's only me that can spot a sea of pain in Lynn's eyes.

I stand and she angles her head to receive my kiss on her cheek. 'Thanks for coming here,' I say, 'though I'd have come to you, I—'

'I was already in Oxford. I'm on duty there for a few days, camped out in some dreary hotel.'

'You look well. Love the hair.' I resist an urge to touch it. 'What will you have to drink?'

'Nothing. Look, do you mind if we walk instead? I've been cooped up in court all day.'

'Sure, no problem.' I pay Jan and we make our way out onto the high street.

She loops an arm through mine. It's something she always does, more to ensure she walks at my pace than anything intimate. 'What a gorgeous evening,' she says, inhaling deeply. 'Now, what was it you wanted to see me about, Jack?' Her face turns towards mine and I sense she's ready for me to say anything but her son's name. For a moment, I don't want to hurt her any more than I did years ago, and I consider swallowing the episode, forgetting it happened.

'Antony.' I blurt his name quickly as her features sink into a resigned sigh. 'He came into the house the other night, Lynn, still had a key.'

'Jesus.' Lynn has stopped walking. She's unhooked her arm from mine and is rubbing her stomach as if she's about to be sick. Beside us, a young mother walks by with a screaming child in her arms.

'Are you all right?' I ask.

She nods. 'What happened?'

'He's been calling me and hanging up and wanted to let me know in person that he's pissed off at me for "dobbing him in". He wanted to yell . . .' I pause. 'Hell, Lynn, I'm not really sure *what* he wanted. Even now, he's still an angry young man.'

Her eyes are fixed on a wriggly concrete line on the pavement between us. The roar of a siren blasts nearby, and it makes me think of all the people I failed in the defence field who went to jail. Some were guilty, deserved it. Some, perhaps not.

'It's all my fault apparently, his going to the young offenders place. He seems to have forgotten what he was doing and wants me to apologise to him.'

Antony was guilty.

Lynn looks up, silent tears welling at the edge of her eyes. 'Did you?' she asks quietly.

I say nothing, and she nods again, wipes her face with the back of her hand.

'I should go,' she says. 'I probably need to get on the motorway home. I—'

'Look . . .'

'I should go,' she repeats, her shoulder strap sliding down her arm as she searches her bag for her car keys.

'Lynn,' I reach for her hand, but she shies away, and I take mine back. 'Is there anything I can do?'

'No.' She straightens up, slides the strap back up to her shoulder, avoids my eyes. 'It was good seeing you, Jack,' she says.

I seem to be blocking moving traffic on the pavement and stand in a doorway, watch her walk away. Biting on a hangnail, I question how I might have played that differently, why most of my interactions with her leave me feeling like I've failed her or failed myself during the exchange. And both thoughts drench me in sadness.

*

Having slept badly, the next day I wake to a flood in the kitchen and a hand-delivered shit through my letterbox. I mop the water, flush the turd down the loo and scrub my hands until they hurt. I'm just about to pulse the digits of Lynn's number on my phone when her face comes to mind – her devastated expression yesterday – and I put the phone back down on the table.

After the plumber fixes a leaky pipe, I finally book my ticket, pay for the most flexible fares possible to give me the right to amend it if I choose, and then sit back, staring at the computer screen. I'm going. I'm really going to do this. Needing to share the news immediately, I call Mum and Dad, forgetting the time difference, and leave a message to call me back. 'I'll be with you soon!' I tell them.

Feeling the need to celebrate, I grab the bottle of champagne Clare gave me from the fridge, plus a carton of orange juice, and walk around to her front door. 'Buck's fizz?' I ask her when she appears.

She frowns, looks at her watch.

'I've booked my trip!'

She invites me in. And then, while she drinks the orange juice and I the champagne, I get drunk sitting in the living room I designed, with a woman I barely know nodding politely. I talk shit for ages, get so pissed that I fall asleep, and when I wake, she's not there and Grace is sitting opposite me, staring.

My head feels as if it's been spliced by a hatchet.

'Oh, Martin,' she tuts. 'Drunk during the day and you snore,' Grace informs me.

My tongue is too dry to reply.

'Mum had to go to work. She didn't want to disturb you.' Walking to the fridge, she pours a glass of water, which I hope is for me. She hands it over, gives me a look that I'm in too much pain to decipher.

'Why aren't you in school?' I manage.

'You've no idea of the time, have you? Today's Saturday!' Her head shakes. 'Mum says you booked your ticket.'

'Uh huh.'

'So, you need to get some practise in then. No more delay. Hand me your phone and we'll get you set up on a dating app.'

My head hurts.

Her hand is out, and she comes and sits opposite me on the coffee table. 'Phone,' is all she says, and I pull it from my pocket and hand it to her. She scrolls through, looking for the app store, and downloads two within minutes.

'I googled the best ones for old people,' she says, and I almost choke on the remaining water before handing her the glass and asking for more. 'When you're sober,' she says, ignoring my request and with my phone still in her hand. 'We'll take a profile picture and—' Looking down as my phone pings she frowns before handing it back. 'You have a message.'

As Grace paces the tiled floor to the fridge and back, I can hear her steps echo in stereo. How in Christ's name did I get so drunk on one bottle of champagne? One bottle of champagne for breakfast, after my regular pain meds, I remind myself before looking at the phone.

I fucking hate you. And stay the fuck away from my mother.

My eyelids lower as I sigh. 'I should probably explain.' I meet Grace's young and very judging eyes.

'It's none of my business.'

I spend the next fourteen minutes telling my teenage neighbour about my ex-lover's teenage son; of how, after his second caution around drugs, I'd found him dealing from the house. I'd informed on him and he spent months in a young offenders institution. Finishing up with a puncutating statement, the type I'd always used effectively in court during closing argument. 'He was wrong. I was right,' I tell her, adding in a shrug for extra measure.

'You still think that?' The girl is eating from a box of Rice Krispies with a spoon. She looks thoughtful as she asks the question.

'I do.'

'My gran had a saying: "Do you want to be right or do you want to be happy?" Which is a bit weird because she and my mum don't talk any more, which means she and I don't talk any more, which means one of them chose right over happy.' Her eyebrows arch. 'They probably both did. I mean, they probably both chose "right" over "happy", which just shows it's all rubbish really.'

'He was breaking the law,' I whisper as I massage my temples.

'Yeah, you mentioned that,' she says. 'What about now?'

I'm not even sure what she means.

'Do you *now* think that you did the right thing?'

I stare at her, resist telling her, this strange young woman, that it doesn't matter. I did what I did in the belief it was right at the time. And when it came to loving Antony's mother or, God forbid, possibly loving Antony, I just couldn't do it right. I couldn't do it happy. I swallow and take a drink of water, stand up and wobble a little on my bad foot.

'I shouldn't drink champagne. Please apologise to your mother for me,' I call back to her as I walk away. 'And thank you, Grace.'

*

'So, what is it?' I persist.

'Well, I don't know, do I?'

I've just asked Ollie to be brutally honest with me and tell me what my worst fault is. He seems exasperated – either by the question or the late-night call. I, on the other hand, have been truly exasperated since Antony's appearance at my house.

'Oliver.' I address him by his full name, a nod to the fact I'm serious. 'It struck me today that there's no point in this trip unless I consider things about me that might need addressing if I'm going to *live* my life differently.'

'That only struck you today?'

'Ha, ha. Be serious.' I think I already know what he's going to say, but not wanting to lead the witness, I allow the silence to grow before he speaks.

'You really want to know?'

'I do.'

'Your worst fault? Only your worst one?'

OK. Maybe I don't know what he's going to say. 'Yes, but if you think there are a few, then tell me.'

He laughs softly before speaking. 'You're sure about this?'

'Speak,' I tell him.

'You snore.'

'Ollie . . .'

'OK, OK. You're black or white, can never see the grey in the middle. There's right and wrong with you, never anything in between. Just too dogged sometimes.'

'I'm a lawyer. A client has to be one or the other.'

'Yes, but *you* don't. You're asking about you.'

I shut up.

'You're a control freak.'

I wince, knew that one was coming.

'Everything has to be organised, just so, no room for error.'

'I refer the honourable gentleman to my earlier answer,' I try to make a joke, but he interrupts.

'You're so completely terrified of fate that you leave nothing to chance. It just means everything is prescribed and there's no room for fun.'

I glance at my mind-map wall, where, thanks to my finding the old planner, the itinerary is finally perfect, and I let out a long sigh.

'So, what do I do?' I ask him. 'When we hang up, do I just google how to have fun at fifty when fun has been missing?'

'You're doing it already. By the way, you're also kind and considerate and loyal, and very funny for a guy who's misplaced his fun. Plus, you're a fabulous singer and musician.'

'Yeah . . .'

'You're a good man, Jack, but April was right. You need to let love into your life and, to do that, maybe just relax and let the you who doesn't give a shit about black or white come out. Find your "grey", man.'

'Right.'

When we do hang up, I google 'finding your grey at fifty' on my phone and am greeted with a host of things about dyeing hair roots, so I look at the dating app Grace loaded for me instead. And ignoring every instinct in my body, after only a few texts, I toss all my natural caution to a howling wind and agree to a date with a woman named Celeste.

Chapter Fifteen

-----Original Message-----
From: GraceBryanson29@gmail.com
Sent: 8th September 2018 18:40
To: TimBryanson@oldhamptoninsurance.com
Subject: Dates to meet

Dad, thanks for last night, goooood curry! We'll go back there again for sure. I thought I'd email you rather than talk on the phone because you just shut me down when I tried last night to talk about only seeing one another every fortnight. During dinner, you told me you got it, that this is an important school year for me. BUT then when you left this morning you said you'd see me here next Friday?!

And while we're on it, Dad, I can come to you too! It doesn't always have to be here. The new place you're renting has a sofa bed, so let's alternate. You here, once a month, and me there, once a month?

Love you Dad. Hope you understand.

Gracie x

-----Reply Message-----
From: TimBryanson@oldhamptoninsurance.com
Sent: 9th September 2018 18:45
To: GraceBryanson29@gmail.com
Subject: Re: Dates to meet

Wouldn't hear of it, love. I don't mind and your mum will be fine with it. I'll sleep on the sofa there twice a month, not a problem.

Dad xx

-----Original Message-----
From: GraceBryanson29@gmail.com
Sent: 10th September 2018 17:05
To: ClareBryansonDancer@icloud.com
Subject: You being stubborn

Mum,

I'm resorting to writing because you won't listen (Don't be like Dad?).

First, I thought I'd scribble this on a note, but that would be too easy to scrunch up and ignore. This way, IT'S WRITTEN DOWN FOREVER unless you choose to delete this email. DO NOT DELETE THIS EMAIL, MUM!

It contains the important list of reasons you should do what you won't do:

1. There's a reason I found the bank book when we moved. There's a reason I took it to town today to update it. We knew Gran had put money in the account when I was small, but neither of us had a clue that she's also done the same every birthday and every Christmas for the last ten years. THERE'S A REASON.

2. The reason is Jack's garage. It's a loan. If you won't take the money off Jack, and you don't have the money, where will you get the money? And if you don't get the money, you won't be able to set up To Dance and that's a chance missed. You would tell me to do it, now I'm telling you.

3. Really, there are five thousand one hundred and sixty reasons. More than enough single pounds for set-up costs. A loan from me rather than Jack. It's money neither of us knew was there. THE MONEY IS THERE, MUM.
   Gracie x

-----Reply Message-----
From: ClareBryansonDancer@icloud.com
Sent: 10th September 2018 17:10
To: GraceBryanson29@gmail.com
Subject: Me being stubborn

You do realise I'm downstairs, don't you?!

You do realise that you don't have to communicate in writing with me to get a point across?

Or maybe I should realise that you obviously feel you do . . .

I'm sorry. Come down. I'll make you hot chocolate and we can talk about it properly.

Thank you.

I love you. Always.

Xx

Chapter Sixteen

'You let him stay overnight?'

Clare bit her lip. 'I did. What can I do, Emma? It's a long drive back to Croydon and he likes to have a beer with his curry.'

'You let him stay on the sofa drinking beer?' Her friend had stopped polishing the handles on the beer pumps and was staring across the bar at her.

'No.' Clare didn't admit that she had also dropped Grace and Tim off and collected them too. 'Anyway . . .'

'I'm not sure if it's all very enlightened, or an awful idea.'

'I'll let you know after the next time.'

'There'll be a next time?' Emma's voice was sounding more and more shrill. 'Er, no. There should be no next time. The clue is in the word "ex"!'

'He's Grace's father. They used to do this every Friday. It's *their* time, though she's managed to persuade him it should only be every fortnight. But still he wants to come here.'

Clare avoided Emma's eyes, hating the fact that she was defending something she was trying to maintain for

Grace's sake, because Grace *did* want her and her father's evenings together to continue.

'Don't you . . .' Emma paused as if she was questioning whether she should say whatever was on her mind. 'Aren't you ever worried about Tim with Grace? That he might . . .'

This time she considered Emma; saw her as the woman she was, someone who was totally loved by Jan, someone who might try but would probably never understand the inside of any relationship with Tim. Emma *was* trying – but who ever *really* understood the inner workings of other relationships?

'No,' she shook her head. 'It's hard to explain, but the problem was always Tim and me. He has never, and never would, hurt Grace. He and I had . . . have,' she corrected herself, 'a toxic relationship. His "love" for me,' she made quote marks with her fingers, 'was obsessive, jealous, isolating, and I was dependent on it for a very long time. *Their* bond is totally different. Whatever happened between him and me, despite what's happened, he's still Grace's father and she loves him.'

For a moment, Clare lost herself in happier memories, times when her daughter was younger: cine-reel images of a childlike Grace and her dad running along a beach squealing with joy, of the time he bought her a new bike a few years ago and surprised her with it outside school, the times he'd lean over maths homework with her and help her work it all out. Any capacity Tim had for kindness was saved for his daughter.

'Be careful, eh? Exes are usually exes for a reason,' her new friend said.

Clare looked over, nodded, a brief acknowledgement to her for caring. A brief admission to herself that Tim *had* in fact hurt Grace whenever he'd raised his hands to her mother . . . Then she shook the can of furniture polish in her hand and sprayed it on the nearest table until she could see Melborough Clare's reflection in it clearly.

*

The cardboard box was the last one she needed to unpack, and thirty minutes before Grace was due in from school, Clare pulled it from under the bed where she'd put it on move-in day. She tugged on the top criss-cross flaps. Removing the items inside she lined them up on the bed, as if they were ready for inspection; all asking the question, will I make it to the new house or end up back in the box?

She placed a silver-framed image, a photo of her and her father taken ten years ago, to the left of the box. Next to join it was another photograph, a family meal – her, aged ten, and her mother sitting opposite each other.

Must you have TWO pieces of toast?

Clare automatically smoothed her hand over her stomach. The first time she'd ever binged and purged was shortly after the photograph had been taken, on her eleventh birthday, when her mother presented her with a cake with eleven lit candles, just after ballet class. The other pupils had sung 'Happy Birthday' to her and Clare had stared longingly at the cake, knowing it wasn't for eating, at least not for her. That night after bedtime, she'd eaten three stolen slices, wrapped in a candy-striped napkin, that she'd squirrelled away in her ballet bag. It wasn't until later, when guilt forced her to purge it, that shame was replaced with new feelings of elation, power, control. Her battle with food was to continue until after Grace was born, when she sought help – not from her mother, whose comments still scarred, but a wonderful counsellor called Nancy.

She took the family shot and placed it back in the storage box next to the wedding image of her and Tim that he'd given her, put the lid on top and nudged it back under the bed with her foot. Her father's image was the only one she wanted displayed in her home. The sepia shot showed him standing at the top of the table with his famous pudding in his hands. Clare could almost smell the nostalgic scent of cloves and the fragrant memory made her head to the kitchen, needing to bake her father's apple sponge.

Earlier that morning, Jack had posted a one-page agreement for the garage through the letterbox for her to sign, along with a note reminding her about the things she'd need to put in place, like building control sign off and insurance. She thought about their previous conversation as she finished beating the sugar and eggs together, where he'd asked her if she believed in magic. She'd told him she did because she could already *see* To Dance working. She could *see* the fitted barre, mirrors, teenagers standing in first position, adults waltzing around the space. She could visualise it and it felt magical. She hated that she'd had to borrow the money from Grace, money that had, whatever way she washed it, come from her mother.

'Stop!' she said the word aloud before she could spiral further and placed both hands on her waist. Thinking of what Nancy might have said to her, she continued, 'If you'd asked her for money, she'd have given it to you. You know this – except it would have come with hidden conditions. This way, you have it, you can build something for you and Grace, and you'll pay Grace back. Yes, it's come indirectly from your mother – but condition free . . .'

Clare began to work the apples, stirring them in a pot over gentle heat before adding the whole cloves that her father claimed made the pudding a 'complete game-changer'. Using her only two Pyrex bowls, she poured the sweet compote equally into both before covering them with the light, airy sponge she had mixed earlier. Into the oven, 190 degrees for twenty minutes – she watched them both through the glass door until the mix began to rise. She breathed the spice, watched as bubbles popped and the sponge coloured from creamy beige to gold.

She only moved when she heard the already familiar slam of the front door. Grace, her saving Grace, was home.

*

'He's forty-nine.'

'Really?' Clare asked as she made custard. She'd been guessing Jack's age, not knowing Grace had the answer. 'He doesn't look it.'

'He has a date tomorrow night. She's a forensic account-ant named Celeste.'

Clare frowned. 'What could possibly be forensic in accounting?' she asked Grace, who had already cleared the main meal from the table and was hovering with her des-sert spoon in her hand.

'Who knows? What do *you* think about him?'

Clare stopped stirring. 'What do I think of the man who probably saved us?'

'I mean, what do you think of *him*? Would women find him attractive?'

She rapped Grace's knuckles as she tried to lower her spoon into the saucepan. 'He's nice, seems kind, so yes.'

Grace grunted. 'Hardly exciting, Mum.'

She shrugged. 'He's a good-looking man.' Grace didn't reply and Clare felt if she could have read her mind it would have been questioning what her mother's preferred type was – someone who beat the crap out of her? Some-one who aided and abetted in her losing every ounce of confidence she'd ever possessed? It wouldn't matter what they looked like. They only had to be someone who was ultimately bad for her. She dipped a metal spoon in the custard and handed it to Grace. 'How do you know all this stuff anyway, like how he's going on a date?'

'We talked out by the pigs earlier. He doesn't really want to go.'

'I'm not quite sure how I feel about your being Jack's love secretary.'

Grace snorted. 'Hardly. I put two apps on his phone. Up to him to do what he wants with them.' She shook her head. 'The Celeste lady is wrong for him though.'

'What makes you say that?'

'She has two teenagers. Martin doesn't do teenagers.'

'Christ alive, Grace, how would you even know that?' Clare began to speak again as soon as Grace tipped the end of her nose with her forefinger. 'How do you know he doesn't like teenagers? He seems to get on well enough with you?'

'I'm different.'

Clare wrinkled her brow at the 'obvious' in the statement. 'You are,' she replied gently. 'For all the right reasons.'

'Mother, do not curdle the custard.'

Clare stirred. 'Do you have homework?'

'I always have homework,' Grace groaned.

'You want to come out with me later, when you've finished, do a bit of a mail drop?' Clare jerked her head towards the pile of leaflets she'd had printed at the library.

'If we go about half nine.'

'Thank you. Have I told you you're the best?'

'Keep moving that spoon, Mother.'

*

Standing at his door, yet again, Clare began to fear she looked as foolish as she was starting to feel. Too late – her hand had already raised the brass door knocker.

'Hey,' he said, when he opened up, his eyes instantly resting on the bowl in her hand. 'Wow, Grace makes amazing cake and now you with—'

'It's apple sponge.' She thrust it forward. 'My dad's favourite, his recipe . . .'

'Thank you.' His eyebrows now raised as he held it.

'Dad, he had this daft thing that he would just do something for someone for no reason, you know, like a random act of kindness, before a random act of kindness was even a thing.'

Jack was nodding.

'If he knew you at all, and maybe you just needed a nice moment, his favourite thing was to bake someone an apple sponge.' Clare began to wring her hands. 'Drove my mother mad because she rarely got her bowls back.' She laughed, a soft, nervous sound.

'I'll eat every bit and I *will* return the bowl.'

'Oh God, that's not what I meant.'

'You meant that your mum hated her bowls going missing. I got that.' He inhaled the spicy scent of the food. 'This was very kind. Thank you.'

'You've done so much for us, apple sponge is a tiny thing, but I just got to thinking about my dad today and wanted to . . . Anyway, enjoy . . . And I also wanted to say, when you go away, if I can do anything, keep an eye on the place for you, anything at all, just ask.'

Clare smacked her hands together and they echoed ridiculously as she stood there, suddenly thinking he might not trust a relative stranger with the key to his house. 'I mean, obviously you might have someone checking in already and . . .' She stopped talking, wiped her palms on her jeans. 'Just ask if there's anything at all,' she added with a shrug.

'If you mean it, there might be something you could do for me?'

'Name it,' Clare replied, hoping anything he asked would be within her reach.

'It's like a Pay It Forward idea,' he said. 'You've been so . . .' Jack hesitated, reached around and placed the pudding on top of a pile of books on a side table nearby. 'Look, it's obvious what the garage means to you and I know how grateful you and Grace are for the house. I was wondering if you'd consider putting in some voluntary hours at a charity I work with locally. I won't be able to do it myself for a while.' He blushed, as if he was embarrassed asking for something.

'A Pay It Forward idea. Dad would have loved that.' She reached forward, without realising she was going to, and gave Jack a quick hug. 'Of course. Let me know what and where and—'

'They do an annual fundraiser, but that's not for a few months, and I just thought I'd flag it as an idea because

you said, if there was anything . . . The charity means a lot
to me and if—'

The sound of his mobile ringing from his back pocket
disturbed them.

'Get that,' she said, already backing away from the
porch. 'We'll talk about this again.'

As she strolled towards the Barn, she went over it in
her head. From the moment she'd found the photo of her
dad holding the dessert, the idea had formed, and she'd
wanted to give her father a nod, while also giving a nudge
of gratitude to the world. She was standing at the precipice
of a new life and was determined to jump – to embrace,
to fight, to live, to be grateful and to give something back,
even if it was at first only a little sweet stewed apple. Now
it seemed that there might be another way too. She pushed
the front door open, not caring that she'd felt awkward
because she'd seen the look on his face when she'd come
bearing gifts. It had been surprise, yes, but good surprise,
like he couldn't believe someone had done something for
him. Clare felt sad and, for his sake, hoped that Celeste,
whoever she was, liked kind, posh boys.

*

The village looked even prettier at dusk, its older buildings
oozing charm and mystery. They were on their way home
after successfully mail dropping quite a few streets. Grace
was telling her that she still needed a website, insisted she
could do it, and Clare had agreed to let her try. Stopped

at lights by the local community centre, Clare followed Grace's gaze towards a floodlit court, where a group of girls were removing shin guards and packing away hockey sticks.

'You should go and ask,' Clare urged her daughter. 'Find out if there's a team, a league. You were—'

'I was. Come on, let's get back. I'm a bit chilly.'

Clare knew her only child. She wouldn't have stared like she had if she hadn't been interested. It had been Tim who had got her into hockey and in Croydon she played in the under-sixteen local leagues. But Clare knew not to challenge her. If she thought Grace might love to take up sport again, the best thing to do was to say nothing now and sow a few well-placed seeds. 'Thanks for your help tonight,' she half turned to her. 'And honestly, yes to the website, it's a great idea.' But the teenager was staring out the window, lost in her own thoughts.

She chewed on whether to ask if Grace was all right. There had been no new friends mentioned, very little said about her old group of friends. She swallowed all the doubts over whether she was settling into school or not, because confronting her with questions would only make her retreat. Grace would talk to her if she needed to. Of that she was sure.

She touched her daughter's thigh with her left hand as she steered the car home. 'It's late, but do you fancy an hour of telly?'

'I'm tired, Mum. I have school in the morning.'

'Right, yes. I know.'

A sudden shower spat noisily onto the windscreen.

'Shit,' Grace said, knowing the wipers were on the blink, and Clare was glad they were close to home. 'You need to get those fixed, Mum. And don't tell me you can't afford it.'

Clare cringed, felt a deep dig at having been responsible for emptying Grace's only bank account. Then she felt a hand slide over her own sitting on top of the gearstick.

'I didn't mean that how it sounded,' Grace whispered. 'I really did just mean get them fixed.'

'I'll do it tomorrow,' she said, flicking the indicator on to turn into the Barn. 'Does this feel like home yet to you?' She blurted the question without knowing it was coming.

'You know, I think it does,' Grace replied. 'It shouldn't, but it does.'

Clare took that. Friends would come in time. Grace was all right. And that was what mattered most.

PART TWO

Chapter Seventeen

Celeste is aptly named. She does, on first impression, seem to have quite a heavenly body. Her nature, however, is a little abrasive, grating enough to make sure I'll never actually touch her, which immediately takes pressure off the 'date'. She has no idea how petrified I've been before coming here. I wrote and deleted at least ten text messages cancelling without sending one. I changed my clothes more often than a model on a catwalk. I'm just beginning to relax when, within minutes of ordering the food, she lays out her set of dating rules. As I listen, I centre the condiments on the white linen tablecloth, refold my napkin along the iron lines, and realise there's nothing particularly unusual in her rules, apart from the strange fact that she has issued them within minutes of meeting me.

I'm trying to be kind. I'm telling myself that the dating scene is a challenging world I'll have to learn to navigate if I don't want to be alone for the second half of my life. She's more used to this and is possibly a bit jaded by it all. I know I am already. I nod along before gently interrupting. 'What's ghosting?' I ask for an explanation of rule number eight.

She raises a manicured hand to her face, as if she's about to laugh but catches my expression. 'You really don't know?'

'I really don't know.'

'Marry me,' she does laugh, and out of pure nervous tension, I find myself grinning too.

'I still really don't know.' My head tilts, questioning.

'Good, I'm glad. Ghosting means when you date someone, probably sleep with them, swap numbers, et cetera, and then you never hear from them again. They ignore all of your calls. They become a ghost to you.' She raises a hand and dramatically flops it outwards at a right angle. 'Ghosting.'

'I've never ghosted someone in my life.'

'Good,' she says again and sips from her glass of wine.

'If I wasn't interested in someone, I wouldn't sleep with them.' I can't believe I'm mentioning sex to a virtual stranger. I do not talk about sex. As a young teen, I ran from the house the second my father raised it in a 'birds and bees' conversation. Alice and I never talked about it because we were too busy practising to bother. Any woman since, apart from Lynn – I rarely got to sleeping with them. I've always been acutely self-conscious of my missing limb, despite working hard to stay fit. I wonder whether Celeste would be delighted or horrified to know I've only had seven lovers in my life. 'Ghosting,' I assure her, 'is not my style.'

'Tell me about yourself,' she says, and as I do, I omit the lover count and highlight the fact that I'm just about to go travelling, because I already know that Celeste and I won't ever be swapping bodily fluids.

'Why are you here if you're about to leave for six months?' She pinches her lips together, her annoyance obvious before her shaking head dips.

I cannot tell her that my teenage neighbour signed me up for the app and filled out my profile, deliberately deciding not to mention my plans. 'It'll put women off,' Grace had said wisely.

'I'm looking for a long-term relationship,' Celeste mutters as she pulls her chair out and stands. 'I'm sorry, Jack, but this isn't going to work, and I'd rather nip it in the bud, so to speak.'

I stand, take her offered hand. 'I understand. I'm sorry. Nice to meet you anyway.'

I eat her starter and mine too. And while I chew, part of me agrees with her. I shouldn't be here. I've never been the type to indulge in meaningless sex and I've no idea why I thought it might be necessary now. Meeting her earlier, though I felt initial feelings of attraction, they vanished as soon as we started to chat. Still, forty-nine and a half and dumped before the starter is a record.

*

Grace thinks the whole debacle is totally hilarious.

'Did you hear that, Walnut?' she says, early next day, over the hedge. 'Dumped before the starter!'

I'm sloshing around the wet sty I've just hosed down. 'Don't mock,' I tell her. 'It's not becoming.'

'I'm not sure it was the travelling,' Grace, mistress of unsolicited advice, advises. 'You can sometimes have this air about you.'

I scowl.

'You do! It's because you're a "DIM" type,' she uses her fingers to form quote marks around the Different in Melborough reference, 'but it says you're not interested.'

'Grace, forgive me here,' I question her, 'but how in fuck's name would you know what air I have around a date?' I'm irritated enough to swear in front of her.

'I don't. I'm guessing. And don't swear, it's not becoming.' She laughs at her own joke. 'It's just I had to persuade you to do it and I'm not really sure you're interested in meeting someone and that will show. You'll wear it on your face – it's like an aura about you.'

'Right.' I empty the last of the food I'd brought into Pecan's end of the trough.

'Wrong,' she shakes her head. 'It's wrong.'

Ollie's conversation with me comes to mind and I concede. 'OK.'

'So, how can you be different?'

I groan, a long, pained sound. 'Go and help your mother, Grace. I'm sure she needs help in the garage.' There have been sounds of electric saws going for the last half-hour.

'Nope, she doesn't need my help, but Jack, you do.'

'How's *your* love life, Grace?'

She sticks her tongue out at me and I smile.

'Seriously,' I ask. 'How's school – are you settling in all right?'

'It's OK.' She pauses. 'The boys are OK, the girls, maybe less so.'

'They're threatened by you.'

She rubs her head absently. 'I doubt that . . . It's early days. Hopefully it'll get better.'

'Has there been any—'

Her eyes widen as she looks at me. 'Any what?'

'Name calling . . .'

Grace sighs. 'Not in the new school, at least not to my face, but it wouldn't surprise me.'

'Grace, if people are cruel, it says more about them than you.'

She nibbles the edge of her mouth, says nothing at first. 'There is one guy. He's a *friend* only,' she holds up a hand, waves it as if to reassure herself that's all he is. 'He's going to help me build Mum's website. We're doing it as a project for IT.'

'Great idea.'

Silence descends as we both walk up towards our homes on either side of the shrubbery.

'You into sport?' I ask.

'I used to play league hockey.'

'You should play again.'

'I'm not sure I'd have the time.'

'You have the time. You don't want to have to start afresh, that's all. School, you have to do. Hockey you don't.

It's a bit like me and dating. Tell you what, if you enquire about a local hockey team, I'll go on another date.'

She grins.

'Deal?'

She fist bumps over the hedge. 'Deal.'

*

The rest of the morning drags, so I end up getting a train into London to meet Marsha for coffee. We're sitting in a coffee bar near the office, surrounded by the aroma of bitter beans, a host of millennial baristas who all look like they have Instagram accounts far more interesting than mine, and too many customers too busy to notice one another. Consuming two piping-hot Americanos and eating the edges of a crispy croissant takes only twenty minutes and then she starts clock watching, even though it's the weekend and she's only in the office 'to catch up on herself'.

'Sorry, you know what it's like. Stan,' she makes a face as she mentions the Senior Clerk in chambers, 'he's snowed under. Hurry back?' she softly pleads.

Looking around me, despite my restlessness, I'm not sure I want a return to this life of people having no life except work. 'I'm not sure I'll go back and I'm not sure if you'd want me back.'

Marsha side-eyes me. 'Jack, we want you back. You're just taking a little rest from it all.'

'I've been working out if I can retire yet or not, looking at my finances.' I haven't, not really, but I might.

'And?' She gathers her briefcase and bag on her lap.

'I'm rich.' I shrug.

'Don't be ridiculous, Jack. You'd be bored. You'd go crazy. You're bored already.'

'Probably.' I stand up. 'Let's wait and see how I feel in six months.'

'Come back. You're missed. Sorry that I gotta run. Keep in touch. Post lots of pictures!'

When she leaves, I head to the National Gallery, spend money on glossy books I don't need and I certainly won't be able to take with me. Walking around, I realise she's right. I'll probably end up marching straight back into the same role I've done most of my adult life because the number of hours to fill, when work is absent, is crushing sometimes. The feeling that I'm only now recognising as loneliness can make a day stretch interminably.

'Get on the next plane,' Ollie recommends when I call him from the train. When I try to tell him that I am going, that everything is planned for certain dates, he tells me I'm not listening, asks what the point is in asking him if I don't listen. 'Get on the *next* plane,' he repeats. Even Ollie seems tetchy today.

When I hang up, I catch a woman opposite glancing at me and I use the situation to try to practise my flirty eyes on her. She reacts by not raising hers from her Kindle for the rest of the journey.

*

'You can't sleep either?'

The voice surprises me and I almost fall off the top bar of the fence I'm perched on. It's a favourite spot of mine and one I can only navigate because of the large step I have permanently placed underneath me.

Clare approaches and leans on the fence.

'I don't sleep so good any more,' I reply. 'Apparently it's an age thing.'

She makes a face.

'What's your excuse?'

'Too hot,' she says simply. 'Apparently that's an age thing too.'

I nod, sip coffee from the mug in my hand. 'I love the view from here.' My head points towards the hills, filled with lines of hedgerows and crops, already showing up so many shades of green in the early light. 'And there's a stream about two hundred metres that way that you can't see from here, but if you listen, you can hear it.'

Clare looks, listens, says nothing.

'Before you moved in, I'd probably be out here singing loud scales.'

'You should still sing loud scales.'

I laugh. 'It's five in the morning. Even if you wouldn't mind, I imagine Grace might.'

She turns to look at me. 'Grace is almost as good at ignoring things as her mother.'

My turn to say nothing. It feels like she just said something important, but I have no idea what she means, so I point to the flask on the floor. 'Take the rest of the coffee if you want? There's a screw cup on the top.'

'Coffee and a view. Perfect way to start the day.'

I'm about to say that we have a lot in common, she and I, that we're both insomniacs who love morning views and coffee. Then, just as quickly as the first thought struck, I realise that's really not very much.

'How often do you do this?' Her voice is now low, just above a whisper. I'm assuming it's a nod to nature's chorus beginning to soar in the background.

'What? Come here and sit?'

She nods.

'"What is this life if full of care, we have no time to stand and stare."'

'Huh?'

'It's a poem from my schooldays by W.H. Davies, about something I've learned to do since stopping work. Just standing, staring, deep breathing. I've shelves of self-help books on how to relax and now I realise that all I had to do was stop.'

The edges of her eyes crease as she seems to imagine me with self-help books. 'Stop working?' she asks.

'Stop whatever . . . just for a little bit.'

'I ain't stopping,' she starts to laugh. 'I'm only starting.'

I watch her look back towards the garage. 'You're excited. You should be. It'll be fabulous.' A soft hum of traffic from the motorway in the distance mingles with the birdsong around us. 'Tell me some things I don't know about you, Clare. You know, likes, dislikes.'

She hesitates a moment before sipping from the cup. 'I've actually thought about this a lot lately – think I'd forgotten what *I* like for so long . . . but I do like nineties Britpop, good coffee, fruit and nut chocolate, drama boxsets, and being independent. I dislike reading, alcohol, stripy clothes and my mother. Your turn.'

'Hang on. You don't drink and don't like stripes or reading?' I deliberately don't mention the mother thing.

'I hate the taste of alcohol and the dust.'

'Dust?' I'm confused.

'Books. They're dust gatherers. Your turn,' she repeats.

'I love reading, jazz, blues, bourbon and symmetry. I hate crowds, noise and judgemental people. And, as it happens, I'm quite fond of my mother.'

She seems to think about what I've said before tossing the dregs and screwing the cup back on the flask.

'It's complicated,' she says.

'Parents are.'

She hands me the flask. 'I should get back. Thanks for the chat. It's good to talk to another grown up.'

I think what she's saying is that chatting might be something she misses about her ex. *I don't get that.* During the one brief meeting I had with him instinct told me not to trust him as far as my dodgy leg would let me throw him.

With a wave, she leaves as quietly as she arrived, and while I watch her, I realise that as lovely as she is, I really have nothing in common with her at all.

Chapter Eighteen

Instagram

GraceD15 Melborough, Wiltshire

. . .

Dad and me!

#hotmadras #currynight #sameeyes

. . .

View six comments:

    AliTyler Ur Dad is #hot!!

    Rickxyx Ur not tho!

    RajERT Fuck u #rickthedick

    Carocals Over 1000 calories girl!

    GraceD15 To whom it may concern. I am exactly the same weight as I was when I was in school with all of you. Quit your lowlife bullying.

    ReyaPurdite U tell em, G xx

-----Original Message-----
From: Enquiries@GoLiveHockeyWilts.co.uk
Sent: 19th September 2018 16:55
To: GraceBryanson29@gmail.com
Attachment: Membership Information
Subject: Hockey League – Your Email

Hello Grace,

Thanks for your email yesterday. I've attached some information on the club for you to have a read of. At the moment, our teams are complete, with no vacancies, but we're always looking for new members and there may be opportunities to play on the subs bench. Please do come along to a taster training session, which are available to non-league players – I've also attached some dates that might suit. If you're planning to come along, just email me on the same day so I can expect you.

    Looking forward to meeting you,
    Vi Haynes
    Club Secretary

WhatsApp Reya & Grace

How are u, G? Haven't heard from u?

OK. Beginning to settle in new school x

U coming back 4 my birthday party?

Need to check with Mum as prob have to stay with Dad?

Stay here?

Will ask Mum! C u, luv u x

Chapter Nineteen

Clare's phone had not stopped ringing. The studio wasn't completely finished yet, but she'd had enough interest, from the mail shot and opening a discussion on the local Facebook Group 'Melborough People', to start her first class the following Thursday. Surprisingly, or not at all if Grace was to be believed, most calls had come from adults wanting to learn ballroom and Latin dance. 'It's all over telly,' Grace told her, 'and it's your UVP.'

'USP,' Clare had corrected her. Now, as she walked up the high street in town, her nerves began to register. Yes, once upon a time she had been national champion, but it all seemed so very long ago. Struggling with imposter syndrome, when her phone rang again, she almost didn't answer it.

'Clare Bryanson speaking.'

'You're still keeping his name then.'

'Mum . . .' The news of her divorce had obviously spread. She stopped walking and balanced her shopping at her feet between her legs, inhaling deeply. 'How are you?' The question felt more automatic than a sincere desire to know how her mother was. It had been many years since they had spoken to one another, and this was the first time she'd called.

'I'm fine. Look, Clare, I'm going to get straight to the point. Can we meet, please? It's been far too long. I hear you've moved away.'

Snippets from the past assaulted her brain. Knowing people were having to walk around her, she moved into a doorway to have the conversation she needed to have.

'No.' The reply was a deep-rooted, instinctive reaction. 'I'm sorry, but that's not a good idea,' she added.

Silence pulsed down the line as people passed by chatting, immersed in their own business.

'Mum?' She felt as if she actually tripped over the word, debated calling the woman Jean. As the thought flashed, she had to acknowledge that she'd really rather not. No further dialogue at all with Jean would be her preference.

'It's been ten years.'

She heard the break in her mother's voice, heard the plea, and forced herself to focus, reading the etched name on the glass signage beside her. Onward Motion – the business seemed to be a one-stop shop for all things rehabilitation – both physical and of the mind. Inevitably, her mind cast back to the one time that Clare had asked her mother to come to therapy with her many years ago. It had been the doctor's idea, and it had seemed like a good one, until Jean had screamed at the end of their only joint session, 'This is *not* MY fault.' She had, even when Clare was in the midst of trying to deal with an eating disorder, made it all about her.

'I need to go now.'

'Clare, could you at least let Grace see me? She's sixteen soon, old enough to decide for herself.'

Clare's mama-bear instinct and natural fears for her daughter coiled into a lump in her throat. Though fear, panic and the need for money had made her consider contact with her mother, she'd come to the conclusion that the very last thing she wanted at this point in her and Grace's life was any hint of influence from her. Grace was a strong young woman – Clare knew and admired that in her only child but wasn't willing to take a chance on Jean Hutton's particular brand of gaslighting anywhere near her. A vision of Jean potentially talking to Grace over her end-of-year school report appeared fully formed in her head. Her mother, fake smile in place, standing proud – almost in a ballet first position, heels together, feet pointed outwards. 'Grace, darling, of course you have good grades, but imagine what might happen if you applied yourself!'

No. Grace had been through enough. She'd already been the butt of several unkind remarks about her body shape in her school environment. She'd had to find a route through her parents' marriage, watching the father she loved abuse the mother she loved. And the guilt Clare felt because Grace had heard and seen things she never should have, as always, threatened to engulf her.

No. She bit her bottom lip to stop it trembling. This was about her mother, and she and her mother were estranged for good reasons. Clare had, because she'd had to, spent her teenage years developing all sorts of survival strategies to deal with her mother's disappointment in her. She could remember Jean withholding physical contact if she'd disapproved of something or if Clare had failed in some way – no hugs or kisses, no approval, no touch . . .

'No.' She repeated aloud the only word that made sense, kept her voice steady and clear. 'I've really got to go now and, please, don't call again.' Hanging up, it was as if the click had an echo button that vibrated through her. Immediately, she blocked the number.

As Clare stood motionless up against the wall of the doorway she was hiding in, she remembered Jack's quote about standing still, seizing the moment – and she breathed it in. The name of the business smacked of irony. *Onward* was the direction she was headed. *Motion* was what was needed. Grabbing hold of the shopping bags at her feet, she first moved aside to allow someone to enter the building. When the door was opened, from inside, she heard a voice she recognised.

Glancing in, she saw Jack laughing with the receptionist. Clare remembered his asking for her help with donating hours to a local charity, but he had never followed it up. Not wanting to be seen lurking in the doorway, she grabbed the bags and walked at pace. Her heart thumped in her chest following the exchange with her mother. She had that effect on her, and the sound of her voice had been enough to tempt Croydon Clare to reappear again. Clare steeled herself.

She simply wasn't going to let that happen.

*

The studio was clear of workmen and the mirrors and barre had been fitted. When Clare let herself in, she dropped to her knees and began to cry. It was stunning: the space seemed even bigger now that the mirrors were on the wall and the light that she'd worried about, coming from the one sliding door at the end of the room, was more than enough with the spotlights that had been fitted to the ceiling.

She rooted for her phone in her bag, looked up Spotify for her favourite dance playlist. Pressing shuffle, she took her shoes and socks off and stood erect in front of the mirror. Then she moved to the music. Samba rolls led to jive kicks led to cha-cha steps as a renewed love of dance surged through her. When the last track stopped and she heard clapping, Clare's head spun around. Jack was stood in the doorway.

'I heard music. Sorry, I'm being nosy.'

Aware she was out of breath, she just smiled.

'Are you and Grace busy this evening?'

I'll be shining those mirrors, Clare thought.

'If not, I'm hoping you'll both come to supper. I'm off soon and thought it might be nice. I'm not the best cook but my burritos are passable.'

'I'm the one who should be asking you to supper.'

He waved a dismissive hand. 'You have enough to do here.'

'If you're sure, that would be lovely. Grace will have homework, so I'm not sure on time, I—'

'Text me,' he called back and then was gone.

She looked around. Two days until her first class. The interested people would try it and then, hopefully, sign up for a course until Christmas. Clare had worked it out – with hard work, she could pay Grace back within a year and then, next year, that piece of paper that she'd signed for the garage gave her an option to renew the studio for a monthly rent payment. She lowered herself to her haunches one more time, glanced in the mirror, and in between dreams of the future, she thought about the evening ahead. She loathed Mexican food with every taste bud in her body, but tonight – tonight she would eat burritos.

*

'She got the moves like Jagger.'

Jack had been trying to compliment Clare, but Grace shook with laughter.

'Is that you trying to be cool, Jack?'

'A little. Was it bad?'

Clare watched the exchange between Jack and Grace, realising that he was probably the only person that made Grace laugh often. Around Tim, Grace was her giving self; knowing she had a role to play with her father and that if she played it well, then she and he and everyone would be happy. But there was, Clare had noticed since they'd moved here, a nervous tension in Grace around Tim. It was as if she didn't really want to play any more, or she at least wanted to change the game. Clare had put it down to her getting older, but now, watching the easy banter between Jack and her, she wondered if it was because Grace had some father fixation on their benefactor.

'Glum face, Mother,' Grace poked her in the ribs. 'Cheer up! You'd swear you didn't like Mexican food!'

Jack gave her a worried glance over the hob. 'You do like Mexican food, don't you?'

'I love it.' Clare side-eyed her daughter.

'How long 'til we eat, Jack?' Grace asked.

'About thirty minutes.'

'Would you mind if I pop next door and finish something?'

'Of course not. Table's all ready, just waiting on the chilli sauce to finish cooking.'

As soon as Grace had left the room it was as if the space was filled with silence.

'I'm not great at this,' Jack said. 'This entertaining lark. I took an hour to set the table. Nothing looked right. Everything was wrong. It's one of my quirks, things have to look right.'

'The table looks beautiful,' Clare said, scanning her eyes over it. He came to join her, handing her a cold sparkling water.

'It has a *precise* look to it,' he said. 'Sort of like a table set by an army officer.'

She giggled.

'Has Grace spoken to you about her possibly looking after the pigs while I'm away?'

He steered her towards one of the armchairs that faced the garden at the far end of his kitchen and Clare sat down. 'She mentioned it.'

'Do you have any objections?'

'Of course not. Though . . .'

'Though?' He played with his iPhone until music filled the air. Clare had expected jazz or blues or classical music and was surprised when Snow Patrol played at low volume.

'I was just going to say something about the winter months here, how it'll be her out there at night, but . . .' she shook her head. 'I'll do it with her when it's dark.'

'If you'd rather I get—'

'No, no, she wants to do it. She's stopped eating bacon since meeting Pecan and Walnut.' Clare smiled. 'It'll just be strange being here alone, the two of us. Not only have you provided this chance for us, but I've come to rely on you being next door.'

'You don't have any other family?' He paused before adding, 'Apart from the mother you dislike.'

Clare cleared her throat. 'Just her. So, none that I could count on.' Thinking of the call from her mother that morning, she killed the topic dead and thankfully Jack did not pursue it.

'So, is that what you think happened here?' he asked instead. 'Chance?'

'Absolutely! This could have happened to one of far too many people. So many unable to see a way out, some a lot worse than we were . . .' Clare heard the emotion rise in her own voice. 'Sometimes I feel guilty that it happened to Grace and me. But something made you offer the charity the Barn. Something made *us* get the call. Accident, chance, a twist of fate, destiny – all of the above, I think.'

He nodded as if he understood what she meant, but Clare doubted it. She was trying not to jump to obvious conclusions, but something told her that, despite his gift to her, the well-bred man opposite had probably been born with a platinum spoon wedged in his lips. She supposed that he had only ever known parental love without a single strand of string attached, that chance had been kind and that though he might have worked hard too, he'd also been lucky without ever realising it.

She noticed, as he moved around his kitchen, as if for the first time, how tall he was. She'd guessed him at well over six foot, yet some of the time it was as if he stooped slightly in order to mask his height. In front of him, the work counter had a bevy of small dishes, now empty, where he'd obviously laid out all the ingredients he'd needed in two neat horizontal lines. As he stacked them and placed them in the dishwasher, she found herself imagining what his dating profile said. 'Tall, middle-aged gent. Velvet buzz cut of dark hair greying at the edges. Kind and funny, looking for like-minded woman for . . .' What *was* it he was looking for? she asked herself. 'Grace said she'd set you up on some dating apps, how's it going?'

He groaned, made a face. 'Awful. I'm so bad at it.'

'I don't believe that.' She didn't. For all the little quirks she'd noticed since meeting him; his love of symmetry and precision and the way he sang to his pigs in the morning, Jack Tate was very easy to be around.

'Believe it. I'm a forty-nine-year-old oddball who has spent the first half of his life considering the best thing to say. Now, suddenly, I say whatever comes into my head. Sometimes, it's perfect. Most times, it's bloody awful.'

The Rolling Stones were playing. She tugged a tiny loose thread on the seam of her jeans. 'Maybe chance will smile on you too.' Clare raised her water glass and clinked it against his beer bottle.

'Truth is, I'm not sure I'm ready to date,' she heard him say. 'But I've learned that not sharing your life with someone can make you myopic. So, I'm trying to dip a toe.'

Clare gave a hesitant nod. So far, her own life experience had taught her that not sharing her life with someone was far better than sharing it with someone who made her miserable.

'Do you miss him?' he asked. 'The man who irons his jeans?'

Clare tried to think when they'd met, blushing as she remembered Tim grabbing her arm on the driveway. 'At least he irons his own now. To think I used to do that for him.'

'Well?'

'I miss being part of a couple. I miss him being around for Grace, but . . .' she paused a moment. 'I don't miss him. Tim. The person. I wasn't happy for a very, very long time.'

She stared at the back door, willing Grace to appear. Talking about Tim out loud was something she didn't do. It felt fine cursing him in her own head but declaring her unhappiness was another thing completely – it required her to hear facts out loud.

I wasn't happy for a very, very long time.

Clare tried to unhear it, to keep all the bitterness she felt towards Tim locked down in her brain. That was the only way she could protect Grace and his relationship. But her mouth had dried in a nervous instant and she drained the water in her glass. Something was happening to her recently and she wasn't used to it. She was talking – first to Emma and now to Jack. It was, she told herself, all part of her rebirth, of Melborough Clare's survival. Tim had distanced her from previous friends, but Tim was no longer there to hinder her.

'Chance,' she tried, without success, to catch his eye. 'Whatever you want to call it, destiny maybe? It brought us all together and now we're friends, so maybe it's already smiled on you too?' When he avoided her glance, she wondered if she'd made assumptions, whether she and Grace were simply his annual charity case. 'You don't seem convinced,' she said, lifting a napkin from the nearby table to fan herself with.

'It's just, destiny isn't always that kind,' he said, a single shoulder shrugging, his eyes still lowered as he plated the chilli sauce she knew she'd hate.

She was just about to ask him what he meant when the door behind her opened.

'I checked the animals on the way back,' Grace said. 'What have I missed?'

Jack smiled. 'Supper is served!'

Whatever just happened, Clare was determined they *were* friends and that, odd as he was, Wiltshire would be a little lonelier without him.

*

It was when she was loading the washing machine at midnight that it came to her. Something had been nagging in her brain since she'd huddled in that doorway in town earlier. Gladys! One of her seventy-something dancers back in Croydon! She'd sold her a ticket supporting a charity her son was supported by. He'd been in the army and lost a limb in Helmand Province. The charity . . . She was certain it was called Onward Motion.

She steadied herself on the machine and pulled herself up to standing. It was coming together like a mental jigsaw puzzle. His gait at times, almost as if there was a hint of a limp. His being there earlier, in the clinic run by that charity. They never did follow up on that conversation about the charity he was linked to, the one he'd asked her to help out at, but Clare felt sure she'd stumbled upon it in town today.

Jack, she thought, she *knew*, as if she'd been shown a picture to confirm it, was an amputee too.

All night she tossed and turned, debating if she was right, what might have happened to him. Annoyed at herself for judging him, boxing him in a 'lucky' box, her heart cracked a tiny little fissure, just for him, for whatever he might have been through.

*

People had come. All insurances and paperwork had been sorted. She and Grace had shone the barre and mirrors to a blinding sheen. The sprung floor had been cleaned. It was Thursday and people had come – eleven of them for the first in a ten-week course in adult beginner's tango. Grace had done several polls on the local Facebook page for her and it seemed like the tango was the ballroom dance people were most keen to learn. Clare arrived at the studio twenty minutes early, read and reread her notes, stretched at the barre and listened until she heard chatter outside.

People had come. And they wanted to dance, and Clare filled with joy. Their sounds, their laughter, their desire to learn, fuelled her. They had all come as couples, apart from one lady, Sheila, recently widowed, whom Clare took by the hand within minutes. 'I'll be your partner,' she whispered.

Clare repeated the class she'd taught for years elsewhere, not needing to look at her notes once. She explained and counted out the man's steps, the lady's steps: slow, slow, quick, quick, slow. She demonstrated the tango hold, the bending through the knees, the slide of the foot on that last count – no, feet slightly apart at the end of the movement – not together. She counted them through it, smiled with them when they groaned, clapped when they got it right. Her first group of dancers were there, working with her in her studio, she thought at one point, before instantly tapping the mirror next to her three times.

People had come.

Chapter Twenty

I'm in a woman's bed and I'm not dreaming. I'm definitely not dreaming.

I'm in a woman's bed and she's sitting on top of me and moving slowly and I'm touching her breasts. A woman, a younger woman, is moving slowly astride me, gripping me, and I don't know if I can hold on for much longer. When she tightens and cries out, I come inside someone for the first time in three years.

She moves off me and lies her head on my chest. Her name is Laura and it's Grace's fault that I'm here. It's Grace's fault because this is the date that happened after she fist-bumped me over the hedge. Laura doesn't know this, but this will be the last date before I leave for the States in just over two weeks. My eyes squeeze shut. I've just had amazing sex with a beautiful woman and I'm going to have to tell her I can't see her again.

'Mmmm' sounds from my chest sometime later and I open my eyes, but as Laura starts to massage my cock, I have to whisper that I'm done, spent, need to sleep.

She gives me a disappointed pout but lies on my chest again.

This is what happens when a forty-nine-and-a-half-year-old man beds a woman of thirty-seven.

Laura doesn't take no for an answer and only lets me sleep for an hour. I know this because I glance at her bedside clock just as she starts to kiss me again. Before long, the condoms are out and we're doing it again. I'm on top this time and her nails are clawing my ass. Briefly, I wonder if there's some new etiquette to asking a woman to be gentler. She moans softly and soon starts to quiver inside. That tightening of her muscles around me is about to set me off and I think of Alice and then of . . . April. It's April's face I see when I come. It's April's hand I feel stroking my back when I lower myself off Laura.

I'm horrified. It feels wrong. And there is only right and wrong, so I force myself to banish her from any thoughts to do with sex. Any thoughts to do with anything other than her being a friend who set me off on this journey to *live*. I am obviously either not a very nice person or someone whose sexual appetite has, like a sleeping giant, been kicked awake. I opt for the latter.

Laura makes tea. Laura has been an awesome date. She works in HR, is charming, funny, good company. She shares my love of music, even plays the piano. She doesn't even seem to notice when I strap on my prosthetic. Exactly the sort of woman I would love to have met sometime in the last few years, or sometime in the near future, just not right now.

When I leave Laura's apartment, we swap numbers and I spend the car journey home feeling bad because I'm going away and have no room in my life for anything other than a one-off sexual encounter.

But I tell her none of this.

*

By midday I'm feeling wobbly. Laura has already texted, and Lynn has just called to tell me Antony has gone totally off the rails and walked out. He won't listen to me, but I text his number anyway, the one I'd been ignoring for ages, which is now the first name in my alphabetical phone list.

Antony, call your Mum. She's worried sick.

Five minutes later I get his reply:

Fuck off.

I do. I fuck off, concentrate on sorting my travel file out, making sure I have electronic tickets in place. Making sure I have dollars. I start to actually pack my rucksack, taking the clothes from the symmetrical piles of warm and cool items that sit on the floor next to my bed.

My phone pings, and, expecting an abusive text from Antony, I'm surprised to get one from Lynn, and my stomach sinks.

This is your fault. All you had to do was handle him right just once. If anything happens to my son, I blame you.

I try to call, leave a message, but she doesn't call back. Unable to pack for The Big Trip now, I toss a pair of jocks and socks and a fresh jumper and jeans in another bag along with my toothbrush and head to the car.

*

Ollie's home has always been a place of comfort for me. Some people want silence and yogic music playing in a spa-like set-up to de-stress. I go to Oliver's – have his two kids crawl all over me, read stories to them before bedtime and hope that Jennifer, his wife for the last fifteen years, will tell me everything is going to be OK while we eat home-cooked pie and mash at supper.

'You got laid!' Oliver wipes his eyes with his napkin.

'Is it really that funny?' I look to Jennifer for help.

She kicks him under the table, doesn't make any attempt to hide it. 'Ignore him. He's jealous. He'd love some younger stranger shagging him senseless.'

'Will you see her again?' Ollie asks, his head still moving in disbelief.

'No.' I don't feel like telling him the rest now. 'Let's drop it. She was lovely, someone I'd like to have seen again if I wasn't going away.'

'When are you off?' Jennifer spoons the last of the buttery mash onto my plate as if I need feeding.

'Seventeen days.'

'You need to send me your itinerary.' Opposite me, Ollie wags a fork in my direction.

'Why?'

'So that if we don't hear from you or you go missing, we know where to start looking.'

'Mum and Dad will have a copy. They're my next of kin.'

'Yes,' he's now jabbing a finger towards me, 'but they won't be keeping in touch with you apart from when you visit them. So how will they know if you're lost, have fallen off a cliff, or been murdered?'

I sit back, fold my arms, and think yogic music in some spa might have been a better idea.

'Ollie!' Jennifer raps him on his knuckles. 'What's gotten into you?'

'What? I'm right. He knows I'm right.' My oldest friend stares back at me. 'Come on, Mr Right or Wrong and there is nothing in between, I'm right, aren't I?'

I say nothing.

'I'll be keeping in touch,' he continues. 'Phone calls, emails, and I just want to know you're all right. This might be your "I'm almost fifty" thing, but there are still things you have to do to stay safe. Including keeping in touch with me. And giving me a copy of your itinerary.'

'OK.'

'I mean, I don't even know exactly what your plans are other than "to travel". Where are you planning to go to and why – tell us.'

I catch another scowl from his wife in his direction.

'What?' he glowers back. 'I'd just like to hear the actual details!'

'The States is first,' I tell them, 'then Europe second.'

'That's it? *That's* the plan?'

I laugh. He's abrupt and sharp, but I know it stems from concern. Ollie thinks I'm running away. From what, I'm not sure. He's never told me. 'This all came about because of April's email,' I remind him. 'And any time I doubt myself, I remember it's about *living* life. But I'm *not* going to be the guy who travels around with a GoPro attached to him while bungee jumping from a cliff, or someone who goes white-water rafting in rapids.'

'Good,' Jennifer whispers.

'There's a structure to it.'

'Finally,' Ollie says, raising his hands to the heavens.

'I found these notes in an old planner of mine, remember the sort we had in uni?'

He nods.

'It was what Alice and I were going to do after our degrees. We'd said we'd travel for a bit before . . . well, the plan was to do that before being a grown up.'

My hosts have both gone quiet. The room is silent apart from the breezy sound of passing tumbleweed.

'We'd only got around to discussing the east coast of America, so that's where I'm starting. Boston, New York, Miami, then New Orleans and the Bahamas. Obviously, I've added in the west coast, starting in San Diego and—'

'You sure that's a good idea?'

'I've heard San Diego is lovely at this time of year,' I reply, knowing that's not what he meant.

He gawps from the other end of the table, any warnings about using the travel plans I had with Alice as a basis for moving on with my life obviously stuck in his throat.

Jennifer pours wine into both of our glasses and changes the subject. 'How are you getting on with your new neighbour? Clare, isn't it?'

'She's fine. The daughter, Grace, it was her who suggested I should date before The Big Trip. Said I'm "a little awkward" and would need the practice.'

Ollie snorts. 'Smart kid. I remember liking her. How old is she again?'

'Fifteen, nearly sixteen, though she's not like any teen I've ever known.'

'To be fair, Jack, your experience with teenagers is a little limited.' Jennifer's eyebrows arch.

'Yes, we all know how I handled Antony and I'm sure you both thought it was badly at the time.' There's a tiny glance between them again, almost imperceptible.

Jennifer kicks her shoes off under the table and sits back in her chair, her full glass held in both her hands. 'You didn't know any better,' she offers kindly.

'No, but I was an idiot. There might have been a way that the threat of the police being called would have been enough, without actually reporting him. I never even tried to talk to the kid.'

Neither Jennifer nor Oliver speaks, which says so much. Lying in the silence of their unspoken replies are the words 'and you and Lynn might still be together, and you wouldn't be such a sad and lonely fuck, needing to run away'.

I sigh, a long hard sigh. 'He came to see me,' I say, running both hands through my hair and rubbing my scalp as if soothing a non-existent itch. 'To be honest, guys, it's been a bit of a week. I had sex for the first time in years and will end up ghosting the poor woman. Antony broke into my house in the middle of the night, except he didn't really because he had a key. And Clare's husband, the one she divorced, seems to be dipping in and out of her life still.' I take a breath, watch their faces.

Ollie frowns. 'Whoa! What exactly happened with Antony?'

'Like I said, he came in and shouted a lot and let me know how angry he still is. Then he deliberately smashed Alice's unicorn before tossing the key at me and storming off.'

Jennifer's hand goes to her mouth and I pull the tiny blue horn from my front pocket.

'I still have this bit.' Leaning forward, I show her, and she takes it, rolls it between her fingers.

'It's the magic bit.' She smiles and hands it back to me.

'And Clare's ex?' Ollie is bunching his bottom lip between his thumb and forefinger like he does when he's nervous.

'I don't often dislike people instantly, you know me, hell, I've had to learn never to judge in work, but . . . there's something about the guy. I don't trust him, and though it seems he's only ever around to see Grace, I'm wary. I suppose I hate going away thinking he's going to slide his feet under the table and I won't be here to stop it.'

Jennifer jerks as there's a heavy thud sound from upstairs. 'You go?' she asks her husband and he's left the table in an instant. 'Probably Agatha,' she tells me. 'She has a knack for falling out of bed. We have a low-lying bed for her, but still . . .'

I nod, gulp some wine.

'Jack, Antony's just still smarting over your part in his arrest.'

'Why now, though?' I ask. 'He only did young offenders for a few months, then left on licence. It was a long time ago and I don't get why *now*.'

She shrugs. 'Because he can. Because he's pissed off. I don't know, maybe something sparked him to blame you again.'

Oliver comes back in. 'Aggie, she's fine, fast asleep still.' He sits down, drinks from his glass and looks me square in the eye from his end of the table. 'Now, I have some things to say to you,' he says.

'Oh dear.' I steel myself to hear what I probably came all this way for.

'You need to talk to Antony, he was a nice kid, and if his stint away didn't mess him up, he probably just wants an apology.'

The mention of the young offender's sentence from Ollie's mouth makes me wince. 'I did message him, and he told me to fuck off—'

'Could the defensive defence barrister just shut up for a sec?'

Biting my lip, I stay quiet.

'Clare's husband? I met the woman. She doesn't strike me as a person who'd mess this chance up.'

'I don't think she is either,' I can't help interrupting. 'It's not her. It's him. It wouldn't surprise me if he just worms his way back in.'

'Ollie's right, Jack,' Jennifer says. 'You have to give a clever woman the benefit of the doubt here. The man has a right to see their daughter. Sounds like she won't let him worm his way anywhere.'

I hope they're right.

'You did a great thing, Jack,' Oliver raises his glass as if toasting. 'They're good people, Clare and Grace. Even the staff who oversee things for the charity who introduced them think they're worthy, good people. You have to trust them.'

My eyes narrow, the cynic in me alive and kicking. I know I'm *willing* to embrace the whole trust thing, but I'm not sure I'm able.

Jennifer stands and comes behind my chair, reaches around me and briefly hugs me. It lasts three seconds before she moves, but I grab her arm, grip it as it lies there beneath my neck, try to make the moment last a little longer. 'It's a decision, Jack, to trust or not. You just have to be prepared to make it,' she whispers before standing upright. 'Who's for rhubarb crumble?' she adds.

Ollie and I both nod before she leaves the room. For a minute or two, we listen to the sound of one of his 'over-dinner' playlists – he's first to speak over the sounds of Rag'n'Bone Man.

'Jack?'

'Uh huh?'

'Since when have you even known what ghosting is?'

We both laugh, and while Jennifer's out of the room, I want to tell him, to ask my friend what it means that I saw April's face when making love to another woman, but he'd probably put it all together and come up with some exaggerated version of reality. It's fine. I'm in control.

So, instead, when she gets back, I just tell them all about Celeste's dating rules and it's not long before they're both crying into their puddings.

ed the door, allowing him through.
over,' Tim whispered conspiratori-

id, they're doing a project together.'
alking and was looking up the stairs.
and whip his ass, do I? I mean, he's
e?'

her natural reply, refused to engage in
ays assure her later, after words might
anger, was mere 'banter'. It was Friday
ub shifts every day for the last week and
ng her first classes. Though it had been
ime, the busy working week left her feel-
anted to do was crash and watch Netflix.
he recently boiled kettle, dangled a teabag
ter, watched Tim take his coat off and put
of a chair. He was working out again, she
ing his biceps. He looked good and smelled
now knew he was doing that deliberately
ime he'd come to take Grace out, he did his
ike an ageing model for a catalogue.
thing happened yesterday.' He took a seat at
able and she handed him a mug of milky tea –
he liked it. 'You not joining me?'
ted, poured the dregs of the kettle over a herbal
sitting opposite him. 'What?' she asked. 'What
ing?'
num,' he said, taking a slow sip. 'She called me.'

Chapter Twenty-One

-----Original Message-----
From: NorseErik@gmail.com
Sent: 10th October 2018 21:09
To: GraceBryanson29@gmail.com
Subject: Website

Grace, think we should use the same provider as the website I did for Dad. It's really user-friendly and free. Can you get photos of your mum's first classes and maybe some old ones of her as dance champion?

We should get together, work out the wording for the main landing page – maybe just get some bullet points from her?

Erik

-----Reply Message-----
From: GraceBryanson29@gmail.com
Sent: 10th October 2018 21:20
To: NorseErik@gmail.com
Subject: Re: Website

Email? I tried to WhatsApp you?!
G

-----Reply Message-----
From: NorseErik@gmail.com
Sent: 10th October 2018 21:25
To: GraceBryanson29@gmail.com
Subject: Re: Website

I hate texting. Just call me or email me.
  Erik

-----Reply Message-----
From: GraceBryanson29@gmail.com
Sent: 10th October 2018 21:35
To: NorseErik@gmail.com
Subject: Re: Website

Good to know. I'll sort out stuff from Mum. Shall we meet for an hour after school on Friday? Might be easier for you to come here, to the Barn. Do you know where?
  Grace

-----Reply Message-----
From: NorseErik@gmail.com
Sent: 10th October 2018 21:09
To: GraceBryanson29@gmail.com
Subject: Re: Website

Everyone knows the Barn. I'll have to go home first and then I'll cycle up for 4.30. See you then.
  Erik

186

Reluctantly, she oper
'So, she has a friend
ally. 'Male or female?'
'Male. Erik. Nice
Tim had stopped
'I don't need to go u
not a boyfriend, is h
  Clare swallowed
what he would alw
have exploded into
night – she'd had
also begun teachi
such an exciting
ing that all she v
  She reboiled
into the hot wa
it on the back
thought, notic
good too. Sh
as well. Any
best to look
  'Strangest
the dining
just the wa
  She rele
bag, befor
strange th
    'Your

'You're n
her until n
it on her fr
she added.
  Her face t
his phone from
act. All part of
  Determined n
Grace has a friend
  'I made a mistak
curry night.'
  'It's not.'
  'You're not at work
around his neck, rubbe
  'Not tonight.'
  'How about a hot drink
Grace and then I'll be on
  Clare glanced over to Jac
  'Come on, Clare, it's cold
and I'll go.'

Immediately, Clare's stomach clenched. 'Called *you*? Why? How would she even have your number?'

'I didn't ask.'

As well as looking good enough to make her realise he was still a gorgeous-looking man, Tim still had the ability to just toss an explosive sentence at her. Over the years she'd learned not to react. Now, she blurted, 'What did she want?'

'I'm still not quite sure.'

'Well, what did she say?'

'Some crap about the fact we'd divorced. And, before you ask, I have no idea how she knew that. It was all about getting your address out of me, I think.'

'Did you give it to her?'

'Of course I didn't give it to her.' He made a face, feigning hurt. 'I wouldn't do that.'

'How do you reckon she had your number?' she repeated as she fanned herself.

'I told you – I don't know. But if I was a guessing man, I'd say Grace gave it to her.'

And with that incendiary sentence, Clare's whole world imploded.

*

'It was a few months ago,' Grace was sitting on the second-last step of the stairs, her arms folded defiantly. 'She found me on Facebook and messaged me.'

'And you didn't think I'd want to know?'

'I knew you'd kick off like this if you did.'

Clare had ejected Tim from the house, which had forced Grace downstairs. In the background, Erik had scurried down the path after Tim.

'You've just made me look like a complete idiot.' Grace was silently seething.

'Probably because you are,' Clare barked.

Her daughter stood and climbed the stairs.

'And where do you think you're going?' Clare's voice rose even more. 'I'm not done. I want you to tell me exactly when and why you've been in touch with my mother.'

'Listen to yourself, Mum!'

Clare ran up the stairs and squared up to her. 'You did it behind my back, both of you!'

Grace shook her head. 'Why would you want me hating you the same as you do her, Mum? Because that's what's going to happen!' And with that she climbed the final steps, leaving Clare breathless.

She sat down, willed the tears to stay inside, fought hard not to let them fall, but fall they did – quietly tracing salty streaks down her cheeks. Less than five feet from where she sat, Grace had slammed the door. Clare bit down on her forefinger, slid herself across the landing. 'I'm sorry,' she said through the door.

Nothing, no reply, just sounds of banging coming from inside her room. Clare was just about to try again when the door opened, and Grace flounced past her. 'I've called Dad back and he's outside. I'm going to spend the weekend at his.'

'Wait. Grace . . .' Clare pulled herself into a standing position. 'Look—'

'No, Mum, you look. I try, OK? I'm the one who understands you no longer love Dad. I get that! And I understand that you and your mum don't speak. But you're the one not getting on with people, not me!'

Clare listened to the heavy tread of her only child running down the stairs.

'I'll be back on Sunday,' she yelled before slamming the second door of the night.

Clare ran down the stairs herself to watch out of the narrow window in the hallway. Grace getting into Tim's car. Tim reversing out the driveway. She sobbed into her sleeve and closed her eyes to the slow sounds of distant trumpet playing.

*

Saturday morning, Clare woke to a throbbing head from lack of sleep. Having texted Grace the night before, her only child hadn't responded, but Tim had. She didn't like it; the feeling that he was somehow more in control of a situation involving their daughter than she was. With her first Saturday class to get ready for, Clare tried to put it to the back of her mind and took a hot shower. She dressed in exercise-wear, paced the downstairs of the Barn with a bottle of water in her hand, before grabbing her folder and heading over to the studio.

Twelve people had pre-booked for the contemporary dance class, most of whom were older girls from the sixth form at Grace's school, and as they began to noisily pile in, Clare felt the standard rush of nerves. Nerves were something she was used to, but the accompanying surging heat wasn't. She opened a fan and began to waft it in front of her face, convincing herself it made her look quirky and Spanish rather than forties and perimenopausal.

After brief introductions she read a small passage from her 'dance bible', a teaching aide her mother had taught from herself. Despite her many faults, Clare believed no other words than the annotations her mother had scribbled in the sides of its pages could be more perfect for her first moments of teaching freestyle. 'Let emotion surge through your veins . . . help your audience feel,' she said as she moved through the room.

Her fear for her own daughter was expressed through wild arms. The irony that her bright, intelligent child possibly having her self-esteem eroded by any contact with the same woman who'd written those sensitive words wasn't lost as she danced. Her desire to hold Grace, to keep her safe from emotional harm, first surged through, then softened her arms, wrapped them around her body in a hug.

Clare stopped, played the class designated music, and went to each girl, helping them through their first moves. When all twelve, after the first taster lesson, booked a course to take them up to Christmas, she felt relief. It was working – something was working.

*

'Everything all right at home?'

Clare was unprepared for the question from Emma when she turned up for an afternoon shift at the pub.

'Of course,' she almost stuttered her reply. 'Why do you ask?'

She felt Emma's eyes rest on her. 'Nothing, just Erik mentioned something so—'

'Wait,' Clare rested both hands on her head. 'Erik with a k and not a c is *your* son?' She hadn't put it together before; though she'd known they had a son, she'd assumed he was a lot older than Erik.

'Yes, didn't you know? And blame the Norse god for that k. I'd have been quite happy with a c.'

'Everything's fine,' Clare said, 'just a misunderstanding with Grace. Teens, eh?'

She could tell Emma was chomping at the bit to ask but didn't. Somehow her new friend swallowed the obvious questions like, 'So was that your ex who turned up and whisked her away from you for the weekend?'

'She's at Tim's until tomorrow night,' Clare confessed. 'To be honest, I don't know what to do with myself.'

'You want to work an extra shift? I know you normally don't work Sundays but it's busy here over lunchtime and, to be honest, I'd love it off – just this once?' Emma pressed both her hands together, prayer-like, as she spoke.

'No problem,' Clare replied, grateful not to be staring out the tall windows of the Barn, alone, clock watching, waiting for Grace to come home.

As it happened, Grace arrived home twenty minutes after her shift ended that evening, twenty-four hours earlier than expected. Thrilled to have her back, Clare accepted her daughter's moody 'I've got that hockey thing tomorrow' and hugged her tight. She put off asking any questions about the early arrival and thinking about now having to disappoint Emma the next day, as behind Grace, Tim, carrying her bag, followed into the house. Within minutes Grace was in the shower and Clare was bombarded.

'What's this I hear about the bloke next door going off for months? I mean, don't get me wrong, he's weird if you ask me. This "friendship" he has with Grace, that's just suss, all wrong. I'll be glad to see the back of him, but I don't like the thought of you and Grace being stuck here all alone.'

Clare refused the bait. 'How was she?' she asked Tim, ignoring his outburst.

'She was fine, ended up going to Reya's birthday party for a few hours. Fear not, I picked her up at a quarter to one.'

Her quick glance upstairs kept him talking.

'I can hear your mind ticking, Clare. Grace told me she'd asked to go and that you said no. My turning up here was nothing to do with anything. That was my mistake. She thought you'd think she planned it.'

She might have planned it, Clare thought but dismissed it immediately. 'Thank you for bringing her home.'

'We're going to get a takeaway,' he clapped his hands lightly together. 'Grace googled a pizza place who'll deliver.

Chapter Twenty-One

-----Original Message-----
From: NorseErik@gmail.com
Sent: 10th October 2018 21:09
To: GraceBryanson29@gmail.com
Subject: Website

Grace, think we should use the same provider as the website I did for Dad. It's really user-friendly and free. Can you get photos of your mum's first classes and maybe some old ones of her as dance champion?

We should get together, work out the wording for the main landing page – maybe just get some bullet points from her?

Erik

-----Reply Message-----
From: GraceBryanson29@gmail.com
Sent: 10th October 2018 21:20
To: NorseErik@gmail.com
Subject: Re: Website

Email? I tried to WhatsApp you?!
G

-----Reply Message-----
From: NorseErik@gmail.com
Sent: 10th October 2018 21:25
To: GraceBryanson29@gmail.com
Subject: Re: Website

I hate texting. Just call me or email me.
    Erik

-----Reply Message-----
From: GraceBryanson29@gmail.com
Sent: 10th October 2018 21:35
To: NorseErik@gmail.com
Subject: Re: Website

Good to know. I'll sort out stuff from Mum. Shall we
meet for an hour after school on Friday? Might be easier
for you to come here, to the Barn. Do you know where?
    Grace

-----Reply Message-----
From: NorseErik@gmail.com
Sent: 10th October 2018 21:09
To: GraceBryanson29@gmail.com
Subject: Re: Website

Everyone knows the Barn. I'll have to go home first and
then I'll cycle up for 4.30. See you then.
    Erik

Chapter Twenty-Two

'You're not meant to be here. You're not even due to see her until next week.' Clare stared at his hand as he placed it on her front door. 'And then, it's meant to be at yours,' she added.

Her face tight with tension, she watched him remove his phone from his pocket and look at his calendar. All an act. All part of his drama.

Determined not to be sucked in, she spoke slowly. 'Tim, Grace has a friend over, they're working on an IT project.'

'I made a mistake, OK? I genuinely thought tonight was curry night.'

'It's not.'

'You're not at work?' Tim pulled the collar of his coat up around his neck, rubbed his hands together.

'Not tonight.'

'How about a hot drink? I say a quick hi and goodbye to Grace and then I'll be on my way.'

Clare glanced over to Jack's house.

'Come on, Clare, it's cold out here. A cuppa and a wave and I'll go.'

Reluctantly, she opened the door, allowing him through.

'So, she has a friend over,' Tim whispered conspiratorially. 'Male or female?'

'Male. Erik. Nice kid, they're doing a project together.'

Tim had stopped walking and was looking up the stairs. 'I don't need to go up and whip his ass, do I? I mean, he's not a boyfriend, is he?'

Clare swallowed her natural reply, refused to engage in what he would always assure her later, after words might have exploded into anger, was mere 'banter'. It was Friday night – she'd had pub shifts every day for the last week and also begun teaching her first classes. Though it had been such an exciting time, the busy working week left her feeling that all she wanted to do was crash and watch Netflix.

She reboiled the recently boiled kettle, dangled a teabag into the hot water, watched Tim take his coat off and put it on the back of a chair. He was working out again, she thought, noticing his biceps. He looked good and smelled good too. She now knew he was doing that deliberately as well. Any time he'd come to take Grace out, he did his best to look like an ageing model for a catalogue.

'Strangest thing happened yesterday.' He took a seat at the dining table and she handed him a mug of milky tea – just the way he liked it. 'You not joining me?'

She relented, poured the dregs of the kettle over a herbal bag, before sitting opposite him. 'What?' she asked. 'What strange thing?'

'Your mum,' he said, taking a slow sip. 'She called me.'

It'll be here in a few minutes.' Turning his back on her, he made his way to the kitchen and opened the fridge. 'There should be some beers left from the last time I stayed over on curry night. Oh, good,' he said, taking one and pulling on the tab. 'I'll kip on the sofa, don't fancy driving all the way back again.'

Clare really wanted to talk to Grace alone, have a heart-to-heart with her. Instead, she ran her tongue over the inside of her top teeth, thought about several responses, before walking to the cutlery drawer and removing three place settings. She swallowed her annoyance at the way he'd walked to *her* fridge and removed *his* beer, cursed herself for having kept them. From a nearby cupboard, she removed three plates, only to replace it all again when Tim said they'd eat from the box. 'Less mess,' he claimed.

She didn't argue.

*

Clare smiled through the pouting images of Grace's friends on Instagram, smiled through her excitement at having spent time with Reya. Having decided to drop any accusation of her plotting to be there all along, she was just glad to have her back, to see her happy. Like a smack in the face, Clare was reminded how much the move had affected Grace, how much she put a brave face on things.

'I'm sorry, Mum. I should have told you about Gran.'

'Your gran and I, it's difficult.'

Beside her, Tim sniggered. 'She's barking mad, not difficult,' he said, nudging Clare with his elbow.

'Tim, please.'

'OK, OK, let's talk about something else.'

'Gran's already explained,' Grace said.

'She has?' Clare doubted it. 'What has she said?'

'That she hates Dad and loves you too much.' Grace shrugged. 'She said lots over time, but that's it, really.'

Clare laughed softly, marvelling at her teenage daughter's way to capture a simplicity in thorny subjects. It was almost easy to forget reality and convince herself just for a moment that they were the family they used to be, just sitting down having a meal.

'Hate is a strong word,' Tim grimaced.

'No, Dad, she does, she *hates* you.'

'Right.' Tim sucked air through pursed lips and Clare couldn't help grinning.

'To be fair, that's not a shocker.'

'Suppose not,' he said, heading to the fridge for the last beer.

'Grace, it's late,' Clare said, ears pricked at the sound of blues music from next door, eyes on her yawning daughter. 'You had a late one last night.' She stood and cleared away the cardboard boxes, placing them straight into the recycling bin.

'I do not know how you put up with that noise,' Tim shook his head.

'I like it,' both Clare and Grace said at the same time. 'Come on, love,' Clare added. 'You're on pig duty tomorrow morning.'

'Pig duty?' Tim asked when Grace had said good night to them both and gone upstairs to bed.

'She's tired, she'll be out like a light before her head hits the pillow after being up so late.'

'Pigs?' Tim repeated.

'Jack's teaching her to look after the animals when he's away.'

'I don't like that guy,' he announced as if it were news.

'I'm sure the feeling's mutual. He's been good to me and Grace.'

'Hmmm.'

'Tell me about the new job,' she asked, knowing the safest ground was to get him talking about himself.

Clare let him speak all about his new sales role. She paid no attention to the detail of what he was saying, just watched him shift around on the old sofa, get up to help himself to tea. She lost herself in the familiarity of his voice and movements.

'I think I'll go to bed.' She eventually stood and rolled her sleeves up to her elbows. 'It's late – now Grace is back I have to text Emma and cancel covering the lunchtime shift I'd agreed to tomorrow.'

'Grace told me about the hockey game. I can take her. Let me do that and you can go to work if you need to.'

Clare didn't respond, not wanting to commit to him being here any longer than necessary. That said, they'd had an enjoyable evening and it would mean she wouldn't have to let Emma down. 'If you're sure . . . ? I'll go and grab the spare duvet from upstairs.'

At Grace's bedroom door, Clare glanced in at the sleeping figure of her daughter, her soft rhythmic snore an instant comfort. She was home.

In the living room, she tossed the duvet on the sofa, gathered her phone and glass of water from where she'd been sitting and, as she turned, realised Tim was standing too, right in front of her.

'She asleep?' Tim asked.

Clare nodded.

'You can't help yourself, always did check on her last thing.'

'Always will, I suppose,' she replied.

'I miss you,' he said. 'Stay, have a drink with me.'

'No, Tim, no,' she shook her head. 'We're not doing this.'

'Just listen, will you?'

Clare watched his lips moving, tuned into the still playing soft music from next door. She'd heard all of Tim's declarations before, didn't believe any of them for a second, yet somehow, after this, his latest statement of regret and love, when he reached for her face and gently pulled her towards him, she didn't resist. She wanted to be kissed. She wanted to be kissed to the backdrop of Jack's music, but after the first kiss, she moved her face from her ex-husband's. 'That was a mistake,' she whispered. 'I'm sorry.'

'No. You want me.' Tim smiled as he pressed her fingertips to his lips.

'Nope.'

'You want me a little bit.'

Clare laughed, but didn't stop him when he reached for her again, didn't stop him when she felt his hand slip under her shirt and cup her breast. Croydon Clare's head arched back as he kissed her neck. She didn't love this man any more, didn't even like him most days, and when his hands moved over her body, she hated herself because it felt so good. She hated herself because he was right. She wanted it. She wanted to be kissed, held, to be possessed by the lost feeling of being touched. Moments later, as Tim led her down the hallway towards her bedroom, she caught their reflection in the long window next to the front door. Melborough Clare closed her eyes.

She could hate herself properly in the morning.

Chapter Twenty-Three

Things I haven't done and things I have done . . .

Things I should do but am too much of a pussy to do . . .

This is what I'm dwelling on right now when perhaps I really should be more present, more 'in the moment'.

I *have* texted Antony a belated and heartfelt apology for not being willing or able to at least listen to him years ago. I know I should try to talk to him, know that it would be the right thing to do, but can't quite bring myself to. Antony hasn't replied.

I *haven't* responded to April's email invitation to dinner with her and her husband. I should but am afraid I'll sit there all night imagining her naked.

I *haven't* ghosted Laura yet.

It's official: I'm a pussy, a fact I'm regretting over a roast dinner in the pub. Laura's a picker, obviously doesn't really eat, even though I've assured her Jan's roasts are legendary. From the corner of my eye, behind the old wooden bar, I can see Clare looking in our direction. Laura's three glasses of Merlot in and I'm three large glasses of water down. It's me who excuses myself to go to the loo first. As I pass,

I nod at three locals lining the barstools, one of whom I recognise as the butcher. They're all nursing black pints of stout. Perhaps I'm being oversensitive, but something tells me I'm the subject of their idle speculation today.

'Jack.'

I hear my name and turn around.

'Sorry to bother you, but I thought as I saw you – the lock on the main door into the studio is sticking and I've tried—' Clare looks awkward, uncomfortable, has her hands backing one another, interlinked, with her fingers pointed upwards. 'I feel bad even mentioning it . . .'

'I'll pop over and have a look when I'm back.'

Clare nods, then lifts her head. 'Thanks. Your girlfriend seems sweet, I was talking to her when she ordered drinks.'

'Laura's not my girlfriend.' I straighten two pictures hanging crooked on the walls, step back a bit and check they're straight.

She says nothing and the two of us stand there, a moment. My bladder is almost at bursting point when she asks when I'm leaving for the States.

'Ten days,' I confirm.

'Does Laura know yet?' Laughter lines sneak into the edges of her eyes and I shake my head. 'You're blushing,' she adds.

'I do need to tell her.'

'She likes you.' Clare says it like it's a warning.

'How can you tell?'

'Women know these things. Let her down gently, eh?' she whispers before heading back to the bar.

At the urinal, I sigh with relief as I take a pee. The wall in front of me is mirrored and I'm forced to look at a middle-aged man whose face says he really has no idea how to let someone down romantically, gently or otherwise.

I decide to do it over the crème brûlée, and by the time I've finished saying what I need to say as gently as I know how, as Laura's eyes narrow and linger on mine for long enough to let me know I'm in trouble, she's suddenly standing, jabbing her phone to call a taxi, and is very upset indeed. I am accused of using her. People are staring. Clare is staring. It's obvious, as Laura storms out of the pub, that I shouldn't have done this here. And once again, as so often in my life, I hear people's judging whispers and, as has happened before, their muted sounds immobilise me. I'm stuck to the chair, ready for rotting tomatoes to be tossed, for the town stocks to be hauled into the pub. But there are no tomatoes, just people looking and then not looking, and the not looking and silence is almost worse.

Clare comes to the table with the bill. She passes it to me, hand to hand. 'Sorry,' she whispers.

My head bobs gently as I press some notes into her hand. 'Keep the change,' I mutter and pull my leg out from under the table.

'You all right?' She looks concerned.

'Never better,' I lie, and I walk away, aware of a slight drag and a pain darting from the stump.

In the car, I swallow some painkillers whole. I've no idea how long I'm sitting there, waiting for it to subside when Clare comes out and climbs into her car. She nods in my direction. Closing my eyes, I hear her turn her engine on, hear it tick over and die. She tries several times and eventually I open my window and yell across. 'Need a lift?'

She gets out of her car and into mine and turns towards me. 'You'd probably have been better just taking her home and saying it then. No one wants to be dumped in a public place.'

'I didn't dump her, I told her I was going abroad for a while.'

Clare puts her seatbelt on, faces straight ahead. 'You dumped her. In public.'

'Ga-wd . . .' I push the ignition on, belt up myself. 'I see now where Grace gets it from.'

My only defence is I know that I couldn't have done the ghosting thing, that I had to say something to Laura, but I decide not to share this with Clare. 'It was for the best,' is all I say.

I stop the car at the end of the drive, fix my eyes deliberately on the ex's car. 'As I'm obviously in the mood for speaking my mind today, perhaps you should get Tim to look at the studio door.'

Clare colours in a way I haven't seen her do before.

'You think I'm not deserving of the Barn, of this chance,' she blurts.

'I like you and Grace, Clare . . .'

'You think that Tim and I are still involved and that means there might be someone else worthier.' Her lower lip trembles.

'Are you?' I ask. 'Is there?'

To my absolute horror she starts to cry. I have no hand-kerchief, no tissues. I sit on my hands.

Eyes glazed, she turns to me. 'I'm a fool, a bloody idiot sometimes, but I'm not involved with Tim, and Grace and I want this to work so much, we really do.'

'OK then,' I shrug. 'You'll need to get your car sorted. I know a guy. I'll text you his number. And I'll have a look at the lock now.'

Clare is staring at the Barn. 'He's in there now with Grace – they went to look at a hockey team play and . . . I'd taken on a shift at the pub and . . . I don't know. Some-how, I'll just have to lay down new rules, but I've . . .'

Suddenly, I don't want to know. I choose to believe her, that she's the right person to have been given this oppor-tunity and, beyond that, especially today, I don't want to know. Exhaustion seems to have filtered through my weary leg and into my bones. All I want to do is get inside and fall asleep in front of *Planet Earth* re-runs.

Wordlessly, because she seems to understand, Clare gets out of the car and walks up the drive.

Grace opens the door and waves to me. My return wave is timid, and I continue up to the house, leave the Bryan-sons to whatever happens next.

*

Mum's been on the phone wanting exact details of my arrival. Marsha, Head of Chambers, has been on the phone wanting exact details of my return. Both got short shrift.

The only person I respond to properly this evening is Lynn after she texts:

> Jack, I'm sorry for my last message. I was angry and upset. Antony is living with some mates in town. Though he's left home, he seems all right. I never really know, but he seems all right. Just wanted to let you know. X

I thumb an immediate reply.

> You have nothing to apologise for. I was the one who needed to do that, and I did – to him. I should never have behaved as I did, but believed by involving the police, I was doing the right thing. What's right and wrong though? I'm realising there's grey in between. All I know is that if I had my time over, I'd do it differently.

When I reread the texts, fear hits in pinprick sensations in the palms of my hand, making me scratch at them. I hope she doesn't think I'm hinting at our relationship. Shit. All sorts of courtroom expressions flood my mind – 'for the avoidance of doubt', 'let me be explicit', 'for the sake of transparency'. My thumbs get to work again.

> I should let you know – I'm away travelling soon for several months, not sure how long yet. On a

sabbatical from work and am deciding to 'live big'.
Hope Antony is happy and you too. Stay well. X

I imagine her face. Then I imagine what Laura is doing
and shake my head. For a man who rarely dates and knows
sod all about handling women, today has been classic.

Armed with the toolbox and the food to feed the pigs
afterwards, I head out to the studio. The lock is sorted
with a bit of oil. I take the time to look around at what
Clare's done. The presence of props is the only sign of
classes: some canes, top hats, a large blow-up ball like
those used in a gym. Locking the door behind me, I feel
something that I think might be pride. I'm proud – of me
because, assuming she really is worthy of the gift of the
Barn, I did a good thing. And her too, because, though I
don't really know her, I feel her sense of achievement in
the walls of what used to be just a garage keeping warm a
car I didn't even need.

*

Walnut and Pecan go crazy when I approach. To the left of
the pen by the hedge, I can just about make out a hunched
figure and the light from a mobile phone and I just drop
the food into their trough, stop moving.

'That you, Antony?' I keep a calm, steady voice.

'Hey, Martin, how's it going? Why would Antony be
out here with the pigs?'

Relief moves through me. 'Grace, what are *you* doing out here with the pigs?' Moving closer, I see she has no jacket on. 'Aren't you cold?'

'Nah,' she looks up from her phone. 'Young people don't feel the cold.' Almost jumping into a standing position, she back-pockets her phone and leans on the pen. 'Didn't you know that?'

'You already know I know nothing about young people.'

'I do. Why'd you think I was Antony?'

'Long story, another time. Your dad still inside?'

She looks towards the lights of the Barn. 'He is. Though he shouldn't be. He's hanging around and—' She lowers her head, so all her hair falls on each side of her face. 'It's my fault. If I hadn't lost it with Mum when she lost it with me, then I wouldn't have stormed off with Dad. And then he wouldn't be here still.'

I have no idea what she's talking about or what to say.

She turns to look at me and I can barely catch her eyes in the fading light. 'They're being completely weird with each other. And Dad being nice is almost worse than Dad being . . . Anyway, it's my fault.'

I doubt that, but don't tell her, instead opting to ask her about her part in our over-the-hedge-deal.

'Did you ever hear back from the hockey people? Your mum said you were going to see a team play today.'

'I did. They've agreed to let me try out next week, just for a subs-bench place, but—'

'That's great. Subs bench is where you get to look at others screw up and learn from them.'

'Not according to Dad. He thinks I'm better than any of the players who were up today and should look for another team.'

'Oh.'

'Grace?' Both of us flinch at the sound of Clare's voice calling from the rear door of the Barn.

'Coming,' Grace yells back. 'Told her I was feeding the pigs about fifteen minutes ago.' She directs this to me in a hushed voice and puts a pointed finger on her lips. 'See ya, Martin.'

'Bye, Grace.' I watch her figure pace slowly up towards the Barn. Tonight, she's slouched, bent over, as if today is one of the days it's hard being her age. My phone pings a message and I see it's from my Instagram account. Immediately I think maybe Grace has taken a photo of the pigs, but when I click on it, there's a picture of Laura, with her phone in her hand, and it clearly shows a photo of me. I pull my glasses from their home in my top pocket and head towards where I know the security light will flick on behind the cottage. With my thumb and forefinger, I enlarge the picture – the image on Laura's phone is the one Grace used for my dating profile. Laura has messaged her followers. 'Do NOT date this man! He is a usurper of souls!'

I have to read it a few times, and glare at it for a few minutes. *A usurper of souls*. I've been called many things in my life, but never a usurper of anything. She has over a thousand followers. I gulp, pass through the dining-room doors and lock them behind me, head towards my bedroom, where I hope to resume my carefully planned packing.

Drawing the curtains, I lean my head briefly against their mass and when my phone rings, I almost don't dare look.

'Grace,' I say, finally answering it.

'Don't react,' she whispers. 'Honestly. Ignore it like you tell me to do with the Porker comments.'

'How—'

'I was stalking you to make sure you're using Insta properly, you know, that you're just posting some great pictures. You are. She's not.'

I hear my slow inhalation just as I hear Grace giggle.

'Some other time you'll have to tell me what you did to her. I have to go – Dad's leaving.'

When she hangs up, something makes me walk to the front of the house to make sure I can see the red tail-lights on her father's car disappear down the road.

Chapter Twenty-Four

-----Original Message-----
From: GraceBryanson29@gmail.com
Sent: 14th October 2018 19:20
To: OldestDancer74@gmail.com
Subject: Mum

Gran,

Mum knows we've been in touch and isn't happy that I've been talking to you behind her back. I should have told her. Gran, can you tell me what happened between you two? She won't. And you just ignore if I ask.

Grace x

-----Reply Message-----
From: OldestDancer74@gmail.com
Sent: 14th October 2018 21:06
To: GraceBryanson29@gmail.com
Subject: Re: Mum

Grace, darling, there are some things that should only be discussed face to face. Let's meet. I know you've resisted doing this so far and this time, this one time, I'd ask you NOT to tell your mum if we do meet. I'm happy to tell you everything, although I did touch on it before when I told you I loved her too much.

Your loving Grandma x

----- Reply Message-----
From: GraceBryanson29@gmail.com
Sent: 14th October 2018 21:32
To: OldestDancer74@gmail.com
Subject: Re: Mum

Gran,

It would have to be Saturday morning when I can say I'm at hockey. And it would have to be in Wiltshire – can you come here?

Love Grace x

----- Reply Message-----
From: OldestDancer74@gmail.com
Sent: 14th October 2018 21:40
To: GraceBryanson29@gmail.com
Subject: Re: Mum

Of course, darling. I can get to wherever you need me to, whenever you need me to. Just let me know.

Your loving Grandma x

Chapter Twenty-Five

It was after she'd kissed a sleeping Grace good night, and she was on her way to bed herself, that she heard a gentle knock on the front door. Clare gripped the top buttons of her pyjamas, her heart rate increasing. Who the hell would call so late?

She walked to her bedroom window and saw Tim's car back on the drive. Clare drew a long, deep breath, tempted to ignore him and hope he'd go away again. From the early hours of this morning, through each hour of the day in the pub, and afterwards, she'd loathed herself like never before, unable to believe she'd let what had happened last night happen. And earlier this evening, refusing to look her ex-husband in the eye when he'd laid out his plan for wooing her again, she'd called Grace in from outside just to stop him talking. He'd left and now he was back for more.

Her phone rang on her bedside table.

'I'm not opening the door,' she spoke into it.

'Clare, open up. If you don't, I'll ring Grace and get her to do it.'

'What is it you want, Tim?' Clare tried to keep the weary tone from her voice. This was all her fault. She should have stopped it. She could have stopped it and she didn't.

'I want you to listen to what I have to say.'

'Tim, I've been listening all evening. I've heard it all before.'

'Open the door.'

'No.'

'Right, I'll wake Grace then.'

Clare shook her head. 'Please. I'll give you five minutes, if you promise to leave then.'

Silence.

She grabbed her robe and crept along the hallway before opening the door. 'Please, be quiet,' she whispered. 'Grace is asleep, and I really don't want to wake her.'

Tim followed her.

'Say what you have to say and leave,' Clare kept her voice low.

'Last night,' he began, before pointing down the hall. 'Last night I fucked you in what used to be our bed and you loved every single second of it.'

Clare winced and clenched her robe tightly.

'You moaned and, just the way you like it,' he neared her, 'I made you come.'

'It was a mistake.' She eyeballed him. 'Something physical that I needed. That's all.' She drew a long breath, aware of his irritation, aware she had to stand her ground. 'Why's it possible for sex to mean nothing to a man, yet it had to mean something to me?' Although on dangerous ground, she didn't stop. 'Tell me, Tim, during those last few years and you had your flings, and you'd always tell me they meant nothing. Why is it not possible in your head that last night meant as little to me? I had an itch that needed scratching. You were here. That's all.'

She felt his hand before she even saw him raise it. And as she fell, knocking over a plant stand on her way down, she realised from the instant searing pain that he'd had time to clench his fist. Scurrying backwards, she struggled to gain purchase on the porcelain floor tiles with her slippered feet as he loomed over her.

'Stay down,' he held a threatening hand above her.

'No,' it was a whimper, and as she tried to raise herself to all fours, she saw him lower to her level, raise his fist again and felt it slam into her back. Clare cried out, fell flattened, felt her tooth dig deep into her cheek.

'You need to leave right now, Dad!'

Through an already swelling eye, Clare saw Grace on the stairs, her phone in her hand.

'Leave this second or I swear I'm calling the police.'

'Grace, baby, you don't understand, I—'

'LEAVE!'

Clare watched Grace pulse numbers on her phone.

'I'm going, I'm going, OK!'

The house seemed to shake as the door slammed.

Feeling Grace's arms around her, helping her stand, Clare whispered, 'Ice, please.'

With Grace's arm around her, she held a tea towel of ice up to her eye and tried to stop her daughter crying.

'I'll never forgive him, this time, *never*,' Grace muttered over and over.

Clare swallowed blood. Her mouth, where her tooth had almost made a hole in her cheek, was still bleeding. 'Don't cry,' she tried to say to her.

'He promised me, Mum. He promised *me* that he'd never do this again.'

''S my fault,' Clare tried to form more words, but they wouldn't come, and if they could – how would she explain to their daughter that she'd known exactly what buttons to press with her father, that she'd almost known what she was doing. It was as if she'd needed to find out, that if he raised a hand to her again, it would confirm that the best-behaviour Tim, who might pop over for curry and a no-strings sleepover, was in fact all a sham, a means of disarming her. Well, she had been well and truly disarmed. And she had made a dreadful error of judgement. And now she had a hole in her mouth and an eye that she knew from experience would take weeks to go down.

She vowed, not for the first time, never to be that stupid again.

Clare felt her daughter move the ice from her eye, heard her suck air, begin to cry again.

'Hold that,' Grace instructed. 'Press it against the eye,' and she did as she was told as Grace steered her towards the sofa, before moving back towards the front door.

'I'm so sorry, I know it's late.' She heard Grace's voice in the hall and automatically called out, 'No, Grace . . . please . . .'

'Something's happened, I need your help.'

Clare closed her good eye, felt a dart of pain through her bad one. She didn't hear the rest of the conversation as Grace opened the door. Moments later, she returned with more ice.

'You shouldn't have called—' Clare began.

'You need to see a doctor, Mum,'

'No.' Clare tried to stand and fell back as silver stars floated in her peripheral vision.

'In here,' Grace called out towards sounds outside. Clare tried to move again, as she saw Jack look down at her and Grace burst into tears. 'I didn't know what to do, I'm sorry.'

'Shh,' Clare heard him say. 'You did the right thing. Grab a coat for her and one for yourself, it's freezing. The car's outside, let's get her to A&E.'

*

Not once, Clare thought, not once during the time she was being seen by doctors, not when she was told she'd have to stay in overnight for observation or when she was advised she'd have to see an eye specialist first thing in the morning; not when Jack told her Grace could stay in the cottage overnight, not once did he ask what had happened. Clare was both appalled and grateful. Appalled that he would know without much guesswork, and grateful because she couldn't bear trying to explain it. She couldn't bear admitting her part aloud; trying to get someone on the outside to understand that it had been her fault, that if she hadn't had sex with him, that if she hadn't goaded him . . . No one, not even Grace, no one understood their dynamic quite like Clare and Tim did. That toxic dependency was why she'd left him in the end. The last few unhappy years, he'd told her he only ever went with other women to provoke some sort of response in her. For some time, she took ownership of that, until she realised that his behaviour wasn't her doing and wasn't good enough.

The next day, all the reasons why she'd divorced him were queuing to remind her in her splitting head. She buried herself under the threadbare waffle-weave blanket, hoping Grace had got off to school, hoping that she was OK, hoping that Jack had given her breakfast. Grace had witnessed the worst attack in a very long time and it had been the first time she'd had to intervene. Clare couldn't imagine her daughter's relationship with her father ever being the same and she felt the loss for her daughter. This Unspoken Thing – the abuse that Clare had suffered in their old home – had now ventured into their new life and there was no going back.

Through a glass window to the left of her bed, she watched the ophthalmology team peruse some scans. They were talking about her, glancing towards her and back at the screen that held images of her eyes and Clare silently prayed that her retina had not in fact detached as the specialist now staring at her had earlier suspected it might have.

She closed her good eye, imagined her new dance students disappearing if she couldn't teach. Along with her job at the pub, as they wouldn't want a black-eyed freak serving . . . Everything that she, Melborough Clare, had tried to put in place could all disappear in a wisp of smoke, just because she'd wanted sex. And because she'd described it to Tim as an itch she needed to scratch. Yes, Clare admitted to herself, that was when everything went to total shit – when Tim and his uncontrollable temper reacted to something she'd said. And that, she concluded, was his fault. She was *not* owning his shit any more.

'The scan looks good,' she heard someone say.

Clare peeked over the blanket. 'You certain?' she asked.

'Absolutely,' the doctor, whose hands smelled of antiseptic wash, declared. 'Bad bruising inside and out. It'll all heal as long as you take it easy.'

'Can I go home?'

'Yes, though no driving for at least a week, OK? Just let the swelling settle and let's make sure you're not seeing any more stars. Come straight back if you do. Have you someone who can collect you?'

Clare avoided the doctor's eyes. He had almost said 'someone else' or 'someone other than the animal who punched you'.

'Yes,' she whispered.

'You're good to go then. Take care of yourself, Clare.'

It was awful. All she heard from genuinely well-meaning people was subtext. People who, she felt, wanted to say, 'Leave him!' and she wanted to yell 'I already did!'

She dressed quickly, stopping only to catch her breath as a fiery heat rose within her. She waited, knowing it was a hot flush and not a temperature spike. She called a taxi company and texted Grace that she was on her way home and would be there when she got in from school.

In the car, Clare refused to read the many texts from Tim, deleting them one after the other. Acknowledging a new and furious urge inside of her, instead, she sent him one.

Tim. I'm no longer listening. That will never happen again. NEVER. Grace is sixteen in a few weeks and old enough to decide whether she wants to continue contact with you. If she does, and that's an 'if' for her to decide, curry nights from now on will happen maximum twice a month, but always only if Grace wants. If you come to Wiltshire and need to stay over, there are many B&Bs locally. You need to stay completely away from me. When I send this, I am deleting your no. from my phone. It's in my head should I ever need it for an emergency, but I no longer need your bullshit in my life. C

At the Barn, she had forty minutes before Grace was due home from school. She stood at the bathroom mirror, emptied her make-up bag into the sink, and started with concealer. Years of doing her own stage make-up, and too many skirmishes with Tim, had taught her all about layers. Two or three different times with concealer, a few minutes apart, followed by the first thin layer of foundation. Dab the black part with a dot more concealer and keep going until the bruising was covered and all that was left was the swelling.

Hearing a car outside, she looked through the window, half expecting to see Jack. At the front door, her hand automatically went to cover her eye. Outside, Emma stood with an enormous bunch of mixed daisies.

'Make-up's good,' she said, peering into Clare's face. 'You'll need sunglasses.'

Before Clare could reply, Emma had walked past her.

'Wow, this place is gorgeous! Vase?'

'By the kitchen window,' Clare said, closing the door and looking at her watch.

'I've already collected Grace from school. They had a free period, so she's at ours with Erik – they have that IT project to finish for tomorrow.'

Her website. Clare hugged herself. 'Coffee?' she asked.

'I drink coffee all day,' Emma shook her head. 'Let's sit and look at this splendid view.'

Clare bit the edge of her lip as Emma sat herself down on the sofa and patted the space beside her. She sat.

'You OK?' Emma asked.

Clare nodded.

'I've not known you long enough to offer advice,' Emma said, and Clare thought there was some coming anyway. 'So, I won't. Grace is worried that you're worried about work and that's why I've come. Please don't. You're a good worker and,' she leaned across and gently touched Clare's eye, 'as you already know, that's nothing ice and make-up won't sort out. The swelling will be gone in a couple of days.'

'Thank you,' Clare whispered.

'You know your car is still in the car park?'

'I need to have someone have a look at it.'

Emma stood. 'Give me the keys and Jan can do it. He's great with car stuff.'

'No, it's fine. I'll get a mechanic, I—'

'Keys,' Emma held her hand out.

Clare walked to her bag in the hall and handed her the keys.

'Will you be able to dance?' Emma asked. 'Your classes? Will you be able to jiggle about?'

She grinned. 'I'll jiggle a little less this week, but I should be fine.'

'Well,' Emma said, 'we could sit down again and try to avoid talking about the obvious or you could show me the studio?'

'Of course!' Clare took another set of keys from her bag and headed out the front door, 'Follow me!'

Outside, the temperature had dropped and she shivered.

'Jack Frost tonight,' she said, looking at the curling smoke from Jack Tate's chimney. Clare felt Emma's arm slip through hers.

'We don't have to talk about the weather either,' Emma said. 'I'm not going to ask anything. And I'm not going to remind you that I thought the ex-husband staying over was a bad idea.'

'Yeah, well, turns out you were right.'

'It is getting colder, though. *You're* right about that.'

Clare laughed and, after opening up, switched on the lights.

'It's amazing! Gosh, how utterly exciting!' Emma clapped her hands.

Clare found her own hands joining together as if après clap, or in prayer, and felt herself uplifted, removed from the previous twenty-four hours. It *was* amazing. It *was* totally exciting, and it *was* something she was making work. 'It is, isn't it?'

Emma walked around, nodding, ran a finger along the barre. 'I remember ballet lessons as a child. I so wanted to take my own child to ballet class, but Erik was never going to oblige, speaking of which,' she looked at her watch, 'I've got to get back. I'll feed Grace and drop her home later, OK?'

At the door, Clare hugged her. She hadn't known she was going to, but it had felt right. 'Thank you. I haven't had someone,' she hesitated, 'a friend, for a very long time. Sorry if that seems foolish, I—'

Emma frowned. 'I suspect that was because he didn't want you to. And don't be embarrassed. Jan can be your boss. I can be your friend.' She leaned in and kissed Clare's good cheek before walking away. 'I'll have her home by eight. You rest up.'

Clare switched out the lights, stood for a minute looking at the dancing evening shadows, realising how far she'd come in a short space of time and how far she had yet to go to get where she wanted to be. Rather than go back to the Barn, she headed to the main house and knocked on the door.

When Jack answered, he held a forefinger up as he tried to finish a phone call. She hovered in the doorway as he walked to the kitchen and spoke to his mum, told her he'd call her back later, that someone was at the door.

Moments later he stood before her. 'You look better than when I last saw you,' he smiled. 'Come in.'

Clare stood just inside the door. 'I seem to have spent so long thanking people, especially you, thank you again.'

'The eye OK?' He removed his glasses from his shirt pocket and, peering through them, winced. 'Still needs ice,' he suggested.

'I'm here because if I don't say this now, I'll file it away and it'll never get dealt with.' She breathed deep, the frosted air she exhaled sitting between her and Jack. 'I'm hoping you might be able to do one more thing for me – I'm embarrassed to ask, but I trust you and think . . . Shit . . .'

'What is it?'

'I want an injunction, or whatever it is I have to have to make sure he can't come near me again.'

'Are you sure that's absolutely what you want?'

'I am. I've thought about nothing else all day.'

'What about him seeing Grace?'

'Tim has never touched her, if that's what you mean. His . . .' she paused. 'His anger, fury, whatever we want to call it, has always been directed at me.'

'I meant access to him seeing her . . .'

'It has to be up to her. I can't tell her not to – I can only suggest limiting it. Strange as it might seem to someone on the outside, she adores him, and he her. Though she hates what he did, what he's capable of, she'd hate not seeing him at all even more. Grace has this infinite ability to forgive . . . I've already texted him, told him that only if she's willing, he could see her fortnightly. If he comes here, he stays in a B&B, comes nowhere near me.'

'Are you afraid?'

Clare swallowed, thought about the question. 'For me sometimes, never for her when she's with him. But I do worry about the effect this latest thing might have on her.' She pulled her phone free from her back pocket and showed him the text she'd sent to Tim.

After reading it, Jack lifted his own mobile from the hall stand and said, 'I've a text to show you too.'

Jack, is there anything legal that can be done to keep Dad away from Mum? I don't want him to ever know I asked, but something has to change.

'Oh . . .' Clare said, both shoulders slumping as she read it.

'Why don't you come in and sit down. I'll make some notes.'

'Jack,' she grabbed his arm as she passed. 'This *has to* come from me. I need him believing that. You can't *ever* let him know Grace sent that text. I don't want her in the middle of our mess any more than she's had to be. I'm the one driving this. OK?'

As Jack nodded and led her through to the snug next to his kitchen, Clare thought about the fact she'd never been asked by anyone if she was afraid of Tim, and was surprised to hear herself admit that she had been. And now that she'd admitted it aloud, she had no choice but to deal with it.

Chapter Twenty-Six

I'm temporarily back at my old desk in chambers and Mabel comes in with a cheery smile.

'Your gentleman is outside,' she says. 'Shall I show him in?'

'Give me two minutes,' I tell her, 'and don't offer refreshment. He's no gentleman and won't be here long.'

Exactly two minutes later she ushers Tim Bryanson, with his ironed jeans, into the office. I don't stand.

'Take a seat, Mr Bryanson,' I say, without looking up, from various pieces of paper. When I do, he's trying to wither me with one of his death stares. 'You wanted to see me,' I say.

He tosses the injunction papers onto my desk. Within moments of receiving it, he'd been on the phone demanding a meeting. 'This is a crock of shit,' he hisses.

I cut to the chase. 'Do you deny being violent towards your ex-wife, Mr Bryanson? Because I urge caution. Your daughter called me on the night of the last incident and I myself drove them both to the hospital. I have several witness statements from medical staff relating to the event and Ms Bryanson's injuries.'

'You're loving this, aren't you?'

'I'm not sure what you mean.'

'You! Sir Galahad on the white steed. You whisk her away to Camelot—'

'I think you know exactly how and why Ms Bryanson and I met.' I let the statement, the truth of their divorce, and her circumstances and involvement with the charity afterwards, marinate.

'You build her a dance studio . . .'

I bite my tongue.

'You behave as if—'

'Why exactly are you here, Mr Bryanson?'

He picks up the paperwork. 'I'll be taking my own legal advice.'

I eyeball him. 'That's your prerogative. In the meantime—'

'What is it you want, Tate? My wife, or my family?'

I can't help myself. 'What is it *you* want, Mr Bryanson? Your wife divorced you. She wants to move on with her life. It could be a great life. You could choose to let her live it. You could choose to let *them* love it.'

'What the fuck do you know about my family, you sanctimonious prick?'

I've been called worse.

'It would suit you, wouldn't it? It would suit you if I just went away.'

Yes, it would. God help me, yes it would. I'd love to head off on my trip without thinking about you, you obnoxious man.

With my hands flattened on the desk in front of me, I watch him take a seat on the opposite side.

'I want to see Grace.'

'According to the terms you can see Grace, up to twice a month, which is what Grace has agreed to for now. However, you need to *not* go near Clare. And Grace is sixteen shortly, should she decide at any time in the future not to see you at all . . .' I shrug for dramatic effect.

'Grace will always want to see me.'

'Maybe, or perhaps she's a little bored of seeing your fists at work. Have you ever thought how hard it might be for her to witness your handiwork?'

'Do not presume to know anything about me and my daughter.'

'I know she's an amazing young woman who gives a great impression of being strong, but no one should have to—' I stop speaking, an image of Grace with her jam-filled cake on the day of our inaugural DIM meeting blindsiding me. 'She's a child.' A part of me wants to appeal to any better nature he might possess, but his fists are tightening in his lap and I'm suddenly aware that this man would love nothing more than to use them on me. Part of me wants him to. I could sue his ass. I would make sure he never crosses the county lines again.

'You know fucking nothing about Grace, about me and her. She *understands*. She understands me.' The implication that Grace is absolutely fine, whatever the hell she's been through, makes me see red and my reply spills out before I've had a chance to filter it.

'Really? It was Grace who came me first. "Is there anything legal that can be done to keep Dad away from Mum?" That was the text she sent me after you hospitalised her mother.'

His lips straighten into a teeth-gritting horizontal line. 'You're lying,' he says. 'Baiting me. Grace would never do that. This is all that bitch Clare's doing. And *yours*. Sticking your nose where it doesn't belong. You're a fucking liar.'

And there it is, the snarling expression that five-foot-six Clare must have had to see before his fists would do their thing. When our eyes meet, mine are daring – daring him to do it, just so that I can hit him back.

I have never wanted to be violent towards anyone. Not even in this room, where I've met all sorts. Not even back when Alice died and in court I watched the man who killed her receive what I considered a paltry sentence for killing her, for maiming me, for . . . Yet here I am, wondering if I could just beat the shit out of this sorry excuse for a human being. I could take him. I have a height advantage. To hell with the fact that he has two legs. And I don't understand why it doesn't terrify me; why doing something so wrong could seem right, and for the first time in my carefully constructed life, I couldn't give a shit about consequences.

I wait.

Then the moment splits and he stands, as if suddenly scalded, as if he's heard my vicious thoughts, as if he's suddenly realised that if he reacts, he could lose everything. Before he turns and walks away, he points a finger at me. 'This isn't over,' he says, his voice no more than a whisper.

After the door slams, I offer a rude hand gesture and a barrage of expletives that I'd forgotten I even knew, all the while batting away the fact that I shouldn't have said that. Clare asked me not to involve Grace. She specifically asked me to ensure that this whole thing was directed from her alone.

'Fu-ck!' I stand up, grab Speak No Evil from his perch, and toss it across the room.

*

My appetite's been absent since meeting Bryanson this morning. I couldn't tolerate even a piece of toast beforehand and, now, the thought of lunch doesn't appeal either. I'm in my bedroom folding clean items for the capsule wardrobe I've planned to take travelling, and it hits me that in amongst my search to find my *emotional* grey, my clothes are already various shades of slate, fog and lead. OK, there are a few white shirts, but most of my casual clothes are – grey. I count my pairs of shorts. One black, three grey, all dreary as shit if I'm ever even brave enough to wear short trousers in public. T-shirts – four white, two black, seven grey. How have I never seen this before?

I push them to one side, head into town and it takes only ninety minutes for me to be back standing in the same spot at the edge of my bed. The new purchases take no time at all to unwrap and behold, a medley of rainbow-coloured attire that before Alice's birthday I literally wouldn't have been seen dead in. The nearest shirt has a label on it saying 'cerise' and my empty stomach heaves a bit. Before I can change my mind, I fold almost everything as small as possible and place the only colour element that I've had for years on top. I've decided Alice's orange baseball cap will help keep the Florida sun out of my eyes. That's it – the warmer-weather element of the trip is sorted. The cerise shirt, for now, stays on a hanger in the wardrobe.

It's the first thing I tell April when I text her later. I inform her all about my new colourful clothes, my rucksack full of rainbow. I don't tell her about my new darker side, where I've thought about hurting someone for the first time in my life – all in just one day.

She's been the one to keep in touch with me, and so far I've managed to dodge dinner with her family. I've managed to banish any sexual fantasies I've had about her by talking it through with myself. *You do not fancy April. You just have an understandable sexual hangover from Alice when you're around April because she is so like her.* And for all the avoiding of meeting the Alice lookalike again in person, spending time with her on text, looking closely at photographs she's sent me of her and her family, it's the differences I now see. Alice had green eyes and April's are brown. Alice was fair-skinned, with dark hair, and April is dark blonde with more sallow skin. April mirrors her mother's looks, whereas Alice was more like her father.

So, the last thing I tell April today as my fingers pulse a text to her is this:

Thank you for sending that first email. Thank you for caring. I apologise for avoiding meeting you again. You're so like her, I find it hard. When I get back from my wanderings, I'll come and see you. You and Greg can feed me, and I'll tell you all about it.

She replies with a single 'x'.

*

'Nice shirt,' Clare winks at cerise-me.

It's the weekend, and during a fundraising event at Onward Motion, Clare, who I'd reminded about our Pay It Forward conversation, has offered to help serve teas and coffees. I introduce her around and she tells some story about how an old dance pupil of hers sold her a raffle ticket for the same fundraiser last year. We marvel at how small the world is and, just as the evening ends, Clare agrees with Pam, the manager, to come and teach willing and able clients, some of whom might be amputees, how to dance once a week. She tells me it's her making good on her offer to help, but the way she looks at me as we're leaving, the way she says, 'And it's the least I can do,' makes me look away.

She knows nothing. She can't know anything. No one in this town knows, with the exception of the staff here, and I can't imagine that anyone here would have had the chance, or the urge, to discuss my missing limb with Clare.

In the car on the way home, she's high on life. Recently, we have, both of us, stopped talking about her thanking me and started talking about opportunity and how it's strange that we're both at junctions where things are changing. I'm excited about my forthcoming travels and she's brimming with excitement about the dance school. Being free of having to see Tim has, I think, made a huge difference in her. She seems lighter, happier.

We reach the entrance to both houses and she says, 'Just park at yours, I'll walk back up.' When I do, she opens her door and looks across the top of the car at me. 'You want to come in for a drink?'

I make a pained sound. 'The last time I drank at yours . . .'

'No problem, if you'd rather not.'

'No, of course. No champagne though. Never again.'

'Gin, I have a bottle of gin somewhere.'

'Gin's good.'

Before long we're sitting in the living area in front of the wood burner, both of us sipping overly strong G&Ts when she just pops it out. 'Are you an amputee?' she asks. 'If I'm wrong, I'm so sorry, but I think I've noticed something, something in your gait that you try to hide.'

There is no reason to deny it, so I lean forward, pull my left jeans leg up a little. 'You mean this old thing,' I say, revealing the socked and booted prosthetic. 'This is me,' I add. 'Not many people know.'

'What happened? Or maybe you'd rather not talk about it.'

Shaking my head, I reply, 'Not tonight. It was an accident. A long time ago, now.'

She doesn't want to push it, is silent for a moment before she says, 'You're going away tomorrow. I know you've sorted the pigs with Grace, and I'll keep an eye on the cottage for you, but is there anything else you need?'

'There are two things actually.'

Her eyebrows lift. 'Go on.'

'Don't let him back in your life.'

She draws breath slowly through an open mouth.

'You've come so far.'

As I've seen her do often when she's not sure what to say, she catches her bottom lip with her top teeth.

'And the second thing – I thought about this when you were talking at the centre earlier, maybe you could teach this awkward guy a few dancing steps?'

She's on her feet instantly and it strikes me that, in her head, teaching an amputee to dance seems far easier than completely staying away from her ex, even when she wants to.

'No time like the present,' she says. 'Come on. A waltz, I think. A Wiltshire Waltz!' She pulls me up to standing, places my arm in the right position. 'Now concentrate,' she says, 'this is harder than it looks.'

She feels slight in my arms as I struggle to focus. She's counting out one, two, three, explaining the basic steps.

There's no music, just a rhythm that she gets me to pace as she stands opposite and claps. I'm listening, hearing her, and gently she slides back into my arms again. She giggles, straightens them, and tells me that actually both my legs are fine, but it's my upper frame that needs work. She suggests setting it to music, and just before she moves away, I squeeze her hand tightly, not wanting her to go. It's as involuntary as a shudder, as a hiccup, but it's there, and she raises her still bruised face to mine, questioning it, yet somehow understanding it.

I kiss her. She kisses me back. Every nervous nerve ending in my body urges me to stop, but every synapse in my allegedly usurping soul tells me not to let go.

*

By the time the car dropping Grace home has reversed out the driveway, with yells of cheery 'Good night!' I'm already out the back door. Very carefully, I tread a guilty path towards the pen and the gap in the laurel hedge. The pigs' snouts noisily grind the earth next to me as I glance back up at the Barn. My heartbeat's racing. I don't know what I was expecting to see – maybe Clare's silhouette at the main window, but I move slowly up my own garden, trying to lower my heart rate, trying not to dwell on what just happened.

I'm leaving this place tomorrow and instinctively I know an immediate refocus is a good thing.

Because what just happened was a very bad idea.

It was beautiful; a night like I've never had before, but it was a very bad idea.

I decide I will never tell Oliver.

And Grace can never know.

And Tim Bryanson would stick a knife right through my throbbing heart if he ever found out.

*

Ollie's words wake me in the middle of the night, and I sit up, drenched in a clammy sweat.

You're so completely terrified of fate that you leave nothing to chance. It just means everything is prescribed and there's no room for fun.'

There was nothing prescribed about what happened between me and Clare and every moment of it was special and fun. Yet here I am shivering, just before dawn, focusing on the other bit. If I hadn't already been leaving, I'd have been ready to run; run from the finger of Fate, because I refuse to allow her to steal anything else from me.

Which I finally accept means I've refused to care deeply for anyone since Alice.

Chapter Twenty-Seven

'It's impossible. What do you get the man who has everything?'

Clare didn't answer Grace's question. All through the time they'd been wandering around the shops, she'd been trying to make sense of the previous night with Jack. She had no idea what had happened. One moment they were dancing, and the next . . . She tried to remember the last time, if ever, Tim had touched her that way. A hand reaching gently for her damaged face, cupping it; a forefinger tracing the line of her lips and a kiss that was tender. There was nothing awkward about the man's lovemaking. There was nothing self-conscious in the way he moved. Any initial unease around his missing limb seemed to disappear as soon as they lay together.

'Mum . . .'

'You know what, we don't need to buy him a present. I think he'd just be embarrassed and, if it was anything heavy, he'd have to leave it behind anyway.'

'Which was what I said! Let's head back, I have homework I'd like to get done before hockey. I'm almost certain I'll get to play today!'

Within minutes, they were sitting in traffic at local lights on their way home. Clare was aware of Grace's excitement about the game, but all she could think about was Jack. Something in what passed between them felt like more than sex. It was as if they'd known each other's bodies for years, known exactly how to be with one another. Clare bit a fingernail. She was being ridiculous. She needed to pull herself together. She'd had a night with a man who wasn't Tim. Of course, it felt different. Of course, it felt special. Jack was different, but that was all there was to it. Now was not the time to be thinking anything else, no matter how bloody good it had been to be intimate with him. He was her landlord. He was her good Samaritan; her *friend*, and she didn't have many friends. Nor was she ever going to hitch her feelings to any man's cart again, she reminded herself, straightening up in her seat. She was Melborough Clare.

'Mum?'

'Oh dear . . .'

'What?' Grace said.

'That word "Mum" with a question mark at the end.'

'We should probably talk about Gran. About what I did.'

'Probably,' Clare relented. 'But we've avoided it so far and that conversation needs more time.'

Grace was quick to reply. 'We have time.'

'But what if I want to yell at you for doing things behind my back? That could take ages.'

'What about if I want to yell back because you make it impossible to ask you straight out? Mum, whatever happened, it happened when I was five . . . I'm nearly sixteen.'

Nearly sixteen. It can't be true, she thought as Grace's life, the life she'd spent most of with *both* of her parents, pulsed through her brain, a feature film of staggered memories.

'Do you miss your dad?' Clare asked.

'Unfair change of subject.'

'Sometimes, I feel guilty because he's not in *your* life as much.'

'Mum! I've always said you were right to divorce him. Now stop changing the subject.'

'I think you miss him, more than you admit.'

'I miss him, sure. I don't miss the fact everything always had to be his way. I don't miss the rows you and he had. And I certainly don't miss hearing the sound of him whack you.'

Clare flinched.

'He's Dad. I'll always love him, but no, I don't miss him like you seem to think I do. Now, Gran . . .'

'The thing with your gran and me . . .' She felt her mouth dry and sipped water from a bottle in the central console before licking her lips. 'The thing with Mum and me.' Her head began to shake; tiny little shivers as if she herself disbelieved what she might say next. 'Is that there isn't just *one* thing.' Having settled on the words, she glanced across at Grace. 'It's a series of feelings, events, and when they all follow one another over years, it just adds up to one big . . . toxic mess.'

'What does that mean though? How?'

Grace, Clare knew, wasn't going to be happy until she had answers. Specifics, which even after all these years were hard to put into words. 'From the time I was a young child,' she began, 'maybe five or six, nothing I did was good enough. There was constant criticism and I was always looking for, and never got, her reassurance. I never measured up to whatever it was she expected me to be.'

Grace frowned. 'She was a dance teacher. *You* were a dance champion.'

'That came later and,' Clare breathed deep and exhaled through pursed lips, 'it came at a huge cost.'

Pointing the car up the hill, she allowed the silence to swell before speaking again.

'I've never told anyone this, apart from a counsellor I saw after you were born, a wonderful lady called Nancy.' Her stomach lurched. 'I was bulimic for a few years as a teen. Desperate to be the weight Mum said I needed to be, desperate to win competitions I was expected to win, desperate for approval from the woman I always disappointed. Even when I was older and became pregnant with you, she screamed at me, "Be a mother or a dancer. You can't be both."'

Grace's hand had found its way to her mouth, where her fingers seemed to hover on her lips. 'Did you hide your . . . your problem? I mean, maybe she just didn't know?'

'She knew. I told her I was struggling, even asked her to come to an earlier therapy session, one that Dad helped me sort. I think I was about eighteen. Anyway, that got ugly.'

Clare pulled into the driveway, and as she put the car into neutral, she felt Grace's hand slide over hers. It seemed to pulse in tandem with her heartbeat, reminding her of the time they'd been attached by an umbilical cord; the times she'd stroked her stomach and sang to her baby and danced through the tiny kicks that had comforted her then.

She had made the choice she had never regretted. She had chosen to be a mother.

'You don't remember your grandad, do you?' she asked Grace.

'A little.'

'I adored him. I mean, *adored* him. Mum felt jealous that Dad got all my attention.'

'But did you . . . *do* you love her?'

Clare glossed over the reference to the present day. 'I adored her. But now? Now, I can't have her in my life. It's been hard, but I'm happier without her in it.' She stared as Grace tried to compute this, a doubtful expression on her young face.

'Surely not forever?' Grace asked.

'As far as Mum was concerned, I had to win, otherwise why dance? She and Dad fought about it all the time. Then, when I met *your* dad, and he was an escape – from their arguments, from competing. And, of course, Mum hated him. Anything that took my eye off winning was not encouraged.'

Clare tapped her daughter's right leg. 'Look, I've never really wanted to talk about any of this. But you've a right to know why I feel like I do. I'd rather you weren't in touch with your grandmother because she has a way of making you second-guess yourself so that you no longer recognise who you are or were, and I don't want you around anyone who's capable of obliterating your self-confidence. I quite like the young woman I see evolving in front of me. She's kind and able and though she thinks she's "odd", she's learning to believe in herself.'

Grace blushed, attempted a smile.

'You're almost sixteen. I can't stop you seeing Jean, but I'd rather you didn't. And if you do, I *need* to know about it. No more going behind my back.'

Her daughter's colour deepened.

'And, whatever happens, you need to respect that I don't want her in *my* life.'

Grace offered a hesitant nod. 'The truth is, I don't know her, Mum.' She hugged herself. 'She's obviously always been good to me at Christmas and birthdays, even though I never knew, and I meant enough to her for her to get in touch with me, but I don't *know* her.'

'No one knows Jean, not really, not even Jean. Dad did and somehow was blind to all her needy ambition. He really loved her.'

'Maybe he saw something . . .'

Clare could hear the naïve hope in Grace's unfinished sentence.

'Tell me what happened that made you stop seeing her? Everything you've said seemed to be happening for years and then when I was about five . . .' Again, her sentence remained unfinished. 'Please, Mum, if I'm deciding whether to be in touch with her, I need *all* the facts.'

Clare blinked slowly. 'Do you remember that one and only trip to Disney World Florida when you were little?'

'Of course.'

'Your dad and I had saved like squirrels for two years. Before the trip, things had been really tense with your gran and me, because I'd retired after you were born, and she was constantly in my ear about competing again, even though there were younger and much better dancers around. I was teaching as well as looking after you, but when you started school, she kept on and on until we eventually had a huge row just before the Orlando trip.'

'The final straw was over dancing?'

Clare could hear confusion and disbelief in her child's voice and turned towards her. 'Not quite,' she replied. 'It was while we were away that Grandad's accident happened.' She dabbed a line of moisture from her top lip with a tissue from her pocket. 'You know he fell from a ladder and was hospitalised with a head injury.' Clare decided instantly that a sanitised, edited version of the truth was the best option. 'We were out in one of the theme parks enjoying ourselves, when he died. Without speaking to me, my mother had given permission to switch off the machine that was keeping him alive. According to her, they could never have waited the twelve hours it would have taken me to get back. Dad was a card-holding organ donor – it was apparently what he would have wanted.' Sudden tears gathered at the edge of her eyelids. 'He was a great man, the best I've known, and I never got to hold his hand. I never got to say goodbye to him. She could have waited. I checked. The medics said that as long as oxygen flowed through the body, the organs were still good.'

Grace was silent as Clare wiped her face with the same tissue.

'*That* was the final straw in years of her shit, and now you know. There's been too much hurt, too much time has passed. Just too much water under the bridge.'

Clare cut the engine and they both exited the car wordlessly. In the cloakroom, just inside the door of the Barn, she blew her nose, avoided her reflection and balanced herself on the edge of the sink. She spoke to her father in her head. 'What do you think, Dad? Should I have told her that Mum never even let me know about the fall?' There had been no urgent call, or no initial message left on her phone, just one voicemail where Jean had said, 'Clare, it's your mother. You need to come home. Your father's dead.' All the explanation about organ donors had only come later, once she was back in England.

She rubbed her tense temples with the heels of both her hands. 'You think I should have told her about Mum telling me I'd gotten fat in Florida, or choosing what I wore for your funeral? Or telling Tim he wasn't welcome at the service?'

Clare smoothed her hands over her hair. 'No, I think she'd heard enough too. Yes,' she whispered. 'I know I was right . . .'

*

'I'm really not sure,' Clare tried to keep the uncertainty that she felt from reaching her voice. She knew Emma was right, that her suggestion of an evening introducing herself and the studio to a few influential locals was a good way to spread the word about the dance school, but self-doubt arrived in the form of a lump in her throat. She was no public speaker . . .

'I am!' Emma said. 'I'm sure! Come on. It's just an intro-ductory chat about what you do. They're a group of my friends who've known one another for years, nine people – and everyone's interested! All you'd have to do is talk for a while; a little about you and your championship background, what classes you're offering and maybe a fun demo of ballroom or Latin. You could do it in the studio. This is a good idea, Clare! It lets well-connected people get to know you and spreads the word about what you're doing.'

'I'm a better dancer than I am talker.'

'You could do this in your sleep – you've performed on the international stage! Come on, no slideshows required. Just an open chat. I reckon you'll get more pupils but, more importantly, every one of them will start talking to their friends.'

She was sitting in a hot sudsy bath as she spoke to Emma on the phone. 'I'll think about it.'

'I'm not suggesting a root canal, Clare.'

Her chin dropped to her chest. 'I'm sorry. You're trying to help, and it *is* a great idea.'

Emma laughed. 'You'll thank me afterwards. I'll sort out a date and let you know.'

Next thing Clare heard was the dial tone. It was one of Emma's quirks she'd noticed. She never said goodbye on the phone, just sort of signed off with whatever her final comment was.

She lay back in the water and began to plan. Emma was right. She *was* only suggesting a casual chat about dance. It would be everything her friend told her it would if she just believed it could be.

Clare plugged her earbuds in, keeping an eye on the time as she listened to an old *Desert Island Discs* edition starring David Attenborough. At 5.45, she got dressed for her 6.30 class, imagining herself as the famous dancer that her mother had always wanted, featuring on the programme. The host would interview her and ask her for the eight pieces of music that meant something to her, and Clare realised, as she fantasised, that one of them would have been Jack's trumpet solo of 'Summertime'. She would tell the host about the first time she'd heard this version and how it had marked a time when her life changed for the better.

She left the Barn with a travel mug of coffee in one hand and a bottle of water in the other, but, instead of unlocking the studio and setting up the music for her class, she diverted up his path and rang the bell. His cab, she knew, was due soon. When he opened the door, she was glad there was no awkwardness, just a smile and a hug goodbye. She tapped his back three times with her hand, pulled away, cupped his cheek and kissed him gently on the lips. 'Stay safe,' she whispered before turning around.

'You too. Clare?' he called after her. 'You too. OK?'

Her head bobbed in agreement. She heard the subtext: Keep him away. Stick to your guns.

She raised a hand to wave.

Melborough Clare had this.

Chapter Twenty-Eight

-----Original Message-----
From: GraceBryanson29@gmail.com
Sent: 24th October 2018 10:19
To: OldestDancer74@gmail.com
Subject: Meeting Up

Gran,

I'm sorry. Stuff has been happening and it's not the right time to meet now. I don't want to lie to Mum. It just feels wrong.

I really am sorry.

Grace x

Chapter Twenty-Nine

I'm in a Starbucks on Lexington Avenue and there's a woman sitting opposite me nursing her baby. She has one of those modesty cloths over the baby's head, yet the child's suckles are noisy. One of its fists slips from under the blanket and lodges itself on the mother's other breast. I try not to stare, to continue reading my *New York Times*. Shuffling a little, I move my glasses up on my nose, but the print blurs.

Junior's noises are getting louder, and I opt to move, to pick up my coffee and wander out into the streets of Manhattan, where it's bitterly cold and raining. Head down against a slanted shower, I walk through Library Walk, studying the brass plaques in the pavement, all quoting literary wisdoms. Unable to grasp what has unsettled me, a recent nature programme on television comes to mind, where an adult penguin regurgitated food for its baby. I pull gloves from my pocket and push the newspaper into the mouth of a nearby recycling bin.

I've been in Manhattan for a week, have already been to a windy Lady Liberty, spent a humbling time at Ellis Island, and been to see *Hamilton* on Broadway last night. I've adored every minute here, just as I loved Boston before, where, according to the plan, I bought a corned beef and pickle sandwich from Michael's Deli and ate it on one of the lawns at Harvard. I could almost feel her whispering on my shoulder.

Now, I'm on my way to the public library, but something has me stopped in a boarded-up doorway in the centre of Manhattan thinking about how penguins feed their young. Thinking of a young mother nursing her child. Thinking of Alice. Regret, I know from years of experience, has an appetite. It can eat away at you slowly, one bite at a time if you let it. I cough into my gloved hands, before clapping them together. No regrets. Not here. Not now. I have a job to do. I head towards the main library building on Fifth Avenue, where, on her behalf, I'm, allegedly, about to write a short story.

*

Once upon a time, there was a boy and a girl. They loved each other very much and planned to be together forever. Then the girl died, and the boy had a wonky leg. He worked hard to build a life and forget her, but he was stuck in the moment when she left him. Until her sister told him to unstick himself and live *life. He did a BIG thing and then left his home to see how the wider world worked and to let love into his life. And love, he was realising, wasn't just romantic love, although the boy was finally open to that possibility. Love, he thought, existed in so many moments of life, if he just allowed himself to really feel.*
    The End

*

Before I arrived in the States, I'd booked a helicopter ride around Manhattan, paid a small fortune for it to be a private experience and the nerves haven't just kicked in – they're stomping all over my insides. Earlier, I walked from the library as far as 34th Street, where a half-naked guy, complete with Stetson and a guitar, sang in the streets and made me laugh for a while. I got a yellow cab down to The Battery and now, after a load of safety instructions, Greg, the pilot, probably because he's checked out my wan pallor, doesn't stop talking on the way to the craft.

I try to be all casual as I walk with him by my side, yet, when I'm sitting in the cockpit, I think about unhooking the harness he's placed on me and escaping. I've never been in a helicopter. The only form of air travel I ever take is an aeroplane and, whenever possible, I travel on the biggest one available, in the front section of the cabin.

'Nervous?' Greg finally asks the obvious and all I can do is nod. Sitting here, I can almost recite every available Tripadvisor comment. I know what to expect. We will take off. We will veer south around Governor's Island and circle, before heading north to the right of Liberty. This, I knew then, meant that I would be travelling over water. This, now, threatens to turn my bowels *to* water.

'It's all good,' I repeat to myself over and over in my head. 'It's all good,' I tell Greg as the helicopter moves upwards before swooshing away to the left.

My eyes remain closed and my sphincter muscle clamped tight as Greg's voice comes at me through earphones. He has a nice voice, one that otherwise might be described as soothing, one that could probably accompany me beautifully on my morning low-key scales. I make myself think of some bad things I've had to deal with in my life, like McDickhead-Bryanson-of-the-ironed-jeans, so that I might appreciate this as a great moment. Finally, breathing calmer, I open one eye, catch a glimpse of Liberty and close it again.

'You going to keep your eyes shut the whole trip?'

I hear laughter at the edges of Greg's question.

'Probably,' I whisper.

'You're British, where's that stiff upper lip?' He might as well have cried 'Pussy' at me.

I bite my limp upper lip and open my eyes. Water. So much water.

'Ellis Island just behind us and the Freedom Tower to our right.'

Trying to look, I have to admit the buildings and skyline are impressive from this height. We fly by the needle top of Freedom and I agree with Greg's mutterings of 'Awesome . . .' Apart from the speed of the Hudson rushing by below us.

'You been to the Square?' Greg asks. 'I've got me some Knicks tickets for the weekend.'

I oblige him with a glance towards Madison Square Gardens.

He laughs, a small, ticklish sound in my ear. 'Empire State, Chrysler just right and in just a moment you'll see Intrepid below.'

And just because I really want to see Intrepid, that warship that sits in dock on the left-hand side of Manhattan Island; just because I look down towards it and the water surrounding it, that's when my stomach gripes uncontrollably and I projectile vomit into Greg's lap.

'Jesus!' he cries, his puke-covered left hand thankfully staying put on the controls. He's trying to wipe second-hand blueberry muffin from his trousers. I rub my mouth with my handkerchief and then hand it to him, apologise and tell him that I'm quite OK if he wants to return to base early.

Back in the hotel, after a nap and a whole ten minutes pacing the bedroom asking myself why the hell I took a helicopter ride when I knew I'd hate it, I finally sit – take in the floor-to-ceiling-window view of a wintry Manhattan. A frosted Central Park stretches beneath me. I'm trying to work out why I'm feeling frustrated and can only come up with the fact that I'm feeling a little like a tourist rather than a fearless traveller. The itinerary that's imprinted on my mind has me doing the things Alice and I had planned to do together. Ollie always hated the idea, told me it still mired me in the past, and I wonder now if he's right. To take my mind off this, I imagine all sorts of idiotic and amazing detours I could take after I've made the first few required stops. Horse riding in Montana. I could ride a horse. Wyoming. I google Wyoming and think, yes, it looks good. Nebraska, just because I like the sound of it. Alaska, because I'd get to wear the warm clothes in my capsule wardrobe.

I post a photo on Instagram of the helicopter with Greg and I, looking all *Top Gun*, before I puked all over him. I tag Marsha and Grace and hope Laura's not looking. I use the hashtag #NYCadventures. The shot I'd uploaded of me eating a sandwich outside Harvard has some comments that I scroll through. Laura has posted: *I hope you choke on it. #soulusurper.* OK, so she *is* looking.

My thumbs are immediately active on the phone:

Laura, I'm sorry I hurt you, but please stop with the Instagram aggression. I should have told you when we met that I had this trip planned – you're right. I hurt you and I apologise, but I have not usurped anybody's soul. This trip is important to me for very personal reasons, so stop – please? I'm sorry. Perhaps some other time, I can explain this better.

The text is sent before I even reread it and, sighing, I know instantly that I'm done with Manhattan. I type a query into the airline's website and within minutes I've changed my flight to Miami from tomorrow night to one leaving in three hours. I'll surprise them.

Mum and Dad will be thrilled.

*

I take a cab from the airport and before long am being driven across Rickenbacker Bridge towards Key Biscayne. Ahead lies the island my parents have lived on for the last three years since moving here from West Florida. As I nudge open the window, breathe the soft air of Biscayne Bay, I regret only visiting them here once before for a brief weekend and am looking forward to spending some time with them in their little piece of paradise. From the car I look back and take a photo on my phone of Miami's urban skyline sandwiched between the turquoise blues of the sky and the sea. I send it to Clare on WhatsApp. She hasn't responded to the last few messages I've sent, and I sense a coolness there. If I'm right, it's probably because she regrets what happened; doesn't know what to say, whereas I've just messaged her as normal, not referring to it, sort of ignoring it. Maybe that's annoyed her – who knows – but if I were a betting man, she's pissed off that my last words to her were about staying away from her wanker husband. Either way, I'm not wasting brain cells on it right now, not when I'm breathing in the scent of Key Biscayne adventures.

Panic. That's what's written all over my mother's face when she opens the creaking door – initial confusion creasing the lines of her face, then immediate wide-eyed panic. I hug her briefly, but only for a second before she's flustered again. The bulging rucksack and the wheelie suitcase, I leave in the marble hallway of their condo, marvelling as I'm stood under the air-conditioning unit that only hours ago, I was freezing.

'Did I get it wrong – you're a day early!' Mum eventually says.

'I wanted to surprise you both! Where's Dad?'

She's rubbing both hands on her tennis whites and I notice the twisted knuckles on her right hand. Warm weather on her arthritic fingers is one of the reasons they moved here. 'Out with his golf buddies,' she says.

'Out?' I glance at my watch. Dad's seventy-four years old and would normally be having a nice siesta at this time.

She points me into the living room. 'I'll give him a call now.' Mum stares as if she can't really believe I'm here. 'Look at you.' She ruffles my hair as if it were still the downy curls I had as a child instead of the tight buzz cut I now wear. There's a loud tut as she touches the beard I'm growing. 'Grey,' she mutters. 'Can't believe that. Sit, son, sit, I'll just give your dad a ring, where's my phone?'

Patting a slim side pocket in her skirt, she heads to the kitchen and I only know she's found it when I hear her voice through the door. I take a seat on one of their cream leather sofas. Opposite me there's a sliding door that overlooks the swimming pool and gardens for the community. It's open, though the screen door is closed to keep the mosquitoes that love to chomp on Dad's sweet blood away. Beyond the door and the wide terrace, where Mum and Dad eat their meals al fresco almost all year around, the tops of palm trees waft gently in the warm breeze and a chorus of cicadas sounds. It's like a musical tropical postcard.

'Right, darling!' Her hand ruffles my head again as she passes. 'Can I get you a drink? Something to eat?'

'I ate on the plane, Mum. I'd love a G&T though. Will probably need a few – can't sleep even weeks on.'

'That's not jet lag, darling, it's middle age,' she laughs as she heads back to the kitchen. 'So, what have you been up to? I want to hear everything.'

When she hands me a drink, she sits on the opposite sofa. 'You look well,' she offers. 'If a little tired.'

'I feel well.' I raise the glass to her in a silent toast. 'Learning to appreciate some time out from work.'

'You sure that's all it is, just time out?'

I smile. 'Don't look forward to me retiring early, Mum. I've still got too much I want to do. And when I do retire, don't look forward to me doing it out here.'

The gin is strong enough to make me wince at first, but the second taste is bliss and it's only when it's almost gone, and we've been chatting about Boston and I've fessed up to puking on Greg, that I realise Dad's not home yet. I'm just about to question it when I hear his key in the door and, within seconds, I'm pulled upright and enveloped in a bear hug.

When I sit, he's still standing looking at me, smiling. 'Doing nothing suits you,' he says.

'I was just telling him that,' Mum agrees from behind his still tall and burly frame. There's nothing old or stooped about Dad's ageing body.

'You too,' I tell him. 'You wear sunshine and golf well.'

He takes a seat next to Mum and together they look across at me as if I'm a performing lab rat in a new experiment. To be fair, it *has* been a while since we've seen each other in real life.

Several gins later and Dad's telling me that they've now got bikes and often cycle down the road to the lighthouse at Bill Baggs Park with a picnic. We could do that tomorrow. For a brief second, I think he's suggesting I join them on a bike, and I wonder if a slight jiggle of my left foot might be needed. It's not something I've ever mastered with the prosthetic, but here, floating in gin, anything feels possible. Or we could drive, he adds, after a glare from Mum, after which he asks whether I'd prefer a lazy day at Crandon Beach. There's a park right next to it where peacocks roam wildly – did I remember that? I didn't. I yawn widely, but Dad doesn't even notice as he regales us with the tale of how last month he and his mate Javier were playing golf and there was a croc on the edge of the greens. Did I know that one had snatched a dog recently? I didn't. I swallow the next yawn and try to catch him between stories. 'Sorry, Dad, I'm bushed. Do you guys mind if I head to bed?'

'Of course not,' they speak together, and the sound is immediately comforting. It's something they often do, reply to a question together, at the same time, with the same words – a sort of vocal synchronicity, and I love it. I say good night, blow them both a kiss and take my bags to the spare room next to theirs.

It's been meticulously prepared. Even though I'm early, the crisp linen is fresh, and rosemary-scented. There is a dressing gown hanging on a hanger on the back of the door. A set of temporary slippers from some hotel they stayed in sit in a mesh bag at the end of the bed. In the en suite, there's a basket of toiletries. I grab the freebie toothbrush and paste, brush my teeth, not even wanting to unpack. Exhaustion has hit and as I climb between the sheets, as muted voices travel from the living room, that feeling of security that still comes from being with my mother and father wraps itself around me.

Chapter Thirty

Clare wasn't a snoop. Even as a teenager she'd never been one of those babysitters who checked out the parents' bathroom cabinet or opened drawers that she shouldn't have. Why then, she asked herself, when she'd just let herself in to get her Pyrex bowl back, was she standing in Jack's bedroom looking all around her? The key he'd given her to keep an eye on the place, to water his indoor plants, seemed to sear the flesh of her closed hand. *Leave*, she told herself as she ran a finger along his dresser. Sitting on top of it was a silver picture frame with a photo of a young girl taken at a pop concert, her long hair falling around her face as she danced. The neon stage behind her screamed '1988 ROCKS'. On the back of the frame was written one word – *Alice*. Clare blushed, as if suddenly aware she was prying, and left the room.

In the hallway, she turned at the sound of the doorbell, rubbed her arms where guilty hairs had risen under her sweater. She had his key, she was merely checking the place, she told herself as she opened the door.

'Hello,' a woman, someone she didn't recognise, said as she looked over Clare's shoulder. Just one word implied a Welsh Valley accent.

'Hi,' Clare replied. 'Can I help you?'

'I . . .' The woman played with the tasselled end of her scarf, both hands entwining themselves in it. 'I'm looking for Jack.'

Clare felt herself appraised. She was in dance sweats, old ones that she used when she was doing housework. Her hand touched a historic bleach stain at hip level. Her curly blonde hair that needed its roots touching up was hitched up in a loose ponytail with one of Grace's bright orange scrunchies.

'He's not here,' she replied.

'Oh.' Disappointment reached every feature of the woman's pretty face. Mid-forties, Clare reckoned, slim build, tall, well-dressed in a tailored way, short pixie-cut auburn hair. 'I should have texted him beforehand. I was in Oxford again for work, so thought I'd drop in . . .'

'Are you Alice?' Clare asked, wanting, for some reason, to seem knowledgeable about Jack's life.

'What? No!' She frowned. 'Do you know when he'll be home?'

'I'm not sure,' Clare answered, embarrassed, as she pulled the door behind her and locked it. The woman stepped back, surprised.

'He's not gone yet, has he?' she asked. 'I mean, has he left already on his trip?'

'I'm sorry,' Clare said, 'but *who* are you?'

The woman rested a hand on her chest. 'I'm Lynn. I'm . . . Jack and I are old friends.'

'Right,' Clare said, pulling her loose cardigan around her to hide the bleach stain, sensing the meaning behind the word 'friend' in this instance. 'Well . . .' She hesitated. Surely if they were good friends, she'd have known when he was going to leave.

'And you?' the woman asked, suddenly turning the tables. Suspicion arrived in her narrowed eyes as she seemed to assess Clare differently.

'We're neighbours.' She nodded towards the Barn.

'Ahh, you're the lady with the daughter. The dancer.'

Clare watched as the penny dropped with Jack's old friend, as she suddenly came to a conclusion that she was no threat. No threat to anything – not to the house, to Jack. To her. She was merely the dancing lady, a mother, a neighbour.

The stranger's head seemed to bob as if she remembered the exact moment that Jack might have shared what he'd done with the Barn, who exactly she was.

'Yes,' she whispered, because that *was* who she was. A dancing neighbour. Lynn had no need for any further detail. 'I'm keeping an eye on the place for Jack.'

Clare wondered if this friend could tell she'd just been in his bedroom when she shouldn't have been. She wondered if she could tell that Jack had recently been in her bedroom when he shouldn't have been. She wondered if this Lynn and Jack were more than friends, whether they *had* been lovers, and instinct told her that, yes, they had.

'I'm sorry I missed him . . . Never mind,' Lynn smiled. 'I should get on the road home.'

'Is home Wales?'

'Where else with this accent.'

'It's lovely,' Clare returned her smile. 'Maybe you'd like a coffee before you head back?'

Lynn looked over at Clare's home and nodded.

*

'It's strange to see it, here, made real. When Jack and I were together this was just a pipe dream. He was always going to do something with the old barn . . .'

So, they were an item, Clare thought. 'He certainly did, something with it, I mean,' she waved a hand about. She was unsure what Lynn might know about her and Grace's circumstances, her reasons for being there, and didn't feel inclined to share it.

'So, when were you and Jack together?' She clasped a hand over her mouth. 'God,' she said through her fingers, 'I seriously didn't mean to say that out loud.'

Lynn laughed. 'Oh, it was years ago, but lately . . .' she paused. 'Lately he's just been an ear . . . I've been having a few problems with my son, Antony.' Immediately, Clare saw hurt in the woman's pinched eyes.

'How old is he?'

'Nineteen going on twelve . . .'

'I have the opposite problem. My daughter is fifteen going on twenty-two, or forty-two. Sometimes she mothers me.' She studied Lynn, tried to imagine her and Jack side by side and she could see it. Physically, they would have looked good. She seemed like a bright lady, someone

who might be his intellectual match. 'Where did you meet?'
she asked. Clare watched as Lynn recalled the memory.

'Through work,' she replied, speaking through fingers
that moved along her top lip gently. 'I'm a stenographer.
I'd met him in court a few times and, well . . . we hit it off.'

Clare nodded.

'He has the most brilliant legal mind, you know, incredible instincts for the law, a nose for right and wrong.' Lynn
sipped her coffee. 'But we were good together for a long
time, until we weren't.' Shrugging, she eyeballed Clare.
'Listen to me. Sorry. You don't want to hear all that. He's
a good man – I'm still very fond of him.'

Clare gazed out at the fence. 'How did he get on with
Antony?' she asked, thinking of Jack's natural way with
Grace.

'Not so good. I suppose you could say that was why
it ended, and I wanted to see him just before he left
because . . .' She drained her cup. 'Listen to me rabbit-
ing on! Tell me about yourself, Clare.'

Without realising it, Clare glanced at the clock and saw
that Lynn had noticed. 'Jeez, how long have you got?' She
tried to make light. 'I'm a dancer, with a new class of septuagenarians starting in forty minutes.'

'Oh, I really shouldn't keep you so . . .'

Clare reached her hand across to rest on the woman's
arm as she went to stand up. 'I run the classes from the
garage, not far to go, and honestly, my life story would
only take two minutes.' She smiled.

'Your classes are in the garage?' Lynn appeared surprised.

'Well, it's not a garage any more, I converted it to a dance studio.'

'Oh.'

With a single word, Clare felt judged and struggled not to launch an immediate defence. She heard the word as confirmation that this stranger had possibly found her wanting; a stranger who had been Jack's lover and shared part of his life. She heard unspoken accusations in her head, even though it was unlikely that Lynn knew her circumstances: 'Oh – it's not enough that the man provides you and your daughter with a free home, but you have to take his triple garage as well.' An immediate heatwave surged through her, the start of a hot flush in her torso that ended in her cheeks.

'That's amazing,' Lynn added, but Clare didn't buy it. 'And dancing septuagenarians? How exciting, what are they dancing?'

'The waltz.' Clare glanced at the clock face on Lynn's wrist. 'Today's the first day for the over-sixties waltz, but I teach all sorts of ages both ballroom and latin.'

'When I lived here, I'd have loved something like that. I often thought how lovely it would be for Jack and I to . . . but, you know, the leg.'

She was fishing, Clare thought. She was trying to find out if she, Clare, knew about Jack's leg.

'Well, he does a mean waltz himself, despite the leg,' Clare looked her square in the eye until Lynn was first to look away. 'I should probably go and get ready,' she said. 'Get these old bleach-stained sweats off me.' She wondered why she'd said that, annoyed at herself for being self-deprecating in front of this woman.

'Yes, of course. Thank you for the coffee.' Clare took the empty mug that Lynn handed to her as she stood. 'I'm glad you're here,' Lynn added. 'Jack's much better with people around. Sometimes he gets so immersed in work that he tends to isolate himself when he's home.' She wrapped the scarf that had rested on her lap around her neck twice. 'It was lovely to meet you, Clare,' she said.

'You too.' Clare led her to the front door, and waved goodbye as Lynn walked back up her drive towards her car. With Lynn out of sight she shut the door and breathed, deep and slow. 'What was all that about?' she asked herself as she headed down the hallway to her bedroom. 'She's a perfectly nice woman, being perfectly pleasant, and you acted like an idiot at the end.' Standing at a window, she stared outside. 'Someone was always going to get this break, Clare. Why the hell not you?'

*

Within an hour her thoughts were elsewhere. Nancy and Stanley could not dance, but their determination to learn made her giggle. Widows Norma and Babs had arrived together and partnered each other around the space like two old pros, and solitary Gene, who bore no resemblance to his dancing hero in looks or foot-stepping talent, was Clare's dance partner for that first class. But it was Hilda and Ernest, a couple of fifty-one years, that had made her heart soar. Insisting on showing her their jitterbug after class, Clare had held her breath until she had clapped wildly at the end.

'It is so good to be back dancing,' Hilda announced when she finally got her own breath back. 'Ernest doesn't hear so well any more, not words anyway, but somehow he seems to hear music.'

Clare's hand went to her throat.

'Says it's through the beat in the floor,' Hilda added, linking her arm through her husband's. 'Same time next week?' she asked, and Clare agreed with a wordless hug.

After everyone had left, Hilda and Ernest in a waiting taxi, she lowered herself on her haunches and touched the sprung floor that had helped him hear. Clare of Melborough tapped it gently three times before checking her watch and glancing towards the corner to a pile of ten stacked chairs Emma had lent her. She had an hour to prep the place for a 'talk' on dance to a group of people her friend had assured her would spread the right word in the right circles. All Clare had to do was chat about what she knew and share her passion . . . Clare's stomach pitched in fear.

As it happened, with nine pairs of eyes gazing at her ninety minutes later, she had no problem talking about her love of dance, with words deep-rooted in her soul flowing as easily as the movements she demonstrated. Her eyes closed as she moved.

'Dancing is about more than moving to set steps! You can't just place your feet in time to the music. A beautiful dancer *commits,*' she said. 'They commit to the movement, to the story of the dance. Life, dance – it's *all* about commitment.'

As the evening passed she noticed their faces change. They had started smiling politely in her direction, perhaps all there at Emma's bidding, vaguely interested in learning to dance. Fifteen minutes in, she had a captive audience as she demonstrated tango, followed later by the waltz.

She couldn't help but remember Jack. 'The waltz,' she danced slowly around the floor, 'is as easy as one, two, three. Beautifully flowing, continuous turns, with lots of rise and fall. It's a dizzy dance of joy.'

Afterwards, Clare took the names and numbers of people who were interested in actual classes. When one woman asked her to talk to the local Women's Institute chapter, Clare readily agreed. There were no sabotaging thoughts; no doubts allowed to enter her mind about what she might be able to deliver. Overwhelmed by a surge of love for everything in her new life, she *did* think about Hilda and Ernest, and her other earlier pupils. She thought of the Welsh woman she'd met at Jack's earlier, someone who'd meant something to him and probably still did. She thought of the dizzy joyous dance she'd shared with Jack. She accepted as she said goodbye to her last guest and locked the studio behind her that the life she now occupied, without Tim, was a whole new story – a whole new solitary tango she could totally commit to.

Without ever having to look over her shoulder.

Joyful, she thought walking up the path. *I'll take that.*

Chapter Thirty-One

Mum is already sitting on her favourite wicker chair on the terrace when I emerge from the bedroom. She's reading a newspaper, her glasses – held around her neck by a string of brightly coloured beads – are perched on the end of her nose. I walk behind her, kiss her head as I pass, and she's quick enough to reach for my hand.

'Two kisses already,' she smiles. 'A woman could get greedy.'

'Morning.' I pour myself a coffee from a filter jug.

'Did you sleep?' she asks.

'I had the best sleep since arriving stateside, thank you. Dad out again?'

'I'm so pleased . . . Your dad's gone to pick up some fresh pastries. I thought we could pretend we're in Paris. Is it on your itinerary? Tell me it is. Oh, how I'd love to come with you.'

She's kidding, I know she is, so I laugh. 'It was on the itinerary, it is . . . I'm not sure yet.'

Mum frowns. 'Not sure?'

The coffee is black, steaming hot and bitter. 'I have a plan – which involves two continents, here first and then Europe.'

'Paris,' she says, reminiscing. 'St Germain . . .'

'But I have changeable tickets, so things are fluid. I've realised since leaving work that part of why I'm doing this must be to see what life is like *without* a plan.'

She peers at me through the top of her varifocals. 'Look at you, all grown up.'

'I'm almost fifty, Mum.'

'Stuff and nonsense! You're permanently twenty in my head.'

I think of all the success I've had in my life since I was twenty and swallow what I might once have retorted. Mum has revelled in my vast professional success, but like any mother, she has always wanted my personal life to be shared with someone. Interesting that her static image of me as a young man of twenty is when I was with Alice.

Dad arrives with enough pastries to feed an army and we sit and talk, the three of us, and I feel comforted, content that the sense of ease that being with my parents brings is still there.

'Enough about me,' I tell them. 'How are you both health-wise? I heard you up and down to the loo last night, Dad.'

There's the tiniest glance between them both before Mum speaks. 'You know your father, he's often up prowling.'

A slight panic hits because I feel like Mum has just lied to me. My imagination runs wild, fearing him with prostate cancer or – thinking of how he'd repeated the same story a couple of times the night before – maybe he's losing his memory. Recently, a client of mine was accused of manslaughter when he drove into a woman at a bus stop. It was a dreadful accident, a terribly sad case. He had just been diagnosed with Alzheimer's and his wife hadn't even known he'd left the house. I swallow the questions – conscious I've just arrived.

'You fancy a round, this morning?' My father is grinning hopefully.

'Dad, I hate golf. I hated it the first time I was here too.'

'I know, I know . . .'

What if there's something wrong with him?

'Tell you what,' I suggest. 'Why don't we just try nine holes? Before it gets too hot? Then I can take you and Mum out to lunch.'

'Sterling!' Dad says and claps his hands. 'You can use my old clubs. I bought some new ones last Christmas.'

'*I* bought you new ones last Christmas,' Mum corrects him.

'Yeah, yeah,' he replies.

'How's your new neighbour?' Mum changes the subject before I have a chance to dwell on Dad possibly losing his marbles.

'Great,' I say, looking out at the tops of the swaying palms and avoiding her eye. My mother would be able to tell at six paces that Clare and I slept together if I let her take one look at me.

*

As predicted, my round of nine holes is shambolic, and my father has apologised for my lack of skill more than once to his two mates who've joined us in a four-ball. Javier, a short, rotund man with a thick mop of silver hair, and two earrings in a wrinkly left lobe, is sixty-two on Thursday. This, he tells me, more than once, as he drives the golf buggy around the course. He's been in 'Our United States of America' for forty years and still has a tiny hint of his Hispanic roots in his accent. Sixty-seven-year-old Mason, who is six foot three and walks with a slight lean to his left, is heir to a sausage empire and has felt the need to discuss the ins and outs of what makes a good sausage with me for the last two hours. All I've been able to think of, as I've been trying and failing to wield Dad's spare golf clubs, is Pecan and Walnut. As soon as we're finished, and they head into the clubhouse for a refreshing drink, I wave, saying I'll follow them in a minute.

Working out the time difference, I see it's seven in the morning at home and send Grace a quick text asking about the pigs. She responds within seconds, telling me they're fine but that she can sense they miss me. It makes me smile. I thank her and ask after her and her mum, to which she replies that they're fine as well, and that they miss me being around too. Finding myself swallowing an unexpected lump in my throat, I don't respond. Everything is good back home.

I rub my eyelids with a thumb and forefinger before turning the corner into the wood-panelled lounge in the air-conditioned clubhouse. 'Who's for a drink?' I ask the pensioners.

'On their way already, Son,' Mr Sausage Heir says, and I nod, take a seat next to Dad. 'We got you a beer,' he adds. When they arrive, and while the men are all chatting, I ask the waitress for a pint of sparkling water as quietly as I possibly can. I'm driving, and Dad has obviously forgotten that I never drink and drive. Nothing. Not a drop. Zero. Without them even noticing I hand my beer back to the waitress and tap my mouth with my finger in a shh motion. She seems to understand and a minute later arrives with my water.

'Just thirsty,' I tell Javier, who's the only one suddenly watching.

'You're a quiet type, aren't you?' he states. 'Don't like talking about yourself much, do you?' Questions he doesn't expect me to answer surely, I think, as I help myself to some peanuts. 'Your dad thinks you're having some sort of midlife crisis. You know, leaving a perfectly good career and, hang on, did I get it right – didn't you give a house away as well?'

A midlife crisis, interesting . . . 'Not quite,' I tell him. 'The house was a philanthropic gesture, to a charity, for a year only. And,' I add, 'I haven't left my career, just taken a break.'

'What happens if you don't want to go back to it when the time comes?'

I pause, lick my salted fingertips and shrug. 'I'll do something else instead. Middle-aged I might be, ready to retire – not yet.'

'Agreed,' he says. 'You're in your prime! When I was your age, I married a woman of twenty-nine! She divorced me three years later and you lawyer types helped her rob me blind, but, hell, the sex was good.' Javier winks.

I feel a little sick. The thought of having a twenty-nine-year-old woman by my side is mildly terrifying. And if I've learned anything in the last couple of months, it's that sex with a woman in her late thirties was pretty sensational, even though she now hates me on Instagram. But sex with a woman in her forties was downright mind-blowing . . . Clare's face fills my thoughts.

'You have someone? A woman in your life?' Javier is looking directly at me.

'No.'

'You should,' he says before breaking the conversation abruptly by standing suddenly and heading towards the restrooms.

Dad has been watching and listening to the last part of our exchange. 'Shall we head home?' he asks, and something tells me he's tired after this morning's activity. 'Your mother has lunch prepared, says she'd prefer to eat in. All are welcome.'

Ten minutes later we're already back at the condo development they all live in. Neither man wants to join us for lunch, insisting we have 'family time'.

'Interesting guys,' I say. Dad walks ahead of me and I follow up the path surrounded by lush tropical plants. 'Have you known Javier long?' I raise my voice a little above the sound of the singing insects.

'He's president of the community here,' Dad replies without answering the question.

I scratch my head. 'Has he been here as long as you and Mum?'

'That last wife of his fleeced him. I never liked the woman.'

I'm trying to figure out why he's not answering a question directly when, in the lift, he presses the second floor, though they live on the third. My hand presses three instead and he taps his forehead with the back of his palm, then shakes his head.

By the time I'm sitting down to one of Mum's salads, which today has walnuts and pecans in it and makes me miss home like a thump to the chest, I just ask them straight out.

'Dad, are you OK?'

Again, there's a tiny pause where my mother looks at my father before my father looks at me and then they both look at me with a matching bewildered expression.

In the absence of a reply, I redirect the question to my mother. 'Mum, is Dad sick?'

'Not as far as I am aware, Jack.' Her head sinks into her shoulders as she seems to contemplate where this question appeared from.

'What in hell makes you ask that, Son? I'm in the best of health,' Dad says finally.

I eat some lettuce and nuts. 'Just feels like something is a little off.'

'I don't know what you mean, love.' This from Mum.

'Everything's good, Son.' This from Dad.

Sighing, I chew a lump of what I think is mozzarella. Soft jazz music plays from an old CD player in the corner.

'You not hungry?' Mum asks. 'I probably should have mentioned we're both vegetarians now.'

'I'm OK, thank you.'

'We've been dying to hear all about your plans,' she deftly diverts the conversation back to my travels. 'Where are you headed next? How long are you staying?'

'I've just got here?'

'Yes, darling, of course, that's not what I meant at all. We've been so looking forward to having you here, haven't we, Joe?'

Dad's tackling a walnut with his false teeth, so just nods vigorously.

'We're excited for you.' Mum again. 'Jealous actually, we should have done that years ago, shouldn't we, Joe? We should have gone off travelling.'

'You moved to America when you were just a little older than me, Mum.'

'Yes, we did, didn't we, and that was such an adventure then.'

I remember when they told me they were going. I was early thirties, a legal career already carved, living on my own in a one-bedroom flat overlooking Battersea Park that I'd bought with a large mortgage. They'd argued that a second-floor walk-up was a bad idea for me, but I'd fallen in love with the red-brick mansion block and its tall ceilings and original fireplace. I felt all grown up and was determined to prove them wrong. As it happened, they were right, and I sold it a year after buying it. But before that, there was that night when they'd come over to see me, I'd assumed just to see how I was. I'd cooked supper, and midway through the evening they announced they were emigrating. Just like that. The feeling still pinches now, all these years later, that sensation of being blindsided by the suddenness of it. Here were these people who had always just been there and then they weren't going to be. Placing my cutlery in the centre of the plate, I remember feeling quite bereft – both at their loss and at the fact that they seemed unaware of how I felt.

'Are you still playing?' Dad asks and I know he means the trumpet.

'Absolutely.'

'And singing?'

'A little less since I have neighbours.'

He starts to sing low, slow baritone scales just like he'd taught me as a boy, and I join him, and before long we're both standing, doing our blended father-and-son version of 'Ol' Man River'. Mum claps and for a few minutes it's just like old times – but without meat.

*

Later that night, unable to sleep, I call Clare, batting away any doubts I have about doing so. I'm a friend calling another friend.

'Jack?'

'Yes, hi, just checking in. I can't sleep.' I don't say: *Why haven't you responded to the photos I sent?*

'How are you?'

I'm trying to figure out if her reply is stilted when she quickly follows with, '*Where* are you? Are you with your parents yet?'

'I'm with people who claim to be my parents, but I'm not sure.'

I can sort of *hear* her smile.

'What do you mean?'

'It's all a bit weird.'

'So, start at the start,' she says.

'Once upon a time there was a young boy, a shy, capable young boy. He was loved. Privileged. His parents, only having one child, adored him.'

'Shit,' she cries. 'That really is the start. OK, OK, let me get comfortable.'

'He went to the best schools, had a stay-at-home mother who was always there, had a father who worked a lot away from home but always managed to find time for him. Are you comfortable yet?' I ask.

'Yup. I'm lying down on my bed.'

She says this as if to acknowledge I know exactly where she means.

I pause a moment. 'The boy was a gifted musician . . .'

And we talk for a bit, starting with my telling her all about Dad teaching me to play trumpet and ending up with my telling her I'm worried about him. I make a joke about the people I've met here, saying I feel as if I've landed on the set of *Cocoon*.

'It's good to hear from you,' she says after a while, in a way that feels like the conversation is about to end. Her voice, I realise, has had a calming effect on me and I find myself not wanting to hang up.

We haven't spoken about the night we spent together. It's there sitting between us, not presenting either of us with a problem, but nor is it something we've raised as what it was – at least what it was to *me*. It was the first time in far too long that I felt something, really experienced something with each and every one of my senses. I want to tell her this but don't want her to have to explain what it did or didn't mean to her. What's the point? I'm here and she's there and the fact that she's not mentioned it at all leads me to believe that more than likely, like I've had to, she's put the event in her memory bank as something lovely that happened but will never happen again.

'What are the chances,' she asks out of the blue, 'of us having met in other circumstances?'

'You could have done something highly illegal.'

'OK, but I've been thinking about the role chance and fate plays in all our lives?'

I remain quiet.

'I mean, we talked about it before or I did, really. Remember?'

I do. It was burrito night.

'Chance,' she says, 'it's about luck, the roll of the dice, but there might be odds stacked for or against something.' It seems she really doesn't expect a reply because she quickly adds, 'And fate, that's more like something we have no control over.'

I was fated to lose Alice, to become an amputee. Is it Chance or Fate that made April send that email or brought Clare and Grace to my door? I'm unsure. 'I'm petrified of Fate,' I admit to her, 'of not having control. According to Ollie, it's made me a total control freak.'

I can hear soft breathing down the line. 'Tell me what happened to you, Jack.' The words are whispered.

And then I do, I tell her what happened to me, I tell her all about Alice and how much I loved her, about the accident, about Alice dying.

I tell her *almost* everything.

Chapter Thirty-Two

The first shock of Grace's birthday was that Clare woke thinking about Jack losing someone he called 'the love of his life' and what that had meant for him since. Since they'd last spoken, a week ago, she'd finally understood that he wasn't running away but was, in fact, running full throttle *towards* something different and exciting. The thought made her smile for him.

The second shock of the day was the postcard. It was a typical tourist picture of London with Big Ben and the Houses of Parliament on the front and a scrawled message from Tim on the back.

Know I've been excommunicated but wanted you to know I've put £100 in your bank account for Grace's birthday pizza night. Tim

Finding it on the mat under the letterbox, recognising his handwriting, she'd held her breath, but quickly exhaled on reading the message. The money would mean she didn't have to put the cost on her credit card. Relief flooded her veins – she wanted Grace to have the very best sixteenth birthday possible.

The third shock of the day was when her daughter asked her to help her apply make-up a few hours before meeting friends at the local pizza parlour. It wasn't a large group of friends like Clare had possibly hoped for her, but Grace seemed more than happy with a couple of girls from hockey, Reya, who was visiting from Croydon, and Erik. Grace didn't wear make-up, had never been bothered with even a scrap of mascara until the day she turned sixteen, and Clare tried to hide her surprise. 'Of course,' she said, smiling. 'Go and get mine?'

Grace ran down the hallway and Clare sensed that already, her daughter was changing.

'Your skin,' she told Grace less than five minutes later, 'it's smooth as a baby's butt.'

'Ugh, aren't they all wrinkly?'

'No, love, they're not.'

Under strict instructions to make it seem as if she wore no make-up, Clare was relieved Grace wasn't interested in the look she saw most younger girls wear – micro-bladed, shaped eyebrows, pumped lips, heavily made-up eyes. She applied a tinted moisturiser, a tiny line of liquid eyeliner on her eyelids, two layers of lengthening mascara, a dusting of rose blusher and some matt lipstick. As soon as she'd finished, Grace ran to the mirror in the hallway and stood there.

'Good job, Mum,' she smiled. 'Thanks. Don't forget we need to pick Reya up at the station twenty minutes before-hand?'

'I haven't forgotten.'

'And, Mum,' Grace smiled through her beautiful matt lips. 'Thanks for the pizza night too. With that and my new phone, I know you've spent a lot.'

It would be so easy, she thought, so easy to take all the credit and have her daughter crown her Mother of the Year. 'Your dad helped,' she told her. 'He sent some money.'

'He did? He already sent me the clothes voucher,' Grace's young, unfurrowed brow raised. 'Wow . . .'

'Yes, I thought the same, but he's paid for the pizza evening, you should thank him.'

'I will.'

Clare glared.

'I will, honestly. I'll text him later.'

'Well, don't forget,' Clare nudged her as she passed, 'I know you're still angry at him, but—'

'We're talking, Mum, stop fussing. I've not been ready to see him yet, but I'll call him.'

'And no booze tonight. Absolutely none, OK? Not a drop of alcohol is to pass any of your underage lips.'

Grace blinked a little too quickly, before uttering a muttered, 'Of course not.'

'I mean it, Grace.'

'Mum, you know Reya doesn't drink, I don't drink, Erik lives in a pub and if he wanted to drink he could but doesn't. And the other girls are nice, you'll like them. Stop worrying.'

Clare noticed she hadn't confirmed the other girls wouldn't be drinking but decided to let it go. It was her birthday after all.

*

After leaving the teenagers, Clare walked along the high street towards the pub, where she'd agreed to pop in for an off-duty drink with Emma. The short walk highlighted just how important the town she now lived in had become to her. The library, a small stunted building with double-fronted windows onto the main street, was where, last week, she and Grace had signed up to the monthly book club. Grace's nose had wrinkled at the size of the novel they had to read, but Clare, who'd always considered books as mere dust gatherers, was now spending the last fifteen minutes before she fell asleep every night engrossed in fiction.

The Onward Motion premises stood under a bright street light with no sign of life inside. Due there the next morning to talk with Pam, the centre's manager, about how exactly she might help with dance, she thought of the time she'd seen Jack in there as she huddled in the doorway while taking a phone call from Jean. She thought of the time she'd helped with the teas and coffees and, afterwards, she and Jack had shared a waltz at home and . . . She thought of Jack and how she missed him being around and how good it had been to chat on the phone the night before – how afterwards she'd had to remind herself of her initial decision to keep her distance from him when he'd left. During those first weeks of his being away, he'd sent photos, texts, and she didn't always respond, wanting him to be free to do whatever it was he might need to do – just as she was.

When she reached the pub, she stopped to look at its frost-covered roof with dim lamplight coming from one of the two dormer windows in the attic. Her hands pushed deep inside the pocket of her coat, she remembered the first time she'd met Jan and how he'd taken a chance on her. Melborough and its people had been so kind to her and the fact that she loved the place was a revelation to her. Clare had never loved a place before. Croydon had been home. She didn't like or dislike it. It had simply been home. Before Melborough, she hadn't even known that a feeling of *belonging* somewhere was even possible. But she felt it here. Here, she fit with the place and the people.

Inside the pub, she removed her coat and gloves and sat on the last barstool as Emma poured her a soft drink. It was quiet in there, 'but not quite quiet enough for me to join you on that side of the bar', Emma said when she'd arrived.

'They all settled in over the road?' she asked, and Clare nodded.

'Snug as a bug. Though I feel for Erik – four girls, one bloke?'

'Every teenage boy's wet dream,' Emma replied before leaning on the bar and whispering. 'So, how do you feel about Grace and Erik? You know, them being "a thing"?'

Clare rubbed her chest with the heel of her hand, then picked up her glass. She'd had no idea. They had, of course, been spending a lot of time together, initially doing the IT project for her website, which had recently gone live. It now looked like it wasn't only the world wide web that was being explored. How had she not known? She shook her head, muttering the single word, 'Shit.'

Emma frowned. 'You're unhappy?'

'Gosh, no! Not with Erik, no, it's just . . . it's just I didn't know. How the hell did I not see it?' Feeling overwhelmed, with a loss for words *and* a heat flush, she excused herself.

In the ladies, she held the edges of the sink with both hands, ran the cold tap, splashed water on her face and patted it dry with a paper towel.

'These frigging hot flushes . . .' she said on her return.

Emma nodded sympathetically. 'I know, and it lasts for years.'

'You're such a pal.'

'Sorry, but no point in sugar coating it.'

Clare reached for her friend's arm. 'You are though. You're a pal to me and I'm grateful.'

'You sure? I wasn't expecting you to run off to the loo when I mentioned my son and your daughter being a thing.'

'When did she grow up,' Clare mock wailed. 'When the hell did I get old?'

'Older,' Emma corrected. 'We're not old until we're as wrinkled as one of those wrinkly dogs and we need help with our basic needs. Then we might be old.'

Clare tried to focus on what Emma was saying. Stuff about them being in the prime of their life. Jan was running marathons and Emma was taking her time deciding what she'd actually do with her prime.

'Emma, you don't think,' she interrupted her. 'You don't think Erik and Grace are . . . you know . . .' She said what had been on her mind since her visit to the ladies. She hadn't known they were an item, so how would she know if they were having sex?

'No!'

'You would tell me, wouldn't you? And are you sure you'd know?'

'I'd tell you and I'd know. Erik and I are close.'

'I thought Grace told me everything and I didn't even know she and Erik were seeing one another.'

'They're not sleeping together,' Emma insisted.

'Tell me I'm a good mother . . . Do you think I'm a good mother?' she blurted the words to Emma, who was hand-drying some glasses with a tea towel.

Emma regarded her. 'From what I've seen,' she offered cautiously. 'You're a good mother, why?'

'My mother was shit at mothering,' she said before draining her glass. 'She didn't notice things either.'

'Jeez, girl. You need to start drinking.' She nodded towards her empty water glass. 'Seriously, have an odd vodka and tonic. It might help you to stop spending so much time in your own head.' She placed a hand over hers. 'I know what you've been through, not the details, I don't need them, but the journey from your mum to here via Tim needs to be deleted from those files.' She pointed to Clare's head.

'I could put up with anything except if I failed Grace.' Clare pushed her glass towards Emma. 'Her happiness is crucial for the move, for all of this,' she waved her hands at her surrounds, 'to work.'

Emma shrugged. 'Well, she looked very happy when I saw her coming out of Erik's bedroom yesterday. Kidding, I'm KIDDING.' She shook her head and laughed as she went to serve a customer at the other end of the bar.

And Clare allowed herself a smile. It *was* a little bit funny.

*

Onward Motion was definitely the right place to be the next morning. She'd avoided any discussion about Erik with Grace by smiling sweetly at her, talking only in general terms about everyone enjoying the night before. She and Reya were going into town until just after lunch, when Reya was due to get a train back to London. Clare headed to the charity's offices, hoping to find a way to give something back to the community she'd come to love and to the place that meant something to Grace's and her benefactor.

'There are more people here that could learn and be helped with dance than not,' Pam assured her. 'Yes, we have some whose disability will always prevent them from being too physical, but, in the main, that's not the case and there's real interest.' She smiled then frowned in one almost continuous expression. 'The downside is it's time-consuming – you can only work with max two people at a time, assuming they have similar needs and, ideally, it's probably best to work on a one-to-one basis. I mean, how much time would you have to give to this?'

Clare held her breath. This had been her worry when the idea was first mooted. She wanted to do this, she really did, but how to do it effectively, without eating into the time she had to earn, was another thing.

'I want to do this, so I'll make the time,' she gave an assertive nod. 'Do you think I could meet those people who are keen and then I can work out how best to deliver it?'

'Of course, let's do that now. I've made a list, there are some of them here at the moment. Also, Simon, our resident counsellor, who's not here today, wants to talk about an idea for a fundraiser.'

'No problem. Show me the way.' Clare smiled as she followed her out of the office.

*

Over dinner that evening she stared out at the moonlit sky.

'What's up, Mum? You've been in a strange mood tonight,' her daughter asked.

'Sorry, just feeling a little distracted.' Clare moved her food from one side of the plate to the other with her fork. 'So, how was your birthday, the party? Did you and Reya have fun in town today?'

Grace's smile said it all. 'Brilliant. It was perfect – just a few important people and they all loved Reya. And she loves it here – we all had a laugh together.'

'And what does Reya think of Erik?'

'That he's cute!' Grace's cheeks glowed and she clapped her hands gently together as if she'd just realised that all was really well in her world.

'I'm glad,' Clare said.

'And I called Dad, thanked him. He was very quiet, but we've arranged a curry night, will see how it goes . . . Anyway, what has you "distracted"?'

'I was at Onward Motion this afternoon. It was pretty humbling seeing people coping so bloody well with such different challenges.'

'Are you sure it's a good idea?'

'What?'

'Are you sure you're able to help? What they don't need is a do-gooder going in there feeling sorry for them.'

'Grace!' Clare pushed her plate away.

'That came out all wrong, sorry. What I mean is you can't fix it, Mum. Fix their problems.'

'I don't expect to. What I'm hoping for is to share the joy of dance with people who want to try.'

'OK, so . . .' Grace paused, laced her fingers together and looked across the table with Tim's eyes. 'What's the problem then?' she asked simply.

'The problem is I now know what's needed and I worry how I'll find the time to make it happen. It's not just a case of throwing a few hours at it. It's a commitment, a big one.'

Aware that Grace seemed to be expecting more of an explanation, Clare didn't want to admit she was afraid.

And she'd only realised it this afternoon when confronted with other people's fears. She'd seen it in their eyes: a blend of excitement and anxiety, and when she'd recognised it, she determined that she was going to do this; somehow she'd make it happen.

'I'll help you do a plan.' She felt her daughter's kiss on the back of her head as she passed. 'And I'll help more at home. It'll have to be worked around your classes, and the pub, which means the evenings and part weekends you have free . . .' Grace shrugged one shoulder, 'well, I suppose they're just not free any more!'

She watched her daughter ascend the stairs, her daughter who had grown so much in the time they'd been there, the teenager who seemed to belong there too. What was vital was that Clare could continue to work enough hours to earn for the future as well as the present, to show her daughter, to really *show* her, that with a little luck and a lot of hard work things can always change.

A Sam Cooke song about change coming came to mind and unaware of the exact lyrics, she hummed the tune as she began to clear the dishes from the dinner table. It was a tune Jack had played often on his trumpet. So far, change had been gratefully received and good for her and Grace, and she was determined to pass on some of the kindness that Jack and Melborough had sent their way.

Chapter Thirty-Three

WhatsApp Erik & Grace

Do you want to talk about it?

Thought u hated texting? And talking about it would be weeeeeird.

Grace, I'd feel better if I knew that you're all right.

You didn't say no. I just want you to know that if you say no, I'd get that and—

Ur checking I didn't say no? Erik! I didn't say no.

But maybe you wish you had?

I might have if u'd wanted to go all the way.

OK. No. Of course not. I mean.

I'm blushing now. U happy?

Sorry. There is something else I'd like you to say yes to . . .

Well?

Would you say yes, if I asked you to be my
girlfriend?

If you asked me to be your girlfriend, yes, I'd say yes.

Really! Are you sure?

I said Yes. Twice now. I'm sure.

Just checking . . . So, yes?

Sure. Why not ☺

Chapter Thirty-Four

Being here – seeing how people greet one another, even me, a stranger, with a smile – has made me wonder if it's because of the sun, all that natural serotonin, or whether people have smiled at me for thirty years under London's bleak sky and I've never really noticed. It's as if I've worn a shielding layer that has protected me from sneers and kept Fate's kisses gentle for years. But the thing with armour is, although no one or nothing can get to me, I can hide behind it too. I can't help wondering how many smiles I may have missed.

I'm reflecting on this and other stuff as I tug on Frank's rein. He's a white Westland terrier and, having delayed leaving Florida for a bit, I've been taking him for a short walk every day since Mason had a fall and ended up in hospital. Mum and Dad, who would have stepped in, are both allergic to dogs. Javier is on holiday. Enter me, the amputee dog walker with a very flexible travel ticket. Thankfully, he's small, and today I find myself ambling along the pathway next to the shore at Crandon Beach. It's hot – the orange baseball cap I wear is pulled low to shade my face and I've given in to wearing shorts.

There's a walkway leading to the water; slatted boards carved into the sand, which I can navigate fairly well, but I stop when I get to the strand, knowing sand and the blade prosthetic I'm wearing today won't work. The air is crisp and briny, and I sit on a bench at the end of the path listening to the sound of the receding tide. It's so peaceful and I have to force myself away after fifteen minutes. Frank obliges when I tug him back towards town. I pass a parade of eateries, breathing in the scent of freshly grilled peppered mackerel. At Betty's Diner, though dogs are allowed, I take the booth nearest the window, beckon to Mum, who's standing talking to one of the waitresses near the bar.

'Darling,' she approaches and kisses my cheek. 'I've ordered us a couple of small cold beers.' She moves along the worn red leather seating, places both her hands on the melamine table and smiles. I notice her normal shade of dark pink lipstick has run into the feathery lines around her mouth. 'Now, what's up?' Typically, Mum gets straight to the point.

'I thought it would be nice to have lunch. We haven't had any time, just us.'

'Lovely idea, darling.'

Two glasses of icy Bud are placed opposite us and the waitress asks if we'd like to order food.

'I'll have a portion of fries,' Mum says. She has the appetite of a bird.

'I'm hungry – I'll try the veggie burger and fries.'

Mum grins approvingly at my choice of food, and as the waitress leaves, I put my hand briefly over hers. Frank slurps noisily from a water bowl under the table.

'Gosh, I will miss you when you've gone.' Her hand twitches. 'I've got used to having you around. You sure you don't want to retire early?'

Rarely do I answer a question immediately. Years of court training have taught me to pause, just for a second or two, give my quick-thinking brain time to analyse what's really being said. Is it a leading question with the real meaning hidden in subtext, or is it as simple as it first might seem? As Mum speaks, my home, the thatched cottage with Pecan and Walnut and Ollie and his family all come into view. I think of other friends – Clare and Grace, Marsha, Lynn and April.

'Jack?'

'Nah, Mum, I won't be joining you under the Florida sun just yet.' Outside, it shines like a bronzed penny in a cloudless, blue sky. 'I see it, I really do. I understand why you and Dad are here. You have warmth and sun, good food and friends. It's a great life.'

'We're very lucky, though you know I've always believed we make our own luck. Son,' she adds, her eyes fixed on mine. 'Come on, you obviously wanted me alone, what's on your mind?'

I clear my throat. 'Is there something on yours?'

'You're not in court now, love. Let's not play with words.'

The food arrives really quickly and is laid out before us. Mum picks a long skinny fry and sucks the salt from it.

How to ask her again if something is wrong with Dad is what I'm grappling with. Still unable to kick the feeling that there's something askew, I know that if I'm right, their instinct might be to protect me. In their eyes, I'm their only son, their little damaged boy.

I spit the words out, 'Mum, if Dad is ill, I'd really rather know.'

Surprise widens her eyes. 'This again?'

'You need to tell me.'

'Jack—'

'He's forgetful, seems anxious around me,' I interrupt. 'Look, does he have Alzheimer's?'

Her shoulders lower. 'Absolutely not,' she says, and I know immediately she's telling the truth. '*Why* would you think that?'

I list examples of his forgetfulness since I arrived, episodes of odd behaviour around me. My mother is listening intently, and I know that she's telling the truth when she announces, 'There is absolutely nothing wrong with your dad that isn't wrong with me too. We're both just getting older, Jack.' The only thing that this lunch has made clear is that there's nothing medically wrong with my father and I'm really not enjoying this veggie burger.

'I thought you were hungry,' Mum stares at the waste on the plate.

'I should have ordered a nice juicy hamburger.'

She laughs. 'You were a picky eater even as a child. You had to have what your dad and I called "precision plating". Everything equally divided on the plate.'

I scratch an imaginary itch on my forearm.

'Do you remember when you took up football?'

I know what's coming before she says it. As striker, the aim was to score goals, but, in my head, I always had to score on the right and then on the left, on the right and then on the left . . . Symmetry.

'You were a funny little thing.'

My head bobs in agreement.

'And all those little nuances seemed to even out when you met Alice.'

I shovel a few cooling fries into my mouth, chew them slowly. *All those little nuances.*

'You still miss her, don't you, even after all of this time?'

My hand automatically goes to the top of my blade.

'I'm sorry. It's just your dad and I worry about you.'

With that, I have the feeling that the tables are about to be turned.

'I hate seeing you alone. Aren't you lonely?'

'Mum, I lead a busy life. I haven't got time to be lonely.' This is a gargantuan, technicolour lie and there's a weighted silence before she speaks again.

'But you've come out of that world just for a bit, allowed yourself to take a breath of air. This trip is great if you know what you hope to get from it.'

'Experience,' I tell her. 'It's all about stepping out of my very comfortable comfort zone and tasting the wider world.' I almost quote April's email.

Mum looks thoughtful. 'Sounds vaguely like a trip to Oz.'

'Huh?'

'*The Wizard of Oz*, your favourite film as a child.'

Every Christmas, I recall being glued to the tiny telly, and before I can reply, she speaks again.

'Well, you already have a heart, a big one. You already have one of the most intelligent brains I know, so it must be courage you're after.'

'I suppose we all need to be brave,' I finally offer.

'Always. Every day, really. To take an occasional risk.' Mum pauses. 'It's strange you being so worried about your dad, because he's troubled over you.'

'Why?' I think of his pal's version of what Dad thinks I'm doing at the moment, *you've left your career and given away a house.*

'Your father thinks you might be gay.' She stares at her fingernails that grip the edge of the table. 'There, I've said it. He'll kill me for doing so, but yes,' she lifts her gaze to mine. 'That's what he thinks. That you're afraid to tell us. And I'm telling you it wouldn't matter. Not to him, not to me, not a jot. I even love that pink shirt you wear.'

I am actually speechless; words won't come out of my mouth. Frustrated that that's what they think, irritated that they couldn't, or wouldn't, just ask me before now, I empty my lungs slowly. Frank nudges my good leg as if to say, 'Time to go.'

'I'm not gay, Mum. Don't, and never have, fancied men, not that I believe it would be something I couldn't share or be proud of if I did. I do and always have liked women. To be honest, I can't believe that you'd think I'd keep that from you.'

She's shrugging. 'I didn't. I told him he was wrong. But sometimes it is difficult to share things, and he worries. It's been such a long time since Alice, darling. We both worry, that's all.'

'You knew all about Lynn. I *have* had other girlfriends.' The blush that has been circling my system finds its way to my cheeks. I haven't really. I'm almost fifty and there's only been Alice and Lynn and a handful of lovers that never made the relationship status, no one my parents would have known about. 'Frank needs a pee,' I state abruptly, placing enough money on the table. A little awkwardly, I stand up just outside the booth.

'We're going?' Mum grabs her bag and slides out. 'Let me give you a lift back, the sun's at its hottest.'

'I'd prefer to walk. It's not far.'

She puts both of her arms around my middle. 'I've upset you,' she whispers to my chest. 'I'm sorry. All I want,' she pulls away and looks up at my face. 'All your dad and I want is for you to be happy. Anything we do or say, and anything we might not say, is with that in mind. And no, that doesn't mean he's ill and we're hiding it – he's not. Son, if this trip brings you happiness, great. We just don't want you to be lonely.'

I kiss the top of her head. 'See you back at the condo.'

'You definitely want to walk?'

'Yes.'

'That happiness you're after, son.' She hesitates. 'The only way you'll find it is by having the courage to let go of the things that make you *unhappy*.'

I place the empty beer and water glasses in a straight line. Mum laughs. 'Still the same.'

'I'll walk you back to the car.'

She links my arm. 'Do you remember, back then, when you moved university to be closer to us?'

It doesn't need a reply.

'We came to see you nearly every weekend, just to visit, to try to help, to make sure you knew we were both there.'

Plunged back in time, I force a reluctant nod.

'We were afraid for you. Me especially, I knew that what had happened was so brutal that I wasn't sure you'd ever recover.' She stops walking, turns to me and with a gnarled hand shields the sun from her eyes. 'I've spent the last few years proudly watching you become the success you are, and I convinced myself that I was wrong, but was I right?'

Mum blinks, long and slow movements, and I'm almost hypnotised.

'Jack?'

I exhale slowly through pursed lips. 'I still feel responsible. If I hadn't drove. If I hadn't left at that time. If she hadn't been with me. If I'd just turned around that first time I saw her.' I've never spoken like this to Mum before. 'What happened . . . It made sure I'd never fully take a chance on love again.'

'Oh, my darling boy.'

The scene is almost Hollywood. My elderly mother clinging to me as she cries, and I try not to. Frank barks as if to ask, 'What's up, guys?'

'Mum, I need to walk now. I need the air, OK? Are you all right to drive?'

She nods, strokes my cheek gently and climbs into her car. I watch her leave before walking back as slowly as Frank will allow. Before long, I find myself back at the bench by the beach.

Gay . . . I fill my lungs with salted air. This is the conclusion my parents have come to, that I've hidden my real sexuality. I can't decide whether I'm angry or surprised but have to concede that we don't talk a lot, not really, and all they see in front of them is a man they love; a man who has lived for five decades, a slightly odd but loving man, a man who spends most of his time outside of his professional environment alone – a lonely man. And I feel it like never before – I feel their concern for me. I won't own it, but I feel it. Her words echo over and over: *The only way you'll find it is by letting go of the things that make you* unhappy.

Suddenly I'm aware I'm already at the gates of Oz and I've been here a very long time. I've always known that hanging onto the life I might have had with Alice has stopped me having another just as beautiful one, but I've never been capable of giving her up. I've never been capable of letting her go, not completely. The tiny unicorn horn in my front pocket is rolled between my fingers and thumb as I'm tossed back in time to the parked Mini that last night:

'You are certain, aren't you? You *need to be sure this is what you want. Alice, don't look at me like that . . . It's your life,* your *degree that would have to go on hold.'*

'You said you were happy.' She adjusts the orange cap on her head and stares at me.

'I am! I just want you to be sure . . .'

'It's probably naïve, but I've never been surer of anything. We can do this. Let's do this, Jack? And I think it's a girl.'

'A tiny you.' I pull her close. 'I love you.'

'We love you back,' she says and kisses me.

Very slowly, I exhale as if blowing her out to sea, and instead of stopping myself, needing to hold onto the last vestige of her inside my mind, I free her. I free them both. I free myself from all of the 'what ifs' and the aching loss they left. Before leaving, I place her cap on the slatted bench, its faded peak looking out to sea.

*

Almost an hour later, Dad knocks on the bedroom door and enters without waiting to be asked. Mum's obviously been talking to him. He has papers in one hand and his trumpet in the other and sits beside me on the edge of the bed.

'Gay?' I raise my eyebrows. 'Really?'

'It made some sense . . . I'm an old man, thought that maybe you thought I'd be odd about it if you were. Just for the record, I wouldn't be.'

'Just for the record, I'm a heterosexual almost fifty-year-old man who's trying to live life as if it begins in the middle. So, you were wrong, and Mum was right.'

'Your mother is always right . . .' Reaching to the shelf in the room where my own trumpet sits, he lifts it and hands it to me with one of the sheets of paper. 'I'll do bass?'

The sheet music is that of two trumpet solos for the Beatles track 'All You Need is Love' and my head shakes, tiny little left-to-right movements. 'I'm rusty.'

'Doesn't matter,' he shrugs. 'Let's try.'

The arrangement opens with both of us playing the few chords of 'La Marseillaise' before Dad begins that background bass and I play the lead chords, in my head singing the lyrics. Together, we harmonise our instruments through to the gentle synchronised end. When we finish, I put my arm around him, because during the two and a half minutes it's taken us to play, I've been reminded of the tenet I was raised with. *Love is all we need . . .* The phone buzzes beside me and I'm tempted not to even look, to bask in the moment a little longer, but seeing her name, I pick it up.

Which is when Fate intervenes to fuck with me again, just because it can.

Chapter Thirty-Five

The idea had settled on her after something Jack had said on the phone whilst talking about staying with his folks, 'Parents matter; we don't have them forever.' His innocent words had left Clare unsettled in a way he could never have understood and now it was as if they'd been daubed in neon paint at the front of her brain – a great big graffiti tag – PARENTS MATTER.

Her feelings towards Jean hadn't altered, but a guilty realisation that she too had moved through life lately, not noticing things in Grace's life that she felt she should have, had left her conflicted. Common sense told her that her not knowing that Grace had a boyfriend was vastly different to Jean ignoring Clare's teenage mental health, but a tiny seed of doubt began to make her wonder if things had really been as bad as she remembered. She'd tried to pay no heed to it, but it was there, niggling her, impossible to ignore.

Her mother had moved back into her head.

Clare parked the car in the wide, tree-lined street in Crystal Palace and looked across the road. She exited the car slowly, determined to give herself the chance to change her mind at any moment by turning around. Once, the well-maintained Edwardian house she stood in front of had been their family home, but, after her father's death, her mother had the first floor converted into a flat and had sold it on.

Glancing up, she saw a line of furry toys on the windowsill of what had been her childhood bedroom. Palms sweating, she stood in a narrow neatly trimmed grass verge, carpeted in crispy leaves that had fallen from the London plane tree next to her. This, she recalled, was the exact spot where she'd shared her first kiss with Malcolm Bonner so many years ago. She opened the gate and walked towards the recently painted front door with its brass knocker gleaming in the low-lying autumnal sun. After the rat-tat sound it made, instinctively, she rubbed it clean with the end of her coat sleeve where her fingertips had left a smudge.

When it opened, Clare took a sharp intake of breath. The woman before her was her mother, but not as she remembered. Jean Hutton, ex-dancing guru, ex-mother, ex-someone who would rap her on the spine for not standing straight and weigh her weekly, now stood, slightly stooped, dressed in a green jumper and dark blue jeans. Her hair, which Clare had rarely seen out of a tight dancer's bun, was frost white and fell in soft curls around her shoulders.

'Clare,' she nodded, as if in some way, she'd been expecting her, and Clare, fighting the impulse to flee, rooted herself to the spot. She had come this far. 'Come in, please.' Clare watched her mother move along the floor to the living room at the back of the house. Closing the door softly, she treaded the old tiles she had last stepped on over a decade ago.

She refused a hot or cold drink, didn't engage in small talk and stood at the rear sliding glass doors, trying to name the birds that were gathering around a small bird table outside. Two robins, a goldfinch . . . Gone was the split-level grassy space that was once their garden, now replaced with a completely flat paved area.

'Easier to maintain,' her mother seemed to read her mind. 'I did it a few years ago, still get some wildlife though. Hedgehogs. There's a couple of holes in the lower fence and I leave them there, deliberately. Mostly cats though,' she gave a small laugh. 'Feral cats or foxes, if I'm honest.'

Clare was still, her hands thrust deep into her pockets.

'I'm glad you came.'

Without being asked, she pulled a chair from the dining table and sat, her coat still on, trying to banish memories of the battles she'd had at the same table. 'I'm not totally sure why I did,' she replied honestly.

'You're here because I'm your mother and you're my only child.'

Clare looked at the woman who'd given birth to her. 'I'm here because I know you've been in touch with Grace.' Was that why? She knew whatever she had to say about Grace could have been said in a curt text. She searched her soul for an answer that might appear now that she'd actually *seen* her mother, an answer she'd not been able to come up with during the long drive here.

The older woman's pale, lined face reddened. 'I needed to,' she replied, offering no other explanation.

'Well, your needs have always been more important than mine. Or hers.'

'You didn't come all this way to fight. Surely not?' Her mother took the seat opposite her. Clare didn't reply.

Together they sat in silence, apart from the backdrop of tweeting birds and the humming boiler in the galley kitchen next to the room they were in. Curiosity made her want to stare, to take in the fine lines on her mother's face that had been absent the last time they'd met, but afraid she wouldn't be able to stop, she kept her eyes locked on the sideboard next to them. It was old, carved from ancient burr walnut and had been in her father's family for many years. If she opened the right-hand door, it would have to be wedged shut again, from where the wood had swollen over time. Behind the same door would be a stack of photo albums from the years she had competed. Or maybe not, maybe her mother had no need for such memory-keeping any more.

'So how is rural life treating you?' Jean broke the uncomfortable stillness.

'Good.'

'Talkative as ever, eh?'

Clare bristled.

'It's a joke. You've always been so sensitive!' Her mother stood and smoothed her jeans with both her hands. 'I'm going to make a cup of tea, are you sure . . .'

Clare shook her head, took the time to look around the room while her mother was in the kitchen. She only knew what she was looking for when she realised there was no sign of it. It was as if, at least in that room, early family life had been obliterated from Jean's life. There were no photos of their family, not one – none of the images she knew her father had taken of them on their beach holidays, none of her competing. Clare swallowed. The only framed picture that hung on the wall of what had been the old family dining room was one of a group of women that looked like a bowls team. Her mother smiled from the centre of the group.

When she returned, she arrived with a tray holding a pot of tea, two china mugs and a dainty milk jug. 'In case you change your mind,' she told her as she placed the tray between them.

'You asked me earlier if I came to fight,' Clare looked up at her. 'The answer is no. But I do have some things I need to say since I'm here.'

Jean poured her tea and sat back in the chair, folded her arms.

'Regarding Grace,' Clare began. 'I don't want you to be in touch with her, *particularly* behind my back. Grace is old enough to choose if she wants any contact with you, but if she does, it's something I would supervise, and it would be without my blessing.'

Jean Hutton's eyes narrowed. 'That seems a little . . . controlling, if I may say so.'

'Between Tim and you, I learned from the best. Take it or leave it.'

'You don't trust me with Grace?'

'No. And I've told Grace exactly why.' Clare's eyes flashed, almost daring her to reply.

'What is it you think I'd do?' Her mother raised both palms in the air. 'Actually, what *did* I do? Really, what?'

Noises blared in Clare's head. Snippets of fights in this very room. Screaming matches that ricocheted against the walls of the house. Worse still – echoes of the silent cries that had never left her lips. She avoided the other woman's steely gaze by closing her eyes.

'Clare, look . . .' A quieter tone had been adopted. 'Things were difficult between you and me. You were always—'

'See, Mum, that's where you've gone wrong already.' Clare's eyes shot open, both her hands reaching the sides of her disbelieving head. 'If we're going to have a real conversation about the past, don't start with "*You* were always . . ." How about you begin with "*I'm* sorry, Clare. *I* really wasn't the best mother to you."'

Jean Hutton looked at her as if she'd lost her mind.

'Or maybe, I could even consider this, Mum, how about "Look, I did my best, but it wasn't great."'

'You haven't answered the question.' Her mother sighed. 'I don't know what it is you want from me.'

Clare laughed, stood abruptly, pulling her bag from the floor and slinging it over her shoulder. 'I've just told you.

You need to apologise for *so* much, for us even to have a hint of a chance of—'

'Apologise for *what* exactly?'

'You pushed me far too hard. For far too long. You made dance the only thing I had access to, withheld your love and approval from me for my entire childhood.' Her voice broke. 'The only thing that ever made you smile was a winning trophy. There was no Clare, only Jean's protégée. During my teens, when I was anxiously trying to please you, you kept me from friends.'

'I never did those things.' Jean shook her head vehemently.

'I became the champion you wanted and still it wasn't enough. By the time I met Tim, I was so ready to walk out of this house, just to get away from you.' Clare paused, held back the tears that hovered behind her eyes. 'But I had no ounce of confidence left. Any intuition I should have had, where I should have known I was heading for another disastrous relationship – gone, vanished.'

'And all of this is *my* fault? Tell me, where was the father you glorified during all of this?'

'Don't, OK?' Clare pointed a forefinger. 'Don't dare defend yourself by attacking Dad! I was sick, Mum, and he was the one who loved me and tried to help.'

Jean pursed her lips.

'And *you* raised the subject of Dad. You know what you did when he died . . . or, more importantly, what you didn't do. That was simply unforgiveable.'

This time, her mother turned her head to look out towards her garden.

'Mum,' she waited until Jean faced her. '"Don't ever love someone and never have children. People you love will always disappoint you."'

Jean's head shook.

'"Be a mother or a dancer. You can't have both." All your words. To me.'

'I never said those things. You're mistaken.'

Clare breathed out the pent-up air she'd been holding in her lungs. '*This* was the mistake. I shouldn't have come. I have no idea why I did.'

'Me neither,' her mother retorted. 'Seems to me like you need to move on, Clare. There is nothing wrong with instilling some ambition in a child! That's what I did for you and you still insult me for it. What is it you're doing now? Oh, yes – dancing. You're teaching dancing. *I* gave you that. No one else, certainly not your father. And Tim? I never liked the man, but he gave you a good life and you walked away from that too. What's the new bloke's name, Jack isn't it? I give him six months before you do a runner. That's what *you* do, Clare.'

Colours darted across Clare's peripheral vision as she tried to gather her emotions. So many replies to that statement scurried to her mouth but none left it. Her head nodded slowly before finally saying, 'You never once cared what my life has been like, so you *would* think that.'

The scene was a version of many that had happened before. Jean, with her defiant arms still folded, would never see any wrongdoing. The untouched tea grew cold on the table. As she'd listened to her mother's rant, something inside calmed the adrenalin that had been surging through her since she'd arrived. Jean would never change. Though Clare had always known it, seeing her today made her recognise that she no longer needed her to. It was as if the little girl who'd cried inside for years had no more tears to spend. She felt the shift in her like a physical thing – from the before moment – where some childlike part of her still yearned for a reconciliation with her mother – to the after moment – where Clare emerged, altered. There was nothing for her here but more pain.

'I'm going now, Mum.'

Her mother didn't move. She didn't look at her or plead with her to stay. As Clare opened the door to the hallway, she wondered if that was the last time they'd see one another and quietly accepted that if it was – so be it.

*

Outside the studio, a queue of eight women and two men were chatting noisily.

'Sorry,' Clare waved as she unlocked the door. 'I got caught in traffic!'

She repeated her apology, but no one seemed to hear as they piled in, leaving their coats hanging on the pegs Jack had put up for her, their bags piled underneath.

Without having to be told, they began their warm-up as Clare searched her iPhone for the correct playlist and, clapping her hands, cried, 'Let's begin.'

Soon samba rolls had them all laughing as Clare dismissed all thoughts of her mother, instead concentrating on embracing these special moments in her new life. Craig, the taller of the two young men, had absolutely no rhythm.

'I'm the son of two repressed clerics,' he explained. 'We're not meant to gyrate!'

This group was always fun, she thought, as she instructed him slowly from inside the curve of his arms. The result was hysterical and, despite herself, she joined in the others' laughter.

After demonstrating the move with Shirley, one of the more able girls, Craig watched, his hand spread on his cheek and chin and nodded sagely. 'All right then!' he agreed.

Class over, as always, the small group asked her to the pub in the village and, about to make her usual excuses, she stopped herself. It was Friday night and Tim's turn to be in Wiltshire – he and Grace were already out. The next morning, she had her 9 a.m. Rock 'n' Roll Saturday, but she had time to be sociable with her students for an hour. Not bothering to get changed, she agreed to meet them in the pub and climbed back into her car.

Emma was working the bar and insisted on her not paying for the first round of drinks. Clare blew her a kiss and carried the tray across to the table, before raising her soda and lime in a silent toast. It was a busy night, the dining area of the pub full of people eating out and the bar area, woven with tiny multicoloured lights, had standing room only. Clare found herself next to the window that she had, only months before, looked through and imagined herself in here with a group of friends. So much had happened in that time and here she . . . Clare flinched. There, looking through the glass, was Tim. She held her breath, whipped her head around and watched the door open, saw him stride slowly through, caught the smile in her direction. Beads of sweat appeared on her top lip and forehead. Though she'd known he was seeing Grace tonight, she hadn't expected to see him.

Muttering excuses to Craig, she apologised, saying she had to get home, and made her way to the bar. 'Emma?'

Emma mouthed, 'With you in a tick,' and finished pulling a pint.

'I—'

Tim stood across the wide bar, and Clare struggled to remember how far the law now dictated he had to be away from her. The memory blurred as she turned and stumbled her way through the throng of people.

She had driven up the road and was parked in the driveway before Emma rang. 'Where did you get to?'

Clare tried to steady her shaking hands as she locked the car and opened her front door. The lights were all on. 'Tim's there,' she told Emma.

'Shit.'

'Grace?' Clare called out.

'Upstairs,' she heard her reply as she leaned against the kitchen countertop, just to keep upright.

'Are you all right?' Emma asked down the phone line.

'I'm fine.' She breathed deeply and slowly.

'Tim, I'm assuming he has the same surname as you?'

'Yes, why do you ask?'

'There's a guy in the bar who's staying here tonight, stayed once before a few weeks ago too, goes by the name of Tim Hutton.'

Clare shook her head. She should have known. The pub had three bed-and-breakfast rooms. 'That's my maiden name,' she whispered.

'I'll move him on,' her friend replied crisply.

'Leave it, Emma,' she said. 'He has to stay somewhere tonight.'

'Well, in future, we'll be booked out,' her friend said before adding, 'And I'm going to let him know I know who he is.'

'Please?' Clare could hear a trace of anxiety in her voice. 'Just leave it.'

'OK. Well, I suppose if he's down here drinking, he's not up there annoying you.'

She thanked her, hung up, removed her coat and dropped herself onto the sofa. It had been a strange day.

'Gran emailed – said you went around.'

The move from panic over Tim to worry over what Jean might have said almost left Clare dizzy. 'She did, did she?'

Her daughter was perched against the doorway between the hall and the open-plan space.

'How come you're home so early?' Clare asked, deciding not to mention seeing Tim.

'It was a *weird* evening.' Grace's head shook slowly.

'How so?'

Grace gave a brittle laugh. 'He doesn't like the idea of me having a boyfriend.'

'What can I say? Daddies and their little girls.'

'It's stupid and hypocritical.'

'Hypocritical?'

'It doesn't matter. Gran? You went to see her?' Grace crossed the room and filled the empty glass she held with water from the fridge.

'Yes, I went to see her. I would have told you – just processing it myself.'

Outside, a fox barked.

'And?'

'It was what I knew it would be.' Clare heard the glass being placed on the worktop, felt Grace's arms going around her from behind. 'The words "I'm sorry" aren't in my mother's dictionary.'

'Will you see her again?'

'Not by choice, no.'

'You really can't forgive her, can you?' Grace asked. 'Not that I expect you to, really, Mum. I've been thinking about it and I'm not sure I'll reply to her latest email.'

Clare lay down on the sofa, stretched out. 'Grace, I've told her that you're sixteen and that it's up to you, but if you do have any contact at all with her, I *need* to know about it. And, as I've already said, I'd prefer if you didn't . . .'

Grace seemed thoughtful as she stood, her back to the wood burner. 'If you think about it, Mum, you sort of married your mother. I mean Dad—'

'Don't . . .' It was something Clare had already figured out years ago and didn't need to be reminded of. 'I'm not so sure I like you studying GCSE psychology.'

'I mean, you really did – you left Gran and married Dad,' Grace continued as if she hadn't heard her. 'And, speaking of Dad, he was a pain tonight, I made him bring me back early.'

Clare noticed Grace's tone had changed. 'Why?' she asked.

'Things aren't completely right with us yet and then tonight he tells me that next time we meet, I can go to Croydon and meet his new girlfriend.'

'Oh.'

'Not sure if I want to, really.'

Clare chomped on a fingernail; her mother's snappy 'Don't do that! It's a disgusting habit!' ringing in her ears.

'I don't think I will,' Grace added.

Clare went to the fridge, poured a large glass of water. 'Don't be worrying about me or how I might feel, because, I'm more than OK with your dad moving on,' she told her, taking a sip, before adding a cube of ice. Then she swirled the icy drink with her fingertip and licked it, just because she could.

Chapter Thirty-Six

I hire a car when I land. It's a long drive and, having barely slept on the plane, I'm tired. Flashes of green pasture whizzing by me, the sleet-like rain and the heat cranked up and blasting through the vents all remind me I'm back in England.

Heading west on the M4 towards Wales, I pass the exit for home and soon, just a few hours after landing in Heathrow, I'm driving the coast road into Lynn's village. When she and Antony lived with me, Lynn rented out the two-hundred-year-old cottage but has moved back here since we split over three years ago. I park on a verge, leave the bags in the car and knock on the door. When she opens it, she throws her arms around me. 'Thank you,' she mutters into my neck. 'I'm sorry, but I didn't know what else to do.'

'You did the right thing.' I pull back and look into her eyes. 'Where is he?'

*

The charges are clear. Antony sits on a chair opposite me at the kitchen table, his resistant arms folded, yet somehow looking contrite. He moves a hand, plays with a corner of the oilcloth lying on top, folding a part of the orange and green pattern in on itself. I've been through the lega-lese. I've told him what's going to happen. There will be a magistrates' court hearing. I will represent him. Without promising the outcome, I tell him I'll do everything I can to keep him out of jail. Antony stares at the floor as if he's counting the ancient quarry tiles and then starts to cry. His mother watches from behind, her fist coiled in her mouth. There's nothing else I can say. Jet lag has finally caught up with me – I'm exhausted. 'I need to go and lie down for a bit, do you mind?' I address Lynn.

'Thank you, Jack.' Antony wipes his cheek with the back of his hand.

'You're welcome.' I touch his shoulder as I pass, squeeze it gently. 'I'll do my very best.'

Lynn leads the way up a narrow stairwell from the kitchen – deep steps, covered in a pea-green carpet. She turns right on a skinny landing and leads me to her small bedroom.

I glance at my reflection in a mirror and groan. 'Christ, I look like shit.'

'I like it,' she says, briefly touching my beard. 'Now rest.' She looks down at my hands. 'Luggage, don't you have any bags?'

Heat colours my cheeks. 'I didn't want to assume. I'll stay in a B&B.'

Her pained face stares at mine. 'Please don't. I—'

The ocean billows towards us outside the window as she doesn't finish the sentence. 'I'd forgotten how beautiful this place is,' I reach for and squeeze her hand. Her nineteenth-century fisherman's cottage is carved out of the rocks, over-looking the sea. Next to the window sits a small desk that doubles as a workstation and somewhere to dry her hair and apply her make-up. Through the window, wild waves, so different to the calmer ocean I'd left behind in Key Biscayne, leap and roar. 'It's rough out there today,' I say.

'It's rough in here too,' she attempts a smile. 'Get some sleep.'

'Wake me in an hour,' I tell her, sitting on the far side of her bed. 'I've got calls to make before day end.'

She nods, pulls the door shut, and I'm alone. I lower my jeans and remove the prosthetic, toss off my lone shoe and lie on top of her duvet. Eyes closed, I try to sleep. Rest will energise me, and I'll need energy to fight Antony's battle. Way over the limit, he drove through a garden, crashing into a house, narrowly missing one of the three occupants inside. They'll want to lock him up, which was why Lynn eventually called me. In my tired brain I start to rationalise a defence, almost startled by the fact that I even want to try.

The next thing I hear is Lynn's gentle knock on the door. 'You told me to wake you.' She peers around it before coming in.

I groan, sit up, am aware I'm in my boxers.

'You should have got into the bed,' she scolds. 'You'll catch cold!'

'Lynn.'

She's carrying a small tray.

'I can't stay here. It would be confusing. To Antony. To you. Hell, even me at the moment.'

'Despite his behaviour, my son is a grown up. And I love confusing you.' She hands me a coffee. 'I made it strong. There's a slice of toast there too. I wasn't sure if you were hungry. Is there anything else you need?'

I take her in, wonder if I'd met her now instead of back then whether I'd have found lasting love with her at home, or maybe even here in this tiny seaside cottage. 'No,' I reply. 'This is great. I'll just make some calls and send some emails. Can I work here?'

'If you give me your keys, I'll get Antony to get your bag in.'

'Lynn . . .'

'Jack . . .'

'It's the—'

'I need you here, please, stay here. I've never asked you for anything.'

The noise of the sea pounding the rocks outside makes me speak louder. 'You asked me to stop globetrotting and come home to defend your son.'

'Apart from that. That and this are really the same thing.'

I pull my jeans towards me, reach into the pocket and toss the keys at her. 'Tell him just to bring the rucksack and laptop bag.'

Dressed and perched at the desk, I'm looking at the foaming surf when Antony comes in and hands me the laptop bag, slides the rucksack under the bed. He hovers as if he wants to say something.

'Mum told me,' he says.

'What?'

'She told me about you.'

'All good I hope,' I'm still trying to crack a smile from a guy who sees his future with barred windows.

'I mean about how you lost your lower leg.'

I place my hands on my thighs, look out the window again. 'Right.'

'You shouldn't have come,' he says. 'It'll rake all that shit up.'

The room is small enough for me to reach across and tap him on the arm. 'You said yourself. I have half a leg. There aren't many days where "that shit" isn't raked.'

There's a silence, filled by squawking gulls and the sound of the water rinsing the rocks.

'I told you I'll do my very best and that's what I'm going to do.'

'I can't go to prison,' he says and his voice breaks.

'Are you willing to do rehab?' I've asked the question I wanted to – sooner than I was expecting to, but it's out. Pleading with the magistrate that he has the chance of being a better citizen, attaching drug and alcohol rehab conditions, could help alleviate things.

His eyes flash. 'I'm not a fucking addict.'

I keep my voice even, aware he's now towering above me, remembering the last time he broke into my house. 'You are.

You drink too much, have done for years according to your mother, who adores you. You took charge of a vehicle, which might as well be a loaded gun, when you were drunk. You could have killed someone. You *did* that, Antony.'

His lower lip trembles.

'Do you remember I apologised to you, about when you were younger, about—'

'I remember.' His voice is gruff, yet I can tell he's terrified.

'Back then, when you were dealing, you had problems with drugs. Even after your short stint in the young offenders place, you had problems with drugs.'

He laughs, a cynical sound. 'There's more drugs in there than out here.'

'Possibly. Either way, what I'm trying to say, as delicately as possible, is that you have substance-abuse problems. Your current drug of choice seems to be vodka.'

'Fuck you.'

I stand. 'Fuck you back. If you let me help you, I can help you.'

'Like you did back then?'

'No.'

We're inches apart from one another.

I whisper, 'Let me *help* you.'

His head darts to the side so I don't see more tears form. 'I know I could have hurt someone, or worse . . .'

'Yes.'

'They'll want to make me pay for it.'

'Maybe.' I pause. 'Do you trust me?'

He doesn't reply.

'You have to trust me.'

'I don't trust anyone.'

'Not even your mother.'

'Apart from her.' His reply is fiery and heartfelt.

'She trusts me – does that mean anything?'

Reluctantly, he nods.

From deep inside my front pocket, I remove the unicorn horn that I keep wrapped in tissue. I place it on the desk.

'What's that?'

'Open it.'

Sighing, he picks it up, stares at it for seconds before he recognises it and something like fear fills his eyes.

'I loved her, the girl that gave me this. She died in the accident that gave me this.' I point dramatically to my leg. 'I fucking *hate* drunk drivers.'

'I said, I—'

'But I've been away, trying to see what the big wide world might teach me, and you know one of the things I've been reminded of?'

Silence.

'Most people are good. Are you a good man, Antony?'

'I want to be.'

'Would you go into a programme? I'll personally sponsor you if you promise me you'd go.'

He sits on the edge of his mother's bed. For moments there's nothing to hear but the rhythm of the tide. 'Why would you do that?'

'Because I can. Because when I can, I should.'

He looks directly at me. 'I've only ever wanted to make Mum proud and it's like every single day I fuck up more and more, and that gets less and less likely.'

'I'll try to get you the chance, now scram, I have work to do.' As he's leaving, I open my laptop. 'What's the Wi-Fi code?'

'Badboy1998.' He pauses, utters, 'Thank you', and is gone.

My fingers are tapping it in when I realise what it means. Twenty years old. The law says he's an adult, yet he's a hurting child in an adult's body. Someone whose father left him and his mother and has another family in Dubai. Someone who came to live with his mother's lover, me, and I too was incapable of ever understanding what it meant to be a father. A young man who's done wrong, who knows it and needs help to break the cycle.

*

Everything done, everything covered that I can think of, I press my eyes with the points of my fingertips. The tide has gone out, the day has turned dark.

'I'm going to keep Antony out of prison,' I whisper to the bearded man in the mirror before heading downstairs to the family I almost had once upon a time.

Chapter Thirty-Seven

WhatsApp Reya & Grace

He loves you!

He does not!

He loves you!

He loves me not!

Nah, he luuuurrrves you!

TBH, better he just likes me a lot.

He likes you A LOT!

Good. I like him too 😉

It's all good

Yep ☺

Chapter Thirty-Eight

'I'm self-combusting,' Clare told her GP. 'I'm exhausted, burning from the inside out regularly. Why does no one tell women about this stuff when we're younger? Why do I have to look it all up on Google?'

Her GP, a lovely lady named Ishita Ramdhani, made a harrumph sound. 'Please stay away from Dr Google,' she said. 'We'll take some blood tests and check your hormone levels. I should ask – could you be pregnant?'

Clare sat perfectly still, stared at a medley of photographs on the doctor's shelves. Three children, all boys, all with glorious arctic smiles. Beautiful-looking, all resembling their mother around the eyes.

'Mrs Bryanson?'

'Ms please, or Clare's better,' she responded. 'I could, but I'm not. My periods are all over the place, but I've been feeling so awful I already did two tests over the last eight days, both negative.'

Dr Ramdhani nodded. 'OK, let's do bloods and see what's going on. You don't have a temperature, no fever, so it's most likely perimenopause, as you say – we'll check your hormone levels. Any diarrhoea?'

'No. I just need to sleep.'

Ever since meeting with her mother, Clare hadn't been able to sleep through the night.

'And there's nothing particular worrying you?'

She almost laughed. 'Apart from an abusive ex, a teenage daughter, an estranged mother, a new business and an approaching menopause? No, nothing at all.'

'If you ever need to talk to someone.'

Clare felt her cheeks redden. 'No, no, I'm honestly fine, as long as you can fix my wonky thermostat.'

Dr Ramdhani smiled and handed her some leaflets. 'Have a read of these. HRT isn't for everyone and family history may affect your ability to take it, for instance whether you have any close female relatives who've had breast cancer. It's all for another conversation, but if it's needed and a decision you decide to make, you'll be more informed.' She tilted her head. 'Stay off the internet and if you have any questions, ask me next time.'

Clare shoved the papers into the depths of her large bag.

'I'll put a rush on the bloods. Now . . .' the doctor's hands tapped her keyboard, 'I've slotted you in, come back on Thursday at midday?'

'I've a class at twelve forty-five.'

'We'll have you in and out quickly.'

Clare nodded as she left, as right on cue, a surging heat flooded through her. 'Got it. Thursday, midday. Thanks.'

*

When she got back, Simon Metcalfe, from Onward Motion, was sitting on the low-lying wall just in front of the studio door, dressed in full black-tie, his wife Lisa perched beside him. She could hear their laughter as she walked towards them.

'Good morning!' she said in the shivering voice of a woman who only minutes earlier had been so warm she'd travelled with the windows open in the car, yet, once outside, a November wintry chill hit her instantly. 'Goodness, you dressed up!'

He smiled, tapped both his feet with his stick. 'I did! And I borrowed these from my dad, who was once a dancer and is the same size!'

Clare looked down at the shining black lace-ups, didn't want to tell him that they, being someone else's dance shoes, would probably be the most uncomfortable thing in the world. 'Great!' she said, opening up, as Simon followed, his arm linked through Lisa's. 'You all set?' she asked as she dropped her bag and turned up the heating controls.

Lisa led Simon to a line of three chairs, guided him into one and sat next to him. She was, Clare thought, a quiet woman who smiled a lot, but she had that look – a look of love for her man that despite his being blind since the age of six made him a lucky man. Simon Metcalfe was loved.

'I, as you can see from my sartorial enthusiasm,' Simon waved a hand the length of his body, highlighting his efforts, 'am raring to go.'

'If I'd known, I'd have worn a dress,' Clare laughed as she scrolled her phone to the track that they'd both chosen to dance to: Tchaikovsky's 'Swan Lake Waltz'.

Before pressing play, she walked over to them, took the spare chair and pulled it in front of them so that she sat opposite.

'We've got the spacing of the room perfect,' Simon spoke first. 'I've learned every angle, every metre. It's all up here.' He tapped his forehead with his forefinger.

'You have?' Clare withheld the word 'how?' yet he seemed to sense it anyway.

'Lisa measured the room last time, then she measured out the same space in our garden and I memorised the steps in a grid,' he announced proudly. 'We've been practising.'

When he'd first mooted the idea as a potential appeal for Onward Motion, Clare wasn't sure. She'd been spending a bit of time at the charity, in discussions with Pam on how to structure her ongoing help, and had met him coming towards her in the corridor, white stick in hand. She'd stopped in surprise, unaware until that moment that Mr Metcalfe, the centre's counsellor, was blind.

'It's Clare, isn't it?' he'd asked. She'd wondered immediately how he'd known, but spending time with him, realising how, over years, he'd learned to read the signals from his other senses, she suspected it had something to do with either the scent she wore or the sound of her footfall.

He'd asked her into his office and there raised the idea of what he hoped would be a major and original fundraiser for the centre. She'd teach him to dance and his wife would film it, posting each lesson daily on YouTube over a few weeks. Lisa, who worked in PR, would ensure both local and national press coverage, hopefully generating some buzz, and the final dance film would be filmed in live time and have a click-link to donate to the centre. The plan was more to increase awareness of Onward Motion and its work, rather than raise actual money, though the hope was that donations would happen too.

Pam, the centre manager, had loved the idea. Both Simon and Lisa loved and embraced the idea. Even Grace, who'd asked if she and Erik could do the film editing for the internet posts as part of a continued media project for school, seemed excited. Yet, Clare was, at first, nervous. Was it something she could do? Her wanting to help at the centre, to share dance with those who were willing and able to try was one thing – but posting it all over the internet was something else. She could almost hear Tim's mocking voice. '*Who* do you think *you* are . . . ?'

'You ready to start?' she asked.

Simon took a deep breath, turned to Lisa and kissed her cheek. 'Lead the way, ma'am,' he said, offering Clare his hand.

It had been agreed between them both that Clare would lead, but he was, in fact, a natural dancer. Though this and the last few lessons were spent counting the steps aloud, his ballroom hold was strong, and she smiled as they moved around the floor, winked at Lisa as they passed.

'You *have* been practising,' Clare grinned. 'Are you happy to try a little out of hold. I can see you in the mirror but want to stand back to check the rise and fall. I'll be right beside you, mirroring it all. You know the room now. Trust yourself. Trust me.'

'I do.'

And with that, he took off, and Clare moved alongside him, her hands poised as if in prayer, her fingertips touching the end of her nose, ready to be there if he stumbled. But if she hadn't known already, she'd never have suspected his challenges, such was his confidence.

'All bravado,' he told her later when she'd commended him. 'I'm terrified of getting it wrong – making a fool of myself, not to mention a fool of you.'

Clare instinctively took his hand. 'You're not going to do either. We've got this.'

'And we don't have to do the final scene live,' Lisa added. 'We can—'

'We said live and we're doing it live,' Simon interrupted. 'As long as you know I won't be letting go.' His free hand covered hers.

'Good,' she laughed.

'Tell Grace I'll email the footage later,' Lisa said. 'It'll be this evening.'

Clare said goodbye, watched them leave, then sat on the nearest chair. Just like the one she'd sat on in the waiting room of the doctors earlier, she shifted uncomfortably. Having recently lost weight, she could feel her bones on the seat. Unlike the earlier stressful years of competition, where she had both starved herself and binge-ate, nowadays she was naturally slim and found it hard to put weight on. She caught her reflection in the wall mirror and stood, placing a padded coat around her shoulders and head. It was raining outside, and running across the pebbled ground towards the Barn, she made up her mind that, as soon as she was safely inside, toasting the cheesiest toastiest cheese sandwich was the first thing she'd do.

*

Clare was surfing on Tim's old work iPad, which had become Grace's iPad, which having managed to get Grace a smartphone contract for her birthday now felt more like Clare's iPad. She was just about to google 'Perimenopausal symptoms' again before she stopped herself. At forty-two, there was something so unsettling about her eggs possibly being redundant. That seemed like a slur on her womanhood she wasn't even close to ready for. She tried to forget, busied herself with reinstalling WhatsApp on the iPad instead.

After the app reloaded, it pinged, and a photo message arrived on screen. The image lasted a mere three seconds, before it disappeared.

Three seconds. Three seconds for her stomach to plummet and settle in the depths of her body. Three seconds, followed by another ten where she realised that Grace's WhatsApp had reinstalled on the device, and where she told herself, firmly, not to move. DO NOT, she told herself, have this conversation with her until you've had time to digest the facts.

Her eyes closed and the image was still there. Erik's long arm, taking the selfie. His other arm around Grace's shoulder – her naked shoulder. A duvet pulled up to cover herself, although not quite succeeding, the nipple on her left breast just peeking out at the side. Grace's duvet. Grace's bedroom, with the full-length window in the background, with the unmistakeable pink mosquito net around her bed. Grace's naked body. It was almost certainly Erik's naked body lurking under the bedclothes too. Here in this house. A Grace and Erik post-sex selfie.

Without knowing it was even close, Clare began to cry. Raising her legs up, she sat on the sofa, her knees pulled tight, hugging herself. Grace and Erik were having sex and she knew nothing about it. The child whom she'd always seen as the person she loved most in the world, and who'd loved her back the same way, hadn't talked to her about it.

Tears lined her cheeks, but, before she drove herself crazy, whipping herself for some alleged failure on her part as a mother, she wiped them away, annoyed at herself. *Why are you crying?* The answer, she realised quickly, had little to do with the fact that Grace hadn't shared it or that she hadn't known. Teenagers *should* have some secrets from their parents, she reasoned. It was more that, under these circumstances, a woman discovering the same thing might call a best friend, or her mother, or have a discussion about it with her husband, partner, ideally the child's father. She was crying because her mother wasn't an option. Her ex-husband wasn't an option and he'd seen off any friends she used to have, and she had allowed that to happen. Her newest and only friend, Emma, as Erik's mother, was not an option.

She was alone and reality hit. Even though she was determined to be independent, the truth of that meant dealing with everything alone. On her own. Single-handedly. Without help. Sometimes, despite herself, that fact echoed in her head.

Grace, before Clare knew it, had appeared at the doorway.

'Mum? You all right?'

'Yes, yes.' She lowered her legs, patted the chair next to her. Almost obediently, her daughter sat down.

'Have you been crying?'

Clare looked at her, committing her to memory. Her hair had grown so much since they'd arrived: long and blonde, it looked luscious and vibrant. 'Your hair looks lovely. Did you blow dry it?'

'Yes. What's wrong, Mum, is it Dad?'

Clare shook her head. 'No, just hormones.' She swallowed, the truth looming large, that the young woman before her had always had a wisdom beyond her years, maybe because she'd had to, or maybe because wisdom was just threaded in her DNA somehow. It followed that she might perhaps have sex at an age that Clare felt was too young. 'You come down for toast?' she asked her.

Grace seemed to accept her hormonal excuse. 'Have you heard anything from Jack?' she asked, already moving on.

Clare shook her head.

'He's normally good on Insta, but there's been nothing up for ages.' Grace shrugged and stood up and, as she did, Clare grabbed her hand.

'Put two slices on for me. And Gracie?'

'Yup?'

Thoughts swirled. Do I? Don't I? Should I? 'I know you and Erik are having sex.'

'Jeez . . .' Grace yanked her hand away.

'Don't,' Clare pleaded. 'All I have to say is, please be safe. First love is a beautiful thing, as long as it doesn't mean you're tied down to a child neither of you planned.'

'Mum.'

'Look at me, Grace.'

Grace was blushing furiously, shaking her head, but caught her mother's eyes.

'I love you. Erik is a great young man. I'm not that old that I don't remember what it's like to fall in love for the first time.' She attempted a smile. 'All I'm asking is that you be careful, always.'

'I'm not stupid, Mum.'

Clare pulled her daughter into a hug and Grace didn't resist. She stroked the hair that she'd once tamed into ponytails, French-plaited for school, lamented the loss of those days. 'I know you're not, far from it, but if anything makes us do stupid things, it's love.'

Chapter Thirty-Nine

'I've been so content by the sea lately that I'm questioning why I live in rural Wiltshire.' Antony and I are walking side by side along the strand. The tide is way out. Days ago, I explained sand's not my favourite surface, especially damp sand complete with uneven wavy imprints of the lapping tide. Since then we've stuck to the path. He has his head bent low, not just against the cold, but I've realised it's the stance of a gangly young man. His hands are set deep in his low-slung trouser pockets. Two friends he hangs around with seem to dress and slope along in exactly the same manner. I feel quite ancient next to them.

'Move down here, back with Mum.'

My eyebrows arch. I'd told Lynn that this would be confusing. 'Your mum and I aren't . . .'

He sets his mouth in a straight line, and somehow I feel like I've let him down again.

'It's complicated,' I tell him.

'Isn't everything?'

There's a trace of resignation in his tone, as if all older adults make things much more complicated than they need be. He's probably not wrong.

'The sea,' I nod my head in its direction. 'It goes in and out, every day. A very simple, non-complicated existence.'

'Until underground fault lines move and there's a tidal wave.'

'You make a good point, young Luke.' This makes him laugh.

'You like *Star Wars*?' he asks.

'Love it.'

'I'll give you a game when we get back.'

'There's a game?'

'There's always a game.'

I agree to play, providing he agrees to a good old-fashioned board game later. Anything to keep him busy. Anything to keep his and my mind off court tomorrow.

'What was she like, your friend?'

I have to backtrack, think for a second, unsure what he means. Yes, he means Alice.

'The girl you loved,' he says, just in case I was in any doubt.

He's curious. I don't think he realises there's accusation in his voice, the unspoken words – the girl who stopped you loving my mother the way she deserves to be loved.

'It was all a long time ago.' I raise my face to the small spits of rain that have just started. 'It really was.'

'You don't remember her?'

I remember her teal blue eyes, the way the left one had a tiny row of laughter lines edging it, yet the right one didn't. I remember her smile, the one she hated because of a gap between her front teeth, which I adored. I remember her scent, a musky one from the men's aftershave she insisted on wearing. Somehow, on her skin, it smelled right. I remember the curve of her back, the way she'd giggle if I touched her just under her arms. 'I remember her,' I tell Antony. 'I do. But it *was* all a long time ago.'

'You've been wastin' your life, man.' Antony has picked up a stick and is trailing it along behind him like a child. He grins at my stretched eyebrows. 'I know, I know, I'm one to talk.'

'Hopefully, you'll get the chance to change.' I hope to Christ we get a good result tomorrow and I hope to Christ he recognises it as the good fortune it would be.

'I do hate what I did,' he mutters. We're almost at the house and my feet just stop walking. Antony leans on a wall and says what I think he's been building up to. 'And for ages I hated you, but I should never have put you in that situation. You apologised for what you did and I'm sorry too.'

After spending a lot of time together lately, I have this overwhelming feeling that right now, in this moment, I have to say the right thing. Instinct takes me back to my court days, where though everything that's said is carefully measured, it appears so instantly.

I place my hands on his shoulders and look him squarely in the eye. 'I think you're a young man with huge potential. I think you lost your way and I think people, probably your dad and probably me, we let you down. I think you made mistakes and the thing when we make mistakes, especially big ones, is that they have to count.

That's not just a hackneyed phrase – we have to learn from them. I think you will, you have already, and I'm seriously looking forward to seeing the young man you'll be in five years.'

His Adam's apple rises and falls and his gaze lowers. 'I think I need to never forget how close I came to really fucking things up.'

My embrace is instinctive, and I whisper to the woollen beanie that covers his ears, 'That too, mate. That too . . .'

When we part, eyes still down, he speaks again. 'If the worst happens, you know, if it doesn't work out—'

I try not to interrupt because he's right to be thinking about the possibility.

'Even though you're not "with" Mum, you'll look after her, won't you?'

'Your mum's a strong lady, but yes, of course.'

'And you really think that . . . that I'll . . . that we'll,' he corrects himself, 'that we'll be OK.'

'I do.'

He sighs with relief. 'My dad hasn't called me yet,' he says. 'He definitely knows, but no call.'

'He's probably waiting to see what happens, so he knows what to say.'

'He could call and say, "Good luck." He could call and say, "You're a fucking idiot and deserve locking up." He could call.'

'Parents. Sometimes they screw you up.'

'He's an asshole. And look, I'm grateful you're here now, but you didn't do the daddy thing well either.'

The words sting. 'I know.' Outside the front door, I remove a glove and root in my pocket for the key Lynn had given me. 'I didn't have it in me back then.'

'What's changed now?'

The question makes me really understand that something has. Even with my jaunt around the world interrupted, something *has* already changed in me and he can see it. The idea that 'seeing the wider world' might not actually mean moving too far away from Wiltshire has been on my mind. 'Maybe you can tell me?' I'm genuinely interested in his reply.

'You listen,' he says, but I'm not too impressed, aware that, in work anyway, I've always had to be, and have been, a good listener. 'But as well,' he shrugs his puffed coat from his skinny frame and hangs it on the back of the door I've opened, 'I think you're more aware of Mum and me as a unit. What she does affects me, and the other way around. Before – you never thought of her. You just wanted me punished.'

I wince again. Truth hurts.

Antony is halfway up the stairs. 'I'll call you when I have the PlayStation set up,' he yells back.

It's all I can do to take off my own outer clothes and stare in his wake. When I hear him call my name, I trudge after him, praying that destroying the Death Star will be easier than defending him in court tomorrow.

*

Later, before Lynn gets back from work, I tell Antony I'll be back by nine and leave a note for his mother. Under cover of darkness, I find myself sneaking into my own home to retrieve my dry-cleaned gown. The house is freezing, and I shiver, check the thermostat in the hallway. It's set to come on, just as I'd shown Clare to do, for a couple of hours in the morning and the evening. My hand on the icy radiator tells me the timer might be a tad off.

Something else I hadn't been expecting surges through me – a longing for familiarity, for my things around me: for the ticking of my dad's old grandfather clock, for the rug from Afghanistan that sits in the hallway, the one that makes me look down every time I pass it to avoid the curling edge, for the way the moonlight shines through the stained glass either side of the front door, throwing dancing rays of colour across the wall opposite.

Focus, I tell myself as I risk turning a light on in the bedroom to help me find what I need quickly. Placing the court-clothes on a chair in the hallway, I pass through the snug towards the rear door, scrabble around on the bookshelf next to it to find the key. I can't, simply cannot, leave without seeing Walnut and Pecan. Carefully, with the help of the light on my phone, I tread the path towards the pen, grateful for the fact that the laurels have grown just a bit.

They begin to squeal as soon as they hear my approach. 'Shh,' I tell them. 'Hello!' With my hands, I nuzzle their snouts and again feel a pang of something unpredicted.

There is food and water in their troughs and plenty of hay under the corrugated roof end of the pen. 'Looks like Grace has been looking after you guys,' I whisper as I glance towards the Barn. It's in darkness, as if they're out, but just in case, and not wanting them to hear the squealing racket, I blow Walnut and Pecan a kiss and leave.

*

We're playing Monopoly from an old version that Lynn had tucked into the back of the dresser in the living room. None of us have played it for years and Antony is the very loud banker because Lynn, having mortgaged us all to the hilt within half an hour, is winning. We've been advancing to Go, moving back three spaces, taking bank dividends and trips to various stations. It's only when Antony picks up one of the fraying, golden-coloured Chance cards and reads aloud, 'Go to jail. Do not pass Go. Do not collect £200,' that there's a collective holding of breath. I'm half expecting him to flip the board over with the back of his hand and yell 'stupid game', like he would have done when we lived together years ago.

'Anyone mind if I take another?' He looks from me to his mum, then places the card underneath the pile before picking the next one. 'Get out of jail free,' he says, staring at it. 'Better. Think I'll hold onto this one.'

'Keep it with you tomorrow,' Lynn suggests. 'For good luck.'

'If we keep you from jail, it won't be free.' I say it because, like earlier, it feels right, and it needs to be said.

'I'll keep it anyway,' he shrugs. 'I know,' he holds a placating hand up to me as he pockets the card, 'I know even with the best outcome, work only begins tomorrow.' He looks at us, one to the other. 'And just so *you* know, I haven't had a drink in a week, nor have I taken any illegal substances since you arrived.' His eyes stay on me.

Nothing is said. Lynn reaches across and squeezes his arm, so I take my go, after which I'm cleaned out.

'Your mother has plundered my reserves. Time for bed.' I stretch and yawn. 'Big day tomorrow.' I pat him on the back as I pass and tell Lynn I'll head on up.

Twenty minutes later, we're both lying in bed and I'm expecting more questions about the defence and how things will unfold the next day. She has needed constant reassurance, so I'm surprised when what she does say is, 'Did you see her when you went back?' Lynn has snuggled up to me and asks the question from the crook of my arm. I know exactly who she means but the enquiry still confuses me. 'I met her, you know,' she says. 'Just after you left, I was working in Oxford and called by without realising you'd already gone.'

'Oh?' A monosyllable seems appropriate.

'We had coffee in the Barn. It looks amazing.' Lynn has placed a hand on my chest. We do this. We cuddle at night, nothing more. She's insisted I stay in the house and so we had a discussion – nothing happens, just two friends helping each other out. It's not always been easy because there's something so achingly familiar about her and tonight I already know I'm pining for the well-known.

'So, did you see her?' she asks again.

'No, the place was in darkness. I just slipped in and out.' All true. I just leave out the bit that I hadn't wanted to see her because I hadn't wanted the distraction. And when Lynn kisses me, as she has done every night, I stop things going any further, as I have done every night, but tonight it's difficult and I tell her so.

'Why more so tonight?' she whispers.

'I want to make love to you right now because we know each other so well and it would feel good. I don't want to do it because if I woke up tomorrow and regretted it, it might screw with my head. Tomorrow I need a clear head.'

She turns from me and, in the small bed, in her small bedroom, her back is edged up against my right side. Her cold feet rest on my one foot and I feel her hand slide into mine. 'I know you need a clear head, but, just so you know, you wouldn't have regretted it.'

Her hand tightens on mine and I close my eyes and try to stop the court notes I've read and reread going over and over in my head. Everything's ready. Apart from the prepared case I can bring to the party, tomorrow, I accept, is in the lap of the Gods of Chance.

Chapter Forty

When Tim emailed with the headline 'URGENT', Clare didn't open it for hours. Tim's understanding of the word might mean anything from him running out of milk to his fighting the legal status she'd placed on him, to some whinge about the current government that he felt he had to share. Her chest felt tight as she went about her day, until finally she thought knowing what was in it was better than imagining what might be. She opened it, resenting the fact that even without seeing him, some moments proved he still had some hold on her.

In bold capitals he told her that he needed to see her. He needed to discuss Grace and it had to be done face to face. Though he understood that the terms of the injunction forbade it, he was asking that she meet him just once. It was about their role as parents and something that required more than a phone call.

Though she was nervous and knew she shouldn't meet him, concern over Grace forced the issue. Clare chose a busy pub near Paddington. It would be busy, full of people, so less likely for him to be on anything other than his best behaviour. Pulling open the pub door, she could see he was already there – sitting in an otherwise empty booth. Clare looked around for another option. It was too close. His sitting across a booth meant they might touch; meant he could reach across and touch her or feel her leg with his. The thought made her shiver.

'This is a little too cosy,' she said on her approach, stopping four feet away.

'You're late and we're lucky to get a seat at all.' His head now raised from his phone, he looked around the pub at the crowds.

Clare wiped beads of sweat that had appeared on her top lip as soon as she saw him.

Tim held his hands up. 'Fifteen minutes, Clare, OK?'

She lowered herself onto the edge of the seat opposite him, double checked that the nearest exit was the one she'd just walked through.

'Drink?' he asked, a pint of lager-shandy in his hand.

'Coffee,' she replied. 'Black and strong.'

Tim slid along his seat and headed to the bar, grazing her shoulder ever so slightly as he passed.

Her senses were heightened, as if something bad was about to happen. Jack's words he'd said to her while drafting the injunction echoed in her mind. "If you do this, you have to stick to it. No meeting him. No going off-piste."

After placing a cup of coffee in front of her, Tim sat down again. 'Grace tells me you met with Jean.'

'I met with her.'

'She still hate me?'

Clare bristled. Ten seconds in and it was all about him already. 'I have no idea. You wanted to talk about Grace. I'm here. Talk.'

Tim seemed to shift in his chair as if trying to make himself comfortable for the afternoon. 'I do. Put simply, she's changed. I get that she's got a new life. Not one I wanted her to have, mind,' he added with a glare. 'But she's . . . she's distant even when she's with me. I think it's this bloke she's hanging out with. Says he's her boyfriend. I mean, she's too young to have a proper boyfriend, isn't she? I don't trust him.'

'This is your "Urgent" need to see me?'

She made to stand up and he reached for her arm, instantly raising both his hands. 'Sorry, sorry. I didn't mean that, and this *is* urgent, OK?'

'Grace may have changed since you put me in hospital, Tim. I doubt it's anything to do with Erik.'

Tim made a face. 'She's far too young to be—'

'To be what, Tim?' Clare could hear the weary tone she'd normally try to hide in conversation with her ex. She wondered briefly what sort of mood Tim was in today. She could tell him about Erik, and he might erupt, which would have her running from the premises, or he might just sit and discuss it properly with her, but she doubted that. 'They *are* seeing one another.' She chose her words carefully, lifting a menu card from the table to fan herself.

'I'm OK with that,' he shrugged. 'She's growing up. But there's still something I can't put my finger on. Look, I'm just going to spit this out. They're not having sex, are they? No way is she mature enough for all that.'

Clare fought the urge to laugh. Her abusive, self-centred and sometimes childish husband accusing their very advanced daughter of being too immature for a relationship. It was actually laughable. Yet she doubted if she, for the first time, could lie to him. It struck her as odd in that very moment, for all the lies he had ever told her, that she had never lied to him, not once. She was due one itsy-bitsy lie, surely. 'No,' she said, 'I think I'd know.'

I do know. But I don't need your drama.

'But would you? Would you even know, Clare? I mean you're busy with your new life. You don't even . . .' He slumped back into the chair, raised his hands, left whatever accusation he'd had in the ether between them.

'I have my finger on the Grace pulse, thank you very much, and she's absolutely fine.' Clare spoke through gritted teeth. 'A happy, well-adapted teenager who's had a lot of change in her life. Perhaps it's your new girlfriend she's not keen on. Apart from her witnessing your handiwork on my face, maybe that's the reason she's distant.'

She matched his stare, willed him to look away first. When he did, she counted it as a mini victory. Clare sipped her coffee.

Moments later, he leaned forward again, and she automatically moved back.

'Louise is sweet. My girlfriend. You'd like her,' he said.

'Well, thankfully, I won't ever have to meet her,' she responded, knowing the only reason he hadn't taken her on was the fact they were in public together.

'How's your fancy man?'

Clare rolled her eyes. 'My *landlord* is away.'

'Left you all alone after all. I told you I never liked that idea either.'

'Tough shit. My decision. And we're not all alone,' Clare lied more easily the second time. 'We have a panic button straight to the police. Jack insisted before he left.' He had insisted on no such thing, but Clare didn't want to look out her window one night and see Tim lurking in the laurels now that she'd gone off-piste once, despite Jack's advice.

'Saint bloody Jack.'

'Don't, Tim, OK?'

'You should know something about Saint Jack.'

Clare shot him a warning look. 'We're here to talk about Grace, Tim.'

'And you've assured me there's nothing wrong, so I believe you.'

'Right,' she set her coffee cup down. 'I'll be off then.' She stood up, removed her gloves from her pocket.

'Sit down.'

'No,' she drew a long breath. 'I don't do what you tell me to do any more, Tim.'

'Sit down. I want to tell you something about Saint Jack. Trust me, you'll want to hear it.'

Her eyes closed a brief second and she lowered herself once more to the edge of the seat.

'Your Saint Jack,' he continued, 'and look, I know I don't come out of this stinking of rose petals either, but, hey . . . Your Saint Jack, he's more like me than you care to know.'

Clare laughed, tilted her head in an 'as if' expression of disbelief.

'I went to see him in his office, up there in Lincoln's Inn. Very fancy.'

Clare felt the creases on her forehead stack on top of one another. She glared at her ex-husband. 'So?'

'He's a liar is Saint Jack. Oh, yes, just to rile me, tried to bait me, telling me that Grace had started this legal shit. I didn't react, *I* know Grace would never do that, but you know what, and this is interesting, *he* was the one who wanted to thump me. I could see it in his eyes.'

Her head felt light. A sudden giddiness stilled her as she tried to take apart what had just been said. *Jack. Violent? No.*

She looked away, studied a small group of people at the bar. A woman sat on a barstool, one that had stuffing oozing out the side of the seating.

Jack had told Tim about Grace's involvement when she'd explicitly asked him not to.

The woman at the bar had one of her legs cocked provocatively around the man who stood nearest her. Her face was turned in the opposite direction and she seemed to be flirting with another man to her right. People, thought Clare, people are strange.

'Not so brilliant now, is he?' He stood and put his jacket on, wrapped a scarf around his neck. 'See, Clare, the thing with you is that you were so anxious to get away from me that you didn't do your due diligence. Did you?'

'If anyone's lying, it's you.' Clare froze as Tim dropped down and kissed her ear.

'You know, you *know* I'm telling the truth.'

She shuddered.

'See you around, lovely Clare,' he said and walked away.

It was a long time before her limbs could carry her to the train station. During the journey, she found she couldn't wait. When the doctor's office called to see where she was, Clare listened to the message and ignored it. Instead, she dialled Jack.

'Hey, look, sorry, Clare, I really can't talk right now, could I call you back in a couple of hours?'

She could hear the sounds of lots of people milling around in the background and checked her watch, for the first time questioning what time it was on the west coast of America. 'This won't take long. I have something to ask you and I want you to be honest.'

'What's up?'

Clare tried to hide her irritation that he was obviously hoping she would indeed be quick. 'Did you tell Tim about Grace's text, about *her* wanting the injunction for me? When I asked for your help, you promised me her part in it wouldn't have to be mentioned, that she wouldn't have to be involved. And were you a hair's breadth away from hitting him, like he claims?'

Silence. Clare chomped on her thumbnail.

'I'm going to need to call you back.' A charged silence, as if he'd moved away from the crowd, waited to be filled. 'I can explain.'

'No, no you can't,' she replied. 'We have an arrangement, which you know I need and I'm grateful for, but this changes things. You crossed a line, Jack, one a friend wouldn't cross. The very last thing I need in my life is someone I can't totally trust.'

Clare hung up the phone. Later, on the train home, she listened to his message asking her for the chance to tell her exactly what had happened. All the way home, Clare wondered what it was exactly that drew her to people who let her down. Her mother, to be fair, she had no choice in – the luck of the draw. Her husband she *had* chosen. And Jack – though she would always be thankful for what he had done for Grace and her, it was time to give him that wide berth that she'd chosen not to until now. It was time to take control of her life properly.

At home, she sat through Grace and her afternoon toast snack, letting her phone ring out. By nightfall, Clare felt an unknown rage build in the pit of her stomach, felt it nudge the roots of her hair, like an electric current. Numb from her still stance, suddenly she stood and, grabbing her coat from a nearby dining chair, she went to the back door and switched on the outside light, picking up the bucket of dry pig feed on her way out. From a distance she could hear the squeals – Grace hadn't fed them when she came in. Clare simmered as she walked. At the pen, she filled the trough. Then she looked up at the sky, before screaming her bubbling fury into cupped hands.

How dare Tim? She pressed her temples with the heels of her hands, freezing fingers clutching her hair. During their marriage, Tim had thought he'd known best, yet, seeing things now, she knew he had managed her life. He had placed her exactly where he wanted, distancing her from friends and even loving the fact she and her mother were estranged. And now he'd succeeded in alienating her from Jack too.

She glanced up at his cottage in complete darkness. And Jack had managed her, manipulated her, too. How dare *he*?

She picked up the pail and, as the rain started to fall, raised her face upwards. From the corner of her eye, she noticed Grace staring out her bedroom window at her, no doubt lining her own excuses up. Clare swore under her breath. She was tired of people doing their own thing. She was tired of people deciding they knew what was best for her.

No more.

In the kitchen she kicked off her shoes and, walking across the heated floor, hung her coat up on a hook near the end of the stairs. From somewhere above her she heard, 'I'm sorry, Mum. I would have done it later.'

Clare ignored her too.

*

After working up a dance-induced sweat, Clare had just stopped practising the new Latin routine and was drying herself with a towel when Grace appeared at the doorway of the studio.

'You calmed down yet?' she asked.

'You should have done the pigs.'

'When have I ever not done them?'

Clare could think of a couple of occasions but was in no mood to argue.

'I came out to show you this and to remind you I need a lift to hockey?' Grace walked the length of the studio to her side, her sports bag slung high on her shoulder. 'Erik and I were working on this earlier. Lisa's already seen it.' She side-eyed her mother. 'I decided to give you some time to cool off, so sent it to her first. Anyway, she's approved it – just you to see it now before they go online.'

Grace pressed play on her phone and Clare watched and listened to an edited version of Simon's lessons to date. Grace and Erik had reduced each ninety-minute-long session to just under three minutes and had captured their essence perfectly. There was instruction, there was fun, and there, in between the lines, somehow, was Simon's disability, without it looming large or detracting from his enthusiasm or ability to learn.

'You like it?' Grace asked. 'Lisa wants the first one online immediately, the next ones staggered before the big finale.'

'I love it,' Clare wiped her eyes with the towel. 'Thank you and I'm sorry for earlier. I had a tough day.'

Her daughter shrugged. 'Hockey – I brought your car keys. Do you have the house ones?'

'Yes, sorry. I forgot you had practice tonight.'

During the journey, Grace chatted, and Clare glanced across at her only child, tapped her three times on her leg.

Gratitude. She told herself. Be grateful for this wonderful human being who you can always depend on. The rest will come.

Chapter Forty-One

----Original Message-----
From: GraceBryanson29@gmail.com
Sent: 23rd November 2018 21:02
To: BadBarrister@TateTravels.com
Subject: Attached photo of your babies

Hi!

How's New Orleans? I wish I was in New Orleans. I wish I didn't have to go to school! I wish it was Christmas already!

I've been waiting to see loads of photos on your Insta! Where are they? I've put the attached photos of W & P up there too.

Thought you might like to see the link for Mum's first lessons with Simon (Erik and I edited them). They've just gone live!

Love Grace x

Chairperson of DIM

Chapter Forty-Two

It's going well. It does look hopeful. Antony's situation, that is . . .

I, on the other hand, have had to pull on every resource I possess. Clare's not to know how badly timed this is – it's not her fault – but the last thing I need now, when I'm trying to do the right thing by someone I once did wrong by, is to hear how I've apparently done the wrong thing elsewhere. She thinks I crossed a line and I find myself really annoyed. Her phone is turned off and she isn't interested in my explaining what happened with her bastard of an ex-husband. Yes, I bloody wanted to hit him, but I *didn't*. Yes, I goaded him with the truth about Grace and I absolutely shouldn't have, but . . . Who the hell does she think she is? She should at least let me tell her what happened before she bloody well ghosts me. Or whatever it's called when I'm trying to explain and she won't even hear me out. I'm also ignoring the persistent, banging question that asks what the hell she was doing with Tim anyway.

Lynn can tell something's happened, has rested her hand on my arm and is asking me if I'm all right. My nod is a little curt, so I follow it up with a kiss on the cheek. 'Nothing to do with the case,' I reassure her, stroking my newly clean-shaven chin. 'Right.' I straighten out my gown and wink at her and Antony. 'See you on the other side.'

*

Before either of them can tell exactly what's happening, it's all over. He has lost his licence for five years and has a suspended two-year sentence, providing he attends rehab and completes community service. I'd warned him before-hand what this would mean – we both agreed – but Lynn is unprepared for the car I'd organised whisking him away straight after the verdict and a long hug. 'I thought . . .' she keeps repeating without more words attached.

Later that evening we're eating a takeaway at her tiny kitchen table when she asks me, 'Will you go back to your travels?'

'I'm not sure,' I answer as honestly as possible.

'Thank you for what you did. I was scared to call you – after what you went through, after—'

'It's what I do. Though I'm not one hundred per cent sure I'll always do it.'

'You'll go back to the law.' Her smile is an attempt to reassure *me*. 'It's in your make-up. You've always wanted to right wrongs.'

'I have?'

'You have.' She pours the end of a bottle of white wine into both of our glasses.

'I want to finish the travels,' I begin, 'finish the journey, but something's changed. It's like I've had to look at everything that's gone before in order to reimagine what comes next, if that makes sense. According to Ollie, I've been too black or white and have no grey.'

Lynn laughs. 'I love Ollie,' she says. 'He's not *quite* right though.'

My eyes question her.

'It's your personal life where you struggle most,' she announces. 'Maybe it's something to do with being an only child, because I see the same in Antony. You both battle with the grey areas of your emotional lives.'

I sip the wine. 'Did I let you down too? Back then? I mean, I know we were finished after what happened over Antony, but . . .' I look at her. 'Before that . . . ?'

'You were just,' she shrugs, 'absent. Emotionally. I tried, but you were wedged in the past.'

I drain the glass. 'I was,' I admit. 'But I let her go. In Florida, I stood on another beach and I let her go.'

Saying it out loud is not easy and she says nothing, though 'About time' is probably stuck in her throat.

Lynn stands and clears the plates and together we move around the small space in an already familiar dance. She loads the two-person dishwasher. I place the takeaway cartons and bottle in the recycling and wipe down the table.

'Heartbreak, real cracked-heart heartbreak,' she says without looking up. 'You're never really whole after it.' She glances at my leg then and looks at me before wrapping her arms around my neck. 'You're a good man, Jack Tate. And you deserve to be happy, if only you'd let yourself.'

God, she smells good and she sounds good, and I know this woman still loves me. If I had a switch inside me with a label on it that said 'LOVE LYNN WITH THE LOVELY WELSH ACCENT FOREVER', I'd flick it now – I'd switch it on and then smash it with a hammer so that it's stuck in that position forever and we might have a chance. She kisses me on the lips and every part of me responds. As she leads me up the narrow stairwell, all sorts of shit is swirling around my head. That heartbreak comment wasn't only about you – I tell myself. It could have been about her too. Maybe you broke her heart last time. In which case, don't do this because you don't actually *have* one of those switches.

Yet, I do it. I do it because we're both lonely and I have to stop thinking that sleeping with a woman is always a bad idea.

*

On Monday, when Lynn's at work, I find myself opening the links that Grace sent and looking at the dance lessons between Simon and Clare. It's remarkable, and while I'm gawping at it again and again, my mind leaps back to when I first met Simon, about ten years ago. I went to see him; just because he was there, in the centre, and all the physios talked about the fact that he was a brilliant counsellor and had really helped many of their amputee patients come to terms with their physical losses. After only an hour with him, I decided it wasn't for me. I can't remember what they were, but he'd had some uncomfortably probing questions at a time when I wasn't ready for any mental foraging.

I stop the video playing on my iPad, freezing the frame when they're in full waltz turn, and I find myself wishing I was him. Not because he has Clare in his arms, but because he dances with an abandon that I wouldn't have imagined he could. He doesn't seem to have a care in the world, yet I'm quite sure he must. His every move seems measured and confident, yet he must feel a hesitancy that's undetectable. His broken eyes are trained on her. He *sees* her. Clare's head is angled back and she's smiling in the frozen frame and it's not lost on me that it's her I told my truth to, not him. It's Clare I revealed my own broken past to. And I find myself wondering if he might also have *seen* the fractured me back then.

When the phone rings, I decide to take Ollie's call, having fobbed him off with texts for the last fortnight.

'He lives!' he yells down the phone before giving me a bollocking about my side of our agreement to keep in touch.

'Jesus, Jack!' I have to hold the phone away from my ear when I finally tell him where I am and why I came. 'Get on a plane and get back to what you're supposed to be doing. What were you thinking?'

I don't reply, knowing Ollie's rhetorical questions don't require one.

'And do not go home in between.'

'Yessir.'

'Have you and Lynn been sleeping in the same bed?' For some reason, Ollie has stopped yelling and is now whispering.

'Lynn and I sleep in the same bed.'

'Oh, for Chrissake, Jack.' He sighs and again I say nothing. 'I suppose I should ask whether you managed to keep "unicorn boy" out of jail?'

'Don't be mean.'

'Do I need to remind you how upset you were when the guy broke into your home?' Ollie sounds completely fed up with me.

'He's gone to rehab, got a suspended sentence and lost his licence for five years.'

'Get on a plane, Jack,' Ollie repeats. 'You want to go forward not back.'

'I will.'

'Promise me you'll do it in the next twenty-four hours.'

'Er . . .'

'Forty-eight then.'

I laugh. 'Right.'

'And don't go home.'

'Right.'

'I'm trusting you, Jack. Just finish what you started, even if you go straight to the Europe leg and don't finish the States.'

I can hear Agatha and Rory screaming 'Dadd-eeee' in the background.

'You should go,' I tell him.

'Call me,' he says as children's tears flow. 'When you get to Paris or wherever, call me?'

'Will do. Give my love to Jennifer and the kids.'

Ollie hangs up first.

*

After the case she was on stenographer duty for is dismissed and she finishes early, Lynn and I are walking hand-in-hand on the path by the strand next to her cottage. We're wrapped up against the elements, she in a fur-lined long coat with a downy hood that frames her face, me in my warmest jacket with a beanie on my head.

'This,' she says, raising her hand in mine, 'this never used to happen. When we were together, you hated any public displays of affection.'

She's right. On two fronts. One, there was a time I'd have hated to hold hands in public, and two, that's what I feel for her – affection, love, even.

'You're leaving, aren't you?' She looks out beyond the wild waves.

For such a brief second, I think about saying 'No', that I'll stay here with her and we can learn to bake bread together and take seascape painting classes.

'Yes,' I squeeze her hand. 'It's not—'

'Don't.' She places a finger on my lips, leans her forehead against mine. 'Don't. I'm glad you came back when I needed you.'

'I'll always come back if you need me.' I kiss her gently. 'Always.'

'But you won't stay.'

My head moves left to right.

'I won't try to persuade you. I won't tell you that we could have a good life together. I won't tell you that you and I only didn't work back then because of Antony and . . .'

A gull swoops and lands right beside us and I'd swear it's the size of a domestic cat. It looks accusingly, squawks before flying off.

'You and he are better now,' she's trying not to plead with me.

I can't tell her that she and I didn't work not just because of Antony. I can't tell her that when we split, I convinced myself that real love was something I was only ever going to have once in my life, and it had been with Alice. I can't tell Lynn that until recently, until April convinced me otherwise, I'd resigned myself to that. I can't tell her that I feel like some sort of chrysalis emerging because I now believe there might be more. I can't tell her that, because I do love her enough not to hurt her. Just not enough to stay.

Chapter Forty-Three

Clare crept into the chapel at the end of the high street, the squeak from the rubber soles on her trainers the only sound. Apart from one older man knelt in silent prayer outside the confessional, she seemed to be alone as she slid herself along a polished pew. A lingering sense of incense clawed at the back of her throat as she tried to pray – the events of the previous few hours replaying in her head.

'Sock it to me,' she'd said to Dr Ramdhani, who had been unimpressed with Clare's missing two previous appointments. 'Tell me what Latin name there is for being burned from the inside out.' Within seconds, the ability to hide from difficult truths, that Clare had spent a lifetime fine-tuning, left her and she'd sobbed like a child. It turned out that there was a very not-Latin-at-all name for everything she'd been feeling lately – pregnancy. Yes, Dr Ramdhani assured her as she handed her tissues, perimenopausal women will get hot flushes and, yes, perimenopausal women can still get pregnant.

Next to her, an elderly woman in a paisley patterned headscarf exited the 'Booth of Sins' and Clare wondered if any middle-aged or younger people actually ever attended confession. She didn't want to think about it for too long. The notice displaying the sacrament's times had seemed to scream at her as she passed the church gates. And here she was . . .

Clare stood, entered the box and knelt down.

A soft voice with a Scottish lilt welcomed her through the latticed opening.

Automatically, Clare's hands joined. 'Bless me, Father, for I have sinned. It has been . . . a long time since my last confession.'

'No problem.'

Clare hesitated. 'I'm trying very hard to be the best person I can be, Father, but there are times when I have unkind thoughts. I think people see me as someone to use.'

Silence.

Jack flashed across her thoughts. It bothered her that she had slept with him, that she had let her guard down just as she was breaking away from her past.

'I slept with two men,' she told the priest. 'In the same week.'

Past the wooden divide, she heard the man shuffle in his seat. 'I see,' he said.

'And now I'm pregnant.' Clare lowered her hands, gripped the sill in front of her and rested her head against the grille.

The silence, as the priest mulled over her words, almost had the tiniest of pulses. At one point, Clare thought she might sit back into the corner and start to rock.

'That's a difficult situation,' he finally replied. 'But any child is a gift from God.'

Clare's eyes gently closed. What the hell was she doing there? She was a grown up, almost fully fledged, something she was still working on, but she didn't need to hear this. What if she'd been raped – was a resulting child a gift from God? Her lapsed religion told her it was, but life had shown her that things were not always that simple.

Clare stood up and pushed the door open, almost running out onto the street. No Latin affirmation over the sign of the cross, complete with a decade of the rosary, was going to change the facts. And as for penance – figuring out what she was going to do about it was more than enough.

*

Clare had brought them extra feed, thinking they might need it in the cold, and Pecan and Walnut had wolfed the lot. One of them, which one she wasn't sure, looked at her as if to say 'Is that it? Where's the rest?'

She leaned on the low fence, looked across at the view shared by the Barn and the main house – towards the swaying, husk-less wheat grasses and lines of erratically shaped shrubbery that separated lightly frosted fields. Circles of cold air escaped through her pursed lips. She had no idea what to do. As a troubled and bulimic teen, she had known to seek help. When the reality of her marriage could no longer be denied, she had known what to do. When she met with her mother, she had known what to do.

Clare pulled her woollen hat low over her ears, touched her stomach with a gloved hand. She had no idea what to do. She was forty-two years old. She was pregnant. She wasn't sure who the father was. Her mother had had words for people like that. As she walked back to the house, her head lowered, in what felt like shame.

In the kitchen, she began to prepare dinner. She spoke aloud to herself, as she peeled carrots, tossing out the pros and cons of having another child at her age. The dance school would suffer just as it was growing. Simon's next few lessons had gone online, and the response had been even bigger, with local radio and television wanting interviews, just prior to filming the finale the next day. Her plan to run the dance school full-time was ready to go.

She washed and cut the broccoli. Full of iron, she told herself, just as an image of Tim and her 'fucking', as he had called it, made her stop and grasp the worktop. She couldn't have another reason to re-tether herself to him, she thought as she watched her knuckles whiten. And what if the child was Jack's? A man who had been instrumental in changing her life so much for the better, yet, when it came down to it, he too had let her down.

'You need to say it out loud,' she told herself, walking towards the window, wringing her hands. 'You need to speak the other option out so loud that you have to listen.' Automatically, her hands covered her ears. She couldn't.

She couldn't even say it because she knew she could never do it.

Clare closed her eyes. Despite the long list of cons, the pro was that there would be a new life, but feeling as she did about either father figure, the only way she could do it was to do it alone. The only way it might work out was if she said nothing to either of them.

The thought festered as her hand rested on her thumping chest, knowing that made her as bad as both of them put together.

*

'Have you heard from Jack?'

'No.' Clare kept the reply simple as she and Grace folded laundry. 'What time is Erik arriving?'

'He'll be here in a minute.'

'I know someone who's almost pleased that her father isn't feeling well and had to cancel curry night.' Clare gave her a playful nudge.

'Dad probably wanted to spend the time with Louise. I'm not buying the "feeling a little off" thing. You haven't heard anything at all from Jack?'

'No! God . . . You're like a dog with a bone!' As usual, denial was her default setting. 'Why are you asking?'

Her daughter shrugged. 'He didn't mail me back – you don't think something's happened to him, do you?'

'Of course not.' She handed Grace a pile of her clean clothes.

'He could have had an awful accident.'

Clare thought fate would never be so cruel, that one awful accident was enough in anyone's life. 'He's fine, he's just having fun,' she said to the sound of the doorbell.

When Grace opened it, Clare heard two voices – that of Erik and his mother.

Emma appeared in the room. 'I've agreed he can come over for an hour only, since he's meant to be studying, so I thought I'd keep you company. Oh, and I brought the dress for you.'

Clare waited until the teens disappeared upstairs, then approached Emma, took the borrowed dress from her and laid it across the back of the sofa, before putting her arms around her. 'It's good to see you.' She almost unravelled under the squeeze of her friend's return embrace. 'I've screwed up,' Clare whispered. 'I could really do with a friend.'

*

It had been beautiful, so much so that if everything went to total hell from that point on, Clare would, for the rest of her life, always be able to close her eyes and remember she'd been instrumental in producing one exquisite dance routine. She had been responsible for teaching Simon to trust in dance. His hold had been flawless, the steps had been perfectly paced. Even the red shimmering dress she'd borrowed from Emma swished and swayed dreamily as they moved together around the floor. Simon's face wore a smile that bore no resemblance to his frustrated expression during the many times they'd practised where he'd counted aloud. A genuine smile told the lie that the whole effort had been simple. It had been far from easy for him, but Simon learned the steps and perfected the dance with the same dedication as he seemed to live. He made the whole thing of a blind man placing his faith in a complete stranger look effortless, when it had been his Herculean effort that had made it happen.

There had been only one live take. They'd talked for ages beforehand. She'd counted his grid with him. He'd asked about her dress, wanted her to describe the colour. 'Poppies,' she'd said. 'It's the same colour and has the same sway as poppies in a breeze.' He'd smiled at that reply.

As she watched the film for the hundredth time, she saw the hit count rise and rise in the thousands. Pam had confirmed earlier that donations had also been coming in, and the sum was already beyond fifteen hundred pounds. Clare allowed herself the moment; a flash of pride in what they'd all achieved, her and Simon and Lisa, Grace and Erik.

Today, she had planned a class-free day, acknowledging to herself that fatigue had crept into her routines and a calmer day catching up on paperwork was needed. The inbox on her website was heaving with enquiries that needed replies and, sifting through a pile of snail mail, including some bills she had yet to open, she made three piles. Recycling. To do. File. To the backdrop of a random playlist, she went through each item methodically, grateful for the fact that she was, for the first time ever, totally in control of her own finances.

She sat back, rubbed a nagging knot in her neck firmly with one hand. It was thanks to Jack that she was sitting there at least attempting to take control of her life. Without him . . . Without him, she didn't want to even contemplate where she might be. It was something Emma had reiterated, insisting that while she was all for Melborough Clare moving forward without a man, and while Jack had been an idiot, she, Clare, was overreacting.

Clare eased the tension in her neck and, picking up her phone, sent an instinctive voice message to the man who might be the father of the child she was carrying:

'Jack, I'd like to try to put what happened behind us but want you to understand how what you did affected me. When I was younger, I had a mother who lived her dreams through me, without ever *seeing* me. I married a man who I thought loved me, but only ever wanted to control me. There's a bit of pattern there, which I'm only recognising now, so for you to do something behind my back when I had asked you not to – it made me feel manipulated again. It's important to . . . Gawd, I'm not sure how to even say this . . . I suppose what I'm trying to say is that because I'm lucky enough to have a chance at a new life, I want every moment, and every *person*, to count. New friends have to be people I can trust, people who can let me be me, because that's what I'm really after, Jack, the me that's in me – somewhere. I hope you get what I mean. I'm still angry at what you did, but I really don't want to be, so let's try to move past it and stay friends.'

Sometime later, the feeling of someone prodding her woke her. 'Bloody hell! I must have fallen asleep.' With the heels of her hands, she rubbed her eyes as her daughter hovered above her.

'We need to talk,' Grace growled.

'What's wrong?' All of Clare's maternal instincts kicked in as she jerked forward so quickly that a spinning ache pierced her head.

Grace waved something in her hand. 'When were you going to tell me?'

Clare tried to work out what was happening as Grace threw it onto her lap. A letter from the 'file' pile – the surgery's logo; the sheet of paper informing her she had missed a midwifery appointment and offering her a second.

'I can explain.' Her insides griped in panic as her voice wavered.

'Save it, Mother.' Grace walked away, grabbing her coat from where she'd put it on the back of a dining chair.

'Grace!' Clare stumbled to her feet. 'Please, I was going to tell you.'

Her daughter turned, glared at her. 'And you lectured *me* about safe sex.'

Clare attempted to move towards her, when Grace's hand shot up in the air.

'Do *not* come near me,' she yelled. 'I'm assuming it's Dad's. Tell me, did it happen before or after he beat you senseless right here in this room?'

Words failed her. Nothing new would form as her mouth dried. 'I can explain,' she croaked.

'What makes you think I want to hear? "You can explain."' Grace pulled the zip up on her coat and, with her hand on the rear door, screamed, 'Why the hell should I listen to anything you say?'

Clare's eyes squeezed closed as the door banged and she steadied herself on the arm of the sofa before following Grace outside. The security light clicked on and up ahead she could see her leaning on the fence at the pen.

'Are you going to keep it?' Grace called back without turning around.

Clare stopped walking.

'I've worked out the timing,' Grace continued. 'It's early enough. You could—'

'Yes, I could.' Clare, coatless in the icy evening, began to shiver. 'But I can't.'

'You should.'

She hugged herself. Though Grace had been through so much already, she'd anticipated shock, with eventual support, but never such vehemence.

'You just watch Dad,' Grace's voice was almost sinister. 'He'll slowly worm his way back into our lives, into your life, into that poor kid's life.' There was a weighted pause before she turned around to face her in the light. 'He hit you. I had to threaten to call the police on my own father! You ended up in hospital. You can't possibly think there's any way some other kid should witness that.'

'I'm not with your dad any more, Grace.'

Her laugh was laced with sarcasm. 'No, just "with him" enough to get knocked up.'

Clare swallowed back shaky tears. 'I'm not with your dad any more,' she repeated. 'And things aren't always as simple as they seem.'

'Are you pregnant or not?' Grace yelled.

'Yes.'

'And it's Dad's?'

Clare said nothing. To try to explain it would make it worse.

'Then you should get rid of it. That's as simple as it needs to be.'

With that, her daughter walked away, back towards the home they'd made together.

Clare stood as still as her quaking body would allow. The only sounds to be heard were the distant hum of motorway traffic and the almost rhythmic nuzzling of the pigs' snouts in the earth. She began to walk towards the house, sobs wracking her small frame. At no time in their sixteen years together had Grace ever looked at her like that before – a look of complete disappointment. Clare had recognised the expression, had recoiled from it. She'd seen it often enough in Jean's eyes.

PART THREE

Chapter Forty-Four

WhatsApp Voice Memo to Erik

You've asked me what's wrong with me? Here goes – my family. Let's start with Mum. I can't go into why, but she's driving me mad. Then there's Dad. I've just had a row with him because he's pissed off I have a boyfriend.

I don't think they even realise they're the adults.

All I want to do is play hockey.

And be with you.

I'm sorry for the moan.

See you later. Be here by eight?

WhatsApp Voice Memo to Jack

Hey, Jack, it's Grace!

Where are you? It's December, so New Orleans, I think – probably playing in some jazz club by now, which is a shame because I saw an ad in the local Melborough Facebook Group for a trumpet player, which would have been perfect for you! I'll find the link and send it, just in case you want to come home early. Hope you're having a great trip. How was swimming with the pigs in the Caribbean?! Your own pigs miss you.

-----Original Message-----
From: GraceBryanson29@gmail.com
Sent: 3rd December 2018 22:10
To: BadBarrister@TateTravels.com
Subject: Facebook Ad

Jack, for some reason, I can't link the ad? Here's the deets:

Wanted Urgently: Trumpet player for six-piece band. We're a local group established for the last six years. We love all things rhythm and blues and jazz – play mostly for fun, but sometimes do special occasions. If you're an established musician who might fit the bill, call Jane on 05553367912.

Grace x

Chapter Forty-Five

The house has a musty scent, and though the first radiator I touch is warm, I still shiver as I pull my bags into the hallway. I leave most of them there, just taking the rucksack with the clothes that need cleaning through to the utility room. After putting a wash on, I head straight to the fridge, where there is always a bottle of chilled wine, before sinking my ass into the contours of the sofa in the snug, full glass in hand.

I'm home. It feels good, and I give myself the time to breathe in the familiar space. Lynn flits through my thoughts. It hadn't been easy leaving her. All the way back on the M4, I just kept asking myself, what now? I left my bags in the hall because I couldn't bring them into the bedroom, which would have confirmed I'm staying, yet I don't want to stay. What would April think? What would Alice think? I know what Ollie would think. My tired eyes close and I ask myself yet again – what do *I* think?

To stop the noise in my head, I open the latest mail from Grace on my phone and read it several times. I'm more of a jazz man than rhythm and blues, but I call the number anyway.

Come on, Chance, you wanna come out and play?

Later, when I do check it out, when I meet Darren, James, Danny, Brenda and Jane that evening, my nerves are jangling. It's obvious very soon that their ad was perfect – they're a relaxed bunch who play together for fun, performing just a few gigs. As I listen to them rehearse, any tension I felt has disappeared and I realise that I'm itching to join them for a track or two. Jane's 'Mustang Sally' is really very good. Their version of 'Summertime' tosses me right back to when Clare and Grace arrived, and yellow rapeseed still waved from the hills at the back of the houses.

'Want to join us for "In the Mood"?' a voice I think to be Danny's asks and I don't need a second invite.

Climbing up to the makeshift stage at the back of his soundproofed garage, I'm moving so quickly that my bad foot twists on one of the steps. I swallow a yelp and take up position, where I'm pointed to. I forget the pain as my fingers move and lungs explode. I hear my sound with the other instruments and inhale the perfect synchronicity and I feel something that I barely recognise. I feel hopeful. Hope flows through my heart and it reacts – beating louder and stronger. If my heart could talk in this perfect moment, it would say, 'Well, hello, Hope, where have you been for the past thirty years?'

Hours later, they want me. I want them, though I have to confess I'm not sure if I want them *now*. I can see each one of the five faces is a little baffled when I'm there to rehearse yet I don't jump at the chance to join them when it's offered. The timing, I tell them, isn't ideal. More bewildered faces. Some disappointed faces. I ask them for a few days to think about it and I can already see a couple of them doubting me. They're thinking I might not be reliable. I assure them I *would*, when my heart is screaming to tell them I *will*. They agree to give me a few days to think, but I can already tell they'll go away and probably come to the conclusion I'm a nutter.

When I get back, I put the fish and chips I've just bought in the oven to keep warm and console myself by opening the door to the garden in the snug. It's bloody freezing, but I know what I'm doing when I blast out 'Rhapsody in Blue'. As soon as the doorbell rings, I smile.

'You're home!' Grace hesitates a moment and then gives me a tight hug. She stands back, pulls her oversized fleece around her and shoves both her hands deep in its pockets. 'You're back early, are you staying?'

I laugh, glance at her with a tilted head. 'You look different.' I don't answer the question. 'All grown up. Must be love . . . I've seen the pics on Instagram.'

Her cheeks flush, yet she smiles that lovely smile that she shares with her mother.

'How've you both been?'

'I didn't hear from you,' she says, her brow furrowing. 'I messaged you and sent an email, and when you didn't reply, I was worried you'd had an accident.'

'I'm sorry, I did get it – it's been a bit mad the last week.'

'Never mind!' She seems genuinely pleased to see me. 'Come on over! Mum's not working and we're just about to eat.' She pulls my arm, but I resist.

'I won't come over tonight, Grace. I'm jet-lagged.' The lie slips out easily.

'Please! Just for supper. Mum would love to see you too. And you'd be doing me a favour. She's driving me mad.' She tugs my arm again. 'Come on. You know you want to!'

'I have chips.'

The words are stupid, and she laughs loudly. 'Leave them!'

'I should— OK, I'll just turn the oven off.'

'Bring a coat,' she rubs her hands together. 'It's bloody freezing out here.'

Before I know it, she and I are walking to the Barn.

'I warn you – Pecan and Walnut have got so fat,' she says apologetically, and I wonder if she has heels on or is just standing more confidently, because I'd swear she's taller.

'You don't look like a DIM any more,' I tell her.

'You neither,' she grins. 'Maybe we'll disband! Mum?' she yells out as she enters the Barn first. 'It *was* him! I told you! Jack's back!'

Clare walks up the hallway from her bedroom and I scratch my neck, say, 'Not back per se, just, well, here for a bit, I think.'

'Welcome home,' Clare air-kisses my cheek. 'Grace thought she heard you play and . . . and now here you are!'

'He's eating with us,' Grace says and heads into the kitchen, leaving her mother and I together. I hear another place being set on the table.

'She insisted,' I tell her.

'She does that,' Clare says. 'You look well.'

My eyes find hers and I see she's smiling. Immediately, I relax a little. Yes, she'd sent me a message saying she'd try to forgive my faux pas with Tim, but that's not the same as seeing her and hoping that she has. It's hard to tell. Clare's a tough nut to crack. Nothing see-through or simple about her, so I suppose I'll know by the end of the evening.

Soon, I'm nursing a weak G&T and listening to their slightly awkward conversation as we tuck into a shepherd's pie. I could be wrong – maybe it's because I haven't been in their company for a while, but something seems off-kilter with them.

'So, your dance with Simon went global, an internet sensation!' I address Clare when there's a lull.

Her response is animated, though little is said about the actual dance. It's all about Grace; how she and Erik were responsible for video production and how she set up and runs the social media account. It's as if Clare wants Grace to hear how proud she is of her. All the while I'm listening, I'm imagining her inner voice as she sees me at her dining table this evening. *You're meant to be in New Orleans. Why are you here?* I'm hoping she can't hear what *I'm* thinking because I'm remembering the way her neck tilted back and she sobbed a little as I kissed her bruised face. I remember loving her scent, and it's a moment before I realise I've said something about her perfume out loud.

Grace looks over at me, her nose twitching in a 'Huh?' expression.

'That's how Simon and I met,' Clare announces, taking control of the moment. 'He recognised my perfume and introduced himself. Being blind, he has the most acute sense of smell.' Clare rubs the reddening area above her chest. 'All of his other senses work that little bit harder,' she explains, and I give a gentle nod as if to say, that little snippet was a good fact to know. 'He can name a flower at a hundred paces,' Clare continues as she spikes a lumpy piece of potato with her fork.

'He's a great guy,' I reply. 'And you two raised such a load of money for the centre. Pam was telling me yesterday—'

'I hate to interrupt, guys, but I have homework.' Grace points at her watch. 'And I want to hear what *you've* been up to, Jack.'

'What do you want to know?' I steeple my hands on the table.

'Everything! Where you went and what you did! Why you came home early. You can't have done the west coast stuff, or any of Europe?'

'No, you're right. I probably only did a quarter of what I'd planned.'

'Why did you come back?'

'A friend in need . . .'

'Oh,' Clare looks at Grace, who waits for me to say more, but I don't. Instead, I regale them with tales of Boston, New York and Florida, and Clare zones out. Her chin is placed in her hand and she's pretending to listen, but I can tell she's now wondering, what friend, what need, what took me out of that travel zone that I'd been so desperate to be in? The mention of Tim's name shakes her out of the reverie.

'And how is he?' I ask Grace, who'd brought him up.

'He's an idiot, annoyed at the fact that I've a boyfriend – but we're going to have to put up with him interfering forever, *aren't we, Mum?*' she glares. 'Would you like a coffee, Jack? Mum's off the stuff.'

*

'What did she mean?' I'm on it as soon as Grace has left the room to start her homework.

'What?'

'When she said you have to put up with him interfering forever. He hasn't been near you, has he?'

Clare shakes her head. 'Teenage drama,' she shrugs. 'Why are you really home, Jack?'

My bottom lip is stuck on one side between my teeth, and with everything I have, I summon the feeling I felt when I played with the band earlier. It was genuine hope, as if I'd really shed the past and whatever happened next was going to be brilliant. I couldn't see or imagine what it might look like, but it was going to be perfect. I no longer cared about the finger of Fate fucking with me, or not having control over every detail in my life, because hope meant I could look forward without being afraid. Yet, right now, I'm nervous. 'Like I said. A friend in need.'

'And have you dealt with their needs?'

I'm not imagining it. There's a little sourness around the edge of her words.

'Yes.' The coffee Grace made before leaving is strong and tepid.

'So, are you staying or going back to your travels?'

'I don't know yet.'

Her eyebrows arch, but she says nothing.

'You know how sorry I am about what happened with Tim.'

'Let's not go there, Jack.'

'It was—'

'I've realised,' she interrupts me, 'probably only in the last few weeks, that I'm OK. I'm really actually OK now. A good friend pointed out that maybe I was overreacting towards you. I can earn a wage doing something I love and that's down to you, so I can't be angry. And . . .' she pauses, 'it's hard to explain. I feel as if I'm only getting back to myself, to the self I used to be so long ago, and she's someone I like. She's strong and doesn't need Tim or anyone else. I suppose what I'm trying to say is I'm moving forward.'

'I'm happy you're happy.'

'What about you? Have you found what you were looking for?'

'Yes and no. I think I've let go of the past as well. I think I'm hopeful for the future.' I drain my glass and stand up. 'Shall I help you clear these last bits away?'

'Of course not.' She stands and notices me rubbing my leg. 'You all right?'

'I just knocked it earlier. I'm fine. I should get back, thanks for supper. It was good to see you both.'

At the door, she reaches up and kisses my cheek, this time touching it with her lips.

'Night,' she says.

'Night.'

'Oh,' she says as I walk away. 'There's a reception tomorrow night at Onward Motion, some drinks thing to reveal the money raised this year. They probably think you're still away. You should come.'

'Pam did message me.' I don't reveal that Pam wrote to thank me for the annual donation I always make to the charity and to remind me of the night, if I was anywhere near home. 'I'll see. Night.'

Normally I'd be there, no doubt, but I'd already decided it might be a bad idea to dip back in, if I'm only here for a quick change-around. The truth is that the European wing of the travel schedule still beckons, and I'm torn between staying and immersing myself in a potential new way of being at home and dusting off my Eurostar ticket because there's still so much to see and do elsewhere.

Clare's question nudges me: *Have I found what I was looking for?* On the short walk home, I remind myself I've come unstuck from historic pain, but have I found *everything* I was looking for? As I turn the key in the lock, I remember Mum's conversation with me: *the only way you'll find happiness is to have the courage to let go of things that make you unhappy.* I think I have a new peace of mind. I have friends and meeting the band today made me think I could have a whole new group of pals and a new release for my music.

Yet . . . to Paris or not to Paris – that is well and truly the question.

*

Ollie's answer is typical. 'Get on the train, Jack.' He sends me a text of the same words too many times to count, one after the other. It looks like a page of one hundred lines I'd have been given by a teacher when I did something wrong in school.

April, who I meet for a catch-up walk the next day, is more subtle. We've chosen Hyde Park as it's easier for us to get into London by train than drive to somewhere halfway. The day is what she describes as 'gorgeous'; bright winter sun set low in the sky has melted the earlier ground frost and has us both donning sunglasses. She wears a lemony woollen hat, 'in honour of Alice', and a long, padded parka past her knees. I have the ski coat that I took away with me on over two jumpers and jeans. The leg underneath is the one I use for harder terrain, even though we've stuck to the park's flat footpaths that are covered in crunchy leaves. As we walk, the fact her hand is looped through my arm feels like the most natural thing in the world.

'I'm meeting the family for lunch afterwards, if you fancy joining,' she says two minutes into our walk. 'The Rainforest Café, noisy with excited kids, so I'll let you off if you say no, but we'd love you to come.'

Somehow, I manage not to answer until much later and soon I discover she knows almost as much about my shortened trip as I do from following me on Instagram. 'Who was that mad woman giving you abuse?' she asks and, without waiting for a reply, adds, 'And that time you puked on the poor pilot over Manhattan. God, I'm sorry, but I laughed.' When we finally get to me explaining why I'd come home early, to me sharing everything about Lynn and Antony, she stops walking, and nibbling her bottom lip, looks right at me. 'You did such big things, Jack. Not just one but lots. Alice would be proud.'

'Stop, OK?' I'm embarrassed and pull her back into our arm loop. 'I feel her around me still, but it's different nowadays. It's like she's there, alongside me. I hear her laughing, remember the actual sound, and . . .' I shrug. 'It's just better, not sad any more.'

April taps my gloved hand with hers. 'I'm glad.'

We walk in silence for a couple of minutes until we reach the Queen Elizabeth Gate.

'What say you?' She places a flattened palm over her eyes to shield the glaring sun. 'Fancy grabbing a cab with me and meeting the rest of my brood?'

This time, I don't hesitate. I just raise a hand and whistle at an approaching taxi. As it pulls up beside us, she tugs on my arm before we get in.

'As for Paris,' she says. 'Why not wait until springtime. It's a place for lovers, maybe you're meant to take someone with you?'

I shrug, because this advice isn't really helpful and directly opposes Ollie's.

'Join the band, Jack! Don't see staying as a failure. You're a musician and you adore playing; the band could be another way of "letting love into your life".'

In the taxi, she sits opposite me on one of those fold-down chairs and I realise that I quite love this woman. I love her simple way of seeing things. I love the fact that she's Alice's sister and is nothing like her, yet so like her. I love the fact that I can think I 'love' her without it being anything other than friendship. It is, I realise, OK to feel this.

I do think she's wrong about waiting for Paris though . . .

Chapter Forty-Six

It seemed by the sounds coming from upstairs that Grace was angry with someone else as well as her. From downstairs, Clare listened as she gripped the timber newel post and glanced up to the landing.

'Do *not* tell me to calm down and do *not* tell me I'm overreacting!'

Erik?

'You're a controlling asshole, Dad, how dare you?'

Her father. Shit.

'Or what, you'll hit me too? That's what you do when you don't like what you hear, isn't it? Come on then – you know where I live!'

Oh. Dear. God. Clare stepped up the first few stairs. Grace held a hand up, warning her not to come any further.

'Don't come on Friday. I don't want to see you. And do NOT come to the house either. You're already not allowed near Mum. I mean it, Dad, I DON'T want to see you right now.'

Clare held her breath.

'Yada, Yada. You're always sorry afterwards.'

From her position, Clare heard her daughter stab the phone, bringing the call to an end, and was sure she heard the word 'asshole' repeated under her daughter's breath as she walked back into her room.

Shit. She couldn't remember a time when Grace had shouted at her father like that, but Grace was right. God, that man could be an asshole.

*

Clare fed the pigs and was washing out the utensils at the sink when Grace appeared.

'Could you take me to school? I've got loads to carry today and I'd rather not wait for the bus in the rain.'

'Of course.' She moved quickly towards her, wrapped her arms around her from behind, and Grace, for the first time in almost a week, didn't pull away or move out of her hold. 'I'm sorry. You're my world and I hate when you're cross. You've a right to be angry with me, I should have told you. I was sticking my head in the sand, couldn't handle it. I'm not sure I can even now.' Grace's long hair smelt of oranges and Clare inhaled.

Grace turned and Clare pondered when she had got so tall. Clare was five foot six and suddenly Grace was looking down at her.

'I hate this,' Grace whispered. 'You and I don't fight.'

'No, and you and your dad don't fight either.' Clare sat down at the dining table, kicked another chair with her foot and nodded towards it. 'I made you toast and coffee. Humour me. Have something to eat before school.'

Grace's eyes wandered to the wall clock before she sat down and took a slice of toast.

'Tell me you're all right?'

'I'm all right,' Grace replied with her mouth full.

'You're pissed off. It's not like you.'

'Does Dad know you're pregnant?'

Clare blushed under her daughter's narrow-eyed scrutiny. 'No, and I'd like to keep it that way. Please tell me you didn't tell him.'

Grace tossed the last of the toast back on the plate. 'Seriously?' She stood up and put her coat on. 'Dad and I were arguing about our own stuff. He's a pain in the ass, capable of being mean and violent, but if you've decided you're having a baby – you *shouldn't* keep it from him.'

'Do you trust me?'

Grace sighed. 'I trust you.'

'Will you leave it to me to talk to your father when I have to?'

'You're going ahead with it then?'

'Yes. And I need you with me, Gracie.'

'I'm with you, Mum.' She shook her head, her hair falling in front of her face like a forelock. 'At least I'm trying to be, but I'm pissed off at him. I wish he'd just realise I have a life here now, a life I love, and all I want is for him to be happy for me, not . . .' she paused. 'Not having something to say about *everything* – hockey, school subjects, Erik . . .' She slumped back down on the chair. 'He's exhausting,' she said, looking directly at Clare before laughing. 'But you already know that.'

'He misses you.' Clare had no idea why she was defending Tim of all people, but some part of her felt sorry for him.

'I know. But I'm not going to let him just think he can control what I do, Mum.'

Clare leaned against the table, took her hand.

'Good,' she said. 'I love you.'

'Take me to school?' Grace was up and headed towards the door in seconds, leaving Clare yearning for but not receiving a reciprocal 'love you too', which would normally be Grace's rote reply.

As the car gasped a route to the school, Clare prayed it would survive until she could afford to take out a car loan the following year. During the silent journey with Grace staring out the window, Clare's brain took off on the anxious tangent her dying car often led her to: Would she be able to still rent the Barn off Jack? Could she afford it? Would she be able to keep working for as long as possible, earn enough money, bearing in mind she had a child to give birth to and look after? Who would look after a baby for her when she worked? Would Tim lose his shit completely if the child was Jack's? Would Tim lose his shit completely if the child was his? And Jack, how would Jack react to any of it?

She'd wanted to do it alone, to carry on alone, but Grace was right. Tim should know. And if Tim should know, Jack should know, and she had to live with the consequences.

Not yet though. Just not yet.

*

Surrounded by people at the charity that evening, Clare watched a calmer and happier Grace, with Erik, sipping soft drinks as they chatted to a young woman Clare recognised as Dawn, the receptionist. Next to Clare, Simon was giving an animated description of their first dance class together. He was self-deprecating, but in a humorous way; with one hand linked through Lisa's he waved the other about as a prop in the story. Clare smiled obligingly but was aware she was watching the door.

She had been certain he'd come. He was home. He knew about it – why would he not come? She glanced behind the group of people she was assembled with, people she was sure she'd call friends in time, a mixture of staff and clients of the services the charity offered. Just above them, on a fairly crude stage made of upturned milk crates covered in a white cloth, a PowerPoint presentation clicked through various facts and figures, revealing monies raised that year. There were no speeches and she was thankful for that, but some part of her had wanted him to see the slide now showing; she'd wanted him to see in black and white that her Pay It Forward to him, with Simon and Lisa's and Grace and Erik's help, had raised £9,087 for the centre. She sipped the flat soda water, rubbed the top of her dress where a drop had fallen.

In the mirror a couple of hours earlier, she'd realised she was wearing this dress to be *seen*. It was one that had lived at the back of her wardrobe for years, one that Tim hated her wearing – a form-fitting, but not too tight, emerald green dress that showed a little, but not too much, cleavage. Eyes still on the door, she wondered, if maybe she'd worn the dress for Jack to see her in it.

But Jack was more than likely packing his bags.

Chapter Forty-Seven

I'm about to leave the house to get into the car and Grace is sobbing on my doorstep, her soggy coat flapping open, her school uniform underneath.

'What's happened?'

'I hate him!' she cries and then looks at me. 'Are you going out?'

'Just into town, I've got physio before I—'

'Can you drop me at Erik's?'

I'm not sure I even agreed, but before I know it, she's opening the passenger door and points towards the studio.

'*She's* busy and, argh, *he* makes me so angry!'

'What happened?' I ask again, throwing my brolly in the back before I crank the heat up. The afternoon is darkening, and automatic lights shine the way ahead through the rapid-fire rainfall.

'He hung up on me. It was just to get back at me because I hung up on him this morning, but . . . ugh, he's such an asshole . . . I hate him.'

'You don't hate him.' The windscreen clears quickly as I angle the heat upwards and pull away from the house.

'I do, I really do.' She looks back. 'And she's no better . . .'

'You definitely don't hate her.' My head shakes. 'You're obviously angry.'

'She's meant to be the adult. He beats her so she can hardly see, and I mean . . . you were there!'

'Grace—'

'You don't understand! She's an idiot! I have an asshole for a father and an idiot for a mother.'

The wipers are on full against the torrent that hit the county yesterday morning and has been relentless since. The windscreen is fogging over again as Grace shivers in the seat beside me. I put the seat warmers on and blast more heat upwards on the front window. Her sobs have increased, and I should say something as I drive down the hill, slowly, turning the car around the bends that lead to town, but I can't seem to find the right words. She hugs herself, and as I glance across at her, blinking fast, I don't even realise that I've veered onto the wrong side of the road.

A car horn blares, and I swerve back into the right lane. Brakes screech. Grace shoots forward, held by the seat belt, but my left arm moves to block her. The sound of a driver screaming through an open window, shaking a fist at me as he passes, urges me to refocus.

'Are you OK?' I turn towards her.

'Jesus . . .'

'I'm sorry, I—'

'Sh-it.' Her hand taps her coat where her heart lies.

'I'm sorry,' I repeat again. 'I—' I look down at my leg, run my hand over the upper thigh. Logic tells me I'm in a rural road near home with Grace in the front seat, that we're both fine and that I've stopped the car just before the verge in front of a line of wet holly bushes. Behind me, another car booms its horn. I'm blocking the way.

Grace's voice reaches me, 'Jack, it's all right. We're all right.'

It's all right. We're all right. I beckon the car behind to pass. My one-and-a-half leaden legs move as my heart pounds behind my ribs.

Grace reaches forward and puts the hazard lights on. 'You're OK,' she whispers, and one more time, I'm shrouded in doubt, thinking I'll never be whole, or ever be OK.

'The thinnest line,' is what I say to her.

'What?' Concern is etched all over her young face. 'Jack?'

'There's only the thinnest line between being OK and not. Between then and now.'

She looks behind as another car passes us on the narrow lane. 'I don't know what you mean but we should probably move . . . Are you all right to drive?'

A nod appears, though I don't remember ordering it. I switch the ignition on and put the automatic transmission into drive.

'The pub,' she says, as if to remind me of her original destination.

Relief surges in my veins as the car moves and, slowly, I navigate the road as I listen to her breathing.

'Over thirty years ago,' I find myself saying, 'I was forced off the road by a man driving drunk on the wrong side. Alice, my girlfriend – she died. She was pregnant and I lost her, lost them.' A quick glance down. 'I also lost my lower left leg.'

She bursts into tears again and I hear her swallow hard as we approach town and I indicate right towards the pub. 'That's an awful lot to lose,' she says, looking out her side window.

There's one space left in the car park, and when we stop, Grace reaches into her pocket for a tissue and, looking in the passenger mirror, wipes her face. It's a snotty mess and I'm not much better.

'I lost concentration back there,' I begin. 'I'd never have forgiven myself if . . .'

'Jack, no one got hurt.'

'Yes, but—'

'I've always known there was a story, that something might have happened to you, but that's too horrible and I don't know what to say.' Her head shakes. 'I really don't know what to say, apart from – we're OK. Come inside . . .'

'No. I need this physio appointment. And I've a few things to pick up before I leave.'

'You're leaving?' There's shock in her voice.

I nod.

'When?'

'Next Tuesday evening. Paris first stop.'

Her eyes fill again. 'Look at us. Sad twats, the pair of us.'

'I'm sorry your father is a prize twat,' I offer. 'And I'm sorry I almost killed us back there.'

She attempts a laugh. 'You didn't. We're both OK. And hearing the word "twat" come from your posh mouth is funny.'

'He *is* a twat. A nosy twat.'

Soon, describing her father with as many adjectives attached to the word 'twat' as she can conjure, she's almost hysterical and the sound is catching. By the time she exits the car, anyone looking would have assumed our red eyes were from side-splitting laughter.

'Will you be long?' She has bent her head and is peering at me through the open door.

'About an hour and a half.'

'Would you pick me up on your way back?'

'You're willing to get into a car with me again?'

'I'll take my chances.' She glances at her watch. 'Five o'clock?'

'See you then.'

*

After a particularly quiet physio session with Jim, who seemed to sense the fact I didn't want to talk as he pummelled knots all over my anxious body, I kill some time with a steaming latte in a coffee shop before collecting Grace. I call Marsha, make the arrangements I need to and tick her from the list I've made on my phone. Looking at Lynn's name sitting there under Marsha's, I text her:

Hope you're all right. I'm off on the second leg on Tuesday. Let me know you're OK and if you've heard anything from Antony. Jack x

Moments later her reply pings:

I'm good. Spending time with Mum and Dad to keep
my mind off him. Haven't heard anything but not
expecting to. Home feels odd – like it had you here for
a while and then you left. Which I suppose is what happened. Miss you. I understand, but I do miss you. L x

When Grace climbs into the front seat, my heart starts
to hammer behind my ribs. It's almost as if she can hear it
because she doesn't say 'hello', she just catches my eye and
says, 'Drive, don't think about it. Keep talking to me.'

'How was Erik?'

'He's great. He has a way of calming me, but there's things
I want to talk to him about and I can't, so . . . Anyway, he
was brilliant, and I feel better.'

'Did you tell him about our little—'

'No.'

'Why not?'

She pauses a few moments. 'I'm not sure. Probably
because it would have led to me talking about the other
stuff you said and that's your story, not mine, to tell. Mum's
been on the phone,' she changes the subject. 'She's pissed
off at me for leaving like I did earlier.'

I don't reply.

'Jack, keep talking to me.'

'My story,' I say. 'Thank you for keeping it private.'

'You should go,' she says, 'go to Paris.'

My sigh is loud.

'There's no disbanding really – we're still both DIMs you know.' Her voice lowers as if that is the secret. Then she fist-bumps me to seal her diagnosis. 'I'm happy that way,' she shrugs. 'Aren't you?'

I'll never know how I'd have answered that question because we've already pulled into the Barn and her mother is outside, rubbing her arms against the cold. All I do know is, before, I remember wanting oblivion, and today, I want to live.

'She's not an idiot,' I whisper.

'I hope you're right.' Her face says she's not convinced as she gets out and I stay put in the driver's seat. Clare gives me a look – of thanks, of something, before they both vanish into the house.

*

Just as I'm getting ready for bed, the power outs in the house and I can see from social media that December winds and rain have brought a tree down on local lines. I look out the window at the Barn and there's still power. I briefly regret not fitting the cottage with the same solar storage. When I hear a knock on the front door I throw my dressing gown around me and, using my crutches, I make my way there. Clare's face fills the peephole and I open the door to her standing outside with a couple of torches in her hand.

'Erik told Grace the whole village is without power. I thought you might need these?'

'I was just getting into bed, easiest way to wait it out.'

She tries not to but is staring at my crutches.

'Have them anyway.' She walks past me and places the torches on the hall table. I'd scratch my head if I could because I have a drawer full of torches if I need them.

'You want a drink?' I ask, suddenly wanting her company. 'You may have to light the way?'

We sit side by side in the snug and, with her standard glass of water in hand, Clare's all animated; tells me all about her visit with her mother. Aware I've just taken medication for pain, I sip some soda water as she sits fidgeting in the dark in a way that makes me question whether Grace said something to her about earlier. I never asked her not to but sort of assumed she wouldn't. Now Clare's glances around the shadowy room, lit only by the torch sitting upright between us, are anxious and there's a tiny line of beaded sweat above her top lip.

'I'm sorry it didn't go differently with your mother,' I tell her.

'Someday I'll tell you all the facts and then you really won't be.' Clare frowns. 'I'm much better without her toxic energy in my life.'

My head rests on the back of the sofa and I find myself closing my eyes.

'What about you, Jack? Have you forgiven yourself yet?'

Eyes shut I speak. 'I forgave myself for being there, for driving that night, for loving her.' My voice breaks a little. 'I stood by the lovely coast in Biscayne and let her go. It felt as if I was blowing her out to sea, releasing her. And me.'

'Good,' she whispers before I hear her taking several gulps from the glass in her hand. 'Jack, there *is* something we should probably talk about.'

'Shoot.'

'We're friends, right?'

I open my eyes, turn my head to face her, and the reality that she didn't really come just to deliver torches she knows I don't need makes my mouth instantly dry.

'Yes, of course.'

'We're friends. And now you're back, I feel like I have to say I can't be anything else to anyone else, including you.'

A frown spreads across my face and I'm not sure if correcting her is the right way forward. I'm not "back" exactly. What does come out is, 'I'm not expecting—'

'I know, I know,' she interrupts. 'I'm not saying you are, but just in case, I want you to know that I can't. Even if I wanted to, I'm not able. He took too much from me and I have to move forward as best I can – alone.'

'All right, but as I said—'

'I need to prove I *can* be alone.'

'Look, Clare.' I sit up straight, and my left crutch falls from where I'd balanced it against the sofa. 'I don't want anything from you. I certainly don't want you to assume I think because we slept together or because you just gave me a friendly hug that that ties us together. I'm not that stupid.'

She seems flustered, her hands circled around her now empty glass.

'Clare?'

'I'm pregnant, Jack. I'm about ten weeks pregnant. And the awful truth is that I don't know if Tim is the father . . .'

My face twitches. Once, twice, two tics around my left eye. Then a tiny tremor settles on my upper lip.

'Or if you are,' she finishes, leaning back into the seat.

Instantly my gaze leaves hers and I stare out the window at the dark landscape, illuminated by a full moon and a top layer of frost.

'As you know, Tim and I are complicated,' she adds, and it feels like such an idiotic thing to say that I briefly wonder if perhaps Grace was right.

'You slept with him around the same time.' It's not a question.

Clare's hand sits above the neck of her sweater, where though I can't see the colour in this sepia light, I'm guessing her chest is flushed. 'Yes.' She hesitates, unsure. 'It was a mistake and you've a right to be angry because—'

'I'm not angry, Clare, what you do is your own business. But,' the reality pierces my heart, 'you *could* be carrying my child.'

'I could. And we won't know until the baby is born. And I'm asking you to forgive me for putting you in this position. You've been a lifeline to Grace and I, and you *are* my friend and I don't know how you're going to feel about this. But I did have to tell you . . .' She chews a thumbnail as both my hands run through my hair and clasp around the back of my head.

How do *I feel about this?*

'I'm sorry,' she whispers.

'Does Tim know? Does he know that he might not be . . . I mean, what has he said—'

'I haven't told Tim yet. I've been pretending that none of this is happening to be honest.'

'You haven't told him?'

'Not yet.'

'I see.' Again, I look away towards the inky Barn and think back to the night that this all started, when Ollie and I sat here and set so many things in motion. 'Grace . . .' I say eventually. 'You'll be a lucky woman if you get another like her.'

Clare rests a hand on my arm. 'Could be a boy who looks like you.'

'Don't, OK?' I try to ignore the powerful lure of hope screaming in my veins once more, telling me that this could be the best or worst conversation to ever play out in this world.

'It's a fifty-fifty chance, Jack, and if this child is yours, well, then there's a you, and a me and a baby and Grace, and – we would work that out. We could work that out, couldn't we?'

'I guess we could.' I have no idea how else to respond. 'And if it's Tim's?'

'Then I'll really need my friends,' she says.

My arm reaches for her and I pull her towards me. Chance taunts me, grins in my direction, nearly convinces me my Fate might lie in something so huge, something awesome.

Nearly.

Chapter Forty-Eight

Clare was pulling a potted Christmas tree through the hall-way when her new life disassembled. She had laid an old towel on the floor in order to pull the pot along the porcelain tiles. It was small, just four feet tall, but the nostalgic scent of pine already filled the space around her. Just as she was about to kick the front door closed with her foot, she saw the car. It drove in slow motion, and even without flashing lights was instantly recognisable. She dropped the edges of the towel, both of her hands resting on her stomach.

Grace, she thought, as she watched the passenger first, and then the driver, exit the vehicle. Both put hats on, as if whatever they were about to say to her would somehow be allayed by hats. Silly, unimportant hats.

Grace, she thought again, steadying herself on the doorway. Grace had left for school hours earlier on the school bus. Clare tried to remember if she'd texted since. The school didn't allow use of mobile phones during school hours, but Grace had broken the rules sometimes. Her Grace, the child who wasn't really a rule-breaker, had broken the silly rules.

'Clare Bryanson?' The passenger, a woman, spoke first, and Clare's instinct was to deny her name. If she lied and said she was Ruth someone-or-other, then they'd move on. They'd take their bad news and move far away from here.

'Yes.' Just to the left of her eyeline, she spotted a tiny speck of white paint on the metallic door frame. She rubbed it with the sleeve of her jumper. *Where had that come from?*

'Hello, love, could we go inside maybe?'

'May I see some ID?' She told herself it was a stupid idea to allow two strangers into her and Grace's home. Perhaps they were tricksters, people who dressed up and pretended to bear news just to gain access inside. Unable to move, she looked at the driver, an older man with greying hair just beneath his cap, as he flashed a badge at her. Silently, she pleaded with his eyes.

'Are you Clare Bryanson, wife of Tim Bryanson?' he asked gently.

'Ex-wife.' Clare blew air through her nose. 'Is my daughter OK?'

'I'm sure your daughter is quite all right, but I'm afraid we have some bad news concerning Mr Tim Bryanson. Perhaps we should go inside,' he suggested, his head nodding as if going inside would be a really good idea.

For the first time in a long time, Clare felt small and insignificant in the Barn, as if somehow she didn't belong there any more. She sat on the small sofa that Tim and she had bought over a decade earlier, both of them still arguing over the colour even as they signed a contract to pay for it over four years. The police both sat opposite her. She forced herself to concentrate, to focus on the man's words, making herself hear and lip-read at the same time.

'Mr Bryanson suffered a massive cardiac arrest in Croydon town centre this morning and was pronounced dead on arrival to hospital,' the woman, who introduced herself as Police Constable Rose Hanrahan, added the detail. 'We are so terribly sorry for your loss.'

Tim is dead.

Clare planted her feet firmly on the floor. She noticed a stain on the navy trainer she wore just to the left of the top lace hole.

'It was instant, we understand. Your husband didn't suffer.'

'Ex-husband,' she repeated, before peering at the man as if she didn't understand something. 'Tim is dead?'

Rose Hanrahan glanced back to the other officer. 'Yes, I'm sorry. You're still named as his next of kin. I'm sorry for your loss.'

Clare seemed to still. Completely. Not a muscle moved as her mind swirled. Tim who caused havoc for her and Grace, Tim who'd forced her to resort to the law to ensure being left alone, Tim who could be the father of the child inside her and didn't even know – that Tim – was dead.

'His mother,' she said. 'You'll need to let her know. She's . . . you'll need to . . . I can't . . .'

'Of course. Don't worry. Can we call someone for you?'

'I need to go and get my daughter.' Clare stood.

'Is there anyone we can call to help? Anyone else?'

Clare shook her head. 'No, thank you.'

Some part of her had counted time: some otherworldly part that perhaps hovered above during the whole episode. No tea had been offered. They had arrived, delivered their news and they had left, assured that she was all right despite the shock of her dead ex-husband. She felt numb. She felt guilty relief that it was Tim, because Grace was OK. Her hand circled her stomach.

'Christ,' she said aloud. 'Dear God.' Her head swept from side to side as memories, only the good memories, of a man she had once loved arrived unbidden and her legs collapsed underneath her.

Approximately six hundred and forty-nine seconds, though she'd not counted whenever she spoke. From the first sight of the car to the moment she crumbled, just about ten minutes is all it took for her life to change one more time.

For Tim to be dead and Croydon Clare alive and kicking.

*

She drove to Grace's school, giving her body instructions to do so and her body obeyed. A stranger, some teacher she'd never met before, brought Grace into the principal's office where Clare waited. Grace's face was ashen. 'Mum!' she cried, running towards her. 'I thought something had happened to you, I—'

Clare held Grace. 'Shh, I'm OK—'

Immediately, Grace stiffened as if she'd just realised why else she might have been pulled from class and she retreated, Clare still holding her by the arms. 'Dad? Is Dad all right?'

And then she fell. Just before Clare had to find the words that she'd worried about finding, there were two people helping Grace into a nearby chair as, all the while, she stared at Clare and Clare held her gaze. She couldn't look away. Soundless words beamed from her to her daughter and back again. There were no questions – there would be time for that later. Right now, Clare knew that Grace knew her father was dead. And in her eyes, Clare saw something like terror, not just fear, but something worse. She reached for her, drew her child into her arms and held her tight, let her know she wouldn't let go. With her right hand she smoothed her hair as Grace sobbed. Each stroke told her that she understood.

During the short drive home, listening to Grace's rhythmic sniffles, Clare thought of the time her own father died – the huge loss it had been for her. She quickly realised, with Tim's death, that her own grieving would be for the father of her child rather than the love of her life. Grace was the love of her life and Grace needed looking after.

She stroked Grace's damp hand.

'I was angry with him,' Grace whispered. 'I told him I didn't want to see him.'

'Shh, he knew you didn't mean that.'

'I did though,' Grace sobbed.

'You meant it for a little piece of time, and you'd have forgiven him, and he knew that.' Clare wasn't only trying to be positive with Grace. If anyone knew Tim's capacity for convincing people to forgive him, it was her. And they always did. At least they always had.

'What are we going to do, Mum?' Grace's tears fell again.

'We're going to do what we do. We're going to get up in the morning and push through it. We'll do the things we have to do, and we'll cry, because we'll remember the good bits. Someday, maybe me more than you, we might remember the bad bits and we'll still miss him because he was Tim. He was Dad.' She tightened her hand around Grace's. 'And we'll survive, and we'll be together.'

*

The rain was relentless on the morning of the funeral. Grace had chosen to wear an orange sweater, that her father had bought her for her birthday, over dark blue jeans. Clare wore a black dress, borrowed from Grace. She had been strangely removed from the arrangements; Tim's seventy-three-year-old mother, Irene, insisting on taking care of everything. When Jack offered to drive to the crematorium, at first Clare shook her head, saying that of course he was welcome to come, but that she would drive her and Grace. It took her a few hours and his expressing concern for relying on her ancient Micra, given the day it was, to understand that he wasn't trying to control the situation but to help.

After agreeing that Jack should drive, Clare sat in his passenger seat, while Grace and Erik sat in the back. Soft music played from the sound system. She and Jack didn't speak, apart from him confirming he was certain that the satnav instructions were correct. In the back, she could hear only whispered exchanges between Grace and Erik. It wasn't until they approached the curved, tree-lined entrance to the municipal building that Clare allowed the reality that she would never see Tim again to sink in.

For the last week, life had carried on in a daze. She had been so intent on ensuring Grace was as all right as she possibly could be that she hadn't allowed herself to think about Tim being gone. Mostly, she felt a guilty relief that he would no longer complicate her life the way he always had. But then there were the parts of him that she had loved, those parts that had existed in him still, somewhere, that insisted on being heard. It was almost as if he was telling her from beyond the grave that he hadn't been all bad. Grief, she already knew, allowed those left mourning to deify the dead. It was something she was determined not to do, but something she probably couldn't stop Grace doing.

Wrapped in their coats, huddled under a couple of large golf umbrellas from Jack's boot, they headed for Chapel B, where the service was due to start within minutes. Inside, Clare searched the crowd – mostly people Tim had worked with – for Irene.

'Who are all these people?' Grace whispered as they began to funnel, single file, into the chapel. Before Clare knew what had happened, she had lost Jack, who had decided to take a back seat and was perched on the end of the last pew. She and Grace and Erik headed for the second row. Just before sitting down, Clare and Grace walked to the front where Irene sat flanked by her brother, Ken, who had been Tim's boss, and a woman whom she didn't recognise. While never exactly close, Clare had always had a friendly relationship with Irene and, after a few words and brief hugs were exchanged, she waited while Grace hugged her grandmother before they both rejoined Erik.

'Nana looks so sad,' Grace sniffed into a tissue. 'Who's the woman with her?' she asked Clare.

'Don't know.'

'You think it could be Louise?' she whispered.

Clare shrugged as the music of 'You'll Never Walk Alone' sounded from an organ. She breathed deep, tried to regulate the rhythm of her breaths by placing a hand on her diaphragm, below which lay a tiny living being, now, according to the pregnancy app on her phone, the size of a kiwi fruit.

Grace seemed to follow her hand, offered her mother a faint smile.

Somehow, Clare checked out of the process as she uttered prayers and sang hymns by rote. Somehow, she and Erik propped Grace up as they made their way slowly outside to where, although the rain had stopped, people shook hands with Tim's mother and the weeping woman by his side, under a temporary canopy.

'You're Clare,' the woman said, pulling her into a tight embrace that caught her by surprise. 'I'm Louise.' Her voice wobbled. 'Tim and I were . . . It's hard to believe isn't it. Forty-four years old and knocked down dead by a heart attack.'

Clare found herself nodding, agreeing with the tragedy of it all, while noticing the size of the diamond ring on Louise's engagement finger.

When she had finished with Clare, Louise embraced Grace, whispered, 'I'd been so looking forward to meeting you, but not like this,' through her tears. Her daughter's pull away from the woman was almost imperceptible, but Clare could see her reluctance to be held by the girlfriend she hadn't yet met. Grace managed to escape, instead hugging her grandmother. They'd been really close until Irene had moved away a few years ago. Clare watched them and hoped they might be again.

'Can we talk a moment?' Irene parted from Grace and placed her hand under Clare's elbow, steering her away towards the furthest part of the gathering still under cover. Clare followed, noticing the stoop in her stance, the slump of her rounded shoulders as she walked.

Opposite one another, Clare took both of her hands in her own.

'Such a shock,' Irene murmured, and Clare wondered if her glazed eyes meant she'd had to be medicated. 'I know you and he had your moments, but my boy, he . . .'

She squeezed the woman's hands.

'You'll come to the Duke's Head?'

Clare would have preferred to suck lemons than sit with Ken, Louise and a half-comatose Irene for the afternoon, but even Tim deserved some public mourning from her. 'Of course,' she said. 'I just want to see how Grace is doing first.'

'She's such a lovely girl . . .' Irene swallowed hard, looked away. 'It was good of your mum to come,' she said. 'Have you seen her yet?'

Clare's eyes darted left to right, landing on a black-clad figure standing on the periphery just to the edge of proceedings. Shit. She followed her mother's gaze to where Erik and Jack stood talking to Jan and Emma, whom she hadn't noticed arriving. Next to them, an emotional Grace was being hugged by Reya, who was apologising for being a little late to the service.

'Clare?'

She shook her head absently as she led Irene back to the group and, with one eye still on her mother, made introductions to her friends.

When she saw her approach, Clare fought the impulse to flee, grinding her heels into the concrete paving slabs that formed a floral-lined path from the crematorium.

'Clare,' her mother nodded before taking Grace's hands in hers. 'Grace, it's been too long, my dear.'

Clare watched the scene as if in slow motion; her mother air-kissing both of Grace's cheeks; Grace's eyes darting between her mother and grandmother; those brown eyes of Tim's seeking her approval when they should have been mourning him.

She tried to reassure her – a small squeeze of her elbow, a tiny nod of comfort.

'And who's this young man?' Jean asked of Erik, shaking his hand while still keeping hold of Grace's.

Clare remained silent during the youngster's polite small talk, only moving from her rooted position when her mother turned to her friends from Melborough. A cry of 'No' that never made it to her mouth, but she heard from deep within, made her grasp her mother's arm. 'Mum,' she said aloud. 'A word?'

'Of course, darling.'

'Join us at the Duke's Head, won't you, Jean?' Irene called to them as they left the group.

As soon as they were out of earshot, Clare spoke. 'You won't be joining us anywhere.'

'Now, Clare,' her mother began.

'This is Tim's service. You hated Tim.'

'Well, you weren't that fond of him either, my dear, and you're here. Besides, Irene has just invited me and—'

'Tim was my husband, Grace's father. We are here to pay respect to him. You're here to cause trouble.'

'Clare, I have come to pay my respects too, to—'

Clare's palm raised. 'Go home, Mum, please. I want Grace to have the chance to mourn with her father's family and neither of us will be doing that if you remain here.'

'I'd like to spend some time with Grace. *You* told me that it was up to her?'

Clare set her lips in a straight line. 'Really? You want her to make that choice now, today?'

'Is that him?'

'What?' Clare looked across to where her mother had pointed to Jack.

'Your sugar daddy. Tim told me about him.'

Her eyes blinked slowly. To be fair, though it was unlikely Tim had spoken more than a couple of times to Jean in the last few months, it sounded exactly like the way he might have described Jack. 'You need to leave now.'

'Truth hurts?'

'No, Mum, that's you, nothing to do with the truth. Just you hurting with your cutting barbs.' A familiar moment of light-headedness that was common in pregnancy made her reach for a nearby wall.

'Are you all right?' her mother asked, something like concern on her face.

'We've just said goodbye to the man I spent over twenty years with,' Clare replied, her hand settling on her stomach, 'I'm not all right, but would appreciate being left to finish saying goodbye the way we'd like to.'

Jean gripped the short handles on her handbag. 'May *I* say goodbye to Grace?'

'Grace can see us talking. She knows what's being discussed and will appreciate no fuss. Maybe give her a wave.'

Clare found herself appraised, her mother's head angled as she stared, before speaking in a low-pitched voice, 'Goodbye, Clare. I'm sorry for your loss.'

She watched for a moment, looked at her mother's back retreat – felt nothing but relief and the beginnings of a light splatter of rain on her face.

'You all right?' Jack appeared in front of her with an umbrella.

Clare nodded.

'That's the mother you dislike, along with alcohol and stripy clothes?' he asked.

'The one and only.'

'Someday, you'll have to tell me . . .' He offered her an arm and together they headed back towards the dispersing crowd and car park. 'You know, what's so awful about stripy clothes,' he grinned, but Clare couldn't even manage a smile.

*

Late that evening, after Erik had left and Grace was asleep on the sofa next to her, Clare listened to the rain and whipping wind outside. Inside the Barn, there was a new quiet, a lull that she sensed might be the calm before the real storm. During the next few days and weeks, life had to go on. Her and Grace's routine had to proceed until one day it might feel like a bad dream. That was Clare's task – to get her and Grace there and breathe in and out and then . . . Then, breathe in and out again. It was all she could come up with. It had been her coping strategy during her darker days *with* Tim and as she felt Grace's soft breathing under her fingertips, as she tapped her three times, it would have to be her coping strategy during the darker days without him.

Chapter Forty-Nine

WhatsApp Voice Memo to Tim

Dad, I know you won't hear this, but I wanted to say I'm sorry for yelling at you. You're not perfect, but you're Dad. You weren't perfect, but you were Dad. Not sure I'll ever get used to using the past tense. I love you, Dad, present tense. I loved you when I yelled at you. Past tense. I found it hard to understand you, but I'll always love you. Because you were Dad. You were *my* Dad. But you can't hear this, can you? So, you don't know any of this and I wish you were here so I could tell you. Dad? I wish you were here so I could tell you . . .

Chapter Fifty

Shortly after Tim Bryanson's funeral, the offices in chambers, where I'd met him last, are already buzzing, even though it's just shy of 8.30 a.m. and a few days before Christmas. A steel-grey sky, obscuring the sun for the last few weeks, has dulled the room I normally occupy here, but the chatter of hive gossip and the clacking of keyboards sound all around us through the open door. I'm borrowing the office for half an hour and Mabel has already brought two large frothy coffees to me and Marsha. I smile my thanks.

'Well?' Marsha says.

'Hmmm?'

'I checked that itinerary you sent me ages ago. You're supposed to be pottering around Europe right now.'

'I'll get there another time,' I tell her.

'Are you ready to come back?' she asks. 'We could really do with you.'

'You know one of the things I've learned being away from here?'

Marsha tries to mask her frustration at my not answering her question by offering a thin smile. 'What?'

'I think I love the law again.'

Her grin broadens. 'Glad to hear it.'

'I also learned that there's more to life than giving fifty-plus hours a week to it.'

Marsha groans. 'Don't tell me you're not coming back.'

I look towards her, over the rim of my cup. 'Marsha, are we friends?'

She seems genuinely surprised at the question. 'Of course we're friends.'

'I mean, I know we're not close buddy buddies, but . . .'

Marsha leans forward. 'We're friends. That may change in the next sixty seconds. Please say you're not leaving for good.'

'Would you miss me?'

'Christ, I've already missed you! Stop messing about. What's going on? Is this because I never responded to that email weeks ago? Is that why you ignored my last one? I'm sorry!'

Just behind her on the shelf to the left of her head, the three wise monkeys, one of which is dented from where I'd thrown it during my last visit, have had a string of silver tinsel woven between them and they're are all off-centre. Yet, today, I couldn't care less about symmetry – I stay in the chair. 'I want to cut back, stay working but work less, take fewer cases on. Can we make that work?'

She scrunches her face. 'You know what it's like here, Jack. Some cases can run on and—'

'Marsha, can we make it work? If not, I'll have to rethink things. I'd like to stay on here, but only if we can find a way for that to work.'

She looks long and hard at me before speaking again, during which time the noises in the building seem amplified. Through the walls to my left, chairs are being shifted around in one of the bigger meeting rooms. To the far right behind the door, I can almost hear Mabel sneak a vape outside her window. 'Did you find the meaning of life out there, Jack – is that what this is about? If you did, please share.'

My reply is instinctive. 'I found the meaning of death. It's final and it lasts forever.'

'Wow,' she mock muses and I laugh. 'Months off work and, wow . . .'

'Life, on the other hand, is unspeakably short and I have so much I want to do.'

'One thing,' she says, eyes pointed at mine. 'Just name one yearning thing you want to do when you work less, impress me!'

'Swim with pigs, play trumpet with a band, sing, make more friends and see more of the ones I already have, live life in the grey lane. And dance, I really want to learn to dance.'

'OK . . .' she tries to hide a half-glance at my leg. 'Thing is,' she leans towards the desk in between us, 'I don't get why you came back? You had so much more time to take and if you'd taken it, you'd probably have got loads of that stuff out of your system.'

'We'll never know.'

'You're very irritating sometimes.'

'So, I've been told. Can we make it work?'

Marsha frowns. 'Fine, fine. You owe me fifty quid, by the way. You're back in under three months.' She extends her hand and I remove five tens from my wallet, hand them to her. 'Right,' she says, pocketing them without as much as a guilty glance. 'I'll find a way forward if you tell me why the hell your plans changed.'

I fill her in on Antony's story and she reminds me she met Lynn a few times.

The story ends with words I'd already said to Clare and Grace.

'I came home for a friend in need.'

I don't say the rest out loud; that I need, no, *want*, to stay home for another.

*

In the pub, Jan comes around to my side of the bar and gives me a big bear hug. 'Welcome back,' he says. 'We haven't seen you in here since you dumped that poor girl.'

Laura . . . I cringe. It seems like a lifetime ago. 'Pint of orange juice, please,' I say.

'Terrible business for Clare,' he shakes his head. In the background the Eagles are playing on Jan's old seventies jukebox. He's bent over replacing a plug-in air freshener right next to me.

I nod my agreement. 'Is Grace here? She's not at the Barn.'

'They're back in the living room.'

'Would you mind if I went through to talk to her quickly?'

'Go ahead, straight on, second door on the left.'

I knock gently, hear movement and footsteps, and Erik opens the door, surprise prompting a few faint lines on his high youthful forehead.

'I'm looking for Grace?'

He stares over his shoulder, whispers my name in her direction, and she comes to the door.

'What are *you* doing here?'

'Can I have a moment?'

Grace closes the door and comes out into the narrow hallway, leans up against the wall. 'What's up?'

'Just checking you're all right.'

'I'll look after the pigs, OK?' She begins to pick at a frayed piece of wallpaper just above the dado rail. 'If that's what you're after.'

'Grace, that's not why I'm here.'

'You shouldn't be going. You shouldn't be leaving Mum. She told me *everything*. And now she has to have a baby alone while you're away finding yourself. That is just not mature, Jack.'

I bite my lip to stop a smile. 'You're right. That would not be mature.' I lean against the opposite wall. 'Maybe I should stay. That said, your mum is a strong, independent woman.'

'I love my mother, but she's an idiot, and don't stay just because you should.'

'OK.' This is Grace, the teenager, who has just lost her father. 'Are you pissed off at me or your dad or both?' I ask.

She starts to cry, and Erik opens the door, only to have her shoo him away. 'I wish I hadn't been so angry with him. Now, I'm just mad at me.'

'I know.'

'No one knows.'

She looks so slight and vulnerable. 'Grace, look at me, please?' I ask her.

By the time she does, she has her arms crossed and her bottom lip folded under her top teeth.

'If I hadn't asked Alice to that concert,' I tell her, 'she'd be alive today. If I hadn't driven, she'd be alive today. If John Hunter, the man who drove his car drunk, hadn't got drunk, she'd be alive today.' I reach for her hand. 'If I hadn't spent so many years stewing in regret, I'd probably be happily married by now instead of debating whether I'll run off to Paris for my fiftieth birthday.'

She sniffs quietly.

'Don't do what I did, Grace . . .'

Her shoulders slump forward, and she pulls her hand from mine. 'Undetected coronary disease,' she looks straight into my eyes. 'Do you think it's genetic, something I might have?' Her voice is suddenly tiny.

'Absolutely not.' I have no idea, but she doesn't need to hear that.

She wipes her nose with her hand, and I fish in my pocket for a tissue, pass it to her.

'I have something for you,' I whisper, taking another tissue, this time from my coat pocket. She looks in my hand, watches me unfurl it, revealing a tiny glass thing.

'What is it?' She touches it, picks it up, and holds it up to the light coming in from a skylight.

'It's a unicorn horn. It's magic.'

She looks sad. 'Do I rub it and get three wishes?'

'No, but it is magic, and it will keep you safe.'

'You should keep it then,' she says. 'For when you go off again.'

'I want you to have it. Alice gave it to me when she was only a few years older than you are now.' I wrap her hand around it. 'Everyone needs a little magic now and then, a little extra help.'

She puts her arms around my neck, whispers, 'Thank you.'

And then the door is opened, and she's gone.

*

'An undiscovered heart problem,' Clare repeats later. 'What are the chances? He was forty-four years old.'

I've stopped in the studio, having seen the lights still on even though I know she's cancelled classes this week. Clare has soft music on in the background and is roaming around the room, just touching things, bizarrely tapping things – the barre, the mirrors, props.

'It's freezing in here,' I tell her.

'What are the chances?' she asks again.

There's no way I, who have had enough skirmishes with Chance and Fate, can answer that. I walk to her side and slip my coat around her shoulders. 'Please don't argue,' I tell her as she's about to tell me to keep it. 'I respect you as a strong, independent woman who can look after herself. I'm just lending you this because it's cold.'

'I've cried all day. I've cried a lot more for him than I ever thought I might.'

'You loved him once.'

'Yes, but he was far from perfect.'

'I'm sure there were some perfect moments and I think they're the ones we remember when we lose someone. Maybe the tears are for those?'

'I'm crying for Grace too. She loved him even though he was . . . difficult.'

'Grace will be fine in time. She'll cry her own tears. Lots of them.' I recall how I witnessed them today. 'How are *you*?' I can't help myself. She's doing that thing that I don't think she realises she does, where her hand circles her stomach.

I see the tiniest shake of her head as if she can't talk about it, not yet, not now, so she offers me the slightest of smiles and tightens my coat around her.

'You'll be OK,' I tell her, and this time she nods because she knows that I know about loss. As I speak, I realise that when I say 'you', I mean not just Clare, but her and Grace and the baby – all of them. Despite her obvious pain at the moment, the woman who stands before me is not the same woman I met that first day. It's as if, with a few lucky breaks and her hard work, her core's grown tall and strong.

I want to tell her that I'm here for her and Grace, but, right now, the words would sound wrong. I want to tell her not to question her sadness because Tim had a cruel abusive streak. I want to tell her if Grace had to have only one surviving parent, she has the right one living. I want to tell her that one day she'll laugh out loud again. I say none of it because grief is such a personal thing and the only thing I can do is be here. In the background. In the foreground – wherever I'm needed, if I'm needed.

The music has changed tracks and there's a song playing that I vaguely recognise, but what I do hear is the beat, so instead of saying the things I'd like to, I opt instead to try to widen her smile.

'You know I practised my waltz while I was away? One, two, three – down, up, up. I'm a lot better.' I move past her, demonstrate my much-improved box step, and it works. She nods as she grins. 'Well, I could be,' I add. I'm by her side again and hold my hand aloft. 'If I had more lessons.'

Her hand is in mine, no reluctance, and immediately we fall into ballroom hold, palm to palm, hands on shoulders. We move in time, perfectly synchronised.

'I'd like to learn to dance. You think you could teach me?'

'I can't teach you to dance. Remember what happened after your last lesson?'

'I do. I still want to learn.'

She stops dancing and moves into my arms. My right hand holds her head against my chest.

'I'd love to teach you to dance,' she whispers.

'Risky,' I whisper.

'I know.'

And we just sway slightly until the track stops playing and I'm more than ready to take Chance on.

*

The morning of my fiftieth birthday Ollie FaceTimes at silly o'clock and sends me a snapshot of today's Eurostar timetable and, after a particularly awful rendition of 'Happy Birthday', he hangs up. Marsha texts at 6.45 to wish me a wonderful day and says she can't wait to have me back in the office, albeit for less time. At 7 a.m. a card is posted through the letterbox and I peek through the peephole.

Clare, walking away briskly, gives a tiny glance over her shoulder as if she knows I'm looking. My eyes lower to the envelope and, picking it up, I wait until the coffee is brewed before tearing it open.

The card is shiny, with embossed balloons all over the front, and inside I recognise both their handwriting. Grace has written on the right-hand side of the card: 'Happy Birthday, Jack, love Grace x P.S. It's only right that you should have cake today – come over at 4.' Her words are surrounded by love hearts and smiley faces. Clare has written on the left:

Jack,

Grace showed me what you gave her yesterday, told me Alice had given it to you. That was a lovely thing. Thank you. I'm sure she will treasure it as you have.

I thought you might like this - it's a little bit of magic too.

Your friend, Clare x

Something flutters to the table surface. It's a tiny square black-and-white image, yesterday's date on top, with Clare's name on it. My eyes focus on the kidney shape in the picture of the scan.

In that tiny foetal shape, I remember what might have been once, so long ago, and I know my decision is the right one. Cake with Clare, Grace and hope in my heart beats a solo trip to Paris any day. I run my forefinger over the image and feel an instant connection.

I see Clare. I see Grace. And yes, whatever happens, I see magic.

Epilogue

WhatsApp Clare & Jack

I'm sorry. So sorry. Where did you go?

Just for a drive. A 50/50 chance. We held off finding out for ages, afraid of bursting our bubble, but that piece of paper says what I think I knew. I want it not to matter.

Does it matter?

Not to me. I want it not to matter to you, Clare.

When Josh was born, you were there. You were there before, and you've been with us since. It doesn't matter to me because you told me you were in this way before today. Are you still in this with us?

WhatsApp Grace & Erik

U should take it. When the time comes, u take it.

It's five hundred miles away.

It's the best course. It looks like a fabulous university and it's an unconditional offer for next year. Who knows what will happen in a year?

What about us, Grace?

If there's an 'us' still, we'll sort something out.

Does it scare u to think there might not be?

Not as much as us still being together. THAT's scary.

WhatsApp Jack & Clare

Is Josh with you now?

Yes ☺ What happened earlier?

Licking my wounds. Tell him I love him.

Come home and tell him yourself.

Tell him to tell his mummy that I love her too.

He says to tell you that even though you don't say it, she knows. See? She's the one who's let love into her life, Jack.

Tell Josh to tell his mummy I'm proud of her and I'm in this . . .

Good. He's happy. We're happy. Come home.

My home is next door to your home.

Home to us. BTW, I have class in 40 mins & you're meant to be Josh-watching.

I'll be there.

Acknowledgements

A published book is never just the work of the writer but also a team of people who go to work after the first drafts have been scribed. A huge thanks to Welbeck Publishing for your faith in this story. I'm grateful to everyone across acquisition, cover design, sales, marketing and PR, but a special thanks to my fab editor, Tara Loder, whose vision really helped shape the final pages. I'm incredibly lucky to be represented by the best agent in the land, Madeleine Milburn, who is also surrounded by a magnificent group of people who help get these words read all over the world. Thank you, Maddy and #TeamMilburn – you rock!

Beta readers are vital to any writer and I think my two writing buddies, Claire Allan and Anstey Harris, have probably read more versions of this than I'll ever admit! You are both incredible – thanks and hugs to you for your valuable time and advice.

This story happens (mostly) in the fictional town of Melborough, which is loosely based on Marlborough, Wiltshire. The Florida journey takes place in Key Biscayne, a truly gorgeous spot, and though I've taken a few writer's liberties, I hope readers will enjoy the settings.

Research thanks must go to the remarkable Lee Spencer, who, in 2019, became the first physically disabled person to row solo from mainland Europe to Mainland South America. Lee, a tireless fundraiser for various charities, gave me valuable insight into the world of an amputee. Big thanks to Red Széll of RNIB Connect Radio for helping me bring to life how Simon might really dance that dance . . . My gratitude too to James Norman, who patiently answered many questions about life in barrister's chambers. Any errors are indeed mine.

A big shout out to book bloggers, reviewers, booksellers, and book clubs – where would writers be without your passion for stories? To all The Prime Writers, my writing group, thanks for the safe haven.

I'm blessed with friends and family that really do complete me. Thank you all – I love you. Finally, to the readers . . .

Without your support, I wouldn't be able to call myself an 'author', something I've dreamed of since I was a little girl. Thank you from the bottom of my heart.

Nell Carter lives in the South East with her husband. Their grown-up daughters have flown the coop but, like boomerangs, keep coming home. From a much larger family herself, Nell likes to write about real people – the dust and dirt that layers their relationships, the light and shade that makes them love and cry.

WELBECK

PUBLISHING GROUP

Love books? Join the club.

Sign-up and choose your preferred genres to receive tailored news, deals, extracts, author interviews and more about your next favourite read.

From heart-racing thrillers to award-winning historical fiction, through to must-read music tomes, beautiful picture books and delightful gift ideas, Welbeck is proud to publish titles that suit every taste.

bit.ly/welbeckpublishing

WELBECK

ANDRE DEUTSCH

MORTIMER

MORTIMER

WELBECK

OH!